Hermann Burger

Brenner

Translated from the German by Adrian Nathan West

archipelago books

First published in German as *Brenner 1: Brunsleben* by Carl Hanser Verlag München
First Archipelago Books Edition, 2022

Library of Congress Cataloging-in-Publication Data available upon request.
ISBN: 9781953861306

Archipelago Books, 232 3rd Street #A111, Brooklyn, NY 11215
www.archipelagobooks.org

Distributed by Penguin Random House
www.penguinrandomhouse.com

Cover art: Phillip Guston (American, 1913-1980) *Friend – To M.F., 1978*, Oil on canvas
Overall: 68 x 88 inches, Purchased with funds from the Nathan Emory Coffin Collection of the
Des Moines Art Center, 1991.48, © The Estate of Philip Guston, courtesy Hauser & Wirth
Photo Credit: Rich Sanders, Des Moines

This work is made possible by the New York State Council on the Arts with the support
of the Office of the Governor and the New York State Legislature. Funding for the translation
of this book was provided by a grant from the Carl Lesnor Family Foundation.

This publication was made possible with support from Lannan Foundation,
the National Endowment for the Arts, the Nimick Forbesway Foundation,
and the New York City Department of Cultural Affairs.

Printed in Canada

BRENNER

I.

LEONZBURG–COMBRAY,
ELEGANT MADURO

My name is Hermann Arbogast Brenner, scion of the famed cigar dynasty Brenner & Sons Ltd. in the *Stumpenland,* the cigar-manufacturing region of Aargau. But I have no hand in production. My second cousin oversees that, along with the three hundred sixty remaining employees and every other aspect of the firm, which is sinking, like the entire industry, into a profound crisis: Johann Caspar Brenner has a brilliant political career both behind and ahead of him – first as a member of the National Council for the Liberal Party in the canton of Lucerne – *Pfäffike,* Pfeffikon, already lies in that Catholic territory to the northwest of Menzenmang – and since last autumn, as a deputy of the Upper Chamber; and it is hardly out of the question that from there he will someday make the leap to the Federal Assembly. A Brenner among the Seven Fathers of the Nation, as Minister of Finance, perhaps, surely this would be the high point of our family's history. A connoisseur of belles lettres on the sly, my cousin, patron, and friend repeats to me time and again that the fall of the house of Buddenbrook was linked inextricably to Thomas Buddenbrook's career in the senate, and that here, as there, the third generation is the critical one. For now, he said to me in the parent company's offices, I see no opportunity for climbing another branch in the family tree, and of course, the business devolving into a holy mess – you remember Dubslav von Stechlin used that same phrase on election day on the way to Rheinsberg – will make my political career equally untenable. One cannot extol the principles of the free market – at any rate, not in Switzerland – while simultaneously sending out pink slips to three hundred sixty employees; as he said this, he chose an onomatopoeia, *Kladderadatsch,* instead of *bankruptcy* or *insolvency,* a word related etymologically to *crackup* or *crash* and the title, moreover, of a renowned newspaper launched in 1848, which would bear out the stalwart maxim *nomen ist omen,* shuttering its doors in 1944; the term means both collapse and outrage or scandal, and indeed, at that moment, *eh shcandal vas efoot,* for January of 1982 marked the demise, after one hundred forty-four storied years, of the Menzenmang firm Weber & Sons Ltd., founded as the *heimzigarri* or hometown tobacconist in the year 1838 by Samuel Weber, a hosier and former bookbinder. Just think of such popular brands as the Rio Grande or the Webstar. Its merger with Brenner & Sons Ltd. led Samuel Weber V, the last of the Mohicans in this family enterprise, to shoot himself with his army pistol, because he had sworn to his father, who lay on his deathbed, that he would avoid this sort of debacle at any cost. And yet, Johann Caspar said to me, as we walked to the so-called showroom, hung with maps of Cuba stained a slight brown from the smoke of many tastings – an elongated bird's head between the shear blades of Yucatan and Florida that girds the Gulf of Mexico, showing the classic growing regions of Oriente, Remedios, and Partido, the Semi Vuelta, and the regal Vuelta Abajo – Weber's liquidation, which reached its tragic-macabre culmination in the suicide of my associate Sämi, whom we had planned to take on as operations manager, has only brought us enough market share to hold production at one hundred thirty million cheroots, cigars, and cigarillos, nothing more. Those are the bare facts. And so forgive me if I envy you. You live on the Chaistenberg at Castle Brunsleben, taken care of by your tobacco pension, furnished to the end of your days with the manifold delicacies of our trade, and inspired by the *pneuma* of the *cohiba*, you are bringing to completion, like a craftsman, your novel of childhood and cigars, free to describe at your leisure what we struggle to bring to market day in, day out. Your epos is a stimulant never to be marred by a warning sticker from the Federal Office of Public Health, and will still be on the shelves, if the nuclear omnicide can be held at bay, long after you and I are dead and buried.

I do not know whether my cousin, who diversified at the right time with a move into the bicycle business, has glimpsed something that strikes him as too dark, too *oscuro,* and is for that reason beset with the pessimism so typical of third generations in family firms. True, it is the founders who are the landholders and architects, the sons the proud occupants who turn the humble enterprise into a joint-stock company, while the grandchildren concern themselves almost entirely with maintenance, but even now, in my final years at Brunsleben, I still possess the salesmanly instincts to stand surety for the *Brennerei* – this nickname for the firm, which means *distillery,* hints at tobacco's origins as an intoxicating drink – far past its hundred-year jubilee, for there will always be smoking, it is simply a question of what and where: *Tobacconists may rest assured / Good men are e'er by good tobacco lured.* And with the leaves of this modest folio, from *viso* to *volado,* I will do my part to keep the baby from being thrown out with the bathwater, and to affirm in our era of hustle and bustle how vast the difference is between a coffin nail tugged impulsively from its packet and a Por Larrañaga – between addiction and contemplative delectation: let the latter be our watchword. The mere sight of the filter, clogged with nicotine and tar, when the butt is stubbed out anxiously in the ashtray, must reveal to the chain-smoker, in the most dramatic way, that his Parisiennes or Marlboros, to take two brands at random, are a carcinogenic pollutant rather than the pure produce of nature. Quite likely his guilt feelings and the longing for self-annihilation anchored in the depths of his subconscious are what compel him to mash it down, to stomp it like a mole cricket and grind it into the street, whereas the cigar, two-thirds smoked, may be laid gently to the side, and dies a natural death upon breathing its last. A Tobajara Real, from Cruz de las Almas in Bahía, Brazil, conceals a bouquet so piquant, there is no need to inhale, nose and palate are thoroughly gratified. This is the future, my dear Johann Caspar Brenner, imports of *habanos* have risen from 3.8 million in the seventies to 5.6 million in 1988, our country boasts the highest per capita consumption in the world, and if I use this statistically prosaic term, *per capita*, I am thinking of the round head of the corona, the panatela, or the Trabuco, cigars for the mind, one and all. My suggestion for a *chopfsigarre* – a cigar with a closed end – is the Montecristo Number One, with hand molded head and foot, an object for the spirit and sentiments, ill-suited to frenzied consumption. What was the adage my grandfather, Hermann Brenner, had hanging up in his inn, the Waldau? *On the third day, the Lord awoke / And planted tobacco and vine; / On the eighth Adam made cigars and wine / That man might drink and smoke.*

I would like to offer those words for your rumination and pleasure before withdrawing from the Gabon cabinet, where its aromas combine with those of its sisters, a Hoyo de Monterrey Des Dieux, tied into a half-wheel with a yellow ribbon, Flor Extrafina, and cutting it as I turn to the pith of the Elegant Maduro chapter concerning the deep kinship between Brunsleben, Menzenmang, and Gormund and Leonzburg-Combray. To begin, we must enlighten the indulgent reader as to why and how this district capital on the banks of the Aabach at the foot of the castle hill, which broods inwardly on hot summer days and never emerges entirely from its medieval twilit slumber, came by its Proustian sobriquet. It was my landlord and patron, Jérôme von Castelmur-Bondo, who drew my attention, during one of our late-morning tobacco colloquies in his *fumoir* or tower room, to the similarity of the Argovian Mittelland and the Norman countryside in Proust. As ever, we were seated in the gloom of the slope-ceilinged Biedermeyer niche beneath the jagged old lambrequin, crimson like a Grand Guignol artifact, recollecting the crumpled curtain of a repertory theater or the fringed skirts of a dancer at the Moulin Rouge. The Emeritus, known simply as *de profäser* down in the village, stretched out at ease on the Louis XIII fauteuil with the Palazzo Bondo pattern embroidered in pale red, its backrest adjustable by means of dentated iron rings, and behind him on the faded corn-yellow walls hung sabers, cockades, and gilded epaulettes, beneath them the red-and-white aiguillettes and cummerbund of a forebear who served with a Neapolitan regiment in the eighteenth century, while I sat at an angle in the cream-white Louis XV armchair with my back to his father's former cigar cabinet, which today conserves, in a manner worthy of the finest *habanos,* costly first editions of Rilke, Thomas Mann, and Proust, the last of these bound in vellum, and on the lowermost shelf, in decorative velvet cases, are his distinctions, the Officier de la Légion d'Honneur, five crosses, the silver medal for service to the Republic of Austria, the award from Charles University in Prague, and, howbeit tucked away, the Order of Merit of the Swiss Confederation, conceded by President Karl Carstens. I still recall, though my short-term memory has begun to fade, the words I exchanged with the chauffeur who parked his Mercedes from the Corps Diplomatique in front of the castle's inner gate; as he watched me bundling leaves, he averred that the gardener's was the most beautiful of professions (of course one should never refuse a post offered to one by chance) and I described to him the vegetation on the three sheer terraces, designed in the Italian manner, and sang the praises of asters and smoldering days.

Jérôme – if I may be so familiar, to hurry things along, though such haste befits neither an Eckermann-like sublessor nor the savors of a Hoyo de Monterrey – Jérôme and I had, after testing other constellations, arrived at the ideal arrangement for the conduct of those talks carried out with my tobacco pages in mind: the guéridon stood between us with its lighting utensils, along with a bottle of Badoux Aigle Les Murailles brought to us by Amorose; the lord of the castle took curt puffs of his pipe, its insides so thickly caked with soot you'd presume the pipe tool had never been invented. I savored the house brand, Rey del Mundo, and we saw, framed by the eight panes of the radius window, far out over the chestnuts, the birch forest and the Lind behind it, stretching out to the timberlands of Leonzburg, *Det's right, mon cher,* as he spoke, his head, imposing like a tortoise shell, gave a twitch, *so it is,* Proust's landscape is of course less hilly than ours, the Côté de Méséglise, where Swann's Tanson-ville lies, opens out onto a broad plain, one of those shimmering expanses our friend Edmond de Mog so loves in France, but the other side, known as the Côté de Guermantes, as I remember from the sketches in George D. Painter's two-volume biography, *de one Unsld put out,* is only accessible over the soft slopes of the valley of the Vivonne, and moreover… And yet, my humble self interjected, in your most recent book, with the hand-some title *Parler au papier,* you described Leonzburg as Helvetia's answer to Proust's provincial village, why?

Look now, I'm not a writer proper, but a *hishtorian,* my obligation is to cleave to what is and not what could have been, as Aristotle says. It is true I've been praised for the literary rather than narrowly academic style of my prose, which led the critic Adam Nautilus Rauch to state in his encomium on the occasion of the Aargau Literary Prize at the Aargauer Kunsthaus that by nature I dwelt among the poets, not the professors, but well, as far as that goes, one just had a notion of Leonzburg as the Helvetian Combray, a whim, if you will, then here you come, the semiretired cigarrier, and want to ask me what for.

De fect is, I can neither justify nor clarify it *en detail,* I simply believe – and take note, this is a man of reason using the word *believe* – that impressions of this sort are based more in atmosphere than topography. There is something you could call the pastoral charm of the provinces, I find this in the Schützenmattstrasse and in the Rathausgasse, in the Schulhausplatz as well as the Aavorstadt, and above all with my friend from my student years in Paris, the composer and painter Edmond de Mog – *he ken turn eh fine phrase too* – we used to live next door to each other in the Hotel Foyot, and when he greets me with a linden blossom tea in the garden at Sonnenberg, his house on the Schlossgasse, and we glance up at the hulking medieval castle, I cannot avoid suspecting, as you may read in my diary entry of April 17, 1982, a distant relation between the Counts of Leoncebourg and Proust's Ducs de Guermantes. And Proust says of novel-reading that it is magical like a deep dream, I have just found the place again in the first volume of the *Recherche* – the 1919 edition with an inscription, dated 12 December 1925, by the Marquise de Villeparisis – it is standing directly beside Grand Duke Wilhelm Ernst's edition of Goethe's Works, *shignificantly* in coquelicot leather – did he know, I tried to interject, that *Unsld* had reissued an edition in red goatskin and Feincanvas with the spine stitched at the Lachenmaier bindery in Reutlingen, but I couldn't get a word in, and settled for a drag from the Rey del Mundo – the place where Proust speaks of the George Sand novels given him by his grandmother, and from this youthful reading during the Easter holidays in Combray the author embarks upon a series of reflections on the relation between novelistic and real experience, touching on that magic we mentioned before, he says more or less – naturally one must refer to the French original – that when we plunge intensely into a book, each of our emotions is multiplied by ten, so that a great work of *littrature* shakes us like a dream, but with far greater clarity than the dreams of nighttime, which last only for fragments of a second in the torpid end-stages of sleep.

What makes this possible is an open question, one depth psychology has hardly looked into, and relevant here is that letter of Rilke's from 1914, when he consults with the Munich psychiatrist Stauffenberg on a course of psychoanalytic treatment, writing that so-called practical people – right away you will see here the parallel to Musil's sense of possible and real in *The Man Without Qualities* – can easily find relief through inducing a "spiritual nausea" that forces them to vomit up their undigested childhood; whereas he, Rainer Maria Rilke – and he affirmed this, *nota bene,* during the great creative crisis that followed the composition of *Malte* – was entirely dependent on what cannot be lived, because it is too huge, too premature, too horrible, *given det… now I've gone en lost de thread.* And he looked at me, somewhat frog-eyed, as if we were sitting for an exam – *aha, yesss,* he required, *dis is de vonderful part,* he depends on making angels, things, animals, even monsters to portray what is too abortive or too horrible. Satisfied that he had managed to put aright that quotation from the letters, which he had clearly dredged up from long ago, Jérôme von Castelmur-Bondo knocked the ashes from his pipe and remarked: *it's de ellegory of de cave,* and in this way came back round to Proust. Wonderment must arise through this sense that an invented figure, event, landscape, or conversation is truer than its real counterparts; truer because subject to the poet's jurisdiction – at this, he raised his index finger in admonition, *dish pehticular poet, mind ye* – and thereby freed from all contingency, he speaks almost like a physicist, *or better yet a chemisht, if ye will* – he said *du* and not *Sie* to me, I treasured it when, from time to time, the Emeritus spoke informally to Hermann Arbogast Brenner – of the ungraspable particles of the soul, which the novelist replaces with an equivalent of immaterial particles, thereby achieving osmosis. That is what staggers us in a person like Proust, with his effortless dominion over every *nuance* – he pronounced it *nü-awnce,* in the French manner – of words with their infinite pliability and every syntactical artifice, we are left speechless, but inside we are that much more alive as we yield to a range of sensations ascending from the deepest anguish to the purest joy – think of certain of Natalie's dialogues in *Indian Summer,* blue as aquamarine – sensations of a kind life cannot convey to us, because these emotions rise up in us so lethargically – he used the English word *emotions* – that their intensity is nearly exhausted, something akin to friction loss occurs, *en bref,* everything I've suffered through in plodding succession, everything that's brought me to rapture in my eighty-seven years on this earth, I can traverse in seven-league boots during the reading of a novel, a liaison, a separation, all that can elapse in the short space of a single chapter. And so the comparison of magic and dreams is an apposite one.

While Jérôme von Castelmur-Bondo took a sip of Aigle, as though to wash down those remarks he had just chiseled into being with the precision of a dentist, then struggled to rekindle the old pipe he had chewed ragged – why didn't he just get himself a Dunhill-Bruyère – I interrupted with the question of whether he would allow a synoptic leap to Hofmannsthal's *Dream of Higher Magic.* The indulgent reader, to whom I cannot stress enough that I, alongside the lord of the castle, Bert May, or Adam Nautilus Rauch, am hardly more than an illiterate, most probably in consequence of that one brutal year in the upper class of the canton school in Aargau when they tortured us with Schiller's *Wallenstein*, should not presume such a poem forms part of any canon readily at my disposal – nor am I acquainted with a single letter of the *Recherche* – but in preparation for our talk on the subject of Leonzburg-Combray, I had copied it down from a pocket edition, lest I were to suffer from my conversational ineptitude. This is a part of my indenture at Castle Brunsleben, not to share readings in detail with this historian so deeply steeped in literature, no, that would be asking too much, but to be *proficient in the lessor's predilect topics,* as per our contractual agreement, and the truth is, this is a double-edged sword. Whoever dwells upon a given writer in hopes of plunging into the magic of dreams will find himself, on the one hand, in a realm of incomparable communicative opulence, with all his antennae played upon simultaneously; at the same time, he is drawn into a dialogical poverty that may take on pathological traits, which, inter alia, sheds light on the phenomenon of professional readers compelled to talk on and on of things they have assimilated in silence, as though, to remain with the dream analogy a bit longer, after every evening they must offer up to their analyst clairvoyantly remembered tatters, with the difference that you have to pay a therapist to *dispel* them, whereas friends, guests, visitors, partners do not charge for such a service.

I no longer recall et, the Emeritus remarked, sinking deeper and deeper into his Palazzo-Bondo fauteuil with a genteel, solicitous nod, what I'd had in mind was the sixth stanza, where it says of the magician, the first, the great one: *He bent, and his fingers creased / The ground, as if it were water.* He fishes giant opals from the water, they fall back in – and this is what I don't understand – in the form of plangent rings, I mean, I reconsidered, abashed at holding the floor so long, I could of course draw an analogy to my own modest art, that of the occasional magician – the first would then be the penetration of matter by matter, while the opal rings would represent both "miraculous multiplication" as well as the principle behind a typical coin magic performance, which I had incorporated into my own routines, turning a one-franc coin into two, a five-franc bill into a *Vreneli,* a *Vreneli* into a Kaiser Franz-Josef ducat, and this last into a five-hundred franc note, which, to my spectator's horror, I incinerate in a dove pan, sprinkling the ashes on his head in commemoration of Samuel 2. *But det megical poem by Hofmannsthal, who incedently formed eh deep friendship wit Rilke in de year 1917, hes nothing te do wit all det, mon cher, es I recall, de magician calls te de "long-departed days" te come back undimmed,* sorrowful and grand, after which – and here, in the eleventh tercet, you find a parallel to the poet's wizardry in the passage from Proust, *classic tercets, mind ye, gif me a moment t' think, ahh yesss: And dreamlike felt the destiny of man / substantial as his presence in his limbs,* which is to say, he's talking about something quite different, keep in mind that *magos* in Greek — Greek, I never learned a word of it! — originally distinguished a member of a learned priestly caste, and only later acquired the sense of diviner or conjurer, of fraudster, too, *I vill concede,* the origins of this Iranian loanword are as obscure as those of magic itself, and we must make a distinction between white and black magic, the latter meaning a capitulation to supernatural powers and thus something quite distinct from the Mephistophelean "penetration of matter by matter," *but eh very diffrent ting, ye know, is det American who just valked through de Great Vall of China es if et vere air, vet is det, en optical illusion, ye simply cut...* No, no, I objected, you must realize resorting to the Blue Box or the Black Cabinet would be the end of televised magic, Herr Professor, but this brings us to a kind of institutional secret, can you keep such a thing to yourself? *Naturly I ken.* As can I, Herr von Castelmur-Bondo, and if I were to reveal to you this old trick of Houdini's, our tobacco colloquium would come perforce to a disappointing end: for you, because you would be forced to accept, even if with a measure of amusement, that you'd been duped, and this would hurl you into an identity crisis, putting in doubt your five senses and your native intelligence, and for me, because I would have broken the magician's oath: Abracadabra, sim sala bim, by Dante, Bellachini, and Houdini, I shall keep secret what I know and never betray my art.

Then again, it was true that Jérôme von Castelmur-Bondo, who just chuckled and remarked, *ferget ebout et,* esteemed literature so highly in part because of the novelist's propensities in the interpretation of dreams, his capacity to hold us utterly under his spell, and was there not, in that, an element of pulling the wool, given that the wondrous apparitions he invokes are themselves sensory illusions? As I admire the first editions of Thomas Mann in his father's former cigar cabinet – among them, *The Magic Mountain,* the hero of which, I happen to know, observes that a day without tobacco is the *ne plus ultra* of vapidity, that indeed, the only reason to eat is that one may smoke thereafter – I recollect the conversation in the studio between Lisabeta Ivanovna and Tonio Kröger. We read this novelette in the canton school, it contains a grotesquely cavalier depiction of the superficial redemption and consummation of feelings through literature, whoever's heart is spilling over need only appeal to the wordsmith, who will analyze your affairs and clothe them in comely words. Did Herr Castelmur-Bondo not agree that the comparison to the journeyman tailor could not be dismissed outright? The afflicted party, according to Thomas Mann, could go home, cooled off, enlightened, and just after that, Tonio Kröger, appalled at his own profession, asks Lisabeta whether she would really care to defend such a vain and frigid charlatan, at any rate, in this shamanism Hermann Arbogast Brenner saw the crass opposite of all that his companion has set forth concerning the magic of reading Proust. And he found confirmation for this view, if he might invoke Hofmannsthal, in the poet's dramaticle *Death and the Fool,* where Claudio says: *Where others take, where others give, / I stood aside, a mute from birth… / Had e'er I gifts of nature felt, / Had jolt or sigh my spirit quelled, / My wakeful heart, to vigil sworn, / Had ever held them in its bourn... / And even anguish! Fragile, frayed, / By thinking sapped, by reverie marred.*

Jérôme von Castelmur-Bondo, whose pipe had gone cold in his mouth, let his meditative gaze wander over the old pink and gold brocade of the wallpaper in the fumoir, which, particularly at the corner where the flat façade of the palas merges with the tower, had suffered some damage from the winter damp in the stone walls beneath the maduro-brown larchwood ceiling. It seemed he was counting each individual sconce on the wall, the holdover *appliques murales* in the Louis XIV style, lingering on the crumbling spines of the tightly shelved editions of Treitschke, Ranke, Mommsen, all from his Berlin semester in the early twenties, even then there were fraternity brothers who would snap to attention at any question as to their political allegiances and proudly proclaim the NSDAP. Only after this interlude, when I had let the Rey del Mundo die away, had taken out my black calf's-leather étui, and had withdrawn an Alonso Menendez Bahía Export, originally packed in a box of reddish smoke-cured sandalwood with a green tax stamp reading *República Federativa do Brasil,* did he resume: I can't say you're completely wrong about the still basically dubious role of magic in *littratur,* let us remember Proust abhorred the daylight and wrote his *Recherche* in a cork-lined room through dreadful attacks of asthma, and then Tonio Kröger, whom you yourself mentioned, tells his friend the rather outlandish story of a banker, an author of stories in his free time, who only became acquainted with his gifts after he'd served a prison sentence for embezzlement, during which this strayed burgher, aching for his habitual pleasures, concludes that those who would become poets must make themselves at home in some kind of jail. Indeed, this is a bitter insight – Jérôme grimaced, and the gold fillings twinkled in his teeth – perhaps, instead of naïve and sentimental, we should speak of respectable and vagrant authors, and the latter's gift would be a piquancy that readily turns to scandal. Think of the *cavaliere* Cipolla in Thomas Mann's "Mario and the Magician," the *forzatore,* the *prestidigitatore,* who tells the young Italian he's encouraged to stick his tongue out at the public, "You do as you wish. Or have you perhaps not done as you wished? Or else what you didn't wish?" Notice how the negation creeps closer and closer to the subject, how the hypnotic destitution of the will is calculated, plotted in the preamble, even if afterward the magician mocks his victim, repeating his words "Bè... that was me," his duplicity shines through here, in fact it is he, with the aid of his medium, who has stuck out his tongue at the public in Torre di Venere. We made it no further, as we took our aperitifs, in the matter of Leonzburg-Combray on this late summer early afternoon, because Amorose struck the gong in the stairwell, as good as saying lunch is served, and Jérôme von Castelmur-Bondo worked his way up from his armchair, took the full ashtray in hand, and dumped the cadaver of the Rey del Mundo from the window over the crowns of the chestnuts, oaks, and elms down into the deep defile of Middle Jurassic stone. Then he reached for his cane and motioned me to go before him down the slightly worn limewood steps with their hundred-year-old hollows, and we descended to the first floor, where his butler stood by the dining room door in his white uniform jacket, hands folded behind his back, red glimmers in his dyed black hair, and he saw me off with a smile that was difficult to decipher. Jean-Jacques Amorose was his full name, Jérome typically called him Jean, and when he did so, he modulated his voice in the tonal pattern C-A-B.

We will return to Leonzburg with its Combray traits when we drop in on the composer Edmond de Mog in the *Landweibelei,* the slumbering Bernese bailiffry in the enchanted garden with its broad, softly sloping roof, perhaps while listening to a work in three movements inspired by Iliers, produced at the request of the conductor Paul Sacher: a fantasia to be understood not as a musical program, but as pure music, the opening of which assails the connoisseur – over and over I come upon this term, not only in regards to tobacco – with a bold theme in D major. But first I must find my way to a neighboring town in search of another tonality, a magic sound from my earliest childhood in Menzenmang in the *Stumpenland* of Aargau.

2.

SCHUCO MALAGA,
WUHRMANN HABANA

There are ur-phenomena of tone, color, and scent often predestined, so to speak, irrespective of their contingent nature, to tune an existence like a stringed instrument; and the adult, when he attends a concert, an exhibition, a theater opening, searches, as though after a vanished picture book, for the traces of these earliest magical impressions. I remember very clearly one afternoon at the Waldau, my grandparents' restaurant, I must have been three at the time, when I was ordered to take my obligatory nap, which was always a torment to me, for just as in the corner in my parents' bedroom in the manufacturer's villa on the Sandstrasse in Menzenmang – *fabrikants,* the noblest genitive – there, too, in the so-called Jews' Salon on the landing overlooking the salon, I was tied down with rubber cords, the door was left open, I could hear the rush of the Wyna coursing through the valley, the hammering of the riveters in the die works or the rolling mill, the shunting of the

Rollbock boxcars at the aluminum factory, the piping of a locomotive, perhaps, like a faraway shriek, schoolchildren on the playground, apart from all that just tedium, counting dead flies, the scuff of chair legs in the parlor, the click and clack of billiard balls muffled at times by felt, my parents often helped my father's sisters during service, if a special occasion was afoot, they'd *shwoop* in, they may have been setting the table for the Frohsinn men's choir, because the swinging door to the office flapped repeatedly open and closed, and a diffuse activity reigned in the *garde-manger.* The child, bound and sleepless on a very bright day in bed — paradox of paradoxes — tries to orient himself, and all of a sudden hears a scattering of piano chords curtly struck, gliding up so softly they bring tears to my eyes, a breath of Sylvester's Day magic in the midst of a summer workday; I was still a little cheroot, I understood nothing of music, but years later, when I had my harmony lessons where my father's cousin lived, at the Pfendsack house on the Ölberg-strasse, I managed finally to grasp what it was that had taken hold of me, to analyze this series of tones that seemed to drift like flakes of gold in bottles of Danziger Goldwasser, a descending melody from major and minor sixths, the series, intended for C major, must have opened with the G-E interval and ended with F-D, that is, descending from the tonic with the 6/4 chord without C from dominant to subdominant — which corresponds to the melancholy of blues — but instead of stopping at A-F, it fell two steps further to D minor.

As we know, the young Mozart could drive his father to the verge of madness with an unresolved seventh, but far more galling was this insistence on F-D, an interval which, with its suppressed A minor, demands the G seventh and a release through the tonic, and I had to endure this tension not only through two hours of nap time in the Jews' Salon, but through the entirety of puberty until my harmony lessons began; and considering it might just have been the servant girl, Irmeli, in a transport of sportiveness or sorrow, who struck the nicotine-yellow keys of the ordure-brown Burger & Jacobi piano, the indulgent reader may gather from these tobacco sheets the ways fortuity reigns in the childhoods of creators, *artistes,* better said, but even more so, how immense is the power of music – here nothing less than magic – over as yet uncultivated natures. Still, I couldn't help but cry, because the descending cadence G-E, F-D, E-C, D-B, C-A, B-G, A-F, G-E, F-D recalled to me the painting of corn fields in the salon, a restrained landscape study in tender lilac, muted gold, and dusty green, showing the stretch of land beneath the Stierenberg, not far from the Waldau, where the Erlkönigstrasse skirts the Wachtal meadow next to *de drüeich,* the three oaks, before wending its way to Rickenbach. All the little oil in its white stucco frame showed was a softly curving path lost in the stalks of a swaying grain field with hints of red poppies under the taut, desolate balloon silk of a summer sky with scant ribbons of storm clouds. Just like the major sixth, with its polka-like opening, the breach in the cornrows ended in a no man's land that presented a riddle to the child stewing in his boredom, yearning all the while for his mother: what happens to the path after it curves, is it even still *there* in the depths of the picture? Decades later, gravely ill, in autogenic training, as I recited over and over the mantra "My breath is calm and effortless, my forehead is cool," I would hallucinate this mauve-gold cornfield; in the deckchair beneath the Canadian silver poplars on the gravel terrace in Menzenmang, I felt the ache for this painting of cornstalks; on Doctor Rohnstein's couch in Buchs, this image from the Waldau materialized; everywhere, always, this single landscape.

Menzenmang, Leonzburg. If I have spoken so profusely of that first encounter with the aural, it is from the certainty – and here I must reach for a robust Wuhrmann Habana, maduro, in its sugar-white wrapping, *cheroot* from the Portuguese *charuto,* cigar, derived from the Tamil for tobacco roll; in German it is *Stumpen,* cognate with stump, and cigars of this kind are cut on each end, the sheath of the Wuhrmann has a red stamp on the foot with the word *feu* – the certainty, if my own memory serves, that we do not awaken, as children, from mythical darkness into chronologically segmented experience; that instead there are aromas, colors, tones that little islands of light become moored to, boring down into them, extracting their ore, and one of these ur-tones was *Malaga*. Malaga wine, of course, on the shelves of the cellar at the Waldau, in the barrel vaults draped with spider webs where I ventured as a boy, but here, in this Wuhrmann Habana chapter, Malaga means Leonzburg-Combray, where my father, an insurance inspector by trade, who spurned a career in hospitality or wholesale tobacco, used to take me now and then on his expeditions, telling mother, *I'm off a-travlin, I'll tek little Hermann wit me if ye don't mind,* and even as a tyke I'd been all over his district, I used to accompany my cemetery grandmother out on her *saunters,* I went with father on work trips, the first of these I can, may, will, or shall remember, was a ride to Leonzburg-Combray. On the lotus-black English velocipede with its cover for the well-oiled chain and a nickel-plated child's seat with two footbeds – these, in particular, were a source of wonder for me – we left behind the park with the manufacturer's villa to the south, four slender poplars flanking its gate, and took the Zwingstrasse down into the village, past the fire depot, the drying plant, the lot with the cable rolls from Brugg, to the Häusler building and the school, that cube of raving madness with its urine-yellow mortar, circled the roundabout where the hooligans left their plunder from the first Saturday in May, onto the Bahnhofstrasse, passing the Weber cardboard mill, the Eichenberger pastry shop where made-leines may well have been available for purchase, the Wildi stationers, and the saddle store, reaching the slight elevation where the SBB train station – *not* the WTB, *not* the Wynentaler Bahn – stood, and they would load my father's conveyance onto the green umber Seetaler mail carriage while he and I waited on the bone-hard third-class benches for the things that were supposed to happen to happen.

It pleases me to emphasize – before the whistle sets us free, along with the signal from the red-capped stationmaster Müller – that we are traveling on the Seetaler line and *not* the Wynentaler, and it likewise seems judicious to me to offer the reader – whose indulgence I have presumed from the beginning, and whom I have prescribed, for this chapter, a Wurhmann B Habana – an initiation, however cursory at first, into the transport geography of Menzenmang; and in doing so, I must reveal something the significance of which will only be clear much later: that my father was an insurance representative for the districts of Kulm and Leonzburg, but not for the capital of *Aarouw*, where his successful colleague Nöthinger plied his trade. These leaps in time, flashes forward and back, these parallel, diagonal, and *contradictio in adjecto* montages, these fleeting distortions of memory intermixed with poppy are in the very nature of my chronicle, because a childhood is assembled from tatters and particulate like the filler of a cigar from far-flung plantations in Sumatra, Havana, and Brazil, not to forget the thin-cut, fire-cured tobaccos of Kentucky or Latakia, and it is on the degree to which this arcana becomes transparent, like a watermark – on the successful *marriage* of ingredients selected by the tasters in the blending room – that the intensity of pleasure depends. To the west, the *Stumpen-land* village is bordered by the Stierenberg, the highest point in the Aargau, and to the east by the ridge of the Sonnenberg, which evens out at the Bruderholz by Reinach before rising up like a Bundt cake again toward Homburg, with its four-legged observation tower and the acclaimed destination restaurant, the Homburg Echo. To the south of Menzenmang, a lateral moraine divides the lowlands of Beromünster in Lucerne, to the north stands Rymenzburg, a fiction once fancifully envisaged as the administrative center of the Kulm district that has sadly become fact through greed and sprawl and the consequent blur-ring of the borders between Reinach, Menzenmang, and Burg, from here we enter the so-called *Rynecher Moor.* The narrow-gauge Wynentaler line, whose formerly greyish-white and cobalt-blue trains were painted blazing orange to mitigate the danger they posed to road traffic, links the Menzenmang terminus to Aarau, while the Seetaler line, a curious relic from the days of the labyrinthine Southern Rail Network, runs from the factory town to Beinwil, *Beuwu* in dialect, note the L-vocalization on the end. There, by bright Lake Hallwil, where we used to ride our bikes to swim when the brown-tinged *baadi,* the swimming holes in the Angermatt next to the cemetery, were too shallow, the trains change to the Seetaler line proper, which links Lucerne, the city of lights, with Leonzburg, and serves as a connector for the east-west line running between Geneva and Romanshorn.

I no longer have in mind the hour or so journey, the SBB will not be thawed out until the Dankensberg chapter, for now, the pneuma of a Wuhrmann B will conjure up within me the light-dappled bouquet of a cool June morning before the summer festivals, my first visit to the city between Staufberg and Schlossberg, when the insurance inspector left me at the Hotel Haller in the care of the innkeeper or a servant girl with the visiting card reading *Hermann Brenner Jr.,* which I was no less proud of than of sharing my father's name – because he had to visit Villa Malaga with a *policy,* another magical word. In vain I must have clamored for permission to accompany him to the elegant mansions of the *widow's quarter,* true, I wasn't afraid, but I felt too small for the novelties with which the big city – the metropolis, even – bombarded me. Among the revelations there was a shunting maneuver I witnessed on the Seetalplatz: gasping, pugnacious, a locomotive – a word that must bear some relation to *perspective* – tugged a lone freight car past the barrier and up the curve that vanished into the shadowy sea of buildings, and after a short while, it reappeared behind the red-and-white grating with an SBB employee in a blue parka in the brakeman's cabin, and automatically, it rolled over the switch rails and onto the dead-end track. O soot-grimy mass of levers, O filigree openwork of the red-spectacled signal arm, O gravel massed between the oaken ties, O double barrier, never before seen, O round roofs of cattle cars, every bit of it inconceivable, things unheard of at the station in Menzenmang, things possible only in a depot-metropolis, thanks to the principles of the hump yard. Still more, I was fascinated – as with the exotic portents of Leonzburg-Combray – by Villa Malaga's Mediterranean echoes, inside me stood cypresses and citrus trees fully formed, and Hotel Haller I lived through as a forced detention, and it wasn't far from one, if we recall the penitentiary with its octagonal watchtower located not far away.

Now there are, as is well known in the science of parenting, two methods for making unruly children compliant, either you punish or reward them, and my father astonished me by pulling something wondrous enchanting, dazzling, extraordinary, rapturous, pyramidal, deathly elegant from his briefcase. Packed in pink wax paper, a toy car or, quite simply *the* toy, *the* car, a superspankingnew shimmering Schuco Examico convertible chosen from among the assortment at my uncle Herbert's store in Burg. To quote the entry on this model in Fritz Ferschl and Peter Kapfhammer's comprehensive Schuco book, *The Fascinating World of Technical Toys:* "What must a proper car have? A clutch, four forward gears, plus neutral and reverse. What model car has had these features since 1936?" The Shuco Examico. It was fire-engine red, with red ribbed upholstery, pinion steering, a painted dashboard, the classic gear shifter with reverse located down and diagonal, a hand brake, a horn, a miniature music box for a radio, a lever by the passenger door, a grille like the one from the BMW it was modeled on, two strips of chrome trim, a windshield wiper, and, in place of the gas cap, a tiny hole for the winding key; the wheels were half-hidden beneath sloped fenders, like on a Fleetwood, silt-brown and running the length of the body; the doors were embossed and shaped like saddle bags – *Satteltasche*, nowadays there's a restaurant in Leonzburg with that name – two soldered grommets for headlights, a black license plate reading *Schuco* graced the trunk, the three-spoke steering wheel had a finger grip rim, the tires were replica Pirellis.

It grieves me that my first mention of my sister Klärli and brother Karli must present them as a kind of wear-and-tear, rubbish-dilapidation consortium, but the fact remains that every single toy ever received, revered, fawned over by the firstborn son, Hermann Arbogast Brenner, was illicitly passed down to Klärli and Kari, then disassembled, destroyed, mislaid, buried in the garden, or consigned in some other way to oblivion sans reimbursement. A horrible trauma, and the beginning of the end of sibling solidarity. But six months ago now, in a Zurich antique shop selling Märklin train stations, drumming monkeys, and tin steamers, I saw, on the glass shelf, that very same model, but cream-colored, correct to the last detail, and the asking price of seven hundred fifty francs did not disturb me in the least; and now, using the one-finger system to draft this episode on a rented Hermes 3000, I can steer with my left hand the fourteen-centimeter long, five-and-a-half-centimeter wide vehicle in a radius of twenty-four centimeters over the thick waves of paper in Dornseiff's thematic dictionary, which lies open to page 242, chapter eight, Section II, with the subject heading *Steering, Routes, Directions*. The critic Adam Nautilus Rauch informs me that this method of novel-writing is known as restitution therapy, though it goes without saying, I have never fancied myself a novelist, at best just a prosaist smoking my existence down to the nub, but still, there's something striking in the technique, which I admire in my friends Irlande von Elbstein-Bruyère and Bert May, and even in Jérôme von Castelmur-Bondo. Through its lens, we can grasp the variance in scale between child and adult, so that now, I may fill in what I couldn't decipher as a three-year-old, the message on the black undercarriage: Schuco-Examico 4001, Patents Applied For In England–Switzerland–USA–Japan–Italy.

And now, as my life has a maximum duration of two to three years, and any parsimony, restraint, or squirrelling away would be absúrd, I have consummated the childhood dream begotten of the Schuco Examico and acquired a *rossa corsa* Ferrari 328 GTS with a removable hardtop and a maximum speed of 166 mph, and may state unequivocally that no make of sports car, however legendary or pedigreed, not even one blessed by the Pope himself, can approach the Schuco brought into service at Hotel Haller, the one I christened the *Schuco Malaga* because my father's clients there took up so much time, and whilst the insurance inspector, Hermann Brenner Junior, and the then-owner of Malaga Cellars on Niederlenzerstrasse talked over the arcana of life, retirement, and disability insurance, premiums, supplementary risks, and double payout in case of death, I wheeled my red convertible over the parquet floor of Hotel Haller, whose herringbone slats marked out a patchwork of streets, and soon discovered it was better to steer by hand than let the mainspring wind down, because that way, you could accelerate forever. On I drove, still ignorant of the castle town's topography, down Bleicherain and Aavorstadt, the Rathausgasse and the Postgasse, shot up Malagarain to Freiämterplatz, then pulled the handbrake to let the crossing traffic through, there wasn't much of it though, so soon after the war. I earned my preschool driver's license, the polished mirror gleam of the Hotel Haller's parquet floor was the world to me, it pushed my tires to the limit, now honking, now listening to the radio – the jingle on the music box was *Falling in Love Again* – I made mountains of tables, meadows of rugs, refashioned the niche for the wood-burning stove into my own personal garage, an ironing board at a slant became a daredevil ramp, I put the clockwork motor through the rigors, look there, the red roadster is taking the hill in first, Leonzburg-Combray was my Maranello. Dropped off for the duration of an insurance consultation, I transformed into the Commendatore. I handled the levers of childhood dominion, steered my time annihilation machine on wheels, I was motorized before my father, and even when he did drive home up the Sandstrasse two years later, anno 1947, in a spinach-green Fiat Topolino whose lone charms were its retractable roof and yellow rims, I, the street sorcerer, felt superior with my Malaga convertible and the two bricks I used as a car lift when carrying out repairs with a ticket punch and my mother's sewing needles.

You, my father, who at seventy-two years old were rammed by a tractor trailer from Dürrenasch on the road running through Birrwil – or *Birrbu,* as you pronounced it – and crushed to death in your Fiat – once a Fiat, always a fiat, *fiat justitia pereat mundus* – so they had to cut you, with your forty broken bones, from the wreckage, you, Father, in those days in Leonzburg-Combray, gave me, for the catalogue price of CHF 7.80, with no motive but to help me brave my boredom, a gift worth more than a Testarossa today, and this only adds to the infamy of my siblings' scrapping it irreparably; a true salesman's son, just like your Hermann, you prospered in what certainly was not the ideal profession for you, you were generous, philanthropic, obliging, first invest, then collect, don't sow before you reap: I learned that from you, I've known it ever since that memorable summer day at Hotel Haller in June on the eve of the summer festival, you started at the bottom, rinsing milk bottles at *de miuchi* – the dairy at Uncle Herbert's – then came your salesman's apprenticeship at the former textile mill of your uncle Otto Weber-Brenner, now the Brenner & Sons offices, you hated it, I know, you would while away half the morning absorbed in your architectural sketches with the excuse of handing out the mail, when the stock market crashed you were pushed to the very edge of the abyss, the last thing you would have dreamed of in your Waldau youth was chasing down clients as an insurance salesman, I will frequently allow myself, as the signatory of these impressions, the privilege of addressing you directly, Father.

As it happens, my Schuco-Examico-Malaga was a faithful replica of the pre-war BMW 328 convertible, prototype for the Bristol 400, and in all sincerity, I should have forwarded the invoice for its cream-white lookalike to my brother and sister – handsomely you should pay today for what you so ignorantly destroyed before – but Klärli and Kari too broke off all contact with me after my wife, Flavia, the jurist from the Grisons, abandoned me at Brunseleben along with – *nolens volens* – my sons, Hermann Christian Laurent and Matthias Wolfgang Kaspar. That's understandable, they chose their longer way, I will take the short one.

What can you do, even in the womb the firstborn has it harder than the latecomers, for them it's a cakewalk, this can be proven gynecologically, the new mother's pelvis is narrower, the path through the birth canal a torment, not to mention the patient's panic in the delivery room, and this can be passed down to her offspring, if the oxygen is too thin, the blood supply interrupted, the lady parts fail, *fiasco;* glimpse the light when you tumble out and you will suffer from agoraphobia your whole life long, will seek out niches and arcades and avoid sunny, bright locales, if it is a forceps delivery, then claustrophobia's the result, and what is my winter pastime, bobsledding, if not the constant attempt through repetition compulsion to conquer the canal, quick and smooth down into the Horseshoe, as soon as you hit the inside curve before Telephone Corner the 4G forces push you into the wall with its snarling icicle jaws that remind one of *Monsieur Winter Go Home,* out with a tightrope maneuver, in, puff, out, precipitate labor on bare ice, a catastrophe, on you glide in the Siorpaes canister, the black tin coffin hurtling back and forth, your helmet dings the track all the way down to Martineau Corner, and then – the finish line. Our siblings may well profit from our pioneering performance, like everyone riding cossetted in the slipstream – this is a term from the world of autosports, Ferrari, the red racer from Maranello with the *cavallo rampante* for its emblem – and now, when the time comes to return the favor, they are stingy, stingy, stingy, never in their lives would it occur to them to offer some small token – voilà, a box of Hoyo de Monterrey Des Dieux – for the simple reason that in squabbles, it was the eldest who always had to be reasonable; a token, my dear Hermann Arbogast, for paving the way for us a bit with *de schnüüzi,* the snowplow, or because our parents found the wooden Flying Dutchman too costly for you, while we naturally got the convertible toy car and the metal rowbike, or because, for instance – I take these instances at random – we not only disassembled and destroyed your Wesa model train set, but were given – unlike you – a Märklin Crocodile with rails, switches, and accessories, or because, thanks to my good word, they let Klärli study German Literature in Zurich, I even got her a two-room apartment, or because I explained to our punctilious mother that Kari flunking school at age twelve needn't be an existential tragedy, and that a secondary school education – as opposed to the district school, where the crème de la crème went – was good enough to find a respectable trade. All this was more than sufficient grounds for a cognac annuity, but instead we are reproached for achieving everything before those born later, condemned for making something extraordinary of ourselves while they remain candidates for mediocrity. But even that isn't true, Kari is now a sought-after landscape architect, and he made it there by the skin of his teeth, while Klärli's had everything served to her on a platter, and dilly-dallies with a part-time job at the high school; *item,* I have recouped the Schuco Examico, have given my sons the Crocodile and the HAG Red Arrow, the brown Lötschberg locomotive and the Rangier tractor, the Re 4/4 and the premium steam engine with coal car and real functioning smokestack, I have always treated the elder Hermann and the younger Matthias exactly the same, naturally I know that as we redress those mistakes we suffered through as *test subjects,* we open the possibility for other childrearing errors, perhaps all this Märklin will drive them to yearn for the Wesa Lilliput set from Inkwil in the Bern Canton – which has now become a costly antique – with the greatest climbing power of any model train, dining car with functioning lights available for delivery.

I ask myself, recalling my Proust conversation with Jérôme von Castelmur-Bondo, why these vessels of childhood memory mean so much, why we are willing so lavishly to forsake, in hyperboles that branch out infinitely in our search for lost time, the entire spectrum of the present *ad interim* for the sake of a single color from the past, honey-yellow or ruby-red and lustrous like a church window. I pose this question, and would reply, with Benn, whom Bert May despises, *I do not know to this day, and must ready myself now to go;* toys of time, Anker Stone Blocks, Meccano Gears, Wesa Arosa train station with real miniature newspapers in the kiosk, the Little Alchemist, the litmus paper, the picture book, now vanished, with the title *The Fairytale Forest and the World of Children* – I believe, no matter how many Examicos we stockpile, we will never again feel what beguiled us back then, or what cut us to the core – not even in the Primal Scream therapy with Doctor Jana Jesenska Kiehl, which I broke off one year ago for the sake of the present composition, the primal scream is never the same scream for the pretty mother hidden behind the seven mountains, the scream bellowed from the children's home-cum-concentration camp high over Lake Walen, or Ache Walen, I should say – for we are creatures of time, even if, now and then, with a deep draw on a Hoyo de Monterrey Des Dieux, a glimpse of all those things may yet glimmer on the horizon. Perhaps the cream-white Schuco Examico with its carousel-red interior is simply a fetish, resurrected for a few seconds of music box bliss when draped in the mist of Havana, Sumatra, or Brazil the way it *really* was in the days of Hotel Haller, gleaming *rosso corsa;* the truer witnesses are my own boys, Hermann and Matthias, and the painful recollection of the first tones they uttered is now tightening its grip around my throat: not Mama, not Papa, but *ka* for car, *tata* for tractor, *wee-ow* for wheel, and then the combinations, *tata wee-ow* for tractor wheel, *ka-man* for driver, *roruh* for steam roller; no sooner did I discover an East German firm was once again manufacturing certain Schuco models, most notably the Mercedes Silver Arrow with screw-on wheels, custom tools, wing mirrors, and tailpipe trims, than I drove them to their own Sigismund Markus – the Hemmeler toy store in Aarau, managed by the wife of my friend Adam Nautilus Rauch, but instead, they chose to supplement their Playmobil collection – just imagine, choosing plastic over stamped tin. Adam Nautilus Rauch, literary editor of the *Schweizer Monatsheft,* need only take the elevator to the first floor from his attic study on Hintere Vorstadt, where 30,000 books line the shelves in alphabetical order – revised annually by the Legissima Literary Institute – and there he stands in that paradise of Furka Alpine train sets and Wilesco steam rollers. O how I loved those visits with my boys to that city with its inevitable air of the museum, its cooing doves, its gate tower rising defiantly over the sloping eaves, the drowsy splash of water in the fountains of Casino Park, the bogen-patterned Belgian block streets brightened by the carillon's pealing, when they needed the G2 gear kit to complete their Stokys erector set, or Matthias wanted to try on gorilla masks for Carnival, I did not hesitate to buy, in addition to the green one, the cockchafer-brown Crocodile CE-3/2 to grace our little Gotthard in the library at Brunsleben, with its two transport trains running in opposite directions on the Basel-Chiasso line, and yet there it stands in black-and-white in my beloved wife's divorce filing: I never cared a whit for our children.

Moving on, my friend and the patron of the present tobacco sheets, Adam Nautilus Rauch, has a comfortable weekend home of his own on Lake Halwil, not far from Leonzburg-Combray, and on the hanging balcony we have often discussed these very questions – he smoking his pipe and I with an immortal Brenner Mocca from the bundle with the mauve emblem, wrapped in a silver ribbon – what is memory, what is the present, what is the future; and in his gruff way he advocated the *carpe diem* stance and modified Proust's dictum about reading's being "as magical as a deep sleep" with a paraphrase of Ernst Jandl, "to the extent that I am present while reading," thereby contradicting Jérôme von Castelmur-Bondo, of whom it was not at all clear *det he was*. What does that mean, he asked again, gripping a mug of beer and squinting into the sea of poplars with his Asiatic eyes, not in the least, Hermann, that I overlook the here and now, my immediate surroundings, my attention to the present, no, I do not flee into Hildesheimer's *Marbot,* into Kleist's feud with Goethe, I sharpen my gaze – and it's true, there is something buzzard-like about him – for the present, reading has more to do with optics than philology, look there at the lake, *de lek,* stretched out, smooth as a whale's skin or crowned with foam when the foehn blows – *salii, Carlo,* he greeted his parrot in its cage by the porch swing – the tones, aquamarine, emerald, turquoise, lead-grey, are by no means those of the studies Hesse executed during his Lauscher period in his rowboat on Lake Lucerne, there you see aestheticism carried to an extreme. At this, Adam Nautilus took a resolute pull from his pipe – what I mean is, through relentless reading of the kind to which I am professionally obliged – just look at the desk, at the Suhrkamp titles piled up there alone – you can also conserve immediate vision in the sense that Goethe speaks of, an earnestness in the enjoyment of life; now as far as the magical dream-depths of reading, there too I would like to correct the Emeritus a bit – *he shouldn't tek it hard* – for as soon as you bring magic into the question, the circus comes into play as well, for me that means the literature industry, jugglers and dancing tigers are a marvel under the marquee, but you can't mistake the sawdust for the grass it's strewn on, or a high wire act with art, or the quiet showdown with a book and the bustling under the spotlights, *ye know,* when I sit down for a theater premier, I stay well away from the rabble in the pit, I think about what I've seen and heard, make a small number of notes, and on Sunday morning at seven I sit down at the typewriter; rubbing elbows with Heinz this and Rüedli that, with the mafia, that's etiquette, polite society nonsense, that's not for us, the critic's task is to judge, and the less chumming and glad-handing you do, the more independent your opinion will be. You see what I'm getting at, once you invoke magic and dreams, the wooly and wistful are just around the corner, adoration, *undershtand, salii, Carlo, saliiii,* the devotion cult, no, I'd rather stick with Brecht, distance, *Verfremdung,* critique, *here, hef a beer, fresh from de tap.*

Your lowly servant, Hermann Arbogast Brenner, who knows a bit about cigars, but next to nothing about literature – significantly, my middle name means "one cut off from his heritage" – could hardly get a word in edgewise, we should have set the chess clock, but then again, it's no great loss, it merely shows that there are authors of the voice, raconteurs – and that earnestness in the enjoyment of life is not enough, you need an audience to brag to about your delectable calamari – and a Bernhard specialist like Adam Nautilus Rauch is not immune to fulmination, and envies the role played by the Jérôme von Castelmur-Bondos of the world, a community can only take one storyteller at a time. In the interim, it struck me that memory likely grows more preponderant as life approaches its end, but when I tried to communicate to my friend the feeling that my submarine was sinking deeper and deeper, and how it seemed that the needle on the depth gauge would never stop turning, Adam Nautilus replied, with his wonted disdain, that no one could say with certainty which of us would embark first on his nautical exploits, alluding, in this way, to the crossing of the Styx: he, of course, was best prepared to traverse the Mediterranean, with his yacht sitting sea-ready at the port of San Remo, but I, his junior by twenty years, was the one with the terminal prognosis. This is plain to see, I thought briefly to myself and swallowed, before he took to crowing about his most recent jaunt, all it takes is one look at the X-rays, but gentle fate has arranged things so that the sick must beg for excuses before the chronically healthy, and not the other way around; it is the privileged who demand consideration, and not those consigned to their doom. The *moribundus* is compelled to ask his visitor how he is feeling, and his friend, depositing his gift of a floral wreath – I do not mean Adam Nautilus Rauch specifically, he would never set foot in a hospital – will not hesitate to stand there at the deathbed gabbing about his migraines or his recent dental checkup. Distinctions collapse, existence has no feeling of proportion with regard to death, when your number comes up, it's best to just slink off without disturbing anybody's sleep, and so, among other things, you get one man claiming he's got no time to lend an ear to reminiscences about a Shuco Examico, while another counters that he'll never be free to skipper for three weeks around the Mediterranean – nothing against sailor's tans or San Remo, but Poseidon, lost in his endless calculations on the ocean's floor, will not have the chance to resurface before the world comes to an end, that's it, don't you see, Adam Nautilus Rauch, my submarine is plunging down without respite, and there's no more point in trying to clear the tanks. Which of us is right? Perhaps that sundial in the south of Bavaria with the banderole that reads: *My time is not your time.* And yet the one shared the same time with the other. *Lookie there, here comes Hetz!*

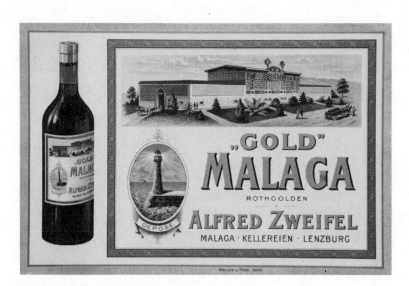

3.

SAND TART MADELEINE,
VORSTENLANDEN SAND LEAF

Climatologists count it as a summer day whenever the temperature reaches or exceeds twenty-five degrees Celsius, eighty Fahrenheit on the gypsum-white jumbo thermometer next to the broom closet under the awning of Castle Brunsleben, regardless of sunlight or precipitation, and if, after midday, the quicksilver climbs to thirty or higher, then the dog days are at hand, and Switzerland can expect a heat wave of this kind to last through to the coming weekend – that is, the moment of writing, on Saturday, July 23 – because, according to the calculations, the air mass boundary between the cooler polar currents and the warmer tropical ones lies at present somewhere over Great Britain and Germany, which is the same path as the Atlantic disturbance. Forecast through Wednesday afternoon: good weather throughout Switzerland, scattered storm formations in the mountains, afternoon temperatures in the Northern Alpine lowlands approximately twenty-eight degrees, rising to thirty in the south, freezing level at four thousand meters above sea level. Outlook until Sunday evening: generally fine, warm weather, light storms on Thursday and Friday. Calendar information for Wednesday, July 20, 1989: week 29, day 222, sunrise at 5:30 AM, sundown at 9:14 PM, moonrise at 12:30 PM, moonset at 11:45 PM, lunar phase waxing. A high-pressure zone assures plentiful sunlight, when the bad weather lifts in Germany, the humidity in Switzerland will rise, and this moisture, combined with unstable thermal stratification, will contribute to the aforementioned scattered evening showers, on Wednesday and Friday the bad weather just north of the country will shift eastward, for the rest, the Azores High should guarantee dry and sunny conditions throughout Switzerland. Thought of the day: *When sunshine toasts his toes and hide / the drudge dreams of the oceanside.* In the same newspaper, alongside this *bon mot:* Nearly 4,000 dead in a heat wave in China, the victims mostly elderly and infirm, these are the ones who suffer most when the temperature rises to forty and above. Public officials were quoted as saying China hadn't seen a drought on this scale in decades. Air raid bunkers had been opened to offer shelter to the *parched.* My mother was a shade plant, better suited to the ice saints than to the dog days. *In hot July when summer scolds, no one knows what winter holds.*

But I must restrain myself in these pages, I cannot range so far afield, my intention is to refract the light, as through a burning glass, and surely the old chestnut *haste makes waste* is pertinent here, to find my way back, with the kindling of an Opalino Forelle, a brand that still exists in name only, from the Lake Hallwil to Leonzburg-Combray, taking

Seonerstrasse along the Aabach, passing the swimming hole, the pentagonal penitentiary on the right, leaving behind the Hotel Haller and heading through the Schulhausplatz and on to the Rathausgasse, my sights set on Schützenmatt Park and Niederlenzerstrasse, because I am obliged, it strikes me, to furnish the indulgent reader – if he is so inclined, I mean this literally, as I imagine him bending over the present pages – with something more than mere local-historical reminiscences of the mansion my father visited in his capacity as insurance inspector in the hot June of 1945 –Villa Malaga, as it was known, not far from the most exotic edifice in all of Aargau, Malaga Cellars, done in the Moorish style, which, I read with relief in the *Aargau Daily* of September 2, 1987, will be preserved, at least in part, after endless wrangling over its restoration, as a mock façade, in deference to luminist ideals – yes, this Spanish bodega with its withered southern splendor stands on the corner of Feriämterplatz, which leads to Gormund in turn – a willfully stereometric outpost of my import-export childhood in Menzenmang, it broods mute in the sun, overgrown with nettles, like so many of the *Stumpenland's* shuttered cigar factories, Eicifa on the Friedhofstrasse, the Indiana complex in Alzbach, Reinach Nord, Gautschi & Gautschi on the corner of Hauptstrasse and Winkel. With their Partagás-yellow and royal blue meanders, the two wings of the building resemble Havana boxes turned on their sides, accentuating the main façade, where a segmented arch conceals the offices; in the pediment, two fantastical winged beasts, in appearance something like dinosaurs, bookend the firm's trademark, a *faro* or lighthouse with the name Alfred Zweifel beneath it, resplendent in Neapolitan cursive; horseshoes crown the blind windows, cradling stylized orchid hearts, in English red a frieze divides the bands of quatrefoil fleurs-de-lys from the basketweave pattern on the flanks with its ultramarine, stelliform acanthus, the middle is Malaga red, checkerboard triskeles alternate with chessboard pawns, curved corbels like abstract caryatids hold up the cornice, licorice-black W's divide window from window, toreador white squares off against oxblood red.

How is it, the wayfarer through the lowlands of *nicotiana tabacum* will wonder, that Leonzburg-Combray should come into possession of this Andalusian jewel, which would demand a rendering in aquarelle – by Edmond de Mog, perhaps – were it not already a painting become architecture? How he loves this extravagant folly, that virtuoso composer and fauvist, well, let's put it another way: Where does an entrepreneur in 1877 find the courage to open a business bottling tonic wine from the Mediterranean under the brand name *El Faro?* Who were the customers, the invalids, who fell for this plonk? What times were those when a hallucination, a fata morgana, sufficed to up and make a go of it just like that? Happily I would have lived in those days, a salesman beside my great-grandfather in the Waldau, a dealer in raw tobacco, brown gold. In my lowermost depths, I am captivated by the specter of risk, of hitting the big one, I ever was, still am, and shall always remain – at least, for another two or three years – a grifter, and magic permits me to juggle – look close, and you will see it – with the certainty of my own death, this alone makes it bearable, and explains my penchant for the market stall, for the circensian, for the illusory, my *do as I do* imagination, where you follow the magician's movements, but something quite different emerges – and there too lie the origins of my obstinate desire to stand before the court on the behalf of a lost cause like Malaga Cellars. I have no need of Castle Leonzburg, admired by all, if only with a genteel, taciturn nod from the backseat of a Buick limousine, when the world offers me a delicacy so abstruse as the madcap, *mental* Malaga Cellars, erstwhile warehouse for tonic wines, now an abandoned circus caravan whose effect, rooted in exoticism or, better, in eighteenth century chinoiserie, explodes with the sorcerer's picturesque virtuosity: a grammar of ornament, a miraculous backdrop, a pyrotechnic one-man show. Why bother shoving off to Chartres cathedral, the gothic has nothing on this.

But wait, O Brunsleben cigarier gone early into retirement, extolling the unhurried leisure demanded by a Romeo y Julieta carefully selected, toasted, lit, and consumed one pull at a time, in even intervals of one minute each: this Felliniesque paean to the magical and circensian ill suits your own tobacco leaves with their late-style pretensions, the Stechlinesque spirit Jérôme so prizes. We shall put this theme aside then, but let us confess behind a hand held forth – as the lord of the castle himself is wont to do – that dry tears fill our eyes when we find ourselves under the big top, especially when the Circus Knie stops in Leonzburg-Combray in the second week of July, for the equestrian, Erica Knie née Brosi, is a pedigree beauty when she wages her three-minute onslaught of artful, archetypal femininity – a free fall, but with no sense of vertigo – not tubercular, no, rather Lipizzan-lissome, limelight blonde, lustrous. We were born in the arena, that is to say, *one* of our births took place there, and so, until we have drawn our final breath, we shall remain in thrall to the circensian Eros, even if we must state repeatedly for the record that creation comprises more than pops orchestras, Turkish delight, and card tricks, and commend ourselves to the sanguine-stoical dignity of being as embodied in the old historian, who, as he can no longer manage the eighty-seven steps from courtyard to castle by foot, hovers now on the platform of his stair lift: down for his daily walk in the Ebnet, up for his reading. Hermann Arbogast Brenner need only stand at the outer gateway between the two lindens that tower over the sloping meadow – the Brenntan, as it is known – bordering the driveway across from the croquet court cloaked in shadows, and he has an oblique view of the castle *au pair,* north-northeast perspective: the crenellated keep, the gate house, and the Bern house; a saddle formation divides the green cone of hill from the neighboring Goffersberg, a flat, rocky crest upholds the fortifications – quite unlike Brunsleben, where a single arched roof joins the palas to the tower, following the Chaistenberg, which drops off precipitously toward the east – over Jura limestone, not soft Südtal molasse.

Brunsleben is a Hapsburg construction dating from the thirteenth century, its tenure fell to Sir Heinrich Gessler of Meienberg, bailiff of Aargau, his widow was at Brunsleben when the Bernese invaded our district in 1415, thenceforward the property was administered by the city of Bern, the heirs fought over the Gessler castle until the Brown Bear lent it to Heinrich Rot of Aarau in 1470 and then to the Segensers in 1472, the Reformation brought further negotiations, Bern assigned Brunsleben to the bailiff of Leonzburg, who leased it to a tenant in turn, and this situation persisted until the fall of the Bernese patricians, in 1804 the castle came into the hands of the newly established canton of Aargau, which turned it over immediately to a certain Colonel Friedrich Hünerwasser, a man who had known Pestalozzi at Neuhof; it then passed down, through the marriage of one of his descendants, to the von Castelmur-Bondos, its current owners. *Round twenty-shix,* in the year 1626, that is, a gale tore off the packsaddle roof, and it became apparent the entire structure was *all rotted out en dingy,* hardly surprising given the centuries-long neglect of any restoration work. The tower was then fitted with *a crook hiddn bek of de vall,* a cruck frame with a crow-step gable, but soon afterward, in 1644, a lightning strike ignited the gunpowder stored there, and only the anchor bolts kept the walls from blowing apart. Not until the dawn of the nineteenth century, during the major renovations carried out from 1805-1806, was the tower brought down to the height of the palas and the entire building placed under a single roof. On the south side, where the enceinte extends to the castle gate, a terraced garden rises up in three stages, the Bernese filled in the outer moat long ago, the service buildings were overhauled, too, the tenant house by the south wall was integrated into the *Zwinger,* the rounded cellar is a vestige of the southeastern watchtower. Before, when the castle bore down on the north wall alone, the courtyard was more spacious, but today, its pitched roof, with double forking beams at right angles, spans the entire precinct. The tower stands compact over the slanting Dogger stone of the moat, describing a semicircle closed off to the west, the stone blocks are rough hewn, at the base the masonry is four meters thick and at the top no less than three, offshoots from the cracks from the gunpowder explosion remain evident to the naked eye. The hallmark of Brunsleben is the seamless transition from donjon to palas, with its slight curve on the south end following the downward progress of the stone ridge. The distinctive windows bring life to Brunsleben's face – now beaming and amicable, now glowering and stubborn – the three-staged gothic recess adds defiance to its expression, the shutters' hue is possibly a blend of magenta, mauve, and *caput mortuum,* a reddish purple named for the blood that flows from a severed head.

Combray, a work for strings in three movements composed by Edmond de Mog, inspired by Proust's house and the countryside of Illiers. Part one, allegro: *La salle à manger.* Part two, presto-adagio-presto: *La Vivonne.* Part three, allegro-molto: *Le Pré Catelan,* the garden where the children played, where young Marcel dove into the magic dream of reading. The initial theme, in D major, comes in after the first few measures, modulating down to C sharp major in pursuit of a second motif of brief intervals, then turns back and braves the leap from seven sharps to two: original impressions, and irreducible to any other kind, as, according to Jérôme von Castelmur-Bondo, the author of the *Recherche* says. The interpolation of a snippet from *Ali Baba,* a hit from the 1930s, should be taken as a boyish bit of mischief, inspired by the plates on which Françoise serves her delicacies, which were painted with illustrations from the *Thousand and One Nights.* Edmond de Mog told me once in his Verona green workroom that an acquaintance of his, the Basel painter Irène Zurkinden, had hummed this melody to herself for weeks like a madwoman – music, he said, was nothing more than the metamorphosis of noise into euphony, however true it was that dissonance continues to haunt it. I couldn't just take Tante Léonie's bedroom as the departure point for my composition, that would have been *shenshless,* even if the view onto the street in Illiers may reveal the microcosm of this French province I hate and love so much, *tonnerre.* In any case, if I am ever to emigrate, as I wish terribly to do before my eightieth birthday falls, it must be there, to that town so profoundly amenable, though I know it only from passing through, and on the back of a maniacal *chopper* no less. *Tonnerre* (you know, Armand – he liked to gallify my name – it sounds like *Tomorrow Augsburg* or *Woodcutters*) but with the arrow-straight canals, the rhythmical arrangement of the side streets, the bluish silver light – up to now no bastard's set up his easel in the heart of Combray – I could just sit there on the little bridge across the Vivonne and try to catch something of the fleeting enchantment. My friend Max Herzog and I roamed all over there, dropped in on the kitchens, heard and burlesqued the palaver of the French petty bourgeoisie, *utterly unbecoming,* you know, and another thing, the green of the room where we are seated is from one of the Louvre galleries on the Rue de Rivoli, I asked the staff whether I might have a sample, but they rebuffed me: "Ah, monsieur de Mog, cela ne se fait pas" – and speaking of Tonnerre, in the town of that same name I had to reckon with further stupidities, *repulshive,* one thing is a Pleyel, another is a Bechstein, but a Bösendorfer no, a Bösendorfer never, I only manage a few bars a day, that little solo passage for violin, *Ali Baba and the Forty Thieves,* I was bent over it for a week, grueling, and when I debuted the damned thing for Paul Sacher in Schöneberg, they cooked me a pot of oatmeal soup that would have fed forty.

Smoking is prohibited in the home of Edmond de Mog, however much I would like to demonstrate for him the madeleine effects of tobacco, no sooner do I light up a Wynentaler cheroot than images I had long thought vanished rise again within me, and it is only, Herr de Mog, amid the pneuma of the *puro* that I hear, smell, taste every single thing, O, the colors of your garden, mauve, phlox, larkspur, rose bosquets, the cobblestones with their fan pattern, the overgrown balusters, the pump house at the entrance, the drowsiness of the driveway, the fountain with the amber mirror under the walnut tree, I must confess to you that I've dreamed of you just recently, and though you were in a violet robe, walking down to the lower grass parterre, the one with the slight slope, I am certain it was you, you were carrying a bouquet of thirty-six Prismalo color pencils, you placed them in a Chinese vase on the back terrace, where the park disappears into the Stallmacher bottoms, and then you began to paint this arrangement, but I was standing between subject and easel and couldn't see the paper, and I wondered the entire time how you would translate madder lake into madder lake, indigo into indigo, green cinnabar into green cinnabar, the 36 Supracolor pencils had sharp tips in place of blossoms, silver and gold stood out among them, you had shoved this efflorescence like pickup sticks into its receptacle and were standing there brushing away wildly, aha, I thought, there must be some difference between Lukas Helio Genuine Orange and the one from Caran d'Ache, but then – and the dream never answered this question – why did you not just draw the pencils with the pencils?

Edmond de Mog sniffed with his greyhound nose and his upper lip peeled back from his teeth, as though in a slightly breathless systolic cackle, *yesh, utter madnesh,* as you know, I only work by artificial light in a corner of the hall, surrounded by concert posters, nature, artifice, *Woodcutters,* the *Pensées,* these stand out better against a backdrop of wrapping paper, and if I cannot finish a measure on the Pleyel or achieve a simultaneous contrast on paper exactly as I have it *en my noggin,* I rush off to the kitchen, shatter one of Frau Stuber's plates in disgust, and *mek a beashtly mesh.* Only once the rage has abated do I turn back to the easel, pick up the chord on the Pleyel, scribble my chicken scratch in the notebooks, iron things out on the Bechstein.

It's been ten years now since he last visited Illiers-Combray, the gothic spire of Saint-Hilaire looming over its plain, the emblem, as it were, of the place's existence, and when he stepped into the little garden with the overgrown rosebush and the rococo statuettes – who was sitting on the bench but Proust's last surviving relative. A crew was there filming from Paris, did I know – naturally, Hermann Arbogast Brenner had not the least idea – that the "little phrase" from Vinteuil's violin sonata had the character of a leitmotiv, really it was the central theme of Saint-Saëns's first violin sonata, there was no composer named Vinteuil, Proust assembled him with bits and pieces from a number of different musicians. Above all, the timid master should be likened to César Franck, whose significance – and this is the way with all revolutionaries – was only recognized after his death. Not a single musical instrument was to be seen in Aunt Léonie's house, presumably the entire *little band* had vegetated there in an inartistic stupor, even if the fine furnishings and bibelots remained, the imaginary invalid never tired of admiring the glazing on the plates, Aladdin's magic lantern, Ali Baba and the Forty Thieves, while Françoise served the *oeufs à la crème,* the primordial essence of the French came to light in the dark-paneled *salle à manger* on the ground floor with the round table and the coral-fringed hanging lamp in poison or eucalyptus green, not to mention the *chéminée* and the Empire mirror, the kitchen, utterly unchanged since Aunt Léonie's day, was in a small annex accessible by a spiral staircase in the corridor, a lead-glazed door with blue and yellow panels led outside, this *cuisine* with its stove, its bulbous tin oven, the bluish white glazed tiles above it, the sideboard where the terrines rested in museum-like imperturbability, the porcelain salver with the cream cups, the copper pans lining the walls, in Combray he had asked himself how two people had ever managed to squeeze in there at one time, everything was *like en eh doll's housh,* he was less surprised by the small size of the remaining spaces, in the room where Marcel slept stood the storied magic lantern that had projected the fairy tale of Genevieve of Brabant on the wall, so that the figures slid across the drapery, on the commode in Aunt Léonie's chambers were not only the missal, the rosary, and the Madonna, but even the bottle of Vichy water she mixed with pepsin drops to aid her digestion, and then, the true relic, the cup that had held the linden blossom tea with an ancient stale madeleine beside it – he, Edmond de Mog, since first reading the *Recherche,* naturally only drinks linden blossom tea – and there were the stairs Marcel's mother hurried up, to bestow on him the ardently longed-for goodnight kiss – *barely more den a chickin coop ledder,* such were the old man's words.

Edmond de Mog lay lolling on this lustrous afternoon, while a

storm seemed to gather overhead, lopsided in his Tyrian purple fauteuil, profile sleek as a greyhound's against the Veronese green of the
wall, the door to the lemon-yellow music room stood open, you could
even imagine the Pompeian red where the massive soup tureen rests on
the marble *chéminée* flanked by two cineraria-blue goblets, the Pleyel
with its Nubian lacquer, the Bechstein matte black and dusty, I lingered
on the still-life to the left, a Brunsleben zopf on a straw-yellow wooden
block, and in the upper corner a glass of *gimfi,* of blueberry confit, rose
up against the ultramarine-streaked paper; in deference to the Golden
Ratio, two meanders, white striped with cobalt blue rhombi framed in
olive green, ran along the vermilion-tinged table, and its encrusted
Delft blue tiles, likely smashed long ago in the kitchen, seemed to glide
toward the observer, a self-sufficient feast of forms and colors. Edmond
de Mog welcomed any subject that might throw him into a tempera-
tube rampage, and to the right of the guéridon, where the latest edition
of the Baden daily paper lay, I was hypnotized by a ruby red cut pinacothèque glass, and knowing the madeleine effect only from hearsay, I
asked Edmond de Mog to recount this quintessential scene for me, so
long as it wouldn't overtax him, as I wished to verify whether the
principle could be carried over to *nicotiana tabacum.*

At once the composer grew flushed, the young Proust's mother sent
for one of those oval-shaped sand tarts on a cold winter's day, I have them
made at the bakery myself, and in those seconds when the sip of tea
mixed with cake crumbs touched his tongue, Proust quivered, suffused
with an unheard-of sense of joy – this so to speak primordial experience
confounds the mind, which glimpses behind it an existential truth, like

the researcher who is himself the veiled terrain he proposes to explore. The experimental phase follows: Proust shuts himself away, concentrates the whole of his being on the attempt to resurrect these fleeting figments, but then, observing how his mind flails in vain, he gives in to those distractions he had labored to refrain from just before, and now, haltingly, he feels something stir in him and shift, as though an anchor were rising from unfathomable depths. But he does not know what it is, he merely hears the murmur of the distances traversed. He had supposed the taste of madeleine and linden blossom had invoked a visual image, but he preserved little more than a shapeless shimmer, which was lost in the eddies of colors; but he could not ask of form, the only possible interpreter, to translate the meaning of this *goût,* and so he repeats the experiment over and over. Ten times Proust tries, and then suddenly the recollection is there – the taste is identical to that of the madeleine Aunt Léonie would offer him in her room on Sunday mornings, after dipping it into her tea, a scallop shell seems to have been used to mold it, and as soon as Proust recognizes this, he steps back into the grey house on the street that had meant the world to the old hypochondriac, and like a stage set before his inward eye, the square where they sent him before lunch appears, the streets he wandered through rain or shine, the paths, the Pré Catelan, *ye musht read all dish, Armand.* The remarkable thing, Edmond de Mog continued, lifting himself up – and in this he was in complete agreement with Jérôme, with whom he had discussed the scene many times – was how the sight of the little cake with its seashell form was insufficient to trigger the mnemonic effect on its own, and Proust attributes this to his having seen the madeleine too often upon the pastry shop shelf, so that its image was disassociated from the one in Aunt Léonie's room, and most likely, it was the sand tarts' staid form, their pious pleating – admittedly, this strikes me as inconsistent – that stripped these geographical and architectural particularities of the motive force which would have allowed them, in keeping with the metaphor of the lifted anchor, to rise up into consciousness.

But you see, Armand, Proust would not have been a poet if he'd found metaphors but no symbols, and so he draws another comparison, referring to a game played by the Japanese, who throw little paper scraps into a porcelain bowl filled with water, they absorb it, unfold, and turn to floating lotus gardens, miniature pavilions, adopt the palpable form of the water lilies in the Vivonne, the inhabitants of the village, the church of Saint-Hilaire, all Combray and its surroundings, this is what emerges from a cup of linden blossom tea. This is one part, but then again, he says that after the people have died, all the things are destroyed, and nothing of an earlier era still exists, smell and taste, I quote him word for word here, will linger, like straying souls, more fragile but also more enduring, living, immaterial yet graspable, abiding and bearing steadfastly in themselves, in an almost insubstantially tiny droplet, the immeasurable edifice of memory. This is the gateway to the second chapter, which begins *Combray, from a distance, for ten leagues around, seen from the railway when we arrived there last week before Easter, was no more than a church summing up the town, representing it...* During Edmond de

Mog's ellipsis, I reached involuntarily into my pochette and began to toy with the trifold calf's leather etui, which is always packed with an emergency reserve of the three classics of the cigarist's art, a Sumatra, a Brazil, and a Havana. I slid off the pliant dark brown cover and pawed the three coronas, feeling for a Brenner San Luis Rey – was it the middle? To figure this out blind is actually quite simple, for as soon as the three specimens – of origins as diverse as Cruz das Almas, Semi Vuelta, and Klumpang Plantation, home of the exquisite Mandi Angin sand leaf – are removed from the constant temperature and moisture of the humidor that has supplanted the cellar at Castle Brunsleben and transferred for a few days to a suit jacket pocket, they dry out in their own ways, the Brazil is the firmest, the Havana loses its elasticity faster than the Brenner Habasuma, and voilà, I withdrew the San Luis Rey from its compartment, rolled it between thumb and forefinger, furtively at first, until the anticipation faded and the desire to light up right here in Edmond de Mog's Veronese green workroom became absolutely irresistible, though I knew from experience no smoking was allowed in the Sonnenberg house. Despite everything, I held back till the point in his monologue when the composer began to quote the second chapter, and the ellipses above are only there to signify how he froze to observe me, for want of a cigar cutter, biting off the tapered cap and spitting it onto the floor, or rather the Persian carpet, as my grandfather used to do, *what, eh raggid shtinkin shigar in my hous-e, ye musht be mad,* and in lieu of screaming *Out!* he pointed with his bony pianist's finger toward the window, the garden, and the ornately lush park, to the furthest corner of shame. Of course I begged pardon for my lack of restraint, picked up the precious crumbs, sprinkled them into my pocket – the head of a cigar is a delicacy, just like the cheeks of a trout, connoisseurs gnaw it like a plug of tobacco – and thanked him for his excursus on the madeleine, shyly inquiring afterward whether I might *perhapsh, down en de pavilion – mais oui, shtink et up down dere es much es ye please.* In the meantime, he had need of the carpet beater to summon his muse, for just then he was revising the Fourth Sonata for Piano from 1975, published by Amadeus Verlag, which Urs Ruchti had debuted at the Seon church on September 11, 1976. To be frank, he was no longer happy with the Exposition in allegro cantabile, the period in 2/8 might as well be Mendelssohn, the suspended ninth in the fourth bar in G didn't work at all, if the theme were to finish in a consequence in G flat minor, that would mean asking the listener to conceive of the dominant G as the fourth step from G flat minor, and nowadays, no one would *jusht shvallow det* from him, music must be clear, Armand, without ambiguities: *Woodcutters.*

4.

SONNENBERG PAVILION,
BRENNER SAN LUIS REY

Truth be told – and nothing but – this jargon was Chinese to me, and understanding nothing, zilch, naught, nada, I bowed respectfully and vanished from the room, the color of which, correcting myself at the final instant, I now saw as Russian green, walked down the dusky hall, lined inch to inch with posters from de Mog's many premieres, the odd location or proper name could be made out in block letters, Lucerne, Salzburg, Seon, Peter Lukas Graf, Orchestre de chambre de Lausanne, Clemens Dahinden, Emmy Hürlimann, Concerto pour deux flutes et orchestre à cordes, Anna Utagawa and Dominique Hunziker; I found my way past the pump house surrounded by reeds to the dark stands of Weymouth and Wellington pines, where life in summer seemed transformed into a dream particularly hard to dream, the scent of resin, dried needles, rustling leaves, a stench, presumably of rancid mushrooms; and I found, in a blind spot amid the nettles, holly, and hazels, almost flush with the wall of the driveway, the pavilion coated with mildew, where I sat in a wicker chair among knickknacks of all sorts and lit a Brenner San Luis Rey, after restoring a bit of its dampness with a leaf of bear's garlic moistened in the pond. This was a superlative long-filler Havana, wrapper, binder, and filler were all from the Vuelta Abajo in Cuba. And as the glowing ember ate its way inward, I couldn't help but think of the minor sensation caused in the soon-to-be-centenary firm Brenner & Sons Ltd. in Pfeffikon when Johann Caspar's younger brother, my second cousin Christian Heinrich Brenner, signed an agreement of cooperation on November 6, 1985 with Juan M. Díaz Tenorio, Deputy General of Cubatabaco, not only securing for the family enterprise exclusive import rights for the venerable old Havana brand San Luis Rey, but also broaching the possibility of a concession to manufacture cigars and cigarillos under this name for the Federal Republic of Germany and the international market. The selection of tobacco from the Vuelta – yes, there it was again, the aroma of the Sandstrasse in Menzenmang, just capital – is the responsibility of Christian Heinrich and Manuel J. Bolinga Facciolo, Jefe de Departamento de Ventas de Tabaco en Rama, the fabrication will be overseen by experts from Cubatabaco, the portfolio includes lonsdales at CHF 10.50 a piece, coronas for 8.80, petit coronas at 70 for a box of ten, long panatelas in cartons of five for 3.40, as well as half-coronas and mini-cigarillos.

The cigar I had toyed with in Edmond de Mog's living room was 14.2 centimeters long, 1.67 in diameter, and weighed 8.97 grams. Eaten instead of smoked, it would suffice to kill two men. Following the habit of connoisseurs, I did not strip off the blue-and-black ring with its cartouche bearing a coat of arms and the circular inscription *San Luis Rey–Habana* – originally these labels served to protect the fingers of Spanish ladies from the film on the wrappers and the dust from the tobacco – surely Zweifel, Malaga monarch of Leonzburg-Combray, was also acquainted with this joy of joys? Already, after a first few pulls, as I had surmised in the Russian green salon, I experienced the very same thing as Proust, whose *Recherche,* if my longevity held out, I would clearly have to tackle in earnest. How did the novelist put it – an anchor lifts? At any rate, I, with my more modest means, will resort to my mercantile heritage: the aroma, bestowed in essence by the volatile oils of the Vuelta sand leaf, fuses with the green meadows of childhood memories locked away in my deepest interior, marrying, to remain with the tobacco tradesman's nomenclature – but what or whom, exactly? As regards the cigar, a *puro* in the present case, it is the three anatomical elements, the filler, binder, and wrapper of my San Luis Rey, and I may add without hesitation, taking a few draws while I compose the present notes in the courtyard of Castle Brunsleben: wrapper from Viñales, filler from Palacios. The binder's fragrance is less important than its resilience, for it will determine the cigar's appearance. The most noble leaves in Cuba come from the Vuelta Abajo in the province of Pinar del Río, each vega or plantation in that blessed terrain has its own peculiar characteristics, the most sought-after varieties thrive in the districts of San Luis and San Juan y Martínez, thanks to their ferrous soils and sandy substrates.

The blending procedure at Brenner headquarters – the Brenner arcanum, if I may borrow a term from porcelain manufacture – remains the secret of Johann Caspar Brenner and Christian Heinrich, and these two cousins would no more disclose it than a magician would the workings of his art. A marriage, then, of what or whom, from the perspective of my childhood? Again, of three ingredients, past, present, and future, what is autobiographically true and by implication correct, or shall we say, looking back with a shred more of modesty, what is even knowable at all depends on my life as it is today and whatever awaits me tomorrow; if over and over, they say of the dying that in the last moments before their surcease, they see their whole lives flicker past as in a time-lapse film, only one explanation suffices: their memory must speed up. If in contrast, the tedium of gymnastics, religion, biology make a child's morning at school stretch on into an eternity, this is because he remains in possession of a future – the progress of which, he hopes, will be more thrilling than his lessons – lying ahead of him. The young person, if the indulgent reader will allow me this paradox, still remembers forward. If I can see now, with the clarity of glass, through the volatile oils of the San Luis Rey, such memories as my automotive tutelage with the fire-engine-red Schuco Examico on the gleaming waxed parquet of the Hotel Haller on a single morning in June of 1945, most likely it is because, at home back in Menzenmang, crawling on the floor of my father's office, I caught a whiff, long before the advent of visual recollection, of something, a gust of flame or the breath of god that binds the universe. In the early phase of his gastritis, the insurance inspector was only permitted to smoke now and again, so when did he light up his Brenner Export or the Rio Six he claimed was *for de road?*

When he was painting or sculpting. The Duden etymological dictionary informs me – as a dilettante writer I rely on such expedients – that *Rauch,* smoke, from the Middle High German *rouch, rouh* in Old High German, *rook* in Dutch, is derived from the verb *riechen,* to smell, in its older sense of *to steam* or *to smoke,* which does not appear until the seventeenth century as a transitive with the meaning of smoking something. In the article headed *Riechen,* we learn further that the Swedish *ryka* has no equivalents outside the Germanic tongues, and meant, as in other Nordic tongues today, *to smoke, steam, spray, expel,* then later *to emanate, evaporate, exude an odor,* and only in the Middle High German period does it acquire the sense of *to perceive an odor.* Moreover, the noun *Riecher* is a commonly used synonym for *nose,* particularly in the locution *to have a good nose for something.* I will therefore assert that Hermann Arbogast Brenner's first word was not *ato* for *auto,* as I recorded of my eldest son Hermann Christian, but rather *'moke* for *smoke.* This was the course my thoughts took in the pavilion, and I wished to share them then and there with my friend, Edmond de Mog, as a composer and a painter, he could have confirmed to me that a tiny mortal's first syllables can weigh on his future existence as heavily – or lightly – as the initial brushstroke of a picture or the opening note of a symphony.

I saw all at once – likely because I was thinking of the finely chiseled pinacothèque glass in the composer's Russian green workroom – that the square gazebo where I was smoking and brooding harbored an additional enchantment. I must have noticed it long before, but without fixing it in my field of vision: the ruby red and cobalt blue stained glass framing the garden window. Then I remembered a book I had bought and read – which are not at all the same thing – as an architecture student at the Swiss Federal Institute of Technology, in connection with an open lecture on Contemporary German Literature. It had cost no fewer than fifteen francs in July of 1963, the equivalent back then of four meals in the university canteen; the cover was like a coat of arms, the left side black, the right side white, and the jacket copy invoked the wonders and abysses of childhood; the back cover, in contrast to these diametrically opposed values – and this made it immediately sympathetic to me – showed the portrait of a man smoking a pipe, as old, I suppose, as I am today. The picture was so crisp, you could make out the clouds of tobacco, in brief, this painter and experimental filmmaker described his earliest childhood impression of looking out into the garden through the colored panes on the vestibule door of his parents' home – first through the red one, then through the blue – and how it entranced him that the same pear tree, the same gravel path, the same leaves looked now iridescent and fiery, now subdued as though undersea. It was while playing thus, the man writes, that he became the person he was, and soon he began painting, after discovering, still knee-high to a grasshopper, that when everything turns red all at once instead of green or grey or brown, the world changes, is endued with its own particular optics, and so it was far more effective to look at the garden through a red or blue pane of glass than to paint a pear tree, a gravel path, or leaves with blue or red pigment.

I climbed onto the wobbly wicker chair in the pavilion and saw for myself that this was true: the Mog possessions, in their entirety, now seethed Bengal red, and now, with the advent of blue, a veritable theater of constant variants arose: a slight movement of the head, a sidelong squint was all that was required, and the beguilement of ruby shifted into that of lapis lazuli, the elements of fire and water triumphed at once over earth and air.

In the midst of my trifling, the San Luis Rey burned out, an unpardonable faux pas for a cigarier worth his salt, but let me say in my defense that a Havana expires easily once smoked more than halfway, because the concentration of tar smothers the ember. Moreover, the *puro's* quasi-natural death is to be desired once two-thirds of it have been consumed, as Zino Davidoff remarks in his *Memoirs of a Tobacco Czar,* the birth of a genius and an imbecile have something in common, and in the same way, the demise of a Montecristo or Hoyo Des Dieux is akin to the dying off of the cheapest cheroot: the last part is bitter, whether in Vuelta Abajo or in Menzenmang, where I shyly experimented with *nicotiana* on home turf during the war. The noblesse of this passion reveals itself in the art of relighting: it is enough to purify the scorched end with a match, to roll the corona slowly for a few seconds over the flame, and look, of its own accord it begins to breathe again, the smoker needn't suck at it frantically like a child at his mother's breast. But it seemed to me wiser, more appetizing, to move on to the Tobajara Brasil Gigante still left in my emergency supply. Right off the difference struck me, the slight sweet notes, the ash white rather than steel grey, but the memory it aroused unsettled me: my own toy car had not been a red Examico, but a different one, the cream-colored Shuco Akustico. It had no gear shifter or radio, only a horn and a handbrake, and my father gave it to me not in Leonzburg-Combray, but much later, on a

Sunday morning in Menzenmang, in the years when I was still allowed to crawl into bed with my parents; yet the surprise, the very thing that makes a gift so beautiful, was consummate, for just then, as I worked my way into the cleft in the middle of the bed – a mahogany sleigh bed, there were two mattresses in the frame – I heard a rumbling, and tried to puzzle out who was making it, and then the car, steered by my forebear's tobacco-stained hand, emerged from under the cover, glimmering an incomparable metallic beige atop the linen. The reason for the gift of the Shuco can no longer be explained. I dressed quickly, it must have been before Easter, because I was still wearing my *gschtäutli*, the slide garters with the straps that held up my wool stockings; I hurtled down the stairwell, with its whitewash tinted violet, through the vestibule, out the oaken door with the basketweave grating over the window, into the open, past the chestnut tree and the gum tree, through the western gate, to the Sandstrasse, where I pushed my car over the masonry base with the iron fence posts till I reached the corner of Furkastrasse; I passed Doctor Auer's villa – *de toktor, de fabricant* – and arrived at the one-family cabin of my friend *Kürtu*, hoping to show off. But Kürtu or Küre possessed one thing my parents had never allowed: a Flobert parlor pistol. How odd, I thought in Edmond de Mog's gazebo, now impregnated with the smoke of Brazil, that when I purchased my present Shuco, an Examico, at the antique toy store in Zurich, childhood nostalgia should drive me to choose the same color as this original, even though, at this most Sigismund of all Markuses there was a red one on offer.

It was the wife of literary critic Adam Nautilus Rauch who kindly lent me Ferschl and Kapfhammer's *Schuco Book* for my studies, and it is there that I find the specifications: manufactured between 1936 and 1957, article number 2002, BMW convertible, two wind-up motors, the second powered the horn and was activated by a button on the steering wheel. Length: 14.5 centimeters. In the early days, the mechanical parts were supplied by the Nuremburg firm Paul Weiss, later Bühler superseded them. The horn was a delight to adults and children alike, when the motor was wound up, it was good for three hundred or so honks, but honk here is a misnomer, technically it was a pendulum striking two washers inside a bell. Some 300,000 were sold, half of these in America, the prewar model had seventeen-millimeter rims and lug treads on its narrow tires. In 1957, the Akustico – along with Shuco Fritz, a fantasy figure with a racing helmet and washable polyester uniform, I alas did not have one – was sold in stores for the price of DM 7.90, nowadays it would cost four figures. After the war, Shuco Fritz vanished, even from the factory: either the supplier folded or else was based in a part of the former German Reich with which Nuremburg could no longer conduct business. Naturally the same key wound both motors, the one for the horn and for the drive gears.

But what about the details for my current Shuco Examico? BMW convertible, article number 2001; four forward gears, plus neutral and reverse; clutch, handbrake, working steering wheel, frame of MSTU stamped tin, .32 millimeters thick, total weight of 190 grams; when the clutch is engaged, you hear the soft purr of the motor, which collectors refer to wistfully as the *Shuco sound* – an analogue in little to the roar of the twelve cylinders from Maranello; to quote the *Shuco Book* directly,

"It must be heard to be believed." The assembly of the chassis was a ten-step process, it was finished with a coat of synthetic resin and heat-treated at one hundred twenty-five degrees Celsius, the finest automotive firms did not shy from saying its quality was in no way inferior to the original. Colors: ivory, light and dark red, green, black with a violet cast, ah, Adam Nautilus, *tek eh look et dish,* mine is a prewar model, as indicated by the markings on the metal undercarriage, the trademark reads "Made in Germany" – *maaadeh,* we pronounced it as children – after 1945 the wording changes to "Made in the U.S. Zone." As a salesman's son I naturally posed myself the question of what the Examico was really worth, more than the Akustico, perhaps; and as an eldest son fleeced by his siblings, I salute its anonymous former owner – an only child, presumably, like Hermann Arbogast Brenner, for six happy years – who so cared for his plaything that not even the delicate windshield – *careful, it'sh delikitt,* my father had said to me – was missing; not to say there were no scratches in the lacquer, that would be something of an exaggeration. By then I had progressed to the Brenner Charuto Fino, *fabricação com licença:* Neapolitan yellow label with a smoke-beclouded *indio* nestled in a golden mandorla. Already two-thirds of it were smoked away, and again, I wondered whether it was licit or even possible to share my discoveries with Edmond de Mog, in the end, for three-quarters of an hour, his pavilion had become a *genius loci,* and his grappling with the revisions of the *Sonate IV pour piano* with its chromatic variations on the dominant tone and its augmented triad, held not the least interest for me in relation to my three trios of filler, binder, and wrapper, past, present, and future, or Sumatra, Brazil, and Havana; this chord, neutral on its own, C-E-G flat, for instance, demands a half-tone step from that major or minor triad and must be combined with sevenths and tonics in some outlying region of the circle of fifths where it becomes, according to the musicologist Walter Kläy, the hub of the harmonic event.

Edmond de Mog, with his persistent carping and vituperation against the pastoralism of Leonzburg-Combray, was oblivious to his good fortune in possessing in the Pleyel, in the Bechstein, instruments that operated like a rehearsal stage at the theater, the black and ivory white keys, the claviature; as was said often at Menzenmang, *practice trumps study,* first the inner ear hears the sequence of sounds, B-E-G, to remain with the fourth sonata, derived from the C minor chord D-E-G, you have the urge to venture an F sharp seventh in the descant, and if, like the author of the present tobacco leaves, you have to do all this on paper, you will give up straightaway; no, enough is enough, B in opposition to A sharp, E to E flat in a half-tone step, the same caper with F sharp and G, and look, you've gotten hold of the monster, and the thing works thanks to the harmonic hub of the exuberant B-E flat-G, and now we easily make our way back to the radiant tonic C, the key par excellence for players of Boogie Woogie, as far from F sharp major as Brenner & Sons is from a cleaning solutions manufacturer. Should we be struck with the madcap idea of animating the reader by embellishing our chapter on the Schucos Akustico and Examico with a quotation from the classics, Jérôme would no doubt turn our attention to the following words of Goethe's: *What you inherit from your father / You must earn before it's yours,* at which point, for want among my inherited possessions of a hand-me-down home computer, we would be forced to graft in the secondhand words with obsolete instruments – scissors and paste; we would insert the citation, proofread the text, cut it back out, shift it to such and such a place, and so on; the painter mixes *caput mortuum,* cobalt blue, madder lake, Indian yellow, then the water effects the glancing intersection. No, I thought better of disturbing my friend, who was busy rehearsing for his upcoming premier, the comparison with the theater, about which, once again, Adam Nautilus Rauch understands everything and I not a whit, may be admissible if we take the notes to be language, the instruments actors, in a way, the Pleyel in the music room is like an orchestra minion for the actors' guild, from one instant to the next it renders articulate what the overburdened brain has studied to exhaustion, B-E sharp-G plus F sharp-A sharp-C sharp-E, and look, the thing works.

And so I clambered out of the wicker chair, took out my Cartier fountain pen, sapphire blue and gold, and executed a sketch of the pavilion – because the writer is only permitted to leave out what he has investigated exhaustively – that *friviloush* witch's cottage measured 1.5 meters or so per side and 3.2 meters from the threshold to the eaves, the wood siding, once painted terra di Sienna, fanned about an array of inlays, frames, volutes, heraldic half-moons, engaged columns twisting and fluted ad libitum, the same extravagance was evident in the cornices. Then the centerpiece, the glazing, here I had to step down from the eastern perspective to Detail A: a rectangular band with alternating squares in ruby red and cool cobalt blue running to the corner of the dusty hothouse window, but there is more, in the center of the checks stood diagonally sprouting, five-pointed fleurs-de-lys, each marked with a tiny blue rhombus, certainly the most *exshtravagant* thing I've ever come across in greenhouse architecture, and now, testing out the nature-estrangement effect, I found it was never-ending. If you looked through the grey square in the direction of the castle, the silver starred panels opposite graded into a cellophane aquamarine blue, while the red, depending on the light from behind, still shone like a chunk of cinnabar. The garden, in contrast, turned a muted chromium oxide green, the strands of ivy in the foreground took on the appearance of *papel picado.* With a change of apparatus, a look through a red square, you saw everything turn purple, if you then looked through a blue pane, the purple turned to oxblood, the blue retained an almost doubled shade of cobalt, white turned Delft blue like the tile wall in Edmond de Mog's still life *The Brunslebener Züpfe,* and I wondered whether, in lonesome hours, the maestro might visit his pavilion and treat his own eye to these enharmonic transformations, I imagined him sitting there in his wicker chair, surrounded by hand rake, leaf rake, spades, and the rotting hose and saying over and over, *exshtravagant.* Indeed it is, Edmond de Mog, nonsense alone makes bearable a world where everything strives for a higher sense. Proust should have dipped his madeleine in the tea here, experienced the magic depths of timeless reading here, dictated his *Recherche* into the memory of his later readers, for nowhere else could he have found a more faithful devotee than under the broad-brimmed roof of the composer's home, Haus Sonnenberg, formerly known as the Landweibelei, not far from the widow's quarter where Villa Malaga stood, if we praise the great novelist's ability to annihilate space and time, then only the veritable master illusionists can live in two different places, at two different epochs at once.

5.

BRIEF COLLOQUIUM ON SNUFF,
LEONZBURGER NR.0

If our friend Edmond de Mog were ever to be induced to the enjoyment of tobacco, and I say this thinking of his ever-vigilant greyhound nose, it would surely be thanks to Leonzburger Nr. 0, even more so if he learned that the little town had once been the stronghold of snuff tobacco production. To appreciate the high regard this local industry enjoyed, it is necessary to keep in mind a number of figures. A shortcoming, in my modest assessment, of many proper novels – as a hurried examination will prove, and just as well, since that is all we have time for – is, ready, aim: their creators' disregard for statistical values. In 1883, 18,487 kilograms of Leonzburger Nr. 0 were purchased by the firm Bertschinger & Co. alone, ten years later that had dropped to 14,000 kilos, then 10,813 on the eve of the First World War, by 1923 it was a mere 2,420. Considering that a pinch of Leonzburger Nr. 0 contains no more pulvil than can be pinched between forefinger and thumb

– you don't just plunge your mitt in, it is too wholesome for that – the quantities are staggering. By the time the tobacco habit shed the air of a fad, it had already found its place in society, and just as the inhabitants of the British Isles attended "smoking parties" to learn to hold a pipe with grace, the diplomat in the European courts at the time of the Rococo was ill-advised not to have a *tabatière* at the ready and to be caught unprepared for the obligatory gesture of taking or offering a pinch. The custom of conferring, instead of a medallion, a costly snuff-box as a sign of favor became a question of etiquette of extraordinary consequence. After the liberation of southern Italy, King Victor Emmanuel gave general Eisenhower a bauble from Napoleon's collection, on one side was a large N adorned with a crown, on the other the Hapsburg coat of arms, and Eisenhower was superstitious enough to think this gift might bring him luck in the field. An alabaster box now found in a private collection once belonged to a resident of Leonzburg by the name Ringier, his friends engraved their names on it as if it were an album, and the student, who guarded it like a *porte-honneur,* was, like Hermann Arbogast Brenner smoking the products of his family firm, eternally enveloped in the fragrance of home.

The Thirty Years' War marked a turning point not only in European history, but also in the evolution of tobacco. During the campaigns of the *Landesknechts* crisscrossing Germany, tobacco smoking took root, and it was soon impossible to imagine a world without it. Where the pipe failed to make inroads, snuff was an object of reverence. We need think only of the "tobacco parliaments" of Frederick William I, where soldiers who shied from stifling smoke and stinging jests struggled to win the Soldier King's trust. Participation in these meetings was so essential that the elderly prince of Dessau, who for health reasons could not smoke, kept his pipe clasped cold between his lips for the sake of form, and when the young king rose to the throne and long clay pipes vanished in favor of the snuff box, this marked a victory of Rococo elegance over the boorishness of the prior era. *A wee pinch of snuff, to put us at ease, / However much it makes us sneeze.* And what do the doctors say? In the volume *Doctor as Destiny* by Dr. Bernhard Aschner – *nomen ist omen,* I think here not just of ashes in urns, but of the curious German word *Schmöker,* a light, leisurely read, from *smauchen,* not simply *to smoke,* but to puff away at one's pleasure – we read: Today we have forgotten a whole range of resources which – when turned to promptly enough – not only hinder cataracts and glaucoma but even age-related farsightedness. Among these is the now rather absurd-looking snuff tobacco, which results in nasal secretions that promote the flow of tears and support healthy perfusion in the eyes. The exclamations *Gesundheit, Salud, Salut* attest to a time when people were conscious of the salubrious properties of sneezing. There's an old adage from Leonzburg that goes: "A pinch clears the nostrils and fortifies the mind / turns the nostrils brown and leaves the plague behind." *Naso otturato, spirito chiuso,* a stuffy nose is a closed mind. The habitual sniffer, however, sneezes very little, every fiftieth time, give or take. On the effects of this strange stimulant, Molière expresses himself thus: "After a pinch, I feel lighter and happier, my black thoughts vanish, my mind works better." It was, once again, Adam Nautilus Rauch who turned my attention to the poem *The Snuffbox* by Joachim Ringelnatz, in which a woodworm, told of the greatness of Frederick the Great by a snuffbox the king had carved with his own hands, is unimpressed, gets a whiff of walnut, and duly bores in.

From this, Adam Nautilus affirmed in his amiably boorish way, we may conclude that snuff-taking was a far less social and sociable act than a smoking party, no, I objected, you must yield the floor to me in tobacconistic matters, in the days when snuff-taking was *en mode,* the *tabatière* reached the height of refinement, after pipes they were the first smoking utensil to become an ornament. When Louis Armand de Bourdon, Prince of Conti, died in 1774, at the apex of the *ancient régime,* he left behind eight hundred snuff boxes, not one of them made of walnut, I am certain; nor does the book about the collection of Frederick the Great, whose uniform jacket was invariably dusted with brown flecks from carrying the stuff loose in his pocket – like schoolteacher Brunies with his Cebion tablets, Adam Nautilus added in – make any mention of wood. These cousins of amulets and suchlike trinkets could not be opulent enough, they came in gold, in ivory, in diamond, even the Sun King was aware of the contradiction between the baseness of the powder itself and the diplomatic-modish nature of consuming it, for this reason, it is hard to find images from the time in which snuff tobacco appears, a visual representation must have offended the character of artist and model equally; an exception is the *shneezed in* handkerchief as a reminder of the indulgence, which court painters depicted in every shade of brown from gold ochre to terra di Sienna to burnt umber and sepia, the gliding motion of sniffing works poorly as a discreet motif, and this noblest of all eras must have sensed that instinctively. True, the occasional figure in Molière's comedies makes use of the tabatière, the playwright needed to stay up-to-date, understandably, as Adam Nautilus said, and he offers the opinion in *Don Juan* that tobacco is a passion of upright people; when Schmidt took snuff in public, Hermann Arbogast Brenner added, he was a more credible politician than Erhardt with a torpedo in his gob, nothing against that, of course, and here one could embark on a long series of observations about whether parallels existed between the SPD Chancellor's vice and that era when *tout le monde* had their fingers in the pie, but let us leave that aside for the course of this brief colloquium, it is beyond our sphere of expertise. Instead we will proceed from the sociological angle. Why does taking a pinch enter the diplomat's repertoire? Because it offers the illusion of spontaneous intimacy as well as the fraternal feeling of having lived through something together, I am talking about sneezing, an *infectious* reaction in the truest sense of the term, nowadays it is rare that the pipe smoker open his tobacco pouch to his colleagues, each boasts of his own *blend, which it took me ages to finally hit on,* no Early Morning for me, he will say, it contains too much Latakia, all the while ignorant of what this word refers to: a lowly, small-leaved bush of the nightshade family that thrives in Syria, harvested as a whole plant and fire-cured, so it develops a particular spicy aroma without undergoing a true fermentation, ergo less distinguished than any of the Havana varieties.

The connoisseur placed great stress on which of the Leonzburg firms supplied him with his Nr. 0. One source from the 1890s classified the companies based there as follows: first, Abraham Bertschinger, second, Heinrich Zweifel, third, Albert Rohr, fourth, Isidor Bertuch. At the end of orchestra rehearsals, the members of the Music Society used to gather in the beer hall, and each manufacturer – apart from Rohr & Co., who only gave out samples on request – would bring a canister of his goods, pass it around the table, and observe the guests Argus-eyed, being sure that each gave his *tabatière* its due. Naturally the mix of spices was kept under lock and key, no fabricant let the others have a peek into his mill. Mrs. Bertuch informs us that the men would wear three precious vials around their necks filled with violet, rose, and clove oil. To impart the right aromas to their house brand, they would drip these ingredients, which must be heated to body temperature, inside the crushed tobacco. Often musicians, who seem incapable of recognizing harmony when not behind their music stands, proved the most disputatious consumers. The business sense ran so deep in Isidor Bertuch's blood that he rarely hesitated to overstep the bounds of tact. Once, when he was looking to attract new customers, he entered the shop in the next district over where snuff tobacco was sold; the owners confessed they obtained their wares from the Zweifel firm. Aha, Bertuch said, then you may pass your orders on to me, because I am the one who provides Zweifel with tobacco. When news of his perfidy reached Herr Zweifel's ears, he proclaimed "that's strong tobacco," his way of saying it took a lot of gall, and at the next recital, where he was to play the violin and Bertuch the cello, he declared he would not sit in the same orchestra with this conman, at which point the conductor demanded stridently the two *snuffy* gentleman settle their Tabachiad *efter de rehearshal.*

The snuff manufacturer generally opts for heavy, oily tobacco, which is left to ferment in brine, individual leaves are formed into *carrotes,* a word that incites special affection in the Aargau, so famed for its carrot cakes; these are thirty-five centimeters long and around eight centimeters thick, the tobacco undergoes its final fermentation in this form, hence the extremely pregnant aroma of the mills. The perfumes the workers spill repeatedly over the leaves were kept secret in the essence house: ambergris, balsam, musk, ess bouquet, heliotrope, lavender, myrrh, spikenard – *don't go on like det, or else de critics'll think ye copied it down from Dornseiff,* Adam Nautilus warned – then the leaves were passed through a mechanical drum with guillotine blades swiping constantly back and forth, every firm in Leonzburg had such a machine, Bertschinger & Co.'s was in Niederlenz. The product was sifted over and over until it was a fine powder. In common parlance, people said Leonzburger, Nr. 0 was a trademark, a rival firm tried to best the competition by naming its own powder Leonzburger Nr. 00. Here is a price list from Bertschinger & Co. from the year 1920: Schwyzer Red, CHF 3.50 per kilogram net, payable within thirty days; Parisian Pure Coarse, CHF 5; Fagon Pettavel Yellow, again, CHF 5; Capuchin and ladies' tobaccos for CHF 4.50; other varieties included Dutch Brown and Prince William of Baden.

For all these particulars, to avail oneself of which requires a pipeful of heavily seasoned W.Ø. Larsen Classic Pipe Tobacco, Hermann Arbogast Brenner is indebted to an article by Edward Attenhoffer in the 1969 edition of the *Leonzburg New Year's Gazette,* and we would be depriving the indulgent reader of the present tobacco leaves of a rare diversion did we not allow the author to speak in his own words. He writes in the style typical of New Year's annuals, which is in turn the pinnacle and paragon of that local beat reporterese I hold so close to my heart: "Around 1920 in Leonzburg there were no more than sixteen persons left who might be considered good snuff-dippers. Apart from these confirmed devotees, there may have been other, clandestine users, the ladies doubtless were not lacking among this latter group. Those who took snuff in secret did so graciously, with a small pocket square, while those who sniffed in the open inevitably had a big red handkerchief at the ready, if not a yellow one with round polka dots" – Adam Nautilus, are polka dots not always round? – "for when the sluices of their sated nostrils opened explosively. The jolly master locksmith Guttermann was a well-known snuffer from the turn of the century in Leonzburg. His family's roots lay in Pfalz in Bavaria, and he had lived through the Franco-Prussian war. In 1870 in Paris he caught a grenade shard in his foot. Since that day, the Swabian walked with a limp. When he met an acquaintance on the road, he would pull his tin from his waistcoat and say, 'Let's have a quick one, now that no one's looking!' Gutterman always left a tobacco tin at the door for the postmen and was infuriated if they didn't take advantage of it. When he took the letter carrier Halder to task and asked him why didn't he help himself, Halder swore he had done so. At that Gutterman replied the man was lying, for there were no fingerprints in the tobacco in the tin. From that day forward, Halder always took a pinch, which he scattered to the gods, to avoid having to answer for himself and sing the praises of snuff tobacco. The chronicle of the old beer hall, in the year 1905, features *A Song of Snuff*, which we reproduce here in a slightly abridged form: *No* sight on earth can be so sweet / As a snuffer sniffing up his treat. / They call it vice, I call it a dance / Of dignity and elegance. // The hand emerges from the vest / And passes out its sweet bequest. / Round it goes, chopped, cured, and dried, / And each man sticks his paw inside. // The cheeks and nostrils flare and twitch, / While each awaits his longed-for pinch. / The powder plucked, the nose bends forward, / The morsels now fly heavenward. // The fragrance rises to the brain, / But woe to him whose caution wanes. / If earth should quake, the skies resound, / The force of the cosmos reign unbound, // We'll turn to sackcloth in our need, / And beseech solace of this weed. / So may the name Leonzburg ever chime / Through burg and field, till the end of time." Signed R., for Ferdinand Rohr-Hase.

Of course, snuff was permissible in Molière's comedies, but not in Racine's tragedies, Adam Nautilus Rauch said, you couldn't, *ye know,* just let Phèdre up and die in the midst of achooing on the stage, and this brings us to another point, that the act of snufftaking cannot in the least be compared to smoking, as the end effect, sneezing, strikes the mind as a symptom of cold – *an inflammation of the upper respiratory tract,* Thomas Mann might have called it, so I learned in this colloquium – rather than as an indulgence giving warmth to mind and soul. To this degree, per Adam Nautilus Rauch, the preference in the theater for cigarettes over the far more potent pipe or cigar spoke to a deficiency among modern playwrights. Were we in an arena, in an Olympic stadium – hold on, my friend, I thought, are you likening literature to the circus? – because if so, Barclay and Marlboro should have nailed their placards to the forestage of the Schauspielhaus in Zurich. Look, there stands an everyman in his hat and raincoat by a door leading backstage. What occurs to the director but to have him light a smoke. With that, he fills the pause the director needs to give weight to his lapidary first line. If a second figure now emerges, the possibilities multiply like chess moves: he can offer her one, can crush his own underfoot, can say through the haze: "Madame, everything's a smokescreen." That says it all, about the theater and about the scene in question. A brilliant opening sentence: Madame, everything's a smokescreen. Madame may react in this way or that, may take the cigarette or decline it, may curse the smoker or fall in love with him. Right away, it is clear why the cigar is losing ground: what person nowadays would think of offering a Partagás Charlotte to a lady? And a pipe – inconceivable. That said, nothing puts the audience more at ease than when a figure from Hauptmann, Ibsen, or Dürrenmatt lights a pipe or cigar. With this gesture he tells them: no worries, we have time to spare. In this way, he thwarts the telos of drama itself, don't you see that, Hermann? The dramatic impulse tends toward peripeteia, peripeteia precipitates climax, it's all the same whether it's a comedy or tragedy. Comedy falls out of the frame, tragedy detonates it. If an actor onstage lights up a cigar, for you, the thwarted tobacco manufacturer – speaking of, why do we never see you at the theater? – that must produce a peculiar sort of tension, to wit: when, on what occasion, with what excuse will it finally be snuffed out? If the character is to actually smoke his Brazil to the end – true, in the theater, we prefer less slavish forms of imitation! – he will need a full hour, that is half the performance. And so we take to heart the lesson: cigarette, cigar, and pipe are dramaturgical clocks, within the compressed time of the play they tell us something about the time perceptions of author and character. Frankly, I said to my friend Adam Nautilus, that's why I don't bother going to the theater, the Lucky Strike cult there bores me to no end, I call for the entire tobacco spectrum to storm the stage, and if you can find me a play where actor number one takes snuff, number two chews tobacco, number three smokes cigarillos, number four a fat Havana, number five a pipe, and number six a gasper, I'll show up for premiere and dernière alike, *Sei personaggi*... What's the name of that play so-and-so wrote? You mean Pirandello. Ah yes, *Sei personaggi in cerca di fumo,* first line same as the last: "Madame, everything's a smokescreen."

Vell, now, that doesn't quite do it, you're overstepping your bounds, but one thing does occur to me, they say that Mitterwurzer, the character actor, was meant to light a pipe in a performance of one of Anzengruber's plays, you know Anzengruber? – beg your pardon, never heard of him – and before the tobacco kindled, he dropped the matchbox onto the rug, surely a rug is out of place in a room in Anzengruber, but that's beside the point, now, pay attention to what happens next, any third-class actor would have tried to correct the error, reach for whatever match lay nearest by and strike it, but not Mitterwurzer, who gathered them serenely, one after the other, and did not relight his bowl until the box was once again full; this so impressed Max Burckhard, the director of the Burgtheater at the time and no friend of improvisation, that he insisted on Mitterwurzer repeating it in every show. No doubt, I said unassumingly, that's why I avoid the theater, that match number was better than any of Anzengruber's dialogue, otherwise he wouldn't have left it in. Something similar occurred when a second-rate shaman tried to recreate Auzinger's famous Black Cabinet, making a roan horse disappear instead of an elephant. You don't see the trick so much anymore, so there's no harm in speaking of it. You drape the animal in a colorful, even garish silk sheet with another one of dark velvet beneath it, when the sorcerer pulls away the top one, the pitch-black beast is no longer visible against the background, to all appearances it has vanished. Well, moving on, our magus manqué is doing his roan horse routine, but he bungles it, the velvet cover slips, and a white tail appears right as he's saying: *Sim sala bim, the horse has vanished!* Thundering laughter on all sides, but in this case, too, he left the gag in, and this is how it went: the next night, the shaman hung a fabric tail on the horse, which was properly covered this time, and at the end of the trick, he removed it and placed it in his pocket. Worry not, Adam Nautilus, I won't get on my soapbox and rant about how theater and magic have nothing to do with each other. Getting back to snuff, my friend said in resignation, if, on the little stage of the Comédie Française, an actor reciting a monologue from the *Misanthrope* pulls out his *tabatière* and absentmindedly takes a pinch, this is credible, absolutely credible in the sense of the classical theater, which functions because the background, the mythos, is known to every spectator, all that is revealed in the arena is, for instance, the players' behavior toward the oracles, and it is conceivable, despite the masks, that something was smoked at that time – I wanted to butt in with a few words about *L'homme masqué* – you know Herodotus, the father of history, says of the Massageteans, who inhabited the islands of the river Araxes, that they would sit around a fire, throw the fruit of the hemp plant into it, and become as drunk as the Hellenes on their wine; and the Greek geographer Strabo wrote at length of the Mysians of Asia Minor, whom he referred to as "the people who eat smoke."

Might Edmond de Mog, when he next visited the old Landweibelei, be inclined to take a pinch if I could offer him authentic Leonzburger Nr. o? Leonzburg-Combray, how else could the five sheaves now behind us be bundled but with the prospect of bringing together the medieval-Biedermeier district capital with its pastoral twilight hues and Bruns-leben, which constitutes both my search for lost time and the seat of Jérôme von Castelmur's senescence? Hermann Arbogast Brenner is thinking now of an evening walk into the Ebnet, a half-hour down in the direction of Castle Wildenegg, to the bench where, framed by branches as in a vignette by Ludwig Richter, the august feudal castle lies some ways off at an angle, looming or serene and distant depending on conditions of weather and light, with radiant merlons, roof, and walls. The path *to the*, *up the*, *into* the Ebnet – characteristically, the German language distinguishes only vaguely among directional prepositions, in these matters dialect is more discriminating; take the Wynentaler in Menzenmang who says *I'm a-goin inte Luzärn,* because Lucerne – in German Leuchtenstadt, literally the city of lights, lies near the Gotthard in the Swiss interior; he says *I'm a-goin up te Bern,* because that midland capital is the crown of the provincial government; *I'm a-goin off te Zurich,* because *Mostindien,* East Switzerland, hence the end of the earth is just as far away; logically he says *I'm a-goin' round te Basel* following the Wyna, the Aar, the Rhine, but he says *I'm a-goin on over te Lake Hallwil,* because to get there, you must cross the saddle land between Sonnenberg and Homburg; when he says *on te Schiute,* Schilten, that is, you may ask what the difference is between *over to* and *on to* — well, the same as a little more and a little less far away; *I'm a-goin down te Äntlebuch,* Entlebuch being a valley strangely hidden amid the cramped geography if you are sitting on the sun-bathed terrace of my family home in Menzenmang with its red and cream awning; *up te Burg, round te Reinach, down te Pfäffike, up te Beromöischter, over te Böiwu,* these words announce, as it were inadvertently, the roads I would take as a cheroot holding my cemetery grandmother's weathered, calloused hand: the *côté chez* Uncle Herbert, the *côté de la cimitière,* the *côté de* Dankensberg; Jérôme, a child of the city, of Bern, prefers to say *up past the Ebnet,* I on the other hand say *round behind,* commemorating both the ascent and the desolation it engenders. We depart — I say *we,* but Jérôme and I never go down together, in the Ebnet a person has to walk alone — through the arched gate with the Castelmur arms on the keystone, past the rubblework walls of the lowermost garden with its wild rambler roses, into the woods till we reach the clearing, to the craggy Malm limestone and the oblique bands of Dogger stone, where the damp of the gulch in high summer has a smell like the heart of a crypt, the once-corn-yellow waymark tells us the altitude is 543 meters above sea level and points the way to Brugg and Leonzburg.

Amid the gaps in the coarsely built ledge, mixed with mustard-gold tresses and covered by tall lindens, with a dim row of steps leading upward, is the former croquet court — what château-roguishness, Jérôme's ancestors playing croquet, of all things, here in this pre-Jurassic landscape, it was, evidently, *en mode* at the time — walk on a bit and the creeping willows and clumps of chestnuts in the Lotan and Brentan sink in tiers toward Bruns, you get a clear view of the village and the valley, the cross street with the arms depot where, for the last mandatory target practice of the year, the men fan out and place the pencil-points of shooting tunnels all around the Bannwald, the Sternen with the Sternenmatt, a multipurpose outbuilding, demolished some time ago, then the clocktower on the forest's edge and the little cemetery, final resting place of Hermann Arbogast Brenner's ancestor, the publicist Emanuel Kindt. The way to Castle Wildenegg rises slightly now, branching off the paved road past a low wall surrounding olive-green comfrey and the banks of the kitchen garden where the servant Jean-Jacques Amorose tends ultramarine larkspurs, red madder phlox, and powder-pink mauves, further up you may choose either the *witches' trail* to Brunsleben or the little road that takes three hairpin curves up to the peak of the Ebnet. You scuttle up through the defile, stepping into the moldy treads between the pale ribs of rock, on the picnic sites marked off by inviting signs – hikers storm the Chaistenberg, if the weather is fine, following the routes marked out by red radio boxes that tell you the story of the region – circle numerous blackened fire pits hardly distinguishable from lime kilns. O rambles in Menzenmang, O fairground of forest, O aroma of bratwurst and cervelat! And here, where the panorama ends, the Ebnet suddenly opens up, a long, unfurled plateau, still rising softly toward the ledge, bordered on three sides by the mixed forest of the Chaistenberg. To the right the holloway continues into a kind of open avenue or half-arcade, I say this because on one side, the birches, oaks, and elms tilt far over the wheel tracks amid the karst, on the field side a few horse chestnuts stand in isolation. A boundary stone marks the edge of the estate, the coat of arms on it is weathered, the runes corroded. *Up past* reigns here in the bend, where I used to push off the bobsled in the bone-chilling winter with my boys, from here onward we say *round behind.* You walk a good quarter-hour in this shifting belvedere of vegetal majesty, man-high hollies, banewort hedged for summer, now and then a patch of wild strawberries, the grass grows thicker and thicker over the path until at last you *circle back* to a niche amid the bushes under a towering tent of birches to a bench which bears the legend: *Jérôme von Castelmur-Bondo – Private Property.* This bench is the goal of our pilgrimage, of course for the man of eighty-seven it represents a tradition hardly graspable to his companion, for me it is enough to smoke my cigar in this chamber of lush greenery, a corner far holier than a lowly household shrine with the crucifix on a tack where the walls meet. In summer you feel you are seated in the Bermuda Triangle of this sea of green, and one lives on long past the Hoyo de Monterrey Des Dieux, which is sweating, too, down in the cellar of Castle Brunsleben – that is a process of fermentation as well, and one looks back without anger, only with a sting of longing, glancing at the benches the Mörken-Wildenbrau-Bruns Improvement Society have set out further up. I think of the joke my friend and benefactor Johann Caspar Brenner would now tell about the old couple trying to explain their reluctance to enter the Society, *et our age, et hardly meks much sense to join eh new soshiety.* It is beautiful to brood and to be here as the steel-blue puro smoke sweeps past your nose, Jérôme, who pays tribute to forest and meadow on this bench in the middle of his sixteen-hectare estate, calls this hideaway Green Stechlin, and here, for once, I am not thoroughly disarmed, a discussion of Fontane's late novel is one of the daily chores of my tenancy, Amorose too must know the Engelke scenes, and just like Dubslav sitting by the lakeside and watching the sun go down, never certain whether the red rooster has actually emerged from the geyser, the Emeritus sits on his Castelmur-Bondo bench, leaning on his cane, he refuses to smoke in the open air, no doubt he is missing something thereby.

6.

WAKING IN SOGLIO,
BRENNER EXPORT

If you drive from the village of Bruns — *Bruuns,* as the natives call it — up the narrow lane to Jérôme von Castelmur-Bondo's estate, you will find to your left the lower meadow where the black-splotched Freiburger cows champ and ruminate in summer, and to the right, an old vineyard wall with crumbling seams of Jura stones the size of skulls, a weed-ridden fence, here it is not electrified as in the pastureland below the Waldau. Only on the occasional turnout can one automobile pass another. The street is paved up to the reservoir, the *vater shtation,* the bunker bears the Bruns coat of arms, a wheel with eight spokes and arrowheads at their ends, what it means, I'll have to ask the castle lord. This is where the asphalt ends and the natural road begins, and you plunge into forest. Brunsleben has four *hektaars* of woodland, not dark pines with sticky resins that seem to cling to your palate, but a bright miscellany, birches, birches, and more birches, a horde of them, still, deforestation is making inroads, here you have the roar of the Zurich-Bern freeway rising up from the valley, there stumps and cudgels, logs and longwood, cordwood and butt logs pile up and crowd onto the road, Rueda, the tenant in Mörken, fells them in January and February. The sun burns down through the tree crowns and casts whorls of light on the bank. Had you not already put it in first, you would have to downshift here, first out of deference to the hikers dutifully following the yellow waymarks, checked flannels and red socks all round, every sport has to have its uniform; and second on account of the tight hairpin curve, which Hermann Arbogast Brenner has dubbed the Winter Horseshoe, after the blood-curdling bend on the St. Moritz bobsled track. Now a connector forks off to the left, leading to a shadowy shrine, a cross in the forest's midst, and then softly down onto Mörker Road, offering a somewhat didactic tableau of the protected flora of the Jura and Mittelland: the cerulean *gentiana verna*, the fire lily and the *nigritella nigram*, edging lobelia, *man's loyalty* is its common name, because the blossoms last no longer than a summer, a morel-like inflorescence of a dubious *caput mortuum* color, the yellow irises whose color agrees most attractively with the corn-yellow arms of the guideposts. They point to the spot where the Chaistenberg reaches 647.4 meters, to Castle Brunsleben and Castle Wildenegg, to the ruins of Salenegg, and to the SBB Wildenau station — wherever you go, wherever you look, SBB delivers the mail.

The turning radius of my childhood dream, the Ferrari 328 GTS, just manages to squeeze around the switchback, there's too little ground clearance to keep from scraping the undertray, you have the man-high wall to the left, where the road rises up like a trough boring into the mountain, we are halfway there now. A rivulet materializes, feeding fat kingcups in the spring, in winter there are often foxes, once I chased off a splendid stag, which the roar of the motor did not bother in the least. After scrub and shrubs of all conceivable sorts and a final pivot to the left, the village appears, a toy settlement with its Lilliputian school, its pub, its post office, tire yard, supermarket, and butcher's, the dear Lord must have forgotten it here while tidying up his building blocks after the creation of the world. We now steer carefully through the Schneck-enwald curves, because everyone – from the postman Surleuly to Amorose to the taxis that bring up the Gesslers' *exshtravagant* American offspring come to pay their courtesies to Jérôme von Castelmur-Bondo – everyone drives like a bandit, everyone thinks they are all alone on the open road. It is not until this bend – especially with a *Rio six for de road* – that it begins to remind truly me of home, when the ancient horse chestnuts and oaks dot the open flank to the right, while on the opposite side the Schneckenwald is so thickly wooded we have the impression, as in the Ebnet, of driving over dusty turf on a country road beneath a half-arcade. The wire fence turns to an enclosure of crooked timbers with gates of crisscrossed boards to let the cattle through, here you can find wild morels big as your fists, here the plateau levels out over the Brentan, here on August first the eighteen members of the men's choir sing the Aargau anthem, here the woodpile blazes, here the professor will speak today for the forty-third time, with no interrup-tions, to the people of Bruns and the multitudinous visitors, *Dear coun-trymen, dear friends from near and far.* And here a long-dissolved picture redraws itself in chestnut green over the prospect of the dirt roads of Brunsleben, the approach to Soglio in the Bregaglia Valley, the granite posts like slender customs officers with holes in them for the long timbers, and in the summer of forty-six, when we drove to that most Italian of all the Helvetian mountain villages, I woke again from the divine darkness of earliest childhood, it must have been before Amden, yes, certainly before Amden, it strikes me as a characteristic of the Mnemoysnian in general that impressions gathered in exile are stronger – fuller bodied, in tobacconese, and what is a vacation for a tot but the painful loss of a hardly apprehended homeland? – than those from trusted surroundings.

Naturally, in order to conjure up and call forth Soglio in the Bregaglia Valley, I must now resort to some of the highest caliber goods from my cigar reserves in the musty castle cellar, then again, I would give a great deal to know the brand of cheroot my father smoked while he painted his aquarelles, for it might, supposing such a product were still available on the market, conduce to an irrepeatable harmonization of paternal and filial aromas, to an inter-Brennerian tobacco consortium, not a doubling effect, for if, in the same half-wheel, no Romeo y Julieta may be compared with another, and the same holds still truer for an Indiana from 1946 and one brought to market in the 1980s, then we find ourselves faced ineluctably with the question: who knows. And we call back to mind the gravest crisis in the family enterprise, the Cigar War or *Stumpenkrieg,* which broke out in late summer in 1937, when Maximilian Brenner hit on the ingenious idea of introducing a five-pack in place of the traditional box of ten. The competition and trade groups, brought together under the aegis of the Swiss Tobacco Union, lambasted his marketing strategy as a peril for the entire industry, which comprised as many as one hundred manufacturers, two hundred wholesalers, and ten thousand small retailers; a boycott was threatened, and thanks to my beloved father's documentarian leanings, I still possess a copy of the scurrilous letter from the S.T.U. dated August 7, 1937, which itemized "defensive measures" against five-packs of Exports priced at fifty centimes – two francs forty in today's money. It is stated there, with arrant hypocrisy, that: "In order to restrict our defensive measures to the absolutely necessary, the executive board of our syndicate, in its session on the sixth of the present month, adopted the following resolutions in reference to the statues and conventions of the S.T.U.: 1. Receipt and sale of the aforementioned five-piece cigar pack from Brenner & Sons Ltd. is prohibited, and all orders are to be withdrawn wherever possible. 2. The sale of all other Brenner & Sons Ltd. products remains authorized. 3. All publicity materials pertaining to Brenner & Sons Ltd., whether for the five-piece cigar pack or any other products, are to be taken down from display and returned to Brenner & Sons Ltd. 4. Cigar, cigarette, and loose tobacco manufacturers as well as wholesalers and specialty purveyors may not sell their wares to any reseller found to be in violation of the directives enumerated in items 1-3, and all sales are subject to Article 7 and specifically 7.iii of our convention. As you [the firm Brenner & Sons Ltd.] can see, you will in the future be permitted to sell Brenner products with the exception of the Brenner Export five-pack at the retail price of fifty centimes. However, all members of the industry will continue to concentrate their efforts vigorously on the defensive war against the five-piece packaging."

If *nicotiana tabacum* is celebrated for inflaming and soothing our mood in equal parts, then the origins of the grotesque *Stumpenkrieg* must be sought in the state of the market rather than in the intoxicant itself, in the press campaign carried on with the same poppycock, taunting, tirading, and bluster, words thought unthinkable in the Switzerland of those days, like "taking up arms," became commonplace, there was even the odd "Sieg Heil," the Syndicate marched on like vandals, and what was it they opposed? Maximilian's creation of a new, convenient, and durable flip-top box, which turned out to be an ideal accessory for the worker, the soldier, the man in the street, fitting comfortably in breast or pants pockets of blue fustian; when cheroots were pressed into bales, you could damage them when you picked them out, and smokers were likelier to skimp on a franc than a fifty-cent piece, so the retail sellers in Social Democratic strongholds like the canton of Zurich called a spontaneous gathering and announced they would not go through with the boycott. An advert from Brenner & Sons Ltd. appealed to the buyer: Show the owners of the tobacco shops who are knocking the boycott off-course that you know how to appreciate reason, civil courage, and liberal thinking. Go with the professionals, and take your business to people who know what's what. This was the hour of my grandfather Hermann Brenner, passionate hunter, keeper of the Waldau Inn, and trader in raw tobacco, who had, over a bottle of "the good stuff" in the same dining room where I would hear the aforementioned mournful cadence not many years later, relied on his country wisdom to bring the *Stumpenkrieg* to an end – and I like to think that as he did so, all by his lonesome, he toyed with the five-pack for three-quarters of an hour, smoking Export after Export and squinting through the blue haze – by suggesting with a wave of the hand to Maximilian, his half-brother, that they offer two of the straw-yellow flip-top boxes sealed together with a single label.

Wonder of wonders, on the evening of September 2, 1937, an accord was reached, a good old-fashioned Swiss compromise you could call it, the S.T.U. was appeased, the Export was now sold in the same syndicate-approved and hence mandatory quantities as bundles of Wurhmanns or Webstars, and the retailers, who had taken Maximilian Brenner's side to begin with, learned quickly to accommodate their customers' wishes by tearing off the union stamp and selling individual boxes of five, which violated not a single statute or convention. The box became known as a golden fiver, the sunflower-yellow *tertius gaudens* of this petty feud two years before the outbreak of the Second World War. By a long shot the bestselling cheroot, it was the revolutionary forerunner to the Cuban single-brand – admittedly the greatest fiasco in the history of tobacco – and having said this, what more can I do, may the indulgent reader permit me an interlude to tear away the cellophane sheath sealing the two boxes of Brenner Exports, slip out a stick, pure as nature in its *Vorstenlanden* wrapper, from the crackling, ecru-colored tissue paper that protects it, and light it with a Pioneer match, either end is fine. I will presume that in Bregaglia – *Bergell* – in the summer of forty-six, when a given *modiv* inspired my father, he smoked the same cigar as I during the composition of the present chapter, but first, with a glance at the dappled ash typical of Vorstenland sandleaf – sumptuous, the Export's oniony aroma – I open the big family photo album with its porridge-beige cover, inside it is like a collage, there I see myself, holding onto the carriage in my Menzo straw hat, trotting behind my cemetery-grandmother and my mother in her folk costume down the Zwingstrasse to the station – for which line, the Wynentaler or the SBB? The pasted-in receipt for four suitcases with a combined weight of forty-two kilograms shows our address in Soglio in Gothic letters, at the home of Giovanoli Peduzzi, and the legend, typed with the – to my mind – so *egsclusif* red ribbon, the H smudged with black, reads simply: *Have you forgotten anything?* On the next page is a shining sun, the logo of St. Moritz, and the yellowed page of a timetable with a box drawn around the train departing Zurich at 9:23, arriving in Chur at 11:32, a tiny fork and spoon indicate the presence of a dining car, in Chur our connecting train left at 11:56, taking the Rhaetian line through Tiefencastel, Alvaneu, Filisur, through the Albula Tunnel in other words, arriving in St. Moritz at 14:30; the Seetaler line, father's insurance inspector line, took us more quickly to Leonzburg than the Wynentaler did to Aarau, but just as it is true that whoever does not enter Venice through the lagoon inevitably steps through the back door of a palace, so for me, every attempt to enter or depart from Menzenmang has been synonymous with twenty-five years of WTB destinations.

I turn the page, noting the refinement of my father's collage technique, to a picture postcard, clear as a steel engraving, which shows the narrow street already mentioned that rose so magically up toward Brunsleben, the granite posts with their timbers – antediluvian guard-rails – a postal van with the top back, the Saurer grille, on the hillside two trees shimmer, the Sciora group towers up behind – and it comes back to me, a few tears well in my eyes, the master of dry drunkenness, the triune honk, the brilliantly resonant six-four chord of the Swiss Postal Service, I can play it here on my secondhand Bösendorfer, in F sharp major, of course, the briefest and most golden of all the golden oldies, the homiest of all the songs of home, the almost propaedeutic apprenticeship in the aesthetics of *Limelight* or *As Time Goes By*, it res-onates down in the Mera, the river running through Val Bregaglia, echoes up to the high campanile across from the pulpit, next to the ruins of a *negozio,* and now, by God, I can rightly say, albeit forty-two years later: Here is… Here in the beginning and always there were words, enchanted, proprietary Latin, the word Bergell is olive-green, Vicosoprano magenta, Stampa granite-grey, Promontogno cadmium orange, Bondo the blue of lead, Castasegna Neapolitan yellow, Soglio burnt Sienna. It occurred to me for the first time in the summer of forty-six, precisely because I could not understand the children I had longed to meet there, that we are, for those who converse in an unknown tongue, a *tertium non datur. Renzo, Adriana* – Van Dyke brown and citron yellow – Matrone bellowed through the narrow, crooked streets, Matrone herself had a henna tone, and here is the washhouse with its shingle roof around the corner from the barn, and dark-haired Renzo sits on the ledge, puffing away at a miniature pipe – one of the many treasures this little mountain boy possessed, among them a small sickle with its own sheath and whetstone. I am obliged to send a letter of contrition to my mother at her present address, for it transpires that she not only packed our bags with foresight, but even found room in one of the four suitcases, of braided bast with licorice-black straps, for my Maggi van, – the Schuco still lay in my future – which I offered to Renzo in exchange for the pipe; my yellow-and-brown company vehicle was stuffed with little Maggi packages, a jar of spices was the crown jewel, you could open the loading door "for real," but Renzo, who appeared to comprehend my sign language, refused the offer – what would he want with a soup delivery van in Soglio, of which Segantini says: "Soglio è la soglia del paradiso"?

I must have complained to my parents of my disappointment, yes, I was feverish with envy, and they held out for me the prospect of a miniature pipe on the trip home, which would take us from St. Moritz to Alp Grüm. If the promise failed to bear fruit, the fault was my own, for in the toy or most likely souvenir shop on the street in front of the station, so many model cars were parked so tight on countless shelves that I buckled under the agony of indecision before settling on a Mercedes Silver Arrow, which, immediately upon leaving the store, I rolled down the base of the handrail, it even had whitewall tires, but then, how tragic, the following night, I lost it briefly at the pension near the swimming baths, it fell through the cleft between the two mattresses. It is striking to reconstruct, through the medium of cigar, the numberless adversities of this kind a parent must redress, and instead of offering them a motorbike or moped or a Golf convertible if they promise not to smoke before their twentieth year, they should rather, for the sake of their own posterity... well, *en bref,* I have smoked since I was five, this is hardly noteworthy in Menzenmang, where the treasures lay there for the taking. It was easy enough to crawl beneath the storage shed of the firm Brenner & Sons Ltd. and pull a few leaves down through a hole in the crumbling floorboards, there you could roll your own *charuto* just as the Indians rolled their *sikars.* If the indulgent reader will grant me a bit more of his patience, in exchange for the consolation of the Alonso Menendez Brasil Import Hermann Arbogast Brenner has just offered him, I will reserve him, for later, another *gavilla* on the Columbian revolution every child undergoes on discovering the uncharted continent of tobacco in his life, portrayed, of course, with customary volatility. Awhile one will have noticed that, in want of the novelist's sturdy know-how, I have permitted emotive words to lead me near and far, soon I shall have to pester Adam Nautilus Rauch with the question of whether a method may yet be imputed to this madness, is it not the critic's job, if I consider his highly erudite labors, to show what the novelist ought to have done, *if he truly is one,* and unfortunately, Shaw's words continue to ring true: Those who can do cannot teach, or that's the gist of it anyway, admittedly I'm no Anglicist.

Making haste back to Soglio, the threshold of paradise − here is the washhouse where the women gab, scrub, wring, stir, and *shplash* in their *blue-en-vite shpeckelt kerchiefs,* cumulous soap clouds with blue-green frays float on the cold mountain water, I was allowed to fetch it when given the order to refill Father's medicine flasks, which lay beside the porcelain dish with its oviform depressions, the golden Eicifa paintbrush case and the black, four-paneled pigment box in the aquarelle portfolio. A photo in the upper left corner on page seven of the 1946–1948 family album documents this memory, which is sharper than the Kodak camera with the accordion lens from those days: he had taken me with him, and the two of us are sitting before the same *modif*, I dip the paint brush straight into the tin can, Mandi – this was his nickname – holds the pad at an angle between his knees, and looks, his hair parted, as always, with Canadoline, at his *aguarell,* mouth tugging downward, this tells me that just then he is thinking *ye goddam fool*. He has made a mistake, a perspectival one, perhaps, in all honesty that was never his strong suit, there is a problem with the vanishing point, maybe the greyish mauve is edging too far into cyclamen green. Dear Father, in late March of eighty-two – this date I should like never to recollect again – when you died in an accident by the train station in Birrwil, on your insurance inspector's route after a visit to the Picasso exhibit in Zurich, it was again the eldest, the exemplar, I, Hermann Arbogast Brenner, who was sent to collect your gruesomely mutilated effects in a plastic sack from the police station in Reinach, the scene reminded me of the airplane crash in Dürrenasch – curious, your death-courier worked for a transport company in Dürrenasch, too – where they marked the severed fingers in the fields with little flags, withal, I took this parcel to the villa in Menzenmang, where mother and the *shiblings* were already busy with the wording for the death notice, but could not linger, because I soon had to move out of the old rectory in Starrkirch and had a guest from Frankfurt staying in my living room who declared that I must, come what may, write a book about my time in Quittigen, because I had peered straight through the church with its dishonorable façade, and so I didn't see every detail of how they ripped you from the crumpled Fiat, the forty fractures and ruptures, but late at night, around 2:00 AM, I did drive the indigo-blue Alfetta two-liter slowly through the Wynental, you veered off the road once there, too, the scar in the tree is still visible, because you were distracted memorizing your wedding speech for your godson, I took the exit toward the *Brome* and reported to the hospital's pathology department, *prosecution* they call an autopsy in Austria – I wanted to look you in the face in that, the most dreadful hour of my adult life, the attendant tried to dissuade me but I don't give up easily, and in the end she removed the screws from your temporary coffin.

And there, I, the frustrated jurist, the Kohlhaas nature, original text by Adam Nautilus Rauch – another masterpiece, this novelette, for which I have no time left – saw first, not the stigmata incised deeply on your forehead, but rather the question of guilt, spelled out without room for error, for you had then, stiffened in death, the same drawn lips as in the Soglio photo, and consequently, O curse this truth-fanaticism in my heart's den of thieves, it was undeniably so, as many witnesses attested, that you had swerved, before the Volg, into the oncoming lane of traffic, presumably in the midst of reverie. How did the semi driver react? Properly, to all appearances, by his own admission he steered to the side, to let the silver Fiat AG 2671, the ghost driver, continue on its way, and you would have scraped through with a crumpled fender, a dented door, had you not at the last moment, *end of the line,* regained consciousness and tried to correct your mistake, the hundred-billionth thought in your seventy-two-year existence was thus one of self-admonition, *ye goddam fool,* and with this, in fractions of a second, you jerked the steering wheel right, ramming the now-helpless three-ton truck from Bärtschi Transport in Dürrenasch, and in shock, the driver of the flattened toy Fiat still managed to maneuver it at the end of its brake path onto the tracks of the Seetaler line, where any old train from Leonzburg or Lucerne could have pointlessly duplicated the work of destruction well past any notion of completeness. I was terribly sorry, as I stood before your coffin, that I could no longer defend you from the judgment of the world.

On your driver's license, which I have kept, the word *Invalid* appears in red stamped letters, a) Light Motor Vehicles *Invalid,* d) Change of Residence *Invalid,* Brenner, Hermann, Insurance Inspector, Sandstrasse, Menzenmang, DOB: 22 September 1910, Place of Birth: Burg, *Invalid,* there is something movingly grotesque about the box stating *Must Wear Glasses or Contact Lenses,* test date 09.13.1938, everything *Invalid,* the whole of your existence, but not for your firstborn, Hermann Arbogast, over and over he will speak to you directly in his tobacco leaves, which here and now declare war on every stamp in the world, on any official empowered by his arbitrary appointment to slam a row of rubber letters down upon a document, no concept coined in rubber will invalidate what I have to say.

7.

THE MAGIC OF COLORS,
BRENNER EXPORT BOX–PRESSED

Fear, loosen thy grip, I urgently require a Romeo y Julieta Churchill to brave the leap in time from March of eighty-two to the summer of forty-six, where the serrated edges of the photos still cling there beneath a drawing from my childhood – a *twain twack* rendered entirely in mauve, the switcher or *switsa,* in my son Hermann's idiom, in gracefully sparse crosshatches – my mother, head leaned to one side, in a white blouse and the skirt with the floral print, is standing in front of Palazzo Castelmur and laughing warmly, a beauté like Edwin's Pretty Mama in *The World of Children and the Fairytale Forest,* I stand in the middle photo with my back to the camera, wearing my father's hat, which he would later lose at the circus, pulled far down over my ears while I piss against a wall of undressed stone. What portion of this still-new conjugal bliss was reserved for the four-year-old in Soglio? This for example: I wet the mattress in the crib at the foot of my parents' double bed one evening when I was told, as it says in the *Struwwelpeter,* "We're going out and you must stay here," squeezing in my hand a tin horseman as I did so, a gift from Countess Kommanda with her pitch-black, raven-black hair, and I envisioned the formal dinner in the palazzo beneath a throne with hand-turned wooden columns, *table, deck thyself,* a richly ornamented, blue-starred ceiling with dangling tassels, mother and father sitting there being served. Yearning drove me out to the street, in a soggycold nightshirt with a red embroidered monogram. I made it to the washhouse and barn, but then, unaware how to further proceed, I felt my way along an endless prison wall that led to the town square lined with chestnuts, but Matrone Giovanoli hurried behind me, shouting her gibberish, led me to the bedroom, and put me back in my *beddie,* without, I surmise, changing the pissed-on fabric, this was, a year before Amden, before the children's home-concentration camp, an initial attempt to recapture the Pretty Mama the prince had driven away.

I discovered, completely *gaga,* a postcard in the family photo album advertising the Palazzo Castelmur wedding suite complete with hand-turned bedposts. How does an abandoned childhood achieve such feats of clairvoyance? And when I offer Surleuly, who has just stepped through the castle's inner gate waving an express letter, which in Switzerland requires speedy hand delivery, a Guinness on this fourteenth of July at 5:30 in the evening, he replies, *Ken't rightly shay no t' one a dem,* and he *sets t' jawin on as us-uul,* remembering, without so much as a glance at my pile of notes, a scene from the recruits' school at Monte Ceneri in '38, *ofer der ve hed a regruit –* what is the explanation for such mentalism? – *en he use t' pish de bed efry night, he took off en deshpair, dey nabbed im by de Italien border, ye know, ve hed orderlies en dere, those er alvays de cruelesht sons a bitches, en det's vy de whole berrecks wound up talking ehbout et, I shtill remember, Recruit Umiker, det vas de bedwetter's name, dey let hem beck on home; es fer yer queshtion ebout de Bruns coat eh arms, if I'm not mishtaken, it's eh eight-pointed shtar on a vite field, de shtaves end en floretties, de chronicle says "The castle gave Bruns parish a shield and a coat of arms," so et's nothin te do with eh millveel, vell now, I told de miss I'd be beck et de offish en ten, de profeshor'll know how te exshplain all det better te ye den I will, natrally, he wrote a whole book ebout his family, ye know a thing or two ebout dat, so I'm off, adieu, vait, no, I hefen't poured de whole thing out, I'd besht hef de last drop, te do othervise vould be impolite.*

Just as in the Gormund *gentilhommière*, so at gusset-shaped Brunsleben castle or the Jura in summer, with limestone far as the eye can see, nothing goes better than a Guinness, the special way it tickles the tongue, a second time, *pisht through and through,* I broke out despite Matrone Giovanoli's custodianship, and since my early childhood sense of orientation didn't let me reach my goal going forward, I wandered back, walking barefoot past the overgrown rear gardens, which belong, as I confirmed sixteen years later, to the extensive Castelmur properties Casa Antonio and Casa Max. As a bedwetter-inmate, I couldn't see the cast iron basket balconies or the blind bull's eye windows, the stepped cornices and the mezzanine, all that caught my attention were the ubiquitous rusty tether rings. Then I fell into the hands of a horde of children who dragged me high up to a park and locked me into a henhouse sticky with fluff and feathers, now – I must have thought –

you are well and truly done for, but there was a small gap in the wooden wall, the postern for the feathered beasts, I had to do it, I had to force myself through this opening before the bailiff let the metal slider whoosh down, it sat propped like a guillotine between two rails, I started crawling through, first one arm, then the head, then the second arm emerged under the blade, the children hung there like apes on the wire fence, it must have been an odd performance, watching an odious foreigner dribbling blood as he worked his way out of the coop, in my mouth was dust and chicken shit, and the startled biddies had lost their minds and ran beating their wings from one corner of the cage to another.

Then my memory blacks out, famously we awaken from our nightmares when the horror is too much to bear, recollection seems to function inversely, we only descend into mythological darkness once *dere is nothing left te shuffer through,* when I was freed, and by whom, from the chimpanzee house now eludes me, but during later visits to Soglio, I devoted a great deal of time to retracing the details of the crime, where, in what corner of which balcony garden did this horrific henhouse lie, even if many had emigrated, there must still be one witness in the village, how was I to dig up this needle in the haystack? Perhaps it was this cage for hens, cocks, and chicklets that inspired me to study architecture at the Swiss Federal Institute of Technology in Zurich in 1962. The name Soglio appears in documents as far back as 1186, the San Lorenzo Church is first attested to in 1354 and belongs, together with the Castelmurs' late medieval tower houses, to the oldest structures in the village. The settlement burned down completely in

1219, in 1662 the Spanish troops razed Casa Battista Castelmur. The original structure overlooked San Lorenzo at the edge of the sloping terraces and forking roads above the church. The monolithic Sott Funtaña dates from 1582. Architectural evidence allows the village's history to be divided into three parts, which reminds me of the sardonic utterance of a painter from Tessin: *my life disintegrates in three periods*. Medieval existence until 1450, prosperity after independence and the conquest wars of the Three Leagues between 1499 and 1512, a final phase of renewal after the road was built in 1875. Sott Funtaña is the name of the village spring with the shingle roof where I saw the bluish soap clouds swim and let the little boat carved from *cheshtnut* and fitted with a paper sail drift into the whirlpool, always into the whirlpool, Giovanoli Peduzzi's house was located in Soglio East, the blueprints at the engineering school in Basel even show the steps where Renzo sat when he refused to trade a miniature pipe for a far costlier Maggi van, and there, in the veil of a Montecristo No. 2, which I have just lit, image after image rises up with its nutty aroma.

Here is the threshold where, livid because I could make nothing out of my bars of modeling clay, I kneaded them into a ball and squashed it flat with my heel, and the blue-grey, egg-yolk yellow, and pinkish red omelet retained the pattern of my soles of my shoes, that did excite me, for I had discovered chance as a principle of modern art. There, in the fusty parlor – Father's sketch in red ink shows the south view from the window, the room is 2.8 meters wide – stands the table where I saw the detested modeling clay transmuted into a tractor in his hands, chassis plate, radiator, two matchsticks for axles, two small tires in front, two fat ones in the back – *tata-wee-ow* – then, as the crowning detail, its veritable distinction, a red seat with real perforations, exactly like those I had seen rolling past in the fields on my graveyard walks with my sectarian grandmother. A bridge leads from the upper corridor to the terrace, where Mother hangs out her washing, I can see the brown leathery farmer Giovanoli shaving in the courtyard, white face foamy before a shard of mirror, while Adriana takes hold of my tractor and crushes it flat on the stone floor, I am transfixed by Renzo's sickle, which cuts the grass on the bank "for real," which you can sharpen as Uncle Eugen does under the barn roof next to the Waldau high up over Menzenmang, there it is again, the honk of the postman's van, *too-ta-too,* Men-zen-mang. It is a sultry afternoon when my father guides me across the village, past endless palace façades to an enchanted park where I hear for the first time the word *atelier,* we step through a wooden gate into a wilderness of grass, then past a furry brown curtain into a hovel swarming not only with painting utensils, frames, brushes, canvas sheets, and tubes of pigment, but also with bees, *bee-yeez,* he shouted, pushing me out, *hernits,* vanishing back behind the drapery. I see the blue and red holes in the wall where they fly in and out and retain the impression of an *atelier* as a place colorful on the outside, but perilous above all, confirmed after an eternity when Father finally parts the fur with a painting under his arm and a thick swelling – a *shting* – on his cheek, which Mother later treats with a salve, *one eh dem goddam be-eyz got me.* There is no photo of the park in the family album, but I can inform the indulgent reader, whom these tobacco leaves may inspire sometime to go up to Soglio himself, that the garden lies on the village's western edge, toward Chiavenna, on the grounds of Casa Max, and is known as Grand Ort, and from the village map I see a middle path leading from the raised grass parterre with a crosshatched shed on the left-hand side down three steps to a rundle whose wavy lines betray the presence of water, from there it travels around the fountain to a small pavilion on the southern edge.

I was able to rent this rather dilapidated Tusculum for ten days in late summer after my father's death, when I was assembling materials for the Soglio *gavilla,* the fountain had long run dry, but the apiary, such as it was, remained in operation, I moved a cot, a table, and a chair into the faded yellow gazebo, washed up in the shingle-roofed fountain to the west, shaved in a shard of mirror as Giovanoli *père* had used to do, ate at midday in the French garden of the hotel that Palazzo Castelmur had become in the interim, in the evenings I sat in the whitewashed dining hall with the vaults over the barred windows and the ruby red filigreed curtains as a backdrop, with no notion that, on Easter of 1983, I would be sitting for the first time across from Jérôme von Castelmur-Bondo, an offshoot of that noble family with ancestral houses in Val Bregaglia, in the fumoir of Castle Brunsleben in my new occupation as companion of the History Professor Emeritus from the Swiss Federal Institute of Technology in Zurich. In the garden, amid the phlox, mauves, roses, and larkspur, a hotel guest mentioned to me a story set in Soglio by an eccentric Swiss writer named Gruber. In all honesty, I tried to read it, but I'd been right not to bother ruining my eyesight on contemporary literature: in syntactical terms, the tale, which starts with an earthquake in Southern Germany, is the most abstruse I have ever come across, first it describes a mad count who dictates his so-called last words to his secretary, who records them in a waxed canvas notepad, but since the author, like many avant-gardists, has the bad habit of dispensing with quotation marks, you are never sure exactly who is uttering what in this essentially ineffable bit of prose, then again, it is brimming with foreign words, a telltale sign, as Adam Nautilus Rauch remarked to me recently at Lake Hallwil, that the author is deficient in his native tongue; going on, this Gruber preposterously asserts that his protagonist could feel the vibrations from the earthquake in the wood-paneled bedroom of Palazzo Castelmur in Albstadt, and this, if you take the Richter scale readings at face value, quite simply cannot be; on top of everything, and this is the peak of confusion, when the novella reaches its end, the count – what's his name again? – who has expired without any apparent cause of death, confuses cause and effect, because according to the notes of his Eckermann in his testamentary declaration, he, the *moribundus* secreting this convoluted thread, is himself the epicenter of the disturbance, I can only say, in agreement with Adam Nautilus Rauch, that a greater charivari, or – since the critic is a skipper, too – a more calamitous shipwreck of sixteen pages can never have been perpetrated before.

On the other hand, it is true that a dilettante like Hermann Arbogast Brenner can learn something from such flimflammery, viz. that the dialect the village elders use to discuss the events of the day on the stone bench in front of Casa Max is called Bargaiot, for them *cuntadin* means farmer, *al balcun* is window, *al peng* is butter, *l'asce* is maple, *al mascum* is bee, *i brascair* are roasted chestnuts, and as I eavesdropped on the murmured words, just the spoken melody, really, sitting under the shade of the chestnut trees, enjoying a Toscano Garibaldi, permitting myself a nip now and then from a glass of Jack Daniel's, something became clear to me about the sense and senselessness in trying to corroborate the scenes from one's childhood. It had to do with the spell a person tries to break by setting primal subjection against orientation, dysphasia against the exact word, unordered against ordered images. As we count the steps between the Giovanoli home and Palazzo Castelmur and compare them with that narrow street straying off into the infinite that the four-year-old couldn't manage, we establish proportions, like Edmond de Mog at the Proust house in Illiers-Combray, finding, in this way, a measure for our childhood, and the delicate question of which is better, to trace out impressions as they actually were felt or to couple them incessantly to present and future, is one only a true novelist – Bert May, for example – can satisfactorily answer. The indulgent reader has my word, I will return to this momentous inquiry on my next visit to Gormund.

Strange, the distortions of scale: of the altogether fifty-nine photos in the Soglio chapter of the family album, thirteen show me with Mother, four with Father – only a single one commemorates the way we used to paint together – yet in Hermann Arbogast's memory, Gertrud, ever clad in the same white blouse and floral printed skirt, appears just three times, on the terrace hanging out the wash, on the afternoon that ended in the henhouse horror, and during the salving of the bee sting; never do I see her cooking, setting the table, ladling, putting me to bed, turning down the lights, kissing me goodnight, never strolling, never resting, never sitting in the chestnut grove, never preparing lunch – though photo fifty-nine shows precisely this, Mother in the middle of pressing together a sandwich while I wait there for it greedily. True, the fathers are the cameramen, only rarely do they offer themselves as subjects, but our inner *laterna magica* unerringly projects onto the walls of the heart the outlines of the parent we feel most drawn to. Even if the most beloved subject of my childhood drawings, the car, was present in Soglio only in the form of the wooden Maggi delivery van, not to forget the clay tractor, the truth of my memory remains that I was always making pictures with my father and never left his side. Of his earthly possessions left over from the indescribable shambles my siblings Klärli and Kari made of his home in Menzenmang on the first day of their weeklong *tidying up* to ready it for the fire sale, I have salvaged three things above all: Father's paint tins, the Eicifa box with the paint brushes, and the porcelain dish with the ten egg-holes for mixing the colors, plus the three prismatic medicine bottles in different shades of brown from Bernese sandstone to rock sugar, still stowed in the insurance inspector's crumbling briefcase, in order – as Jérôme von Castelmur-Bondo has said with regard to his collecting of relics – once more to acquire what I already possess. After lighting his Brenner Export, father would spread these utensils over the grass, there was neither folding chair nor easel, and he would let me open that holiest of holies, the black metal case, to delight in the four-tiered spectrum of lickable colored tablets, which started in the upper left with white, spanned every shade of yellow from cadmium orange to minium, a musical keyboard of chromatism, descending from cinnabar and carmine red to madder lake and *rose véritable* through the brown regions of umber, sepia, and sienna, followed by complimentary greens, Veronese, sap, Paris, olive, permanent green light, the illogically named earth green, the cake of which stood out brightly in the row, finally the blue values, cerulean, cobalt, ultramarine, indigo, Prussian and Parisian blue, and a scant number of violets, mauve, lilac, amethyst. My father, who never sat in the sun without his grey hat cocked and crinkled in the front, squinted his eyes through the cigar smoke and fixed his *modif,* perhaps it was a hut in Löbbia with chestnuts, the foreground specked with alpine flowers, wild pinks, perhaps, the Scoria Group in the hazy distance, *do as I do* is the motto, just as in the eponymous magic trick, but the cumbersome underdrawing with the Faber Numero 4 bored me; he did let me scrub his Schminke Original watercolor pans, this allowed him to practice his geography of the vanishing point and show me what to do with the water. Bottle one, probably still with the fretted label reading *Muriatic acid,* was used for mixing colors, the second flasklet was for washes, the third for rinsing the brushes.

First came the miraculous multiplication of compartments, when you lifted the pressed cake tableau from the case to reveal five porcelain squares and three rectangles in the base. Here I found myself in the labyrinth of indecision, for I was drawn, on the one hand, to the ten resplendent ovoid depressions in the porcelain dish, on the other to the four lavish compartments in the paint box's lid, but no less tempting were the coy swatches in the center of the palette, and there I was, given my place in this avocation in which my father showed such virtuosity throughout his life, able to mix *for real,* and so Renzo and his little kid's sickle could take a hike for all I cared, my labor was that of a true aquarellist on a one-to-one scale. Here, the indulgent reader will break our concord and object: This cannot be, this Hermann Arbogast Brenner is styling himself a child prodigy. And I concede to him that this endless flitting over scales of red until the precise color of the wild pinks was revealed would have bored me the same as any other *liddle cheroot* were it not for the immense seductiveness of doing the very same thing as my father. Not until he began to prepare the ground for a chestnut tree with a very fine glaze did I abandon the procedure, dunking the paintbrush boldly into the cake of geranium and coloring the fenders of the impossibly sleek *amerikaner,* giving it Neapolitan yellow windows and a sky blue tail end, most important of all, perhaps, was that now and then my father would let me take a pull of his cigar if I promised solemnly to blow the smoke out right away and never, ever to tell my mother.

Another thrilling moment during these *modif-aguarell*-studio excursions, which always took us under, over, west, or east of Soglio, even if its hallmark, the campanile of San Lorenzo – its bells tolled like blocks of lead tumbling down in the afternoon – always remained in view, was when the brushes with the black or English red shafts and the Rowney trademark were taken from the Eicifa case and I was allowed to unseal a new color cake, first from its proprietary wrapping, then from the silver foil inside, and was encouraged to lick it like the caramel fudge when my cemetery-grandmother took it out of the oven, you paint with the tongue, you must eat the *caput mortuum,* this word beset me like none other, something dead, something broken – kaput – was a spur to my contemplation, then my imagination was steered toward the local *cimitero* on the Angermatt, because the blackish brown wooden crosses with the oxidized tin canopies brought to mind the exquisite mushroom dish my favorite aunts Ideli and Greti used to make in Stierenberg and at the restaurant at the Waldau with black trumpets, the name of which translates in several languages – *Totentrompete, trompette de la mort, trombetta dei morti* – to trumpets of the dead. What words the world held in its bag of wonders, they modulated the child's temperament like a piano, throwing it out onto the ski slopes of associations, contrasts, parallels, where did we learn this technique if not in the chestnut green, Scoria-bright midsummer of forty-six, high above the wild spray of the Maira, where again and again the postman's triad let loose tears of longing, in the ancestral homeland of Jérôme von Castelmur-Bondo – not, to put things plainly, in the ABC-barracks the four-year-old as yet had no notion of, no, certainly not there. The artist's formation in general commences, like early sexual dreams, with a rudimentary aesthetics quickly extinguished in the cadet's drill of one-times-one and capital and lower-case letters, every so-called pedagogical intervention that interrupts the virtuoso nature of youth is a capital offense perpetuated by the state, only with the advent of puberty – if training in the *proper* perspective, abstinence from all but the *proper* color schemes, has not spoiled everything for all time – can a new impulse begin to take hold. My magician mentor and friend Wolff Baron von Keyserlingk confessed to me one and a half years ago during a private lesson in one of the pantries of the Frankfurter Hof that already in first grade he had mastered Dai Vernon's forcing technique and could even do it in his sleep, slipping away the ten of spades deftly during the Injog shuffle, fanning the cards out, letting them glide subtly until five cards before high noon, then slowing the tempo, faking an offer, pushing forward the lead card, the queen of diamonds, with the right thumb or the little finger on the face side; the mark thinks: there's the card he's trying to palm off on me, so he doesn't bite, after all, this guy's no fool, and you go on fanning them out, with the ten of spades you do the very opposite, simulation, dissimulation, and there, when you start to pull it away, the mark reaches out – but thanks to compulsory education, I can't do that one anymore, even if I was card magician of the year for 1985-1986 – or at least, I can no longer do it in my sleep.

The oblong box adorned with gold leaf, which held the brushes and extra paint cakes, produced by Eichenberger & Co. in Menzenmang, showed a dark-skinned beauty on one side arrayed with flowers, offering up a bunch of tobacco leaves, to whom? To a sailboat dropping anchor to her right. Today I recognize it as a topsail schooner with fore-, main-, and mizzen-mast, in the middle is a triangle enveloped in brown tracery with the name Eicifa and the family's coat of arms, a priapically erect acorn wedged between two oak leaves. *Overseas* was one of the magic words of my childhood, and for this reason, too, I would stand before the court on behalf of Malaga Cellars in Leonzburg-Combray, for even if *El Faro* meant lighthouse in Spanish and not *far* as I might have hoped, still I could lose myself for hours in this visual riddle, I knew nothing yet of Columbus and his discovery of tobacco, of the shipping of stamped bales in the harbors of Cuba and Brazil, the symbols of the beauty, the leaves, and the ship had to suffice, along with the silver coins that framed the whole scene. What would happen, I asked myself, if the outsized woman with the four-leaf clover in her hair boarded the diminutive ship, I made no distinction between fore-, middle-, and background, even my *amerikaner,* pasted into the family album and dated with the green ink office stamp 10 July 1946, already concealed the lineaments of simultaneous perspective. In sleep, in truth, it is given to us, and it is taken away in the sudden exorcism of waking, and for this reason, we must support the child artist in his somniferous phases, and it is much to the credit of my father in Soglio, even if I never did become a painter, that he recognized so early everything I might have been, if my health had only played along, and that he gave me, a *liddle cheroot,* this chance; inert, as if trapped in Bernese stone, the hum and winging of nature around us, time stopped, he oversaw the lofty business of mixing the colors. The leathern briefcase must also have held the premium tables and the actuarial handbook of the Swiss Life Insurance and Pension Company, you never knew, even a mountain farmer by the name of Giovanoli or Torriani might need a bit of insurance advice, which would later bear fruit in the *büroo* at home in Menzenmang with a grey sheet of paper bearing the light blue legend, *New customer enrollment.*

And I heard, as his *aguarell* marched on toward completion, the gently rasping intake of air, in the critical stage of the final brushstrokes you could no longer take your cigar from the corner of your mouth, this was the sequence of events: left eye squinted, lips slightly parted, so the Export tipped upward, expansion of the lungs, in smoking there are two sorts of joy, as Adam Nautilus Rauch writes in a jubilee volume devoted to Opal – *the fine cheroot:* the inhalation and exhalation of the fog of Havana-Sumatra-Brazil, the systolic and diastolic rhythms of the heart, and since he let me now and then, as I have already mentioned, have a puff at his horribly gnawed-at stump, this idyll was a conspiracy of father and son occurring far from the eyes of Mother, never did she come to disturb us, never to look, *te come en goggle,* to see the progress of the aquarelle – remarkable that it should rhyme with Bergell – never did she shout with delight when the picture with its vertical, diagonal, horizontal washes stood on the stuffy chair in the kitchen while the mat, the *passbartut,* was being trimmed, this was a particularly solemn proceeding, for only in the viewing box, the white window of paperboard, was the deep green study severed from its coincidental surroundings, my father revealed to me the secret of framing by holding an ordinary piece of paper cut in a right angle against the whitewashed wall, look, he said to me, inside it the finest structures are revealed, things hardly to be seen on the rest of the wall adjacent, as a four-year-old I could not grasp all this in a comprehensive way, today, however, I believe I am entitled to memorialize it in these *doble claro* tobacco leaves as an ur-experience of the kind which, the perhaps still indulgent reader may rightly suspect, will only become clear to the architecture adept during his study of Klee's *The Thinking Eye.*

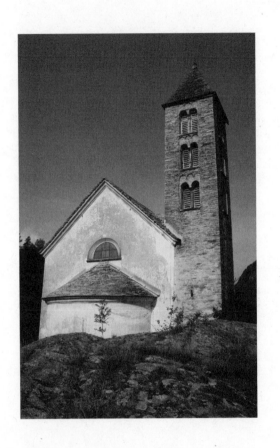

8.

VISITORS FROM JAVA, VORSTENLANDEN

Though it is only late in life, via a gratifying digression on cigars, that I have finally put ink to paper, let the apprehensive rest assured, *l'appétit viendra en mangeant,* my debut in this dubious métier will likewise be my farewell, but there is one thing I know, to second Bert May: our backbreaking labor is an archeology of the soul, there is no remembrance without fiction, no recollection without invention, true poets, from whose ranks this thwarted tobacco salesman is naturally excluded, are those who live by lying, *who lie like print,* as the German adage has it, and as we note here a certain consonance among the words *lie, lure,* and *louche,* we cast doubt on how things really were and cajole the indulgent reader to follow us into the regions where the subjunctive reigns, how things might have been; we use metaphor – from the Greek *metapherein,* to carry across, according to Bert May – to grant coherence to that which simply cannot have occurred, for life is a dice game, through a long night of play you may wait in vain for the six to come up, out rolls one after exasperating one; or else a wheat-blonde fairy announces six lotto numbers on the TV screen – a stroke of luck that never comes for millions but lands twice for a select few – hence the high art of creation may be thought superior to life, because the scribbler does not leave the order of the balls to chance, literature is the award of that once-in-a-lifetime jackpot. Here my friend Adam Nautilus Rauch will vigorously object, that still and all, the world has its laws, physical, botanical, chemical, astronomical, and it would be a deep affront to his earnestness in the enjoyment of life – a credo for which I would declare my utmost respect, were the duration of my existence not curtailed by a terminal diagnosis – to see literature and art confounded with magic and games of chance: what do craft and trickeration have to do with the linguistic organism, the swindler relies on the marvels of a moment, the epic poet is an artist of perpetuity, the sorcerer's appearances deceive, the creator's, however much he lies, do not. And the critic – my two boys' local Sigismund Markus – has urged me, after a cursory inspection of these pages, to stick to the relevant facts of my life as a cigarier, *ye hef te know how te dishtinguish relevant en irrelevant.*

Inclined to pay heed to this wise bit of advice, we will return to the summer of forty-six in Soglio, where the legend on page seven of the family album reads in dull chromium oxide green: *Many lovely days in the chestnut forest.* Just below, on the Parisian blue label: *From Soglio through the chestnut forest to Castaseigna, where we bought fruit on the Italian side, then wandered at midday over the old bridge to Bondo. From Promontonio by taxi back up to Soglio.* Edwin's Pretty Mama will have chafed at the chromium oxide green and Parisian blue, and because it is Castasegna and Promontogno and not Castaseigna and Promontonio, and these poorly pronounced and/or badly transcribed terms would plague my father right up to his accident in *Birrbu,* he said *granofong* for gramophone, *simeetrie* for symmetry, he christened Cavaillon, famed for its asparagus, *Cavilion,* he was a playful sort of person, my mother a correct one, and that, in spite of his shortcomings, he *maneged te mek it* as an insurance inspector was entirely thanks to his *disiplin,* not discipline. I recall nothing of what the Kodak photos reveal from this expedition to Castasegna, Bondo, and Promontogno, which requires just two hours, according to Kummerly + Frey, on the other hand, I do remember a crooked tunnel beneath a waterfall, and in the middle, faint and shadowy amid the scant sunlight that reached inside, a handcart, put down in such a way there was no telling whether it was entering or leaving. This wagon would crystallize into a colored pencil drawing, a rectangle on two spoked wheels, but how should I represent its ambivalent position in the tunnel? Simple: I scribbled to the left and right two horseshoe portals and omitted the conveyance's drawbar. There was no way to say now which was the front end and which was the back, whether it had entered through one side or the other. Then, unforgettably, the moment near Castasegna when the church tower soared up in withered orange ochre in the midst of the crowns of trees, at first just the arches over the belfry windows in their oblong frames. A campanile was something you could experience from above *and* below, because once the road rose up, it descended steeply into the village. In Soglio I always asked to climb up and see the bells of San Lorenzo, the thought of the lead blocks resting there enthralled me, the request was dismissed, *too dangeroush,* but at least Castasegna offered a simulacrum of this enchantment. No sooner was the octagonal cupola seen and compared with the one from Soglio than we took, if memory serves, the same road back through the chestnut groves of the Brentan to retrieve Giovanoli's haycart, and I was allowed ride inside with Renzo, crooked pipe in his mouth and tiny sickle in hand. But this is not true, image twenty-four shows me in my crisscross suspenders in a deep sward of grass following close on mother's heels; as far as the black taxi, all I see of it is Uncle Fritz trying to jump on the running boards as we drive off from the square paved with cobblestones in front of Palazzo Castelmur, he hopped up and down next to the windows until we reached the pinched side streets, where he was pressed into the wall of a building. Java–Rotterdam–Zurich–St. Moritz–Promontogno–Soglio was the itinerary my third-favorite – because third-cutest – Waldau aunt undertook with her colonial consort to spend a few *idillische* days in Bergell. In the collage on page twelve, the postage stamp on the blue-and-white airmail envelope reading *Dunedin C.I.* bears the date 10 April, 1946 and the address Mrs. E. Lüning-Brenner, Waldau – crossed out – c/o 53 Djamboelaan, Batavia-Centrum – crossed out scrupulously in pale red – Menzenmang, Argovia, Switzerland – strike-through – then, aslant on the left-hand side: Forwarding Address Brenner-Pfendsack Residence, Soglio, Bergell, Schweiz. On the sepia-brown stamp from New Zealand, an alligator rests on a rock, underneath the flyer for the La Plota–Stampa hiking trail is a rubbing of a reptile's hide with Father's comment: Snakeskin, followed by three exclamation points.

One evening in Bregaglia – or was it at the Waldau? – I lay *nekkid es eh jaybird* on my belly in bed, Uncle Fritz was next to me, he stroked me tenderly on the buttocks, and said: This one is the Homberg and this one is the Stierenberg. Only decades later did I understand what had happened, when my father revealed to me that this wealthy colonial lord from the Netherlands, who had lost his shirt in the war, had most likely turned homosexual, *homoo,* in the prison camp in Java, Doctor Vogt had called once in horror from Reinach because Fritz had been found in the waiting room attempting to undress a child. And yet, Fritz lent enormous distinction to the summer of forty-six, no one could play pranks and act a fool like he, and there he stands in photo twenty-two between Elsa in her Aargau folk costume and my mother in her white blouse and floral printed skirt, his shirt is dark, his hands on his hips, khaki pants and sunglasses, an overgrown Boy Scout. And here he is squeezing me between his knees, whether before or after the Homberg-Stierenberg groping remains uncertain. I would like to do justice to him in matters of tobacco as I go down into the vault where my cigars are stockpiled. Java, the gates of Hell, in the Sunda islands alone are more than a hundred active volcanoes, the perilous, fire-spitting Galunggung, Galung Agung, and Galung Dieng could blow at any time, they fling forth their masses of lava – a magical word that cast a peculiar spell on me when Blandi told me the story of Robinson Crusoe – over that fertile strip of land where the two distinguished representatives of *nicotiana*, Vorstenlanden and Besuki, thrive alongside pepper, cinnamon, and tea. The first has a captivating savor of fresh nuts, also a scent of onion, and shimmers velvety from blackish-brown to silver-grey in color. As filler it aerates the cigar, it is elastic enough to serve as a binder, which must stretch like a muscle around the cocoon, but to use it to these ends – unless you're a *Pietjes* smoker – is almost a waste, only as a wrapper are its exemplary virtues revealed: the onion and nut aromas develop, tiny silver kernels arise on the snow-white ash when the tooth – the pockets of oil in the leaf – begins to smolder. Johann Caspar Brenner uses the costly sand leaf for the wrapper of the Export. Besuki is hardly inferior to Vorstenlanden, which has no well-defined cultivation zone, but thrives in those provinces once held by the aboriginal princes; its no less delicate hues range from Sumatra light to chestnut brown, it grows in the southeast of Java in the Djember region, and is divided into three grades: Mark B is straight-packed whole leaf, well sorted for binders and wrappers; Mark HK is Hangkrossok, generally only appropriate for binders; Mark K is Krossok, bottom-grade chopped tobacco for filler.

I would question whether my mother truly welcomed those guests from the *Waldau clan* in those days, on the next page already we read *Adio Soglio,* another spelling error of my father's: the journey home over the Alp Grüm through the Bernina Pass, the coveted sunglasses – a desire surely stoked by Uncle Fritz – casting evening shadows over my face on the restaurant terrace, my father found them further down in some *sufenir shop,* I can still see him tramping through the summer snow, and here he is in another photo, inevitable Menzo hat in hand, he would carry it across the entire country before losing it in the gullet of a predatory beast at the Circus Knie, he has hoisted me onto his shoulders as he did during the steep ascent to the Alpine prairie Plän Vest at 1821 meters, where today there is one double stable and fourteen individuals, eight residential huts, three dairy huts, two cheese cellars, and seven ruins attesting to the devastating avalanches, we had to spend the night in one of these half-stone, half-wooden buildings, because mother fell into the slurry, which was stored in a rowboat covered with hay sacks, and the whole night long a miner's lamp burned behind its grate in the corner; I slept that night not in the cleft, but at the very foot of the bed, and I remember very clearly the words *headache tablets,* my mother must have gotten one of her migraines after her unintended manure bath, *it like te creck her head open,* she groaned and yammered and called out over and over, "Mandi, Mandi," and now and then I caught a foot in the belly, the embryo was no longer inside kicking at his mother's womb, instead the begetter was kicking her firstborn, but still, the adventure pleased me, as did every improvisation that neutralized Gertrud's stern parentage, there it is, another reminiscence of mother, the fourth from the summer of forty-six.

Every farmer has one or more stands of chestnuts in the *selva,* the fruits are dried on the spot, in the anterooms of the drying houses – in Menzenmang, at the plant just down from the fire station – the *cheshtnut hushks* are kept next to the cordwood for the smokehouse, when the fruits are spread over a wooden grating on the upper floor, the fumes blanket them and remove the final hints of moisture, the older buildings are asymmetrical, either of stone masonry or wooden frames, their drying beds lie crosswise to the direction of the roof ridge, in the newer buildings the exposed beams in the ceiling rise up over the partly white-washed walls. The floor plans of both types are almost identical, with the exception of the timbered stairwells. Nor has time much altered the look of the stable barns, the combination of *rasa pietra* and cornerstones distinguishes the newer buildings. Prior to 1800, the lower floor, which housed the stables, was still whitewashed or infilled, and the loft made of horizontal logs. Double stables typically have right-angled roofs, gable ends on double barns come from the older building tradition, hip roofs the new. The *ingradä*, the preliminaries for drying the chestnuts, take place in the rear of the building, the *mechine* is divided into several compartments, the *mottfüür*, not an open flame, is fed by the *fufa*, the chestnut shells from the previous year. The thirty-centimeter layer of chestnuts should be turned after three or so weeks – the resemblance to tobacco fermentation is striking, I must tell Johann Caspar Brenner – then the fruits are scooped up with a *vandal*, dropped into sacks and baskets, and laid out again on the grille, but at a distance from the fire. The process lasts four to five weeks, depending on the weather conditions and the thickness of the layer. The smoke from the chestnuts leaks out between the beams and the stone shingles on the roof. The *pastä* – the process of cracking them – is so laborious, families have to help each other out. They fill small sacks of unbleached cloth with two kilograms or so of dried chestnuts and thrash them against tree stumps until the shells burst open, then they shake them into a *vann* of willow strips, sifting out not only the *güscia*, the husk, but also the *geja*, the thin skin. During this coarse treatment a good many of the *cheshnuts* break, then the people say *farciam* – let's grind them, for the *farina dulcia,* the flour used for that local delicacy, chestnut pizzocheri. Finally, the dried fruits are sorted by quality and size and emptied into sacks, they can be stored up to two years, the leftover bits, the *farciamin,* are fed to the chickens, and with this, we return to the grisly backyard monkey cage on some never-to-be-found balcony in Soglio. The largest drying center is in the heart of Plazza, halfway up the narrow, curvy drive to the terraced village where the footpath branches off toward Castasegna.

I own one aquarelle of my father's from the summer of forty-six, done in olive green, sap green, moss green, grass green, leaf green, gravel grey, and light steel blue, the inscription in pencil reads *Chestnut forest below Soglio,* the signature is the BR seal, square with rounded corners, it shows, from an aerial perspective, the roofs of four barns in the foreground next to a mowed field with little sheaves of hay, and further on, the leafy tumult of the chestnuts. The edges of the gabled stall roofs with their stone bases to the lower left are mirrored in the mountain to the right, on the other side of the valley; in the midground stands the hex green slope over Bondo, ending in the hill where Nossa Donna rises up like Napoleon's hat, its right flank following the caterpillar line of the crowns of the trees; in a zigzag Val Bregaglia opens up, and the eye traces an imaginary path to the Scoria Group, lying bright in Parisian blue beneath the lowering rain clouds; the ragged mountaintops in the background are reflected in the horizontal lines of the drying houses and the slight convexity of the Bondo meadow. The technique has, viewed against the earlier works, progressed toward a detaillism that will terminate in pointillism – the stables on the earlier painting *Mountain Brook in Gadmen,* 1943 show hardly any indication of the beams, but now the gneiss roofs are marked with crosswise flaring brushstrokes; if before we had balloon trees with light radiating outward from their green core, now individual branches are perceptible amid the bushels of leaves, and in the Scoria Group the summits of Ago di Scoria, the Gemelli, Cengalo, and Badile are clearly visible over the glacier, greyish blue like the plumage of a kingfisher. No red, just light ochre for the warm stone foundations, sepia brown for the timbers. Sixteen years later, when the whole family of five stayed in Palazzo Castelmur in Soglio, we have another view of the Bondasca, this time from a high meadow on the village's western age, the campanile of San Lorenzo materializes against the hill of Nossa Donna, forming a golden section with the light ochre swatches on the left and right edges of the picture; oblique in the foreground a stone ridge and a stooped boulder, the brim of Napoleon's hat hugs a chestnut bending into the valley, daubs of madder lake offer a complementary accent to the ever-more-sovereign green, which deteriorates into cinnabar in the midground. Recess of the Bondasca Valley, glacier and Soria Group in rosé, pearl white, Sahara beige, diluted cobalt, a sky of cerulean and Heliogen Blue above. Next to it, again from 1962, is my *Church in Stormy Weather,* a view from the window of Casa Alta not far from Grand Ort: to the upper right you can see traces of the soffit in Delft blue and Sienna yellow. Deliberately arranged in the foreground are two pots of geraniums and bellflowers, their scarlet and cinnabar tints against the earth green give the sense – implicitly, of course – of a pointed vault in the center. Architectural harmony arises from the rubblework arch of a cream-colored house with green shutters to the left and an older one, scratched in with charcoal, on the right, its six-paneled windows the same charred black hue as the chimney. We plunge here into a narrow lane that ends in a door of the same raven black. There, too, the golden section of the lines curving upward from the rear of the storm-swept house points past an imbroglio of clustered gneiss roofs toward the slender penstroke of the campanile's western face, while the left edge of the northern perspective, crosscut by the roof, sinks down through the thick anthracite strip of the cream-colored house and expires in the bulging pot of geraniums. Playfully, a segmented clock face with Roman numerals. Belfry windows with clockworks inside, crown cornice, eight-sided tambour under the cupola. Stormy sky, two-fifths of the composition, lead grey mingled with *caput mortuum* and mauve, in an oblique golden section with the rear edge of the tower and the right window embrasure stands a transmission tower with glass insulators, the wires against the clotted clouds describe a parabola over the openings in the spire, which delimits the background to a conic section mirrored in the arcs of the flowers. The black blotches of the windows in the house of undressed stone, the door at the vanishing point of the narrow lane, and the apertures in the bell tower form an isosceles triangle which is repeated, in a smaller form, but overturned, in the gable to the left. The larger of the flowerpots rests diametrically across from the higher building, the smaller one across from the shorter. O the flourishes of the Vorstenlanden wrapper!

I read just now in *The Tobacco Times:* Will Smoker's Lawsuit Unleash an Avalanche? Fallout From Litigation Following a Chain Smoker's

Death From Cancer. The case is as follows: fifty-eight-year-old Rose Cipollone died of lung cancer in 1983 after forty-plus years of smoking. A year before her death, she sued three firms. The court reached the verdict that the cigarette manufacturer Liggett Group Inc. had falsely understated the dangers of its product in its advertisements. The two other producers, Philip Morris Inc. and Lorillard Inc., were acquitted, because Rose Cipollone only began consuming their cigarettes after 1966, by which time companies were obliged to print a warning on their packaging like the one required by the Federal Office of Public Health. Is this a crack in the dam? Richard Daynard, head of the Tobacco Products Liability Project, believes this verdict from Newark shatters the myth of the invulnerability of *nicotiana* traffickers, and many in the legal profession predict a boom in cases of this kind. In an earlier suit, the producer was forced to pay $80,000, this time the damages are $360,000. Compensation claims are likely to be limited to the years before 1966, when advertisements claiming the benefits of smoking were still permitted, and the firms insist, to use their words, there will be no *flood of new verdicts*. If it is reasonable to take Wall Street's reaction as a reliable barometer for the ramifications of the Liggett case, then cigarette makers may sleep easy, on the day of the verdict Liggett closed at $7.625, a drop of only fifty cents per share. *The Wall Street Journal* cited an analyst from the securities firm Kidder, Peabody & Co. as stating the decision was a "non-event" and neither demand nor pricing would be affected. At the foot of the article was a portrait of a young American blonde in profile bringing a cigarette to her lips with the caption: *This pretty, self-assured young woman knows how to appreciate the flavor of a cigarette.* Eight days ago, Hermann Arbogast Brenner signed a petition for the Federal Council to put a stop to the country-wide campaign against smokers, which now has millions of adherents, because it defames a significant portion of the population, provokes an utterly unjustified psychotic dread in the rest, and is therefore a human rights violation, moreover it is squandering millions in tax moneys that could better be spent on insurance programs for the elderly, widows, and indigent children, as well as on environmental protections. We are, the petition closes, under the rubric FT for freedom and tolerance, an independent organization, beholden to no political party or religious denomination. The Cigar War of '37, my dear Johann Caspar Brenner, has now become a tobacco world war, and there's no need to ask why the Americans flew to the moon, they'll soon be opening a satellite outpost where smoking is still permitted, that may be why John Glenn, upon returning from the stratosphere, received a gift of his bodyweight in Havanas; but all this is beside the point, I must ready myself for today's colloquium with the Emeritus, Jérôme von Castelmur-Bondo, who in his student days drew that family tree now hanging on the wall in the knight's hall facing the palas, with this late interest in the chronicle of his ancestors he has returned to those inclinations that destined him as a secondary schooler to the study of history.

9

THE PRIMAL SOUND IN PALAZZO CASTELMUR,
HUIFKAR TRABUCO

It was already past five on a midsummer afternoon when I sat in the terrace garden of Brunsleben with its classic triad of mauve, larkspur, and phlox, corresponding, as you know, to the ternion Havana–Sumatra–Brazil, waiting for Jérôme von Castelmur-Bondo, a box of Hamers & Co. Huifkars on my knees. The Emeritus asked me to bring something light, something wholesome in view of the thirty-two degrees in the shade, at the hour of our Rilke-and-Soglio colloquium, not a Partagás culebra, in other words, though it must be said that the heavier Havanas, so long as the bowels play along, help us hold out against the heat: in my role as companion, I acceded to his wishes, besides I love this box of *reservados,* which reminds me of my boyhood treasure hoards. To my honor, I never trapped, and never would have trapped, the small tortoiseshells – *Nymphalis urticae* – that were lurking in the rose garden, I never built an herbarium, I cared only for dried *nicotiana,* the dark bronze gleam of the Médaille des Beaux Arts de S.M. le Sultan and the Croix d'Honneur d'Amsterdam 1895, cerulean sky arcing over the Hamers firm's covered wagon on its purple-red ground, the emblem Sigarenfabriek Oisterwyk colored in blood orange, a bit of green earth, cadmium yellow banners, the wood slightly smoked, well suited to the *pajizo* tint of the torpedo, which had first to be extracted from its sugar-white tissue paper, then from the bulging silver foil. At this temperature, Amorose's hair dye begins to run down his temples and chin, by the pond, on the back lot over the shadowy ravine, he filled the cocktail shaker and chilled the Martini Dry; he looked at the palace, then at the guest, it's a Huifkar today, I reported, and just then came the rattling of chains announcing the Emeritus had stepped onto the stair lift platform in his pulpit by the main door, and would soon be appearing like a *deus ex machina* over the glass awning shielding the peach espaliers, white linen suit, straw hat on his head, big paws resting on his cane, floating down from his lectern to the plane of conversation, which he loves and practices as a fine art. *Vat hef ye brought us teday, aha, intrishting, shuppose I'll tek te dis one?*

His comment persuaded me to draw his attention to the conical tip of this nearly ovoid specimen, that was the foot, I explained; he delighted in the charming packaging and quoted Fontane's Gundermann: "Ah, capital, a few pulls of that will do you better than soda water," it also merits mention in the memoranda of our talks that at the moment in *The Stechlin* just cited, the author omits mention of a house brand, though elsewhere he archives every last stone in Brandenburg; a Schlottmann would have certainly been fitting, but no, unlike the liquor, where Danziger Goldwasser is specified, Woldemar speaks only of "the little case." Jérôme had, he recalled, brought up this very issue once to a scion of the Burger-Rössli dynasty during elective exams at the ETH, and the young man replied readily, completely at ease, that it was not yet becoming for young Stechlin to go boasting of the treasures of the house – of his Havana imports, among other things; and returning to the professor's specialty of history, he told the story of Bismarck, who offered the last of his Punches to a wounded soldier on the Königgratz with a grave need for succor, and remarked afterward that no cigar had ever tasted so good to him as one he hadn't smoked himself, could one not extend that to *The Stechlin* and say: never has a corona so occupied our imagination as one that goes unnamed? Now, then, or as he liked to punctuate his remarks: *item*. Amorose sidestepped the yard sprinkler and poured the urine-yellow beverage from the silver shaker, placed a pierced olive into the goblets, *on de rrocks* he remarked with French severity, then he prepared a cool footbath for the lord of the manor, who placed his pale flippers in the tub with a quick word about this splendid summer, which had been prophesied correctly in the hundred-year calendar, fiery days, muggy moonlit nights, storms, sudden shifts of weather, hour-long games of ninepins under cloudy skies, *enyhow meks ye think more of Eichendorff den of Stechlin,* all that's missing is a marble Venus moved by Bacchanalian magic to open her eyes beneath the spell, *Klingsor's Last Summer* comes to mind as well, *yesssh* he had known Hesse well, he said, had been often to Montagnola to visit, Hesse had shown him Casa Camuzzi with the balcony over the Siebold's magnolia: *We children of July do prize / Pale jasmine's sweet perfume / And wander hushed through garden's blooms / As potent dreams draw closed our eyes. // Our brother is the poppy red / That burns on flickering plains, / On blazing walls, on fields of grain, / Its windblown petals rend and spread. // Like a July night our life will stand / To dance before the song has ceased / In thrall to dreams and harvest feasts / With wreaths and poppies in its hand.*

True, the last stanza falls short, he commits one of the four deadly sins of lyric poetry, coming out and saying *like, like* a July night, so are our lives, there's nothing new there apart from the harvest feast, and here you have greetings from the Grim Reaper, in the story he's there grinning between the branches in August, *yessssh, bacchanalia,* Hermann Hesse was fond of tying one on in the *grotti,* the taverns with their earthenware mugs of blue wine, in that same summer of 1919, when he was composing *Klingsor* at Casa Camuzzi, that branching, plump palazzo on the sunny side of the Collina d'Oro, Rilke was in the library at Soglio writing *The Primal Sound.* Yes, I've read that, dear Professor, I readily confess I didn't understand a word.

As Jérôme von Castelmur-Bondo regaled me with feudal relations in the Sottoporta and Sopraporta of Val Bregaglia, my memories took me back twenty-six years to that visit to Soglio in 1962, when I painted the watercolor *Church in Stormy Weather.* I had come straight from Thun to my family, I'd had to leave the officer's school for tank corporals after six days on account of a psychosomatic gastritis – that was, in all likelihood, the greatest act of liberation of my existence, and I will never forget it. It was a Saturday in July that the Azores High sun had transformed into a hellish furnace, I deposited all I had to leave behind in the arsenal of the main barracks in Thun, traveled in my fatigues with the quince yellow collar tabs for light and mechanized infantry with sack and pack and assault rifle through Bern and Aarau to Menzen-mang, where I hastily stuffed a suitcase with summer clothes and a few books, taking along the Olivetti Lettera my father had given me as a graduation gift. I was in Zurich at 3:15 PM, transferred to the Rhaetia Express, and gorged on Valais cheese toast in the dining car. Around 4:30 I passed through the curves of the Albula Tunnel, crawled into the maize-yellow post bus in St. Moritz headed for Majola-Chiavenna, an hour later my father picked me up in Promontogno, my mother made a nasty scene in the restaurant at Hotel Willy, overseen by *Patron* Torri-ani, it just made no sense for me to quit officers' school on account of some supposed gastritis – the very illness my father had suffered from for years – and then come there that night hoping to dine on risotto and chestnut pizzoccheri, either the thing about the illness was true, and I would have to go on a diet, and should restrict myself, *like Mandi does,* to a plate of gruel; or else my stomach complaint was made up, and I would have to return to officers' school in Thun that coming January; moreover, the family had been looking forward to this holiday without my presence and had rented two double rooms at Palazzo Castelmur, and with it being the high season, who knew whether Herr Torriani could find me additional accommodations. Alas, this was but the begin-ning of the *via crucis* that would lead me away from this Cold Sophie's clutches, and so I acquiesced and ate my gruel and scurried upstairs to the French Garden where I stood on the lawn *behrfoot* and felt it rising up in my through my toes: freedom, you are free, the barracks are behind you now with their iron commandments CCC: Command, Control, Correct, and lying before you are the three Cs of art, which is so long, while life is so short: Comprehend, Commence, Contrive, I still wasn't sure, on the eve of my twentieth birthday, whether to study architecture or art history, but the summer in Bregaglia was chestnut green and the semester didn't start till the end of October, Kari was fourteen years old, Klärli thirteen, who cared if I was disrupting the family's idyll, they gave me a room on the fourth floor of the Cas'Alta, the outbuilding, the *dépendence* as it was called, curious that term, I painted and read for four weeks uninterrupted, and by chance I came across that trace of Rilke...

Monsieur, has monsieur fallen asleep? Amorose was bending over me with a cool washcloth, a few ice cubes bundled inside, no, no, Jérôme then intoned like a drumbeat, he too thought it necessary to awaken his dozing companion, the Cas'Alta was built in 1524, and it became the main monument to the late Middle Ages in the village once the Castelmurs' oldest residences in the center were destroyed. Casa Gubert, which dates from the mid-sixteenth century, is likewise a simple, almost primitive structure, Dietgen von Castelmur was Bailiff of Castel and a captain in the service of the emperor, his descendants embellished the living spaces with coffered ceilings and sculpted stoves, Leu, in his Swiss Lexicon of 1762, had already described the Soglio we observe today: "Leading up from there was a steeper road, furnished with several hundred stone slabs or steps as though in a staircase, accessible to pack animals as well: and yet the three imposing palaces that lie unremarked along this route, with their rare and precious pleasure gardens, are among the possessions of the Castelmur clan." Casa Max or Casa di Mezzo, the middle of the three houses, was the first one built, in 1696, a thoroughly Renaissance structure, but one that betrays a longing for the Baroque with its flared balconies and the portal at the central axis; the stallazzo, distinguished by its extraordinary grimacing faces with tethering rings in their mouths, joins it to Casa Battista with its open courtyard, erected in 1701 over an older core across from Casa Max; Casa Antonio was not completed till around the middle of the eighteenth century – my dear Professor, you've let your Huifkar go out – Rilke spent the summer of 1919 there, yes, I thought of its endless frontage, how I felt my way along it in search of my parents, especially Edwin's Pretty Mama, once I'd slipped Matrone Giovanoli's clutches. Today I can grasp its advent in light of the principle of ordered planes, first the viewer must content himself with the side you wish to show him – here, with the prospect of the village – then the façade is pierced with as many windows as possible, to look out onto the mortal rigidity of the Bondasca and the Scoria Group, the square between the rear of the building and the mountains was used for one of those gardens inaccessible from without, so beloved of the eighteenth century – another cigar, Herr Professor? *Mehny tenks, but I'm te limit my tobacco consumption, tree pipes eh day, det does me.* Yes, and so, what about Rilke and Soglio? Well, the Emeritus continued, letting Amorose change the water in the footbath, after the war and a creative crisis, Rilke was taken with this refuge in Bregaglia, his feeling of deliverance is clear to us from his letters, he wrote to Aline Dietrichstein on August 6, 1919, here, *I've brought de book along wit me:* "A map of Switzerland will show you perhaps the situation of Bregaglia, the haste of this valley to reach Italy; over the valley, halfway up the mountain, lies this little nest covered in sheets of gneiss, a (Protestant, unfortunately, and therefore empty) church on the slope, extremely narrow streets; one lives in the middle of it, in an old estate of Castelmur (of the Bondo line), amid old furnishings, and moreover the palace has a French terraced garden with old stone borders, traditionally trimmed box trees, and in between a throng of the brightest summer flowers. Another time, however, I must tell you of the chestnut groves, which descend down the slopes toward Italy with magnificent beauty." Then, in a letter to Countess M. on August 13, 1919, the description of the library, an old-fashioned room, still, facing the garden, the Castelmur coat of arms over the chimney, a Louis XIV fauteuil, a spinet, a square table from the seventeenth century, an iron coffer with an immense many-bitted key, cabinets full of books, memoiristic literature from the eighteenth century in attractive leather bindings, Albrecht von Haller, whom he reads during the day, and Gaudenz von Salis-Seewis in the 1800 edition, for which Rilke reserves his evening hours. "Now you understand, dear Countess, that I am doomed. How could I resist this room, where I still make discoveries every day – and then the garden calls to me, and I recollect the chestnut woods: there is no getting by and no finishing, this Venusberg encircling me, where an overgrown rosebush is the Venus and books gleam like the alluring rocks in the mountain, has me in its power, I don't care to plan beyond it, let alone think of winter, for which I can imagine neither place nor mode of life. Munich doesn't appeal to me in the least, but where? Where?"

Notice, *mon cher*, how the erotic dimension permeates that unusual prose piece Rilke called "The Primal Sound." The text begins with an experience from his school days, the boys in physics class had to build a phonograph from rudimentary materials, they fashioned a cone from a sheet of cardboard and sealed the hole in the end with a membrane of the kind you could easily get from a preserving jar, they perforated it with a bristle from a stiff clothing brush, then a thin layer of candlewax was poured over a roller, if the experimenter now spoke or sang into the makeshift horn, the needle sticking in the parchment transferred the sound waves to the cylinder, and when the needle was made to retrace its path in the varnish, the person's voice, distorted, warbled through the paper chamber. In his Paris days, Rilke was a zealous attendee of the anatomy lectures at the École des Beaux-Arts, and became so fascinated with the human skull that he purchased one of his own, and one night, by candlelight, he noticed with astonishment the similarity between the cranial sutures and the crowded, sinuous lines of the wax phonograph roll from his school days, and he asked himself what would happen if the needle were to run over a track that was not the graphic translation of a sound – for instance, along the coronal suture of the human skull. He was so taken with the idea that he could think of no better term for the notes that might be produced in this way than "the primal sound," and he suggested the artist was one who developed ever finer spiritual capacities in the five-fingered hand of his perceptions, in contrast to the telescope or the microscope, the technical discoveries of which lay on a different plane, for the cells between lamina of glass or the whorls of the thumbskin no more penetrated the senses, and hence could no more be experienced, than the magnified moon; while the artist, with quite simple means, works to broaden the optical, olfactory, tactile, auditory, and gustatory; but as his proofs were impossible without a "miracle," his extension of the territory could not be recorded in the atlas laid open before us, whereas the experimenter's needle, by means of the primal sound of the cranial suture, conveyed everything all at once, articulated it, so to speak, in a paleolinguistic medium. A tone, notes, music would necessarily arise, Rilke says, yet feelings of skepticism, timidity, awe kept him from proposing a name for it, at a time when he began to interest himself in Arabic poems, which seem to owe their existence to the simultaneous and equal contributions from all five senses, it struck him that for the modern European poet, only one of them – sight, overladen with the world – seemed inevitably to predominate; how slight, by contrast, is the contribution he receives from inattentive hearing; and a lady had exclaimed to him that this harmonization of the optical, auditory, olfactory, and so on was nothing more than the mental presence of love. But even then, the lover is in such splendid danger because he depends on the coordination of his senses, knowing nothing of them but that they meet in that hazardous center where, renouncing all extension, they intersect, and where there is no continued existence. If one represents the entire field of experience in a complete circle, it is immediately evident how much greater are the black sectors which cover over the incommensurable in comparison with the lighter segments that correspond to the spotlights of sensuality. Now the position of the lover is this, that he feels himself placed all at once in the center of the meridian, where the familiar and the ungraspable converge on a single point, become a possession through the abrogation of all individuality. The poet, so Rilke in "The Primal Sound," is ill-served by this position, for detail must be constantly present, he is constrained to employ the snippets of the sensory according to their extension, and he must also wish to extend each individual one as much as possible, so that, to quote him directly, "his girded delight may leap through the five gardens in a single breath."

I had long since exhausted my Huifkar and had moved on to a *maduro*-brown Partagás culebra, the noblest rendition in tobacco of the shape known in Switzerland as a crooked dog, and I looked up at the taut scalp of Jérôme von Castelmur-Bondo, now dotted with bits of leaf, straining to make out the thin trace of the cranial seam, which Rilke had hoped to take as the subject for his experiments, what the *profässer* had said struck me as characteristic of the primal sound in the sense that, despite the heat, despite the occasional white noise that broke through in the midst of his monologues, the pen, the needle at the earthquake station, attention, seismologically attuned, followed a path that left a flash of inspiration in the wax of our minds, how was it that storm clouds produced electric charges, no matter, the tension between two parts of the clouds or between the gathering cumuli and the earth grew too great, the lightning clove its way by propagating a conductive channel a few centimeters in diameter in a discontinuous process called "stepping," when these partial discharges came close to the ground, then a low resistance path opened up between it and an upward leader. Men of old had interpreted the subsequent primal sound, thunder, as the language of the gods. Turning this over in my mind, I watched how the graceful servant Jean-Jacques Amorose prepared a tartare for the lord of the castle, mincing the steak with a butcher's knife. Well done, the beef must be trimmed by hand, not run through a grinder, and he laid the red frays over ice. Then he stirred together a bit of olive oil and ketchup – *Not se much temeto puree, Jean,* the Emeritus shouted as he did so – mustard and egg yolk, Tabasco, garlic powder, Worcestershire sauce, and a bit of cognac – *No, no, de cognac at de end, Jean* – mixed parsley, chives, capers, chopped onion, and sardine fillets inside, then seasoned with pepper and paprika – *Easy der, Jean* – to finish off.

Every good story, Jérôme von Castelmur-Bondo said, can fit on a thumbnail or the cuff of a shirt, where bad students – to whose ranks, alas, I never belonged – write out their crib sheets before their exams, Rilke's "Primal Sound" is naturally a *mise-en-âbime,* as they say in French, of Herder's famous *Treatise on the Origin of Language,* to put it briefly, the bee buzzes as it feeds on nectar, the bird sings as it nests. What, though, is the natural way for man to speak? There is none, nor can he act from nature like the animal. He is the first free being in creation, therefore he must communicate digitally. The lyricist, take Rilke, uses analogue language, preferring the archaic image, the symbol, to the discursive sign, whose relation between *signifiant* and *signifié* is *arbitraire* and therefore highly dubious. "Symbol" comes from the

Greek *sumballein,* to throw together, also to hold jointly, here to unite the particular and the general. A symbol in this sense is the skull in Rilke's text, he means a part of the human skeleton but also death, or life. The crown is a pointed gold hoop worn on the head as a sign of dignity and power, the *sutura coronalis* or crown suture is a forensic concept transferring the jagged lines of the royal ornament to the surface of the skull itself. If, like Rilke, one places a phonograph needle inside, the membrane of the cone will produce a kind of sound, *Schall* is the term Herder uses, that is more primordial than the articulated word, is also more legitimate, for it corresponds to the mew of the cat, the bark of the dog, the chirp of the sparrow, the coo of the dove. And so, in the course of a primitive experiment in physics, Rilke, long before the therapists, tapped into the primal scream, the primal sound of the human species, the poet, like the phonograph, is only an amplifier and translator, for the most beautiful, the purest poetry – *now de cognac, Jean* – is a perfect variation on themes the world itself has dictated. There remains the relationship to love; here Rilke employs another symbol, the circle, but in its geometric purity it enters the purview of physics. Here, with all due respect, we may correct the author of the *Duino Elegies.* Grace or mental presence, to use his terms, are not identical with the midpoint of a circle, but with the geometrical position of every point X that maintains the same distance from the center Z. Love, Frisch says, does not mean fixing the other in an image, but following her through all her transformations. Thus X can persist interminably without ever broadening the radius R that emanates from Z. That is grace, that is what the guest in the Palazzo Castelmur library in Soglio with its airs of Venusberg had wished to say.

By now Amorose had scooped the tartare from the bowl onto the plate, where he scored the meat diagonally with a fork and garnished it with slivers of ice, black olives, and a bit of capers. Whoever drives from St. Moritz to Silvaplana will see *in natura* Lake Silvaplana, famously painted by Ferdinand Hodler. Those coming from Milan to the Italian-Swiss border will have another historic painting, Segantini's *Becoming*, before their eyes. In between these lies Bregaglia. Amorose worked for some time as a waiter at the restaurant Couronne-Les Halles in Zurich, that was where he learned to perfectly serve this tartare that made the professor mad with hunger. Upper Bregaglia is known as Sopraporta, the lower valley as Sottoporta, the border is at Promontogno, where the road passes the Porta, a narrow ravine. Amorose had crisped the bread slightly on a charcoal grill. The excavations carried out on the rock sill from 1923 to 1927 gave incontestable proof of the Roman station of Murus on the Antonine Itinerary, the foundations of a large stone building were discovered, fragments of a canal and a bath consisting of frigidarium and caldarium with hypocaust and heating ducts. Amorose had glazed the toast points with garlic butter according to the custom of the house and slipped them inside a napkin pocket. In October of 1939, seven years before our stay in Soglio, a soapstone domestic altar was found at the eastern foot of the second defensive wall west of the Porta, its inscription: *Mercurio / Cissonio / Pro Bon(o) Cami(lli),* the god Mercurius Cissonius would have been the patron of the carters, as his name recalls the Gallic *cisium,* a two-wheeled cart. Jérôme von Castelmur-Bondo wolfed down the tartare, offering not a single forkful, not a taste, to Hermann Arbogast Brenner, who was allowed to smoke away at his leisure, this is not to say that he didn't invite me now and again to dine, but sparingly. The district of Bondo, which appears relatively late in the documents, encompasses the entire left bank of Sottoporta, the name is unrelated to *ponte* or bridge, the root is the Gallic *bunda,* which means soil. Pouring correctly, with the left hand behind his back, Amorose served the lord of the castle a Château Lynch-Bages *grand cru classé* to accompany his tartare. Bondo was part of the parish of Nossa Donna of Porta, reformed under the influence of Vergario in the year 1552, in the first documentary mention of it we read: "bergalliam vallem cum castello et decimali ecclesia," intended here is the Castelmur stronghold, the ancestral home of the history professor's clan. From time to time, Jérôme seasoned the tartare with black pepper and spit the olive stones into the ravine. After the breakup of the greater parish in the course of the sixteenth century, the church fell into disuse, by the beginning of the nineteenth century it was nothing but a crumbling ruin, Baron Giovanni von Castelmur acquired it in 1839. The blue Havana veil, tremulous in the heat-refracted air, was now evaporating; even as he ate, the lord of the castle rested his feet in the tub of water. The house of God rose up on the southern rock shelf of the Porta, consisting of a rectangular nave and a semicircular apse, nowadays, the steps led to the new crypt, on the north side a campanile rose up, thin, in the Italianate fashion, of undressed stone with solid stone blocks at the corners, the twin barrel windows of the three upper floors are set in shuttered niches capped with a motif of three blind arches, the tented stone roof dates to 1100, the imposts and engaged columns with shaft rings are of soapstone.

10.

STUDIES IN SOGLIO,
BRENNER BRANIFF,
WILD CIGARILLO

In August 1982, after Father's death-catastrophe, after I had checked myself into the hospital pavilion at Grand Ort Park, I walked, over and over, the two opposing paths, one through the mountain meadow west to the ravine, where dozens of deadly looking, shimmering green lizards crisscrossed the trail, and the other along the Granadasträsschen to the bench on the grass promontory high above Bondo, where I saw, looking like a little toy in the French garden of Palazzo Castelmur, a cadmium yellow parasol that spoke of the merriment of midsummer siestas. I thought, gauging the distance of the drop, once again of the sense of proportion in childhood, and realized the walk down to the much-praised flagstone path of La Plota would last little more than an hour, that my view of it, right when the postal bus blew its 6-4 in F sharp major, would endure just minutes, and yet, for the plot's sake, I would have to get through La Plota, and with a plotter, that device for the automatic graphical representation of diagrams. To take full advantage of my bird's eye view, I must first know that this palazzo was built from 1765 to 1774 by Pietro Mastoco and Martino Martinojo in collaboration with the plasterer Domenico Spinelli from Como for Count Hieronymus von Castelmur-Bondo, the English Ambassador to the Three Leagues, husband of Mary Fane, descendant of the Earl of Westmoreland. The edifice, extremely austere on the outside, owes its dynamism to its interior architecture, the order of the rooms proceeds from the garden hall in the center and is staggered, terminating on either side in small corner chambers. In contrast to the style of the South German Baroque, the staircase is given a separate chamber and has no fluid connection to the corridors, which are striking in their sparseness. The interior décor, like the building style as a whole, stands at the threshold of Louis XVI, neoclassical themes mingle with rococo motifs in the liberally applied stucco, especially in the upper salon with its fluted ionic pilasters and thin foliations and festoons. The plasterwork in the vaulted bedchamber on the ground floor exhibits a pronounced *italianità,* while the unpainted paneling of stone pine in the dining room marks a concession to the domestic style of the natives, a corner room, following the fashions of the time, boasts Japanese ornamentation.

Lesenes divide the two halves of the façade into sections with three axes each; forbidding granite frames the two portals with curved pediments and cartouches bearing coats of arms, a perron leads down twelve exposed steps from the western entrance to the garden arranged in a breezy imitation of La Nôtre; it was there, at that moment, that the cadmium yellow parasol stood open, and I dipped my brush in a cake from my traveling paintbox to daub it out in sepia. Worth mentioning, Jérôme von Castelmur-Bondo said in the dining room of Brunsleben, which some sources incorrectly call Salenegg, are the masonry oven with its architectural elements and the little landscapes painted on tile, and in the bedroom of the first of the upper floors the round stucco stove with the brightly colored three-dimensional eagles; among the family portraits is one of Rodolfo von Castelmur-Bondo from around 1660, and another attributed to Van Dyck of Lady Rachel Fane, Countess of Bath, deceased 1680, it is a life-size likeness of her in a champagne-colored dress and green shawl – was it Veronese, Russian, chromium oxide, Hooker's, cinnabar, or Helio Genuine green, when it came down to it, the historian couldn't say, even if he were sworn with Aristotle to relate what happened and how, while we, the independent scribblers, depict what might have happened, and how. Did we visit the ruins of Castelmur on our wanderings through Soglio, Castasegna, and Bondo in the summer of forty-six? Neither my memory nor the family album attests to that marked interest in history on the part of my mother, from whom Hermann Arbogast inherited, along with a number of personality traits, the sense that the manifold past permits us to grasp the contingency of "today." The first documentary mention of the fortifications in the Carolingian urbarium of 831 reads: "Providet Castellum ad Bergalliam." In 960, along with the valley between Segantini's *Becoming* and Hodler's painting of the Silvaplana Lake, the fortifications were deeded to the Bishop of Chur, and they are expressly named in the confirmation of Otto III on 20 October 988: "insuper bergalliam cum castello." Anno Domini 1120 we find the fortress in the hands of the burghers of Chiavenna, a papal rescript demanded its restitution. For four years during the feud between Bregaglia and Chiavenna from 1264 to 1272, Porta was occupied once more, the eastern walls were reinforced and the gate system built up, the tower was raised around 1300.

The ministerial family from Chur, which appears with the name Castelmur for the first time in 1186 – later they will receive the more specific designation Castelmuro de Porta – was evidently long enfeoffed with the castle. In 1341 the bishop mortgages it to the Plantas, and later it will pass back to the Castelmurs, the Salis clan, and others. The complex dominates a rock ledge running north to south, up from the Mera in three stages over Promontogno. Above the plateau of the lowermost terrace, where the Roman station of Murus once stood, runs the medieval road, still preserved, here barred by fortifications. The eastern side is the best preserved, the walls are 3.7 meters thick, a recessed battlement sits over three arches on the northern section, and in one of these niches, we find an oblique embrasure overlooking the road. The lower part of the opening to the gate still exists, there are deep gaps in the jambs, but the breadth and the angles don't match up, most likely they held not a portcullis, but irregular wooden crossbars. The north wall, being inaccessible to invaders, measures only 1.4 meters. On the crest of the second rock ridge runs another defensive wall, a transverse descends from it into the hollow to the south, intersecting with the Roman road. The tower ascends from the third of the ridges, a stark, square donjon, without quoins, five stories of undressed stone. The elevated entrance faces east on the second floor. Looking higher, you see flues, on the fifth floor two arched windows facing east and south, the one serving the aesthetic purpose of contemplating the landscape, the other the military function of lookout – a succinct demonstration, if you will, of the reason why the elective courses I attended in literature, history, and philosophy before breaking off my four semesters of study for an architecture degree at the Swiss Federal Institute of Technology had to be shared with the Department of Military Sciences. The church of Nossa Donna in the depression to the south of the castle keep, which was covered with a hipped roof; over the slope of the Mungac, the Torraccia observation post, the ten square meters of its foundation unfortunately covered with rubble. All this was the material I gathered in a sketch in pen-and-ink in August of 1982. The method of the captioned sketch, as opposed to the snapshot taken with the camera, I owe to my first-semester drawing lessons with Professor Hans Ess, it allows us a horizontal projection with four planes, same as the ones I executed as a child absorbed in simultaneous perspective; in contrast to the photograph, it puts not everything to paper, but only what corresponds to the inner architecture of our intentions, we may magnify details, scale becomes flexible, and, let me add, the drawing takes us an hour, whereas controlling for lighting, fiddling with the bells and whistles, pressing click takes no more than a few minutes. In this hour's work we see more, and more precisely, than during that post-mortem pasting of our memories into an album; we are not like tourists reminiscing about having been "there," even if, admittedly, these tobacco leaves attempt to share with the reader how, for the span of a brief, heady happiness, we were allowed to be citizens of the earth.

When the experts in the tropical growing regions wish to test a tobacco for its aroma and mildness, they roll themselves a crude cigarillo. The Brenner Braniff Original is prepared the same way: tobacco rolled around tobacco, nothing more. It looks like one of those muskets that brought the Mayan priests into contact with the gods. The sepia legend over the gentleman in the medallion, who looks a bit like Nietzsche, dominates the mocha brown tin, light ochre prevails throughout. May it be known to all dry drunks, if only for the sake of thoroughness, that Hermann Arbogast Brenner, in the summer of 1962 in Soglio, immediately upon escaping his military serfdom, not only painted watercolors, but also drafted sketches in words, which he called, quite simply, Soglio Prose, trimming them and preserving them in a black binder following the tradition of his father's documentary collages. The question arises in Ludwig Reiner's *Guidelines for Novelists: An Introduction to the Novel Technique* (Göttingen, 1952) as to whether such materials may be in the public's interest at all. But surely, it strikes me, the consumers of my bales and gavillas will wish to know something of what Hermann Arbogast Brenner might have done had he gone in for a career in letters. Here we read: The village is dry and thirsting. The mountain dwellers flee the light. The sun has sunk behind the arid slopes, has sucked the last sap from the withered pastures, has bleached the colors from the flowers. In the distance hovers a haze: blue, water, cool. Even the graves are parched. Why do I suddenly speak of graves? A wet grave is the coolest thing I can imagine. Cool, I mean, not cold. The heat weighs like lead on the roofs, it wafts up, mixed with the scent of wood, from the open door of a ramshackle stable. The church tower seems to tremble in the glare, barely distinguishable from the rest of the torrid chorus. The sun is too close to the earth, yet unseen, as if it were fleeing its own fire. So runs one of these *études*, and every reader will concur with my diagnosis: thank god the poor bastard put writing aside. Utterly different in character is a dream note of July 28, 1962: I was painting a picture, a primitively rendered city, the houses were like toy blocks with tiny square windows. In the foreground was water, covered with crescent-shaped ice floes, to the left a sturdy tree trunk, on the upper edge green leaves, and past the tree trunk, snowfall. At the same time, it is summer all around. A diagonal splits the sky in two, the upper wedge is stormy green, the lower ice blue – summer and winter – and each of the two colors belongs as much to one season as to the other. On the right-hand side was a modern shop, I had taken especial care with the details in the door, glass from top to bottom, with a slender frame of red iron, and in front of the door, an ellipse, set at an angle from the iron frame, shimmering whitish-pink, divulged but not properly described. This doorway to Hell was the birthplace of Pablo, the sax-playing tempter, and the picture is entitled *Pablo, or Early Summer Snow.*

This offers two points for the consideration of my one-time psychotherapist Jana Jesenska Kiehl: first, I must have been reading Broch's novel *The Tempter* and Hesse's *Steppenwolf* at the time, otherwise Pablo would not have appeared to me in such a guise; second, the summer snow she will see as evidence of my mental illness. I still remember quite clearly the morning after the dream, in the interim I had moved my things from Cas'Alta to a small corner room in Palazzo Castelmur, where I could look down from the window onto the narrow lane from the kitchen wing to the French garden and voyeuristically observe the serving girls from my crow's nest. They couldn't tell they were being watched. This invisibility-cloak-situation I found extrarodinarly arousing. Before breakfast, I typed out this dream on my red Olivetti Lettura and made a few notes with my fountain pen in the margins: Why an ellipse in this city? Was it the birth of Lucifer, that angel whose beauty God couldn't bear the sight of? And the snow? Death – dying and being born. Memories of the sickly November snow in Aarau. How I had smelled the scent of death on those endless afternoons. A neighborhood street, buildings to the left and right, in the distance the stern stares of the manors, high firs, a thin sheet of dust on the asphalt, a broad track running through it – such is my image of the access road to the kingdom of the dead. That all was not well with us in Soglio at the time can be deduced from a letter to my second cousin and friend Johann Caspar Brenner, who was finishing up officer's school at the time. For my twentieth birthday, he had given me Hermann Broch's *Death of Virgil,* I made diagrams of its interminable sentences. My friend, who was one year older, and who answered to the name *Cigarillo*, I thanked in the following words:

I am here in Soglio for the holidays, you must know, and so your present has only just reached me. Painting and writing, atimes – I was rather proud of this coinage – reading as well, I am trying to come to terms with nature, and this, more than ever, is driving me away from chromatic representation, driving me toward – I know not where.

Because, if truth in painting exists, it lies beyond all philosophy of color – my father used to say that, *vat ye need is eh philosophy* – beyond all conscious originality, but also outside the unconscious – far too often we are tempted to situate everything we fail to define in the unconscious – lies just beneath the fingertips – but not mine. And yet, since people are pleased to see me as a painter, since they deem this a fit role for me, like it or not I must fulfill their expectations. But the painter's world lies behind me like a romantic Arcadia. With greater or lesser aptitude, I will trace out postcard pictures from a long-lost youth. For my part, I am happy to have stumbled, like you, onto the writer's path. Stumbled, I say, for there is no promise I won't be led astray. Lured off by the myriad, by the longing to see the myriad, by the false paths of fidelity or infidelity to nature, and not least of all, by fear before this dreadful false path – fear, to be plain, of a misspent life – which keeps one from writing over and again. And the brief instants of creation are like opening one's eyes after a thousand-year paralysis. A paralysis that makes itself felt in the brain, the sensation one sometimes has in dreams: you just must run away, but your legs fail you. The sensation of unspeakable impotence, not only in art, but in life, impotence even before the pretty serving girls who walk past my window into the garden, then back into the kitchen, sending fleeting, inquisitive, tender, eager looks – perhaps this is only vain illusion – eyes full of expectation, will he do something, the intellectual, will he woo her, O most burning, O only question of the female sex, foretold in the strolls of the village brats, question of eyes, question of hips, question of rouged lips, and he does nothing more than search repeatedly for her gaze, for him, the question is too vaguely posed, too easy to mistake. He sees more and more through their transparent courtesy, their smile, at first misty with the hope of love, the courteous love-smile of the first evening, source of O so much joy, devolves into a mere smile for the solicitation of a tip, infinite rejection, the rejection of a bore. Aware of his dreariness, aware of his impotence, he recognizes in his intimations the concrete form of his wish: to banish impotence forever, to subdue time – through death. I hope, dear Cigarillo, you have made it through the loneliness of your first days in the service. In sooth we have no need of it, this voracious, sterile solitude. I will try to be constant, and send you the odd jotting whenever possible, even if you may not always find time for an answer. Kindest regards, Your Hermann. P.S. The description of Lake Hallwil was truly vivid, and will live on in my memory, for a bit of manuscript that means a great deal.

This letter of August 3, 1962, which I would not have dared to try the indulgent reader's nerves with had I not offered him a selection from my store of cigars stockpiled in the castle cellar – a Brenner Brasil, for example, which at the time of my epistle was still marketed in the ecru etui with the family's coat of arms, a lone flame behind a trellis over the trimount of Eichbühl – illustrates, in many ways, my struggle for a future vocation, as well as my difficulties with women. I should have been able to speak of these at least with my father, who was fifty-two years old then and a militant adherent of Moral Re-Armament, an ideology born in America that had established its headquarters in a lavish palace-hotel in Caux-sur-Montreux overlooking Lake Geneva, with its four overarching principles of Absolute Love, Absolute Purity, Absolute Honesty, and Absolute Unselfishness. Every morning before getting up, in lieu of a cold shower, my parents talked over what the dear Lord God had shared with them in the *schtiui zyt*, the quiet time, to wit: Yesterday I had impure thoughts about Aunt Sibylle. Here I must turn back to the family album of 1946-1948, which documents Caux on pages seventeen and eighteen, again in the form of a *collasch*. The composition included a pale blue sheet of lined notepaper from my father's *shtiui zyt* booklet, dated August 1947, the period when I was interned in the children's home in Amden. In his looping, sensuous script, with generous flourishes for the capitals, in words that can only be deciphered with the aid of an Eschenbach handheld magnifier, it is written: Where do things stand with us in Switzerland today? In our land, we have privilege. It is a fact that – underlined – the – illegible – relationships better than in any other country in Europe. Most Swiss are aware of this privilege. But only a very few ever consider that privilege must be accompanied by duty. They forget that the fate of our country depends on the wellbeing of Europe. A statesmanlike thought for the year 1947, when we recall that even today Switzerland is a member neither of the European Community nor the United Nations, but instead, belonging to the neutral countries, only participates in them as an observer. Father's legend on the outspread Moral Rearmament castle on the postcard from Caux reads: Already, countless friends from all over the world have sacrificed their homes, their jobs, their time, and their savings to contribute to building a new world. Is it not natural, then, that we too give up our holidays to attend this once-yearly conference to try and do our part – underlined – to help? The newspaper excerpt pasted in below, *The World of Caux: Impressions From the Conference for Moral Re-Armament,* reports under the initials MG: Caux-sur-Montreux, known at the turn of the century, if at all, for its two large and luxurious hotel-palaces, has in recent years become an international meeting point of a totally different kind. Its grandiose hotels are today the seat of a spiritual – italics – world center, a small state within a state which, if the wishes and hopes of its inhabitants are fulfilled, may become a world power. That its connections already span the globe, from East to West and North Pole to South, is evident in many ways: in the course of this summer, 10,000 people have visited Caux, coming from all continents and from approximately seventy countries.

Here the same scissors with which the nurse at the children's home threatened to snip off my *tea spout* bring this report to a partial end, of the second column, nothing can be made out except: More than thirty union leaders, presidents, and secretaries assembled, all of them ready to speak of their experiences with Moral... Germans, Eng... French, Swi... in public and in... because the... hear best with their own ears... A president, who A... from Miami... strike the last... harsh. Finally... In the upper corner of the article loomed a group portrait with the founder, Frank Buchman, in a semicircle of people yellow, red, black, and white. An article in English: Millions in Europe are hungry for a constructive answer to totalitarianism. National leaders from all over the world will be meeting during the next two months at a

World Assembly for Moral Re-Armament at Caux-sur-Montreux, Switzerland. At this training center last year, 5,000 representatives from fifty-three countries planned for ideological preparedness for their nations. The address by Mr. A. R. K. Mackenzie, printed on this page, was given before delegates from twenty-four countries at the Moral Re-Armament Assembly at Riverside, California. It outlines the steps statesmen can take to bring a Renaissance to their countries. Then a half-page photo: A thousand delegates at Caux celebrate Swiss National Day with the traditional *fire of freedom*. No, I could not confide in my father during quiet time that I'd had filthy thoughts about the serving girls in the white blouses.

Johann Caspar Brenner, alias Cigarillo, wrote me back from Pfeffikon on August 5, 1962, at the address Hermann Brenner, Jr. Hotel Wittig, Soglio, Bergell (GR): My dear painter, August is come, verily, August: yellow-grey clouds blow across a deep blue sky, there is something pronouncedly melancholic about it, this blowing, the buzzing of flies, the birds chirping softer, more meager than in spring, but more intense, more anxious, ruttish, all the sounds are strangely muffled, even the smells, even life itself. One should wander through the country now, from morning to night, one should lie now beneath the trees, one should – . One should do so many things. O eternal damned longing for the feminine! I thank you for that intense letter of yours, that august letter of 8.3, which reminded me that August was here, my military service had made me overlook it. Make good use of it in Soglio, this August, even if its harvest is melancholy above all else. Melancholy is one of the noblest feelings we possess. And the loneliest! I could tell you all about my current assignment, which in a certain way is quite different from the others. It promises to be extremely rigorous, but at the same time interesting, however much this interest may be a danger for the introverted soul. I must note in passing that our superiors are highly intelligent on the whole: they welcome discussion, take part in it ably, they manage to demand the utmost from each and every one of us, but with reason rather than coercion. My comrades – they're nice, they're bright as well, they have everything a person could ask for, but in my heart, I have not yet found my place among them. An example: we are talking over our faithless, outward-oriented way of life. The captain guides the discussion. Many thoughts that are intriguing, many true. All wish to see a remedy to their grievances, a renewal of the church, a return to the contemplation of the soul, humility before God and not before oneself, modesty, etc. It all seems so utterly simple, we are of one mind, we chatter on ardently. Then I speak up: and I mention the arbitrary, misguided religiosity of our century, the cultish devotion to boxing, pop music, and so forth. Displeased interjections, the conversation turns cool, everyone's embarrassed, as if I'd said something thoroughly inappropriate. Is this because certain depths are inaccessible to some? Did they feel themselves somehow targeted? Am I no longer allowed to state something reasonable? Here is where my surroundings grow foreign to me. Whether the fault lies with myself, with my environment, or with the circumstances, it is a sad fact, I feel this foreignness. With kindest regards. Yours, Cigarillo. Current address: Corporal Brenner, Johann, Class 2 Armor Branch D, Wil Barracks, Stans. PS: And, so you have something to smoke, a bit of *tubake* as we say in the Wynental, here's a few boxes of Brazil and Sumatra. Twofold shame: that he never became a writer, nor I a manufacturer of cigars.

II.

MENZENMANG,
RIO GRANDE, WEBER & SONS LTD.

Menzenmang: how many are the byways, crossroads, holloways, and false paths I have taken, how many the years of illness endured, how many the cigars smoked, it must be ten thousand now, in order to come closer once more to this triad the postal bus in Soglio brought back to mind, Havana and Brazil blaze in bright major, Sumatra takes care of the minor tones, *Mänzmi* you say in the Wynental dialect, with its vocalization of the final syllable, and now I withdraw from the antiquated regulation carton, loser of the cigar war in the year of thirty-seven, a finely veined Rio Grande, not yet showing plume, and I roll the foot back and forth in the flame as millions before me have, factory men in the aluminum works, United Carpenters Ltd., laborers at the Plaggi and the Riemi, cigar makers in the gypsum grey high rise – the *houptgebäu* – on the banks of the Wyna across from the WSB Menzenmang-Burg terminus, first and final stop for my journey through the world. And even if so-called *dents de bonheur* are an auspicious sign for travelers, thanks, perhaps, to the *gat-tothed* Wife of Bath who *koude muchel of wandrynge by the weye,* it hasn't been much of one, in terms of itineraries or time. The Rio too has an onion scent, but with more Kentucky than the Brenner Export, and proportionally less Java and Domingo. Aarau was my first stop, where I attended the baccalaureate section of the canton school, but in the metropolis of carrot country, formidable on its rocky knoll and glowering at the Aare River, there was no university, no theater, no shopping center, no library, no art museum, no government office, only an infantry barracks; and so my conquest was nothing more than the city where I was born on the tenth of July, 1942, a muggy Friday during the town fair in labor room B of the canton hospital, son of Hermann Brenner, insurance inspector, and Gertrud Emmy Brenner-Pfendsack, at six on the dot; after the meeting on the terrace at the reform church had adjourned, having decided on the good weather program for the local fair, I, the patient, helped along by the customary clap on the behind, uttered my first cry.

As though my life simply depended on never living anywhere from which the Wynentaler – yes, I will stick with this designation, even if today the tram is called the WSB, the Wynental-Suhrental line – were not reachable in the shortest possible time, I avoided the capitals in my home country and beyond, and if I commend to these nicotine-yellow tobacco leaves the declaration, home is only ever a breath away, I mean both the breath drawn in the death-defying, big-holing, caterwauling peanut roaster and the "poison" breath of tobacco, which was only ever grown in Menzenmang on a trial basis during the war. In Zurich, where I studied architecture for four semesters and took a few courses in the school of design, I didn't yet have a Deux Chevaux, even if, as a saxophone and vibraphone player, I could have used a set of wheels, every weekend I took the SBB to Aargau and then the *dinky* into the valley, as if plunging into a tunnel, for *Mang* means *within;* no rambler in a cap, in blue fustian or coveralls, with a bindle or a lunchbox for his daily fare, would ever say *on up te Mänzmi,* true, there is a difference in altitude of 177 meters, and it is not – or is only slightly – a lie to say that in December, we are already sledding and skiing when there's nothing but mud on the ground in Aarau, but it doesn't matter, one always travels *on down te Mänzmi.* When I married Flavia Soguel, the jurist from the village of Davos in the Grisons, on October 7, 1967, we looked for a three-room house in Baden, but in the end wound up on the Gonhardweg at the so-called Bürgen-stock in Aarau, twice we moved houses in the city of Swiss cadets before they offered us the old rectory in Starrkirch-Quittung, and from the pastoral hearth along the Aare and over the Inseli it was just thirty minutes to the WSB station. If one wished to draw an analogy between state railways and established religions and the private lines and sects, then Swiss Federal Railways would be easily recognizable as the Evangelical church; the Rhaetian Railways, which cover the Grisons and Valais, would be the Pentecostal movement, on account of its proclivity for climbing, the faithful must toil upward, for God will not come down to you; the Wynenthal-Suhrental Line I would not hesitate to compare with the New Apostolic Church, its twelve disciples appointed by a charismatic circle around 1830 in Albury Park in southern England correspond to the twelve iconic stations Aarau, Suhr, Gränichen, Bleien, Teufenthal, Unterkulm, Oberkulm, Gontenschwil, Zetzwil, Leimbach, Reinach, Menzenmang-Burg, or, ordered from highest to lowest or inner- to outermost and voiced as a prayer: *Mänzmi-Borg, Rynech, Leymbach, Zetzbu, Gondischwiu, Oberchoom, Underchoom, Teufetu, Bläje, Gräneche, Sohr, Aarouw.*

The obstacle-ridden journey lasts a scant fifty minutes, in Aarau, on the Buchserstrasse, you are already reminded of home, because the tramways laid in the pavement run so close to the dusty lilac and box hedges planted around the suburban villas that you can reach out and touch them through the open window, *ne pas se pencher en dehors;* in numberless dreams, above all in the first years of my mental illness, when it was still concealed beneath the diagnosis of genital migraines, this stretch always prefaced a fit of dry coughing that would overtake me around Reinach-Unterdorf, when the main road narrowed to a leafy tunnel, where the old, immense trees of the Hediger & Sons Villa cast their shadows over the whole of the track. Here is where the graves were, I should begin by saying that it was as a three-year-old on the Angermatt, where my grandmother Ida used to go talk to the dead and pick snails off the marble gravestones, that the idea of *home* was impressed on me, *yer et home here, boy,* it is true we spoke of going *out* to the cemetery, but for me, the feeling was always one of inwardness, because the labyrinth of yews and box trees was a sealed domain, and there is a certain irony in the fact that the former Menzenmang station, the terminus, lay near the Wynental restaurant where the Friedhofst-rasse – Cemetery Street – branched off from the Oberdorfstrasse, there the conductor of the C Nr. 31, which was purchased secondhand from the city of Neuchâtel, used to knock one back before embarking on the thirty-two-kilometer stretch inaugurated on March 5, 1904, when my grandfather, Hermann Brenner, was twenty-two years old, in eighty minutes you were in Aarau, free from the clutches of the New Apostolic Church and entrusted to the sect of the SBB. There, in this eternally august, dusty green manufacturer's villa with its gardens at the entrance to Reinach, with the aid of a few meditative draws from an Indiana, the first memory arises. I am sitting on my father's knee, we are in my parents' bedroom, I know because I see the black-and-brown streaks on the mahogany nightstand with the rubber truncheon in the drawer, ready for any and all possible prowlers – Mandi, an auxiliary in the Swiss army, kept no rifle in his closet – and he told me a story. Once upon a time, there was a lad – not a boy or kid – who was allowed to go with his father to the parish fair, he could choose – *chuuse* – between a ride on the carousel or a balloon. And so my life with high literature began, and I kept interrupting Papa with the question: But what if? What if the lad, Edwin with the Pretty Mama, decided on the carousel instead of the balloon, or vice-versa? I must have reflected on this a long time, for it was not so easy to say which of the pleasures was the more alluring. Initially, you preferred the horses, they undoubtedly had the advantage, for rocking back and forth beneath a baldachin, putting your feet in real stirrups and grabbing hold of the bridles, surely that was earthly splendor. But then the roundabout's spinning would suddenly halt, and when the blaring and crashing of the organ died down, it became clear that fortune favored the lad who had asked for the balloon, which you could tie to your wrist during an afternoon nap, letting it float up safely toward the ceiling. Naturally, like every child, I despaired at the abrupt either/or and struggled to solve the problem of how to enjoy both pleasures on the fairground, unaware that in doing so, I was following the trail of Aristotle, in logic the following is valid: A is by definition either equal to or not equal to B, and cannot at the same time be equal to C, the *tertium non datur* would be the lad with the balloon on the carousel horse. Like all stories, this parable too ended in tragedy, the lad chose the *kerushel,* fell from the saddle, and bloodied his head on a *cobbleshtone.* Now King Subjunctive takes the throne: *ef only he'd teken de balloon!*

Every three months, on the last Sunday of the month, there was a market, *en märt,* in Reinach, and it must have been on this dazed and motley day that I found myself in the same position as the mythical lad, but now, life was writing the story, I owe this phrase to my cemetery-grandmother, who would return from her *saunter,* catch her breath on the tile bench, tell some anecdote about someone from our family circle, then stand up with a sigh, saying: *it's jest one eh dem stories life writes.* You learn from your mistakes, as the proverb goes, but really I'd learned from the mistake of the young man in the story, and with his fate in mind, I prudently chose the balloon. We rode home on the ponderous English bicycle with the black oil in its gears, I stood over the cargo rack with the two foot pegs below, the green droplet was tied to my wrist, and near the village of Litzi just before the Fischer Wireworks it happened – no, the thread didn't break, the balloon simply crinkled and sank, the gas seeped out, my father dismounted, *damn de luck,* untied the knot, blew with full cheeks, and I was terribly scared, I imagined the leftover gas was streaming into his lungs. Nights on end, the same dream haunted me, I would sit up in bed *soppin wet,* Father had died from poison gas and it was my fault, *ef only I'd teken de kerushel ride.* Today I hop into the Jet Star 3, the roller coaster with the wildest twists and turns, bobsled in winter on the Olympic run in St. Moritz, race the Ferrari at 170 on the four-lane highway, all this most likely because I should have chosen the carousel back then; and it reappeared to me years later in a dream, abandoned in a Bengal night, its canvas cover buttoned shut. As I pushed in through a slit, I entered a fairground Gehenna: sharp scent of camphor, everything mothballed, wildly swollen nostrils on the varnished horses, dangling canopies on the carriages with moth-infested pompons and tassels in plum compote brown, the organ, the hissing bellows; *cawusew* my boys called it when I took them to the market for the first time, they would get their *tertium non datur,* the balloon and more rides than they could count, Matthias picked a motorbike with drag bars, sat in his seat like an angel petrified with joy, legs gripping the motor; Hermann waved from the Zurich tram with the light-up logo for the fair, honked the horn on the driver's side, and even father let himself be lifted from horizontal to vertical, whirling and rotating in a kind of mop bucket, sealed in a monkey's cage, and the towers of Aarau spun sharply, one past the other, and the boys stood right by the barrier. Hoping, fearing – for what? Was this madcap bucket not riskier than the gas in the green balloon?

The Weber & Sons Ltd. Rio Grande is pulling in air from a crack, I will have to cut a patch for it with a razorblade and press it on tight. Menzenmang, how often I returned, not because my mother sang *Boy, come back home,* it was my father's house, I explored it lying on my back in the crib, surrounded by bars in the corner of my parents' bedroom, when I awoke with the darkness, Ur mated with Ur, the ur-flash was the moment when the light shone in, ur-essence and ur-blending are the elements, a chaotic ur-amalgam, shot through with ur-lightning, ur-glimmer when the night birthed Erebus, then Thales, then Anaximenes, then Heraclitus, the volcanic bubbling, the ur-mass, the magma that formed the dinosaurs, shaped by a hulking hand, monstrous beasts like the Brontosaurus, Plesiosaurus, Ichthyosaurus, how gruesome to see the mammoth crocodile draw open its maw and sink its fangs into its victim's scaly, armored skin, tearing away dead chunks of damp flesh while our ur-ancestors wallowed in blood, wandered through the man-high ferns, splashed in brackish waters, the canebrakes crackle and everything cannibal that creeps and crawls along the earth is there as we flee the mythological darkness, grasshoppers big as biplanes with razor-like jaws, monstrous spiders with poison fangs long as spears, bats with lissome outstretched wings, butchery, annihilation, massacre, carnage, murder, endless ritual slaughter of nature, cave salamanders, horned toads, midwife toads waiting bug-eyed in damp hollows in walls for the coming of day. I lie there tied with elastic bands, just as in the Jews' Salon in the Waldau, and walk with my eyes along the ceiling, immerse myself in the riddle of the patterned wallpaper, the never-ending ribbon, a brown jagged band on sand-colored fabric, strange, mythical creatures cross my path along the way, a prised-open pear with a herringbone pattern, an ochre-edged starflower, impossible to say, are these plants or hieroglyphs; and when the line breaks off at the corner, rhomboid butterflies and intricate shamrocks emerge dancing just below and slip behind the curtain, which is flesh-toned, stitched carnations of dried blood, and on a string, a brass bell hangs down over my bed, but I am tied down and can't touch it, tell me, muse, how are we to find our way. It was war, my mother told me when I asked why she'd put me in the elastic straps, we couldn't get it warm enough in there, and I was a *hellion* and always thrashed and kicked off my blanket. But in my memory, it is summer, the door to the terrace stands ajar, it is painted a shrieking minium orange, all of outside, which I am forbidden to access, is a single orange ochre, and a noise sharpens the hours for me, it comes from the nearby workshop, from the builders, where Rota is finishing the newly molded window ledge with a mallet and a drove chisel, this monotone tapping set the tempo for my dance across the ceiling, I have, to entertain myself while I lie in my own urine, discovered the adventure of turning the bedroom upside down, using the plaster ceiling as a floor, treading barefoot on the stucco roundel, inspecting the amber mushroom of the lampshade: is it edible, poisonous, or merely suspect? And what is the magnetic miracle that makes the bun feet on the weighty mahogany wardrobe cling to the carpeted ceiling, over the windows the lintels turn to little benches, scale the barricade and you reach the bathroom with its vanilla yellow tiles, the Glenburn toilet bowl I imagine as a porcelain awning in an alcove, the longer I play, the more I start to reel, I can no longer tell whether the olive green ottoman at the foot of my parents' sleigh bed is crashing suddenly upward or downward. For my two-year-old self, or maybe even younger, these architectural studies were a taste of freedom, but at the same time forced labor, I was in a race against Rota, the master mason, I devoured time, and it tasted of Valhalla, of the plasterboard walls of the eternal hall.

Suddenly we flee to the cellar, a siren is blaring, Father has grabbed wool blankets, we stand like mummies pressed flat against the wall; flush on my left, next to the coal chute, on the safe side, in other words, stand Mother and Grandmother, my protector is on the right, the door to the washroom stands open, and in the grated window, as if hurled into the frame by a foreign hand, is a careening airplane in flames. The next memory may be still older, from a deeper stratum than the story of the carousel and the balloon, maybe even my very first impression of life: a dark-skinned man in colorful clothes on a boat on Lake Geneva extended his closed fist, turned it over, and when he opened it there lay, in the brightness of his palm, a yellow sugared mint just for me; gladly would Hermann Arbogast Brenner have commenced his thwarted salesman's existence with an act of such largesse extended across racial lines, but most likely in the beginning was the war; sometimes, when the English and American planes were hit, they strayed into Swiss airspace, that pilot in particular had bailed out in Erlosen, at least that's what they said, people found wreckage smoldering all the way down in the village, the wool blankets tell me it must have been winter, maybe 1944 or '45. And here stands the Christmas tree in the living room, aromas of candlewax and gingerbread fill the air, the fir with its ornaments has transformed our home into a lordly abode; when the Christmas child rings the bell, father opens the clattering sliding door with its mandarin silk curtain, the forest of lights glows in the inner sanctum, the branches abound with dangling balls of cognac-gold, beet-red, and dusty silver; the candlesticks look like reeded tiger's claws, garlands of lametta swing from branch to branch, tinsel shimmers in white and gold, on top is a five-pointed star; when you light them, thin slivers of anthracite shed wild showers of sparks, the surfaces of the balls reflect the rain and bend the image of the window in the door.

And there it is, the building kit, the crate so heavy I *kent lift et up* alone, not plain blocks made to fool the child into thinking the world his workshop, not coarse-grained beams and cubes and triangles unfit to make a pyramid, let alone a whole temple, no: in a container more alluring even than Father's parrot-yellow boxes of Partagás, a real, complete Anker Stone construction set, fresh from the stockpile of my godfather in Grabs, when you grabbed the brown handle and slid the lid back in its grooves, the orderly splendor of architecture before the creation of the world was revealed, their arrangement, in two layers, was so ingenious you hardly dared reach in to grasp a sand brown, rust red, or Prussian blue piece, and my father sat cross-legged on the carpet, he alone was allowed to disturb this primal order because he alone was capable of restoring it, he demonstrated to me anew the invention of the wheel, sliding a plate with beveled edges over two column drums, alternating the rollers until the load had passed beneath the Christmas tree, a car – *cah,* my boys would have called it – when you smacked two blocks together, it sounded like Roda nidging on the worksite, two pillars go up, an arch bridges them at the top, now the gate, *de tunnew,* was done, *finisht,* the most striking thing about the tunnel pieces was the impost blocks and keystones, their *correctness* – here, too, we have an ur-memory, my view from a train window of a softly sloping avenue, and a door with a round arch in a rusticated frame at the end of a row of trees, without this, I could not have grasped this idea of exactitude in proportion. Whoever devotes himself to the study of childhood becomes a detective *pro domo*, I have traveled down every possible stretch in Menzenmang and the surrounding area, now on the left side of the tracks, now on the right, and it was there, on the Buchserstrasse in Aarau that I clung spellbound to the handle by the window of the WSB train car, then plunged four decades downward in an instant. I saw it again, greeting me across the row of plane trees, austere like a train station, the rusticated door with the round arch leading into the old canton hospital, an architecture from elsewhere, exactly as it stood beneath the Christmas tree, and it is no exaggeration if I write today, slipping a Brenner Mocca from its silver sleeve with the cardinal purple inscription, that my father's hands, which he never raised against me, resurrected Alberti's Palazzo Rucellai with the Doric order on the ground floor, the Ionic pilasters on the second, and the Corinthian capitals on the third, with its archaic jutting cornice and the mullioned windows under the twinned arches, their exacting proportions suited perfectly to the façade, and what I later read in Alberti was no less true of the Anker construction set, the harmony of parts was such that nothing could be added or taken away, this was a basic principle of the Renaissance, unlike a Gothic parish church, where a side aisle could be built on later without destroying the overall effect.

On the glimmering, sea-green lid with the medallion windows and the red Anker logo was the image of the masterpiece, the acme of my own kit, the Imperator: a bridge with two towers and metal railings, the iron sections steely blue in contrast to the cornflower blue of the pyramids, quarter moons, and triangles, in the instruction booklet, entitled *The Little Anker Master Builder,* a pale boy kneels, aware of its perfection, before the gateway to a German city, of course, they were German to the core, these slabs of basalt and rustic brick; the blocks, the architraves, which left a furry feeling on your palate, screamed out for a Märklin steam locomotive, for a soot-blackened wheelhouse, for a gravel-covered rail switch, for the deep red of a crossing signal, and on the base of the box, each piece was drawn and numbered in the order of installation, like a puzzle, what a wonder for an artistic soul on this Christmas Eve, of which I remember nothing else – no, that isn't true, there is that phrase from father's story: *And they found no room at the inn.* What an inn was, I just had to know, and look, with the Imperator you could build one of those too, using the hinged bridge slabs as roof ridges, the crisscrossed railings for a garden fence, with the flat tiles of stony blue resting in the cardboard box, my father laid a parquet floor with a diagonal pattern of rhombi. This toy, too, which I treasured like a jewel, was annexed by my siblings, perverted from its true purposes: my sister Klärli put a rectangular block in her doll oven like a loaf of bread, Kari had the atrocious idea of building something with real mortar, he set up his half-finished monstrosity in the middle of the sandbox, in brief, it was embezzled and destroyed like everything I ever held dear, right down to the vile Mammonolatry of their *total liquidation* of our Menzenmang home in the summer of 1985.

Menzenmang on the Sandstrasse, now long sunken away, no more notes of Chopin from the living room with the cinnabar green jalousies and the decorative helmeted soldiers on the latches; no more does the smoke-cured office door creak as when father, ever cheerful, ever game for a prank, used to emerge from his insurance inspector's atelier. We were, as a family, too weak to preserve and perpetuate our former holdings, from the cemetery our parents looked down on us dismayed as we plundered, one truckload at a time, the substance of their estate: built in 1927 by Otto Weber-Brenner, occupied in 1941 by Hermann Brenner and Gertrud Brenner-Pfendsack. We deliberately destroyed what two generations had built, he was right, Johann Caspar Brenner, there was no point in denying it, the third branch is the rotten one, my siblings sawed off the fork in the tree where we used to sit, and with this, in accordance with the puncta of inheritance law, Hermann Arbogast Brenner was summarily ousted, an iron curtain fell between his Brunsleben days and his childhood, the partition of the two Germanies was repeated in miniature at Menzenmang, my estate lies as far from me as Hohen-Cremmen in Brandenburg, by car I can travel faster to East Berlin or to Rheinsberg than the Wynental, it is easier to go through customs there than to cross the ridge in Bowil.

12.

THE PLANT,
PURO HABANO

The leaf of the finely veined, *colorado-claro* brown cigar I smoke with delectation while fitting a sheet of paper into the typewriter was neither grown nor treated in my first homeland, the *Stumpenland* of Aargau, it comes from Cuba, from the regal soils of the Vuelta Abajo, which lie west of Havana on this sickle-shaped island between the Atlantic and the Caribbean; around Pinar del Río, Sierra del Rosario, and Sierra de los Órganos; but also from the heart of the country near Santa Clara, where the most storied firms with the most illustrious names have their headquarters, and the fertile regions with their swaths of green leaves are known as villas. Herrera, a biologist specializing in *nicotiana,* writes that the seed germinates some ten days after planting; between the thirty-fifth and the fiftieth day, generally in October, the shoots emerge, a month or so later the first signs of ripening appear, the matte green leaves turn softer, more luminous, and shed their nap;

the grower, the *veguero,* as he is called, attentively observes the stems and ribs, when he wants light tobacco, *claro* quality, he picks the sand leaf, the *centro bajo,* the *centro medio,* the *centro alto,* and the *corona* prematurely; if he is looking for *colorado* or *maduro* shades, he waits a few weeks more. It is a sight to behold, after you have cut the corona, when its glowing wreath eats into the edges, the symmetry between the steel blue of the ash ring and the hazy blue of the smoke; the first drag is capital, already it contains the full savor of the aromatic oils. After picking, the leaves are laid out in spacious sheds, so-called tobacco cathedrals, where they lose some of their moisture and starch. The brown gold may be dried in three ways: air drying is most frequent, the bundles are hung from the steps of a lath ladder under a roof thatched from fronds of guano palm or palmetto, and as the water content evaporates, they are placed higher up. This method demands close attention and fine adjustments depending on the climate, if the relative humidity exceeds eighty-five percent, the leaves must be taken out and laid in the sun, otherwise they will start to swell, this stage is a foreshadow of the finicky nature of the final product, a hand-rolled Havana will lose its freshness and elasticity unless stored in an old vault or a humidor with constant temperature control.

Swelling must be avoided at all costs. If it is too rainy, a fire of wood charcoal can help reduce the ambient humidity. If it is too dry, you sprinkle the floor and cover it in wet rags – the work of art we indulge in when the process is over owes a debt to the dexterity and instinct of the tobacco house's custodian. Sun drying is reserved for leaves not plucked individually, but harvested with the entire plant: the bushel is laid on wooden grates and must be constantly turned, if it yellows as it ages, it is brought in for air drying. This method requires less room, but in this land of riches, the only one where the *puro* thrives, you must give the plant the space it demands, even a humidor cannot be built too narrow, the Partagás, the Romeo y Julieta, the Hoyo de Monterrey must be allowed to open up like an old Bordeaux in a decanter. There is not much to say for fire drying except that it arose along with the fashion for *doble claros* or *clarísimos*, the green wrappers popular in the United States and falsely thought to be lighter in nicotine. For the veteran *vegueros*, artificial heating is a disgrace, it strips the tobacco of spice and pliancy. Drying is followed by fermentation, which removes the resin and nitrogen compounds from the leaves, to achieve it, they are taken from the drying shed and bundled, this is done in damp weather, so the now-brittle *viso* and *volado* leaves won't crumble. The *gavillas* are layered over a bed of guano or banana leaves, the height of the mound hints at the quality of the tobacco, a dry year brings an exquisite crop. The mound – the *pilón* – of tobacco thus prepared is wrapped in palm fronds or light fabric on all sides, and when, in a few days, the interior temperature begins to rise, this tells you fermentation has begun. What does that mean, in concrete terms? The proteins and residual sugars break down, and important aromatic compounds develop, while the nicotine content drops by some ten percent. The temperature of the tobacco must be precisely controlled, if it exceeds or falls below the desired fifty to sixty degrees Celsius, the bale is unraveled, the tobacco from the middle pulled out, and the outer tobacco placed inside. This is done at least three times, with the entire process taking around six months. And so, passing from its first heat to its second, from its second to its third, *nicotiana* leads an intense life of its own before its eventual deflowering by the smoker's kiss.

The dried and pre-fermented material is sent out to the warehouses and factories. Following a secret recipe, the overseer prepares a decoction called bethune, the main ingredients of which are water and tobacco stems. He sprays this on the leaves, which are then sealed in crates. The next day they are taken out and sorted into *capas* and *tripas*, but this is only the beginning. In each category, whether for wrapper or filler, there are more than ten sub-categories, with the goods being graded for thickness, color, shape, and texture. It is in the art of selection that the true connoisseur distinguishes himself. But he is also rewarded on the other end of the globe with earnestness in the enjoyment of life, as Adam Nautilus Rauch is accustomed to say. Before packing, another fermentation occurs, with the leaves bundled into *gavillas*, the still-damp tobacco – and what true cigarier would fail to acknowledge the rare delights of a fresh cigar – is wrapped in palm fronds known as *tercios*, this form of aging is particularly prized for the brown gold of Partagás, Montecristo, and Punch. The *tercios* in the warehouse, like champagne bottles in the Reims cellars, are constantly inspected, turned, and rearranged until the process of fermentation has run its course. Then the first phase of manufacture begins with the removal of the *gavillas* from their coverings. You must be a true tobacco serf, a master of dry drunkenness, to bear the sharp, piercing, numbing scent of fermentation at this stage. Whoever steps into a storeroom at Brenner & Sons Ltd. in Pfeffikon or Burger & Sons Ltd. in Burg, where wares from

Sumatra, Brazil, Java, and Domingo lie, will get some sense of what I'm talking about. I recommend, as I rotate my Romeo y Julieta a quarter turn with every draw, that the consumers of the present tobacco leaves treat themselves to an olfactory inspection of this kind on a summer afternoon, in doing so, you enter an ICU of tobacco, as it were, and will grasp that there exists between morphinomane and cigarier, between the infatuation with poison and with the pneuma of blue haze, only a slight – albeit vital – difference.

One last time, the workers moisten the *gavillas*, then shake them, so the liquid drains away, before placing their harvest into separate baskets and handing them off to the destemmers – who are almost always women. In his memoirs, Zino Davidoff writes: "And these are the true stars of tobacco, the barelegged beauties of legend. In them lives on the memory of Carmen and the girls who worked tobacco in the factories of Seville. Mostly young, alluring creatures, their skin shimmers in all shades from white to dark brown, joyous, lively girls who sit there in the gigantic workshop, in the *galleys*, on their little leather-topped stools." Their task is to strip out the middle vein. They lay the damp leaf on a little board set across their hips and skillfully remove the stem with their thumb and forefinger. Then the tobacco is layered in barrels and stored for the third and longest fermentation. If it is heavy, thick, and succulent, it may stay there for years doing its work. It is a long way from plant to cigar, as long as the journey from my cheroot childhood, and the aficionado must keep this in mind as he opens a golden box adorned with exhibition medals and Havana muses and dreams his fill at the mirror. After the third fermentation comes the blending, on this the aromatic harmony of taste depends. This is where specialists step in, each responsible for a given brand, and their task consists in finding, from one year to the next, the proper tone to assure the continuity of the Montecristo, Partagás, and Romeo y Julieta names. Their gift is their supreme olfactory organ. A fine restaurant only becomes a first-class destination when the turbot arrives fresh from the market and the preparation never varies — whether slow roasted or quick-seared — when the cook heats the cast-iron skillet to the same temperature every time, sealing in the flavors of the tenderloin; at the same time, the Montecristo freak who swears by his torpedo — like the Ferrari driver who balks at the offer of a red-paneled Maserati from Maranello — will fail at first to see the virtues of a Davidoff in its brown wrapper. As the cigar is the culmination of every *menu gastronomique* and, indeed, one only eats in order to smoke, when this moment arrives, the connoisseur must under no circumstances be deceived. And so we must imagine the blenders, these wonder-workers of pneuma, walking thoughtfully back and forth through corridors where leaves hang from the ceiling like precious silken threads, letting themselves be guided by their noses. These palate-tinkerers are the masters of ceremonies for our most beautiful aimless hours, recall that the influence of tobacco on the taste receptors, on the olfactory organ, on the skin, has only barely been investigated. The volatile oils, which can be extracted through steam distillation, clearly play an important role in aroma formation, the importance of the resins is likely overstated, while smoking, the sugars help soften the flavor, some tobaccos, like the oriental varieties

Zichna-Basma, Akhisar, Selçuk, and Giaour Keni display browns spots that are thought to indicate spiciness.

As soon as the odeur-funambulists have composed the blend, the batch is moistened slightly and packed in boxes so the aromas will *marry*. Unsealing one of these after many years, you will feel the aromas of the Vuelta Abajo streaming toward you, this is no longer remotely like the stifling opening of the bales of fermented leaves in the warehouse. A tea box left long in the attic offers a similar bouquet, though naturally in an entirely different octave. We must chastise Davidoff for having ushered in quality cigars under names like Château Margaux, Château Latour, or Château Haut-Brion, when the essential thing is to distinguish Camagüey y Oriente from Semi-Vuelta and Sierra de Nipe from Sierra del Rosario. With such blunders, the marketing strategists evinced their bankruptcy vis-à-vis the description of tobacco's aromas. The person concerned with his own childhood must sniff out the earliest vestiges of scents. Now is the hour of the cigar-maker himself, who forms the leaves into a roll – with Havanas, only whole strips, long filler, are employed – covering it with the binder and producing a cocoon that can be measured with a ruler. Then the wrapper, a diagonal strip cut from the heart of the tobacco leaf, is placed over the binder and held fast with a special glue. This is why all true boxes imported from Cuba read *hecho a mano,* the cigar is not, as legend still has it, rolled over women's thighs, instead it takes shape on a small work table, in the hands of an experienced man who works with a clockmaker's precision. The wrapper is too delicate to be rolled by a machine. The final phase of production is no less picturesque than the beginning. The cigars delivered from the worktables are tied with silk ribbons into bundles of fifty. Each of these is called a half-wheel. In Cuba, it is said of a person over fifty that he has passed the half-wheel of his life. The bundle rests for a few weeks in a cedar cabinet where the cigars sweat out the heat of the third fermentation. A month later they are re-sorted, spread out and ordered by color from *doble claro* to *claro* and *maduro* to *oscuro*, each firm has its own scale for the wealth of hues. Finally they are boxed up, and here again, a trained specialist is required, with the lightest examples placed on top – this upper layer is called the mirror – and arranged in such a way that the fine veins lie on the underside. The interior of the box is of Cuban cedar, by far the best for preservation, though today we must often resort to Gabon wood.

And here we enter the magic realm of the treasure chest *hecho en Cuba* with its sumptuous, exotic labels, had I ever owned a magic lantern, like Edmond de Mog and his beloved Marcel, it wouldn't have mattered, couldn't have possibly compared, no hocus-pocus contraption from Franz Carl Weber Toys could have caught me in its spell like the parrot-yellow Partagás box with its gold meander, its royal blue banner, its label in citron yellow with a dangling scroll in antique pink and the brand name in an arch of cinnabar red, *Flor de Tabacos Superiores de la Vuelta Abajo, Habana, Fábrica de Cigarros Puros,* then, stamped in an almost bleached olive green, the flag of the Republic of Cuba, the medallion with the palm trees, Havana's coat of arms, *the country of origin guarantees the authenticity of the exported product.* With a paper knife, you carefully slice it open at the edge, press the little golden nail in the lid, and an even deeper yellow astounds you, corn-color, almost, the interior, as if inlaid, is replete with pale blue and fleshtone markings, decals with garish tobacco-muses, plump putti, gold exhibition medals crowding in on a sarcophagus speckled with turquoise stones, *un rappel de médaille d'or,* and only when you pull back the glossy protective paper – the bastard title, they call it in publishing – do you see the immaculate *claro* mirror. Distinct is the subtle vanilla yellow of the Montecristo box with its six crossed daggers forming a double triangle and three cadmium red trapezoids reading *Monte Cristo Habana,* around the edges is an ochre-gold checkerboard frieze, on the inside the same insignia in white and gold, the signature of Menéndez y García and the inscription: *Los tabacos que utilizamos en la elaboración de esta marca son seleccionados de la más alta calidad que se reserva en la Isla de Cuba.* For Romeo y Julieta, a border of pale cinnabar green with vignettes from the island's history in blue and orange, on the fabled balcony, under a pink banderole, the beloved looks down at her suitor in his cobalt purple doublet, Cedros de Luxe No. 1, the band gold and dark olive green.

And yet this box is still not in our hands, it awaits that adventure we call exportation. Import-export, such was the twofold grace of drawing breath in my childhood. The cigar now has its three main fermentations behind it, until the fourth, which will occur some five months after shipping, it can be sold as a fresh, or green, Havana. To smoke it in this state is a peculiar delicacy, you come closer to the leaf, the feel of it is more tender, there are customers whose dealers notify them immediately upon receiving a shipment that has yet, if you will, to enter its final menstrual cycle. Afterwards, another year must pass, no sooner has the shipment reached port than the tobacco comes to life again. Good sellers will advise their customers to stockpile their still sweating *puros*. For this purpose, a first class shop will have a maturing room on site, it is essential that the tobacco rest undisturbed, the discriminating connoisseur is party to this tranquility, and will take no more than a single pull per minute. This unique blend of stimulation and appeasement, of distraction and concentration, is highly fruitful for the epic mode as practiced by Hermann Arbogast Brenner, to quote Reiner, we must let detail drive us far and wide, even into madness, at the same time, our lens must focus the light so sharply that our object glows like fire. You could almost say, borrowing a concept from psychotherapy, that the Havana in the maturing room is engaged in autogenic training, to visit it now and then without disturbing it during this phase is a part of the tobacco-idler's devotion, as if the champagne drinker were to descend to the catacombs to stare at the flared bottles during riddling.

The cigar must be stored at the proper humidity, sixty to sixty-seven degrees is ideal, and sheltered from abrupt changes in temperature. As the pneuma of my Romeo y Julieta subsides, I remember the cellar labyrinth of the manufacturer's villa in Menzenmang, the *carceri* with the conches facing out toward the graveyard at the parish house in Starrkirch, and the cracking of my heart reminds me that once, I had a family there. Here in Brunsleben, my treasury is in the dungeon of the old lookout tower, but on dry nights, I take my boxes to the stables to provide them a bit more humidity. The Upmann Aromáticos – mandarin meander around the edge, medallions in a sky of gentle blue – I store in the home of my friend Irlande von Elbstein-Bruyère, in the so-called hunter's room with the stuffed armadillos and the poisonous serpents preserved in jars. I am aware of the neophyte smokers' custom of setting their brass-trimmed mahogany humidors in the center of the living room, like a TV, to advise their guests from the moment they enter that this is a house where tobacco culture reigns. This is a mistake, Havanas must be tucked away in their original packaging. Soi-disant experts recommend the removal of one stick to allow the others to breathe better, this too is a travesty, each cigar must remain with its family members, it is only in communion with them in its original abode that the Montecristo will ripen to perfection. Cuban cedar aids in the process, stacking in layers ensures an ideal development. There is one thing that cannot be stressed enough: a well-preserved Havana loses nothing of its virtues, to the contrary, it grows nobler with age. A seasoned tradesman like my friend Walter Menzi from Dürr on the Bahnhofstrasse in Zurich knows the excellent years in Vuelta were 1962, 1967, 1976, and 1981; the 1940 and 1980 harvests, by contrast, were *malas*. He can tell us unerringly whether the goods on offer have been twelve or forty-eight months in the store, whether the cigars are still sweating before reaching their prime or whether they are now at their peak.

For this reason, we should spend as much time considering additions to our stores as we do on a visit to the tailor's. For me, the anticipation is always mixed with a bit of stage fright, as when we were allowed to visit Franz Carl Weber in Zurich as a child. Herr Menzi knows what I am looking for. Did you know, he tells me, the great cigar lovers in England have not only a fumoir, but a maturing room built right into their home? Ah, I reply, then my cellar dungeon at Brunsleben is a barbarity by comparison, I might as well stick my fresh Romeos and Partagás directly into the fridge. Not at all, Herr Brenner, those old rubblework walls provide an absolutely ideal environment. You know, when I still lived in the parish house in Starrkirch, which even then was fit for demolition, I let my boxes rest so long in the mildewy vaults that a verdigris patina covered them. But the cigars stayed as supple as if they'd just come off the boat, and the *doble claro* effect was exceptional. Ah, yes, the Americans with their mania for bright complexions! In Spain, *oscuro* still triumphs just as it did at the dawn of the century. And now we drift back into history as we look for a Rafael González from the province of Pinar del Río. You see, Herr Brenner, what we have here is a marriage of poetry and tobacco, in the fifties of the preceding century the custom in the workshops of Don Jaime Partagás was to read Victor Hugo aloud while binder, wrapper, and filler were rolled, and in the days before the war for Cuban independence, the galleys were hotbeds of agitation. They banned reading or commenting on the news of the day, and this led to popular uprisings. In his memoirs, Zino affirms that the Cuban independence movement, which finally proved victorious in 1901, had its birthplace in the historic cigar factories. Radio first made inroads at Cabañas y Carbajol, a top brand that is sadly no longer around; nowadays, Castro's teachings and pop music have pushed poor Hugo aside. Imagine if, instead of the oldies, they recited Gabriel García Márquez, whom admittedly I myself have never read? And so on and so forth with our disputation as we take the staircase down to the climatized inner sanctum. The financier may feel something similar when he descends into the cold *sous-sol* of his bank, the door to the vault opens silently, and he presses his key into the lockbox to fetch one of his gold ingots or even just to give it a quarter-turn, but what is a lump of gold compared to the treasures housed at Dürr on the Bahnhofstrasse? A disdainful glance at the gleaming wood humidors and the Davidoff scissors in their jewel boxes: the true cig-arier bites the cap off with his teeth, knowing it was attached there with that purpose in mind. Herr Menzi shows me the most alluring mirrors of Hoyo de Monterrey, Larragaña, Upmann, Punch, Ramón Allones, Montecristo, Partagás, Romeo y Julieta, no effort is spared me, I may sniffle or pinch, as adepts say, press down with my thumb here or there, complain of a slight discoloration, I am not yet convinced by the pro-verbial Alonso *oscuro*, and what are these La Paz doing here among the treasures of the Vuelta? In the end, I will always return to my tried and true triad: for solemn occasions, the Romeo Number One, especially on afternoons of Azores Highs and deep-summer August nights; the half-wheel of Hoyo des Dieux with the egg-yellow silk band for work and midday reminiscing; the Partagás corona or culebra or Charlotte from the romance of my childhood, for it was in these very same golden boxes, which looked no different in the nineteen-forties than today, though memory has bleached them to a light ochre, that I used to store my boyhood treasures, the aluminum scraps tossed from slits in the freight sheds of the WSB and SBB, labels from cheroots and Churchills, no butterflies or stag beetles, I told you that before, nature never inter-ested me especially, I preferred to it a ruby red button from my dear mother's blouse.

13.

JOURNEY TO GORMUND,
RIO 6 FOR THE ROAD

I fear – and so console myself, as it is still early in the morning, and my stack of ELCO foolscap with the Brunsleben watermark remains essentially untouched, with a Danneman Sumatra Espada, Havana short filler, fresh as on the day of purchase thanks to its foil wrapper, *the silver arrow* as it is commonly known, and my second cousin, Johann Caspar Brenner, will not begrudge me this foray into the competition, even less so as true gourmandise is inconceivable except through comparison; it astonishes me how little the Mandi Angin wrapper from the Klumpang plantation in Indonesia contributes to the Danneman filler as against the Brenner Habasuma, maybe it is a touch more metallic, yes, in brief – I fear, and moreover regret that no order will be imposed on these tobacco leaves running from *viso* to *volado,* for yesterday was the first hot August day, though still with a stretched taffeta sky of a Julian blue – Swiss National Day, I will get to that later – a grain-laden, corn-pregnant day of the kind where earth blows on us from all round, and in the bright zenith something of the rage of the reaping archangel is palpable, no wonder the verse "Never lonelier than in August" is now a commonplace, the red and yellow fires, hour of plenitude in the fields, the sun blazed down with leonine might, the side streets of the little cities of the Aargau, medieval, vaguely brooding, were packed, perhaps because it was Saturday, the convertibles wheeled out, polished to a high glow, shopping baskets were filled with mineral water, cider, and bottled beer, the world was new and shiny like a toy, a vegetal seduction emanated from the glances of the women in their flimsy fabrics, but in his late period at Brunsleben, Hermann Arbogast Brenner can confidently let that pass without getting heated, the swimming pools were full and festive, the mopeds wedged in one over the other, this sculpturesque assortment of scrap metal in the park bespeaks the youth stampede, air temperature thirty-two degrees, water twenty-four, slight breeze from the northeast, the family cabins a leaden blue, and on the distant horizon, beach huts turned toward the bottle-green Baltic sea, the tops of parasols spinning white-red-white, *Melkfett* and *ambre solaire,* refreshment stands, the fire red of a sugared strawberry beckoning from summer at Menzenmang, the fine prickle of Kontiki popsicles on the tongue, delicacies from the kiosk in the blackish-brown bathing house by the graveyard and the Rösli hut across the Wyna dam: all this must be told, for behind every chew of Bazooka lies the ur-gum, which must be dislodged with an archaeologist's care.

Item, the day began with a mood as on the eve of festivities with the post, brought by Bruns's own PTT autocrat, Surleuly, counter clerk and letter carrier all wrapped up in one, not to mention mayor of this municipality of three hundred souls, he slips it into the mailbox around 9:00 AM under the awning between the doors to the stall and to the house, both of a mauve color gone dark with the decades; the shade appears unnatural at first on the wood, but it matches precisely the patina of the shutters of the great hall of this old ministerial dwelling that rises high over the vessel-shaped courtyard; among the newspapers and flyers was a citron-yellow envelope with the red seal of the abbot Gerold Haimb: The poetess Irlande von Elbstein-Bruyère invites you to afternoon tea in Gormund, Bert May will be among the attendees, Hombre the butler will set the table over the graveled half-rondell alongside the wall of Virginia creeper, if the Azores High holds out, as it shall, we can stay outside late into the summer evening, and this gives a special splendor to the August day, which harbors already a whiff of September; the castle lord, the Emeritus, the politician, my companion Jérôme von Castelmur-Bondo, should be able to agree ad hoc to this invitation to a tea-à-tea, his calendar is hardly packed with obligations, I may go, so long as he does not require my services as private secretary, and on weekends, this happens quite rarely, I will use the rotary phone in the cloister room on the ground floor with the green tile stove and the sunken Biedermeyer window niches to see if I have carte blanche to accept this petition from Gormund. Custom dictates I or Amorose must clean the courtyard, I got at it early, just after sunup, with a broom, later, after a breakfast of ham, eggs, and coffee, I took the trash bags to the dumpsite behind the croquet court, and as the heat rose up, I stood a while in the canyon-cool emptiness of the leaf-strewn path in the shadows of the beeches and chestnuts to the left and right running from the driveway to the Hapsburg Forest, rising up here were the walls of Dogger and fissured Malm limestone, exposed as though for pedagogical purposes; over this former moat, the rubblework walls of the three nineteenth-century Italianate garden terraces ascend, and on the highest, very narrow promenade along the wall, bordered with berries and privets, lies the foot of the sturdy keep, the conical roof of which blends seamlessly into the main building; a faded waymark, once the corn yellow of the postal service, reveals our altitude, five hundred forty-three meters above sea level, and the walking directions to Brugg via Birrli-Löpfen and Leonzburg-Combray, one more reason, on a day that threatens to turn to a furnace, to choose this twenty- or thirty-foot-wide ravine – to the south of the Aare, a geological oddity in and of itself – where the Jura damp never quite evaporates, as a preamble to Gormund, to let the bitterness of the Chaistenberg take hold, to immerse oneself, because one is unaccustomed to taking the marked route, at the ostensible peak of two excursions, in the desolation of the molasse valleys, which swells with the summer heat, not with the proverbial black bile, but with the melancholy of the morels not seldom to be found there.

Amorose has not yet donned his white livery, preferring a brightly speckled apron – as if decked out for a grand finale – for the preparation of a cold soup, he announces around midday there are no objections to my traveling to Gormund, the lord of the castle has not yet finished his reading of Kleist, naturally it will be necessary to note a few things down, especially concerning the feud between Kleist and Goethe, at any rate, they were expecting at midafternoon the *arrivée* of the former ambassador Jean de Rham, who ten years ago had researched the significance of Switzerland's neutrality in the Second World War, in the open windows, Jérôme von Castelmur-Bondo can be seen in the knights' hall working away at his family history, manic the way he drew from this document and that, please greet Frau Irlande – the witch! – on his behalf, and Bert May, too, they shouldn't be strangers here at Brunsleben, all this Amorose tells me in his broken German with its bits of French, which reminds me of the magicians' *conférence* and those wonder-workers who mangle their pronunciation, knowing this is yet another way to lead their spectators astray. Off I drive around three-thirty to the Freiamt in my spanking new lustrous Ferrari 328 GTS, leaving Leonzburg-Combray behind me, the castle to my west. A cancer, hyper-susceptible to mood shifts of all kinds, I owe an explanation to the indulgent reader of the present tobacco leaves if I mention the desolation of the valley – what that might mean, no matter – as I take a brief pause to light up a Rio 6 for the road. Just as Bregaglia seems to hurry toward Italy, so the Aargau has a natural inclination toward the Federal Republic, intuitively the motive may lie in its many north-south tributaries, the Bünz, the Aabach, the Wyna, the Suhre, all of which flow into the Aare, joining the Reuss in Turgi and flowing on toward the Rhine. The Aargau is the only canton that borders both the Swiss interior and its much larger neighbor. Whoever grows up in Menzenmang, Beinwil, Muri, or Zofingen will yearn his whole life long for Aarau; the natives of the canton capital dream of Bern, Basel, or Zurich; and those from Bern, Basel, or Zurich feel the pull of the immense conurbations of West Germany. Yet no sooner has he emigrated than the boy from Muri or Zofingen is seized with nostalgia for the molasse ravines, the furrows of the southern valleys like the convolutions of a brain. If you sit a while in these hollows, a sort of storm front starts to form, a tension between the cumulous precipitation of the longing for home and the cirrus proliferation of the need to be elsewhere, this is what I mean by the desolation of the valley, which drives you to leave home on a hot afternoon in Menzenmang and drink a beer on the Lindenplatz in Reinach, full of envy for every WSB customer traveling toward Aargau with his suitcase, but only because, in the same breath – to wit, of the Rio 6 – you see yourself getting off again at the Menzenmang-Burg terminus. This molasse melancholy backs up for the first time at the explosives factory in Dottikon, the terrace over the Bünz Valley has completely leveled out, the water runnels descend from Lindenberg; the oblong basins, former proglacial lakes, offer a striking image to the wanderer out for a stroll from, say, Boswil over the mountain meadows toward Buttwil and Geltwil, which conjure up a landscape of sweeping lines and moraine ridges running parallel to the distant mountain ranges of the midlands, and when suddenly these longitudinal valleys stop, for example by Horw, and the prospect of the Ruess valley opens up – a tongue basin replenished after the ice age, in contrast with the flavio-glacial Würm stage deposits below Bremgarten – it is pure astonishment. Tschuppert compared Aargau to a closed hand – not to say a fist brandished against Bern – with the index finger, Freiamt, pointing toward the Swiss interior. The Michelskreuz Pass closes off the mountains like a barricade, at times the

Rigi rises swathed in darkness and spectrally close, of the Schwyz Alps you see nothing but a shimmer like silver foil. We have not yet mentioned the site of the monastery in Muri, the name likely goes back to the Roman settlement, its ruins discovered during the construction of the seven hundred twenty-five foot perimeter, the walls of which enclose the church, a sort of rotunda with three spires, as well as the four-story-high abbey, the convent house, and the inn. Founded in 1027, the cloister was suppressed in 1841, a politically significant year for the Swiss. Today, the abandoned cells and spacious halls house the Muri district school and the *Spittel,* a cloudy yellow mutant structure combining nursing home, madhouse, and hospital. To judge by its plasterwork, it took its inspiration from the nearby Fremo juice factory. Whenever I drive by it, I believe I can hear the walled-in cries.

These are some of the highlights we ought to keep in mind on the heavily trafficked highway route as we leave the go-kart track behind us near the stretch of outré-provincial oaken railroad ties from the time of the Südbahn imbroglio, overtaking a local Aarau-to-Muri push-pull line with a conspicuous mail car from the forties, before glimpsing the cheese wedge roof of Boswil's Old Church, one of the few architectural landmarks on the northern border of Irlande von Elbstein-Bruyère's domains. The church was profaned in 1913, leased, along with the parish house and the chapel of St. Odilo, to the painter Richard Arthur Nüscheler, who set up his studio in the nave and adorned the choir windows with glass fragments from Königsfeld, this first attempt by the muses to exorcise the necrotic spirit of this museum to God would result in the eventual sale of the property to the Boswil Old Church

Foundation, which converted the parish house into a residence for has-been figures from the worlds of visual art, music, and literature, a sort of companion piece to the Muri *Spittel*, and now these clinically depressed pajama dwellers dream their way off toward their *opera omnia* – O, Hermann Arbogast Brenner knows well what it means when the neurotransmitters cease to fire – roaming through the former high medieval church with the meter-thick Bering walls on a moraine hill in the Bünz lowlands. The church, whitewashed as a monument to tastelessness, and its brawny tower from the late fifteenth century, whose thick ashlar cornerstones seem rather to extort than to merely gird the rubblework masonry, has been thoroughly divested of its sacred adornments, looking, with its parquet floor, like a gymnasium devoted to high musical art. The slightly bowed galleries, the lancet windows, the narrow quatrefoils and lunettes adorning a ceiling somewhere between a squinch vault and a plafond, do nothing to dispel the germinating reminiscences of horizontal bars and pommel horses when, for example, Edmond de Mog's finely chiseled composition *Les Charmes de Lostorf* reverberates against the no less rocaille curlicues of Andreas Tschanet's stucco work in the choir. Irlande von Elbstein-Bruyère's factotum, one Hombre, often does double duty as orchestra minion, crouching in the vault of the sacristy in his lice-ridden tuxedo while these post-tonal enharmonic artifices of modulation resound against the acoustically antagonistic floor. The ominous Saint Odilo chapel, rebuilt around 1700 on the parish meadow, is a two-story ossuary where the Queen of Heaven once sat enthroned over purgatory on a cloud divan amid a throng of putti, the paint was a most lascivious salmon red and muffled ultramarine, now the bones are what catches your eye, screaming of typhus and pestilence.

True to the Hellweg rituals outlined in *The Handbook of German Superstition,* before passing Odilo's shrine, the altar of which – long since sold off – the prince-abbot Plazidus Zurlauben consecrated in 1781 to saints Odilo, Apollonia, and Ottilia, I always drop in at the Sternen in Boswil, where I tip back three shots of fire water in the name of Satan, the Antichrist, and the False Prophet, only then am I free to go to Gormund, but first, we must make our way out of the village where the narrow, arrow-straight road turns into a racetrack and the northern face of the Muri Abbey drifts ever nearer. It perhaps suffices to inform the indulgent reader in passing that this cloister, which broods tyrannically over Upper Freiamt on a terraced plateau sloping downward to the northeast, haughty in the August heat like a fata morgana rendered in stone, is an example of what we might call umbrella architecture, thanks to the effect of the towers, which measure thirty-two meters at the height of the unusually steep and slightly concave gables. The octagonal spires resemble wind-twisted pyramids, inevitably they remind me of Flying Robert in the *Struwwelpeter.* On top of that, a dome weighs down over the martyr's chapel between towers and transept, its octagonal tambour illuminated by no fewer than seven lunettes, the tented roof culminates in a two-stepped cone crowned with a ball, where a copper archangel, like the ornamental putti on a hand organ, blows his trumpet till the end of time, keeping the decimated remnants of the population, once clad in black habits, in a constant state of alarm.

Let us discard this ineffable Benedictine backdrop as we take the underpass and cross through the premises of the Muri marshland labor colony, which in the years of its foundation, just before the Second World War, so raised the hackles of the Grand Council. No relics remain of this erstwhile strife or this former outpost of Muri but the splintered boards of the Grimsel barracks – which resemble tobacco huts demolished in an earthquake – built for the accommodation of eighty ex-prisoners, and whom should I thank but Jérôme von Castelmur-Bondo for the record of the plea of an upright farmer who asked the State Council what evil the fine people of Freiamt had done to deserve a penal colony planted there in the middle of their wetlands, after much heated argument the *Freiamt Courier* declared the rhetoric and expert opinions had so drained the region that there was no more peatland in sight. This revitalization of the peat industry, this sanctuary for prisoners and physical and mental defectives or "difficult elements" in the words of the *Courier,* was seen as an affront to the healthy pursuit of private property as well as public sensibilities, a threat to the small landowner, whose little plot of peat provided him with wood and straw for the stables, and whoever failed to champion the sinking of federal funds into the Muri wetlands was suspected of antisocial tendencies. "Are we to rejoice at the arrival of these dozens of failures," Jérôme quoted, "whether through their own fault or the fault of others, who arrive here, bringing insecurity to our region, so women and children can no more walk alone to work through the peatlands?" A reporter for the *Aargau Daily* who covered the administration and the courts wrote on September 6, 1932: "Clear for action: yesterday the Grand Council smelled of swampland, and a fighting mood was in the air. The speaker who opposed the exploitation of the Muri wetlands transformed into a veritable Abraham a Sancta Clara as he railed against the political terrorism of the arrivistes. Not even Zarathustra enjoyed such a rapt audience. The clock had long since struck midnight. A whole troupe of speakers were yet to take the floor" – we find here an error of subject-verb agreement, shame on the proofreader of the time – "but their moment would never come, for the presiding committee avoided the issue." We will be forgiven for attempting in these tobacco leaves to give pride of place to the journalist's poetry, especially when it comes arrayed in verse, as in the following rhymes of an anonymous author printed in cursive under the title "The Old Moor of Bünz": *Old moor, once peaceful, there ye lay / A place where all we children played. / Where wind whipped birches, war breaks out, / The brown coal brings the bandits out. / They grin and fling their gleaming gold, / And 'fore we know, our moor is sold. / Says not a word throughout this strife, / Nor protests at th' end of its life. / But bids its heirs in their abjection / To labor for its resurrection.*

With exemplary concision, particularly in the apostrophes, the archaic *ye,* the omission of the subject in the penultimate phrase, the poem whips up the emotions; but strong personalities cast just as long a shadow as great events, and so what the Sunday poet so deeply yearned for in the early years of the labor colony came to pass through the work of my friend Irlande von Elbstein-Bruyère, on this August Saturday, which seems to have stretched taut in the heat, bringing to mind the nighttime splendors of the lakefront in Lucerne, of bottle rockets popping off with a hiss, of golden rain and bouquets of purple roses in the heavens. I will have to ask her again about Charly, the legionnaire of legend, whose accordion enchantments beguiled her in her far from easy girlhood no less than the white clown playing the concertina in the circus did me (later, the virtuoso Riemi Weber would have the same effect on Sylvester's Eve, or at the end of National Day at my grandparents' inn, the Waldau). You come to a stop at a crossroads, try to get your bearings amid the fields of ripe grain, turn off into the Hasli forest where my irrepressible fairytale mistress Kommanda capered, and as soon as you have left the dark treetrunks behind, you espy the ridged roof of Gormund. With its gables covered in Virginia creeper overlooking the park walls and the rows of apple trees and the window wreathed in twined and shady flowers, this country estate discloses to me, every time I drive up its gravel road, something of the enchantments of the garden of paradise: how it glows here with the residue of home, with its airs of the late Romantic, and the spell it casts on this side of Eden has grown painfully stronger since Menzenmang was lost. We park below the broad barn, before the gate where the farm machines, the harrows with forking hands, stand like disarticulated insects, rather whiling away the summer than waiting for their errands to begin; we pass the wayside cross and stop before a walkway flanked on both sides with climbing roses, it pierces the elongated, slightly bulbous fieldstone walls built atop a bank of dusty grass, comprising a terrain of around eighty acres on the morning, evening, and southern sides – this, along with the modest sandstone architrave, is the reason the manorial façade, lying in the shadows of the shade firs and locusts, is only partly visible from my perspective. The roofing tiles atop the outer walls remind one of a cottage in Brandenburg, but the jointwork is reminiscent of Brunsleben, and if I ask myself what it is that makes the Gormund landscape so forlorn, there emerges from the depths of the toddler's investigations in his parents' bedroom a painting hung to the left of the changing table that engrossed me in a way akin to the picture of grain fields at the Waldau: it showed a shrine, a crucifix under a gabled roof on a pastel-glowing knoll, the ochre street rose gently, topped the crest of the hill, and vanished past a slope of infinitely mournful grass. This out-of-doors *natura morta* made me cry, no need for a falling cadence of sixths – for the grey sky hung vast and heavy, and the pedestal stood aslant, and where – that was the agonizing question – to what country did this lane lead, to what aporia, a meadow of asphodels, perhaps? And there, where the footpath starts to the home of my friend, Irlande von Elbstein-Bruyère, I see a kindred monument to desolation, weathered, mute, silently marking two points of the compass, transfiguring the meadow into a hill of the dead. O isolated refuges of all saints, crosses of heathens and cholera, conciliation stones, sylvan chapels, columns, cairns, obelisks, pillars to Mary, brotherhood plinths, sacred birches, pedestals to the redeemer, crosses in the countryside, at forking roads, in fields, it is this statuary alone that makes the breadth of the landscape graspable, the solitary sovereignty of these INRI timbers, and I hear, quite far away, the murmur of the Ascension Day procession in Selben above the commons in Menzenmang.

14.

INTERIOR ARCHITECTURE OF MENZENMANG, MONTECRISTO NO. 2 TORPEDO

Whether crawling on all fours or walking upright, I no longer know; all I see is myself being freed from the elastic straps and lifted from the grated bed with its brass rings and fold-down railings, then a myriad of ground-level details mingled with the scent of floor wax and the stone-sweet coolness of the corridor. Except the architect, who surveys a building in need of renovation, none will come so close to the decorative moldings and doorstops, the thresholds and tile surfaces, as the child who sets forth like Columbus to discover nothing less than America, later, in the vanished children's book, which Klärli and Karli must have torn to shreds, came the full-page tableau of the abandoned brood who transformed the dark-paneled living room to an endless ocean. We must assume I drew on my under-the-Christmas-tree apprenticeship to build the vehicle from two sand-yellow Anker columns and a single rust-red beam that I would drive over every square inch of my parents' house in Menzenmang: here is the dining room in invulnerable *doble claro* brown, the wooden grate over the radiator below the window with the flower bed, you can park the car in the dark zone underneath the heater, its bent tubes become viaducts, and if you opened the barred doors with the sharp corners, you could squeeze in under the knob, this gives a reference point for my stature at the time, since Father never notched my centimetrical progress on a roof post down at the shed, what early pleasure, watching the goings on in the parlor without being observed. Here is the tile stove gleaming green with black gaps between the stubby hounds' feet splayed out beneath its weight, the *chouscht* as they called it, the heated bench where mother sits to do her knitting, she calls out tongue twisters and bids me repeat them, *I vish ye'd veaf me eh shtack of shtockings,* over and over I bumble, *vish ye'd veash* I say, the ball of twine, Schaffhauser wool, is a trove of secrets, now and then a mint or a chocolate square falls out from its rimples, later she told me Father would roll the skein up that way to make her handiwork less dull, in its depths was a tiny hot water bottle, all of this I see, quickened by the Montecriso No. 2, *no diffrent from if it vas yeshterday.*

A mishap occurs, no bloodshed, but I am made to swallow charcoal, because I have licked the bile green fence posts of the wooden Thurgovian village, you know how children just have to put everything into their mouth, the charcoal powder turned my tongue licorice black, my salvation happened in the kitchen, that's why it's so clear in my memory, because the sticky black flaps of the furnace were in the corner next to the door, the coal cellar, the scene of multitudinous nightmares, is the darkest of the house's dungeons, there, our parents can no longer protect us. In later summer the sooty journeymen come, park their truck by the garden gate, and schlepp their sacks to a shaft by the wooded stairway, the chunks tumble ton upon ton down a chute to the underworld, I overhear the word *anthracite,* which strikes me as no less exotic than *perspective,* the mere threat of being taken to the coal cellar would make me weak in the knees. When we fled underground and saw the flaming airplane in the window, there was war behind the soap blue door with its Z-brace, the coal porters had come from the war; in bed in the evening, I hear father fill the furnace, I wince, the shovel's scraping tells me the coal cellar is open, and the danger isn't banished till he mounts the stairs and shuts the door in the corridor. Once, in a dream — or was it at the Waldau? — a witch with pigtails and a rumpled face came creeping out of the opening in the stove. Shudders. Considering the outsized role such spectral women would play in my life — the worst of the nightmares didn't come till after Amden — the indulgent reader will grasp the importance to Hermann Arbogast Brenner of retracing the physiognomy of the doddering females he encountered as a boy. Why the pigtails? Well, there was, between the post office and the WSB train station, a paper shop owned by the Merz sisters that looked out onto the main road, and these two old ladies, the spitting image of one another, did wear their hair tied in pigtails. The shop was the epitome of a forgotten provincial stationers, with last year's bestsellers and birthday and condolence cards napping away the afternoon. Even when the doorbell has rung, everything stays still until you hear the precentor start to shift, in her way, she brought to mind a harbinger of death, chatting with herself in the stairwell; before she served you, she used to always push aside a stack of cardboard boxes, toppling them, maybe, to sweeten the wait for little Hermann Arbogast, who remained there holding his mother's hand; at the Merz shop you waited for hours, and that was what the decals were for, those garish bouquets of flowers and childhood idylls recalling Ludwig Richter, they stuck to your hand miraculously, and later, as a student, someone told me the pilgrim's dilemma: to get to Rome, he must rely on the aid of two sisters, one of whom always lied, while the other always told the truth, but he didn't know which was which, this inevitably made me think of the two saleswomen, one of them, Jordibeth, seemed not to be there at all, she would emerge unpunctually amid her dominion of envelopes, notebooks, carnets, and letter boxes, a Siamese cat on her hunched back, and ask what you wanted in a cracking, nasal voice, fiddling incessantly with her merchant's utensils, for me she was the very archetype of a witch. I will allow myself a deep draw on the Montecristo, sliding the label down to mark off the final third, which you are wise to lay aside to let the cigar die a natural death.

Here is the staircase in Menzenmang, the violet whitewash, the shaft where later, in dreams, phantom dogs and corn spirits would creep, the nickel-plated stair rods with their screw-off fittings delight me, in the banister are tiny locked wooden doors that deliver me to the sylvan root kingdom, what I like best is to crawl on the landing five steps before the upstairs hallway, this is my childhood dwelling, I place a bed, table, chair, and lamp there, it offers the best view, partaking at once of the house's upper and lower floors, for us, what differentiates them is that Mother reigns in the big kitchen, my cemetery-grandmother in the *kitchinet*. There are struggles for supremacy between these two realms that the child can cleverly exploit, an essential part of my early years were the nights when the hall door stood open and Grandmother would tiptoe over to bring me a *tablit,* though this was forbidden, because I had already brushed my teeth, and later, Mother would complain she had heard perfectly well when the cabinet door *got pullt,* not only were many of the original boxes for my toys tucked in the green cupboards of the kitchenette, but also the blue-and-yellow striped Franck Aroma brand chicory, the slate blue Rupperswil sugar cubes, the Wenger egg noodles, Bienna 7 and Persil detergent, the glass with the sour candy from Uncle Herbert's store, sugared raspberries, garish glass cylinders, *breekets,* corrugated cookies, and the homemade caramel fudge that broke the ban on sweets and was smuggled on secret pathways to my room. The opportune moment was when the rasping of the coal shovel told me Father was in the cellar filling the oven, Mother would be sitting on the bench in the parlor and knitting, I could plead for sweets and they'd be none the wiser, *Auntie, ken I hef a goodie,* and what auntie could resist this call, the sweets were doubly sweet when licked at under the covers, too often my parents left me in the care of Ida Weber-Brenner: in the evenings, when they helped out with the service at the Waldau, the Saturdays and Sundays afterward, when they would sleep in till noon, I will have much to say later about the Côté de Dankensberg. Here, let me clarify provisionally how it came to be that my father's aunt became my grandmother. Otto and Ida Weber-Brenner, factory owners, proprietors of Weber & Heinz knitting works in Menzenmang, had no offspring of their own, and when my father started at the district school, they took him into their home and brought him up as their own. We were only tenants at the villa on the Sandstrasse, it belonged to my grandmother, at the end of each month I would take the rent, *de rint,* upstairs, the franc I got for my troubles would subsequently vanish into the slit in the oval metal cash box, which opened and closed when unlocked like a pair of jaws, the black emblem on it read *Bank of Menzenmang,* Aunt Ida was Menzenmang's empress, for this reason, the humble sectarian reserved for herself the prerogative of furnishing me with bonbons when I had only just brushed my teeth.

Here is her empire, the former loggia, a space little more than four meters square, situated over the vestibule at the end of the upstairs corridor, this landing done in the late post-*Gründerzeit* style at the top of the dusky cobalt violet staircase, inside there was room for a wardrobe, a table, two tabourets, a heating element and a washbasin, a drip tray, and a chafing dish, on the grating of the windowsill the fat geraniums gave off their strong scent, on the western, the windward side, you could see the upper gate, the chestnuts and sweetgums and the Waldau rising over their crowns, this tiny witch's workshop saw the birth of luscious artworks, from chicken noodle soup to the blackish-brown roast rabbit prepared once a year, while the fudge was prepared in Mother's kitchen, which also belonged to my grandmother, and in the Therma baking oven, the rows of caramel fudge turned yellowish gold and swelled into little dunes, here is the box beneath the table in the corner, where my treasures lie in a tattered tumult, the picture scroll with Buster's adventures, the stack of calendars for the blind, the book about alpine railways. Without the fat album where my father glued in my childhood drawings, proud of my development as an artist, dating each with his office stamp in permanent green or carmine red, it would be hard to express, in the language of the archaeology of the soul, what exactly it was that captivated me about this rowdy rascal in his sailor's suit – the antics certainly, cutting open the old man's mosquito net while he slept, I remember how it billowed over the bed like a balloon; slinging horseshoes over the fence, not just to bother the gardener, but actually to ding him in the head; the sudden substitution of a spiny cactus pad for a pillow; I always pick up Buster first, then the alpine railroads, then the calendar for the blind with a boy standing on a sap green hill amid blazing light, you could tell he was blind from the soft stitching around his eyes, his fate moved me, what if, I wondered, I had dead flaps instead of eyelids, what if my child's mind had been unable to stand my parents' bedroom, the entire house, on its head – but my grandmother consoled me, saying this boy would enter into the glory of God and be made to see again, a doubtful proposition if you believed the artist, who had placed the flaming halo behind the boy rather than in front of him. Of a distinct, because earthly allure were the tiny funicular compartments with their stairstepped windows, Braunwald, my grandmother said, she had apparently traveled all these routes, Wildhaus, Rigi, Pilatus – *de twain!* I used to shout over and over, so I was told, there again the symbol proves more magical than reality, for I no longer recall my mother pushing me to the WSB building to reverence my small-gauge idol, but I do see the placard before me with the stylized black locomotive, the customary warning against carelessly crossing the tracks, and perhaps, but only very faintly in the murk, the apparition of headlights between the foundry and the hosiery, where the train screeches left across the main road and steers its way to the station. Perhaps.

Conjectures built upon conjectures, sure to remain unpalatable to the indulgent reader despite my assurance that the principle of chance is no less in force in the blending room at Brenner & Sons, when the Java, Domingo, and Kentucky leaves tumble through forced air to aid the arcanum in penetrating the filler. It is essential that certain seasoning tobaccos, Besuki, for example, be avoided in cigars meant to convey an accent of Havana. Now and before, we have striven to impose a tolerable order upon the images that assail us. Hence the assertion by that writer who experimented with the blue and red bits of glass that however much the garden shifted, over the course of his game, from bright ruby red to frigid undersea blue, its essential traits remained immutable, and nothing betrays our character so much as selection and rejection. A good waiter could compose a taxonomy of the guest through his reflections on the one lady who opts for turbot and the other who prefers filet mignon. Adam Nautilus Rauch, my constant companion in the redaction of these tobacco leaves, has enjoined me to embrace economy, the *pars pro toto* approach, and has urged me to read Hans Boesch's *The Maelstrom,* masterly, he says. And how. But the masterly is the very thing that cannot interest us, who proceed from a blank page with no sort of perfection in view, even less is the critics' and connoisseurs' notorious *and how* of any use, because in essence, no scribbler can learn from another. Otto F. Walter's childhood is Otto F.

Walter's alone, we should only listen attentively were Adam Nautilus Rauch to compare us to Hermann Arbogast Brenner, and yet, this would be naturally asking too much, how can the critic, who must struggle with the fine points of valuation, establish a scale of measure for a thing he cannot know – and therein lies the futility of dialogue with literary experts, which I have always sought out passionately; we writers must achieve what they think impossible, between us stands an unbreachable wall, if only of glass. Creation demands the solution of a problem with three variables, X is the plot, Y the material, and Z the definitive form, and their functions remain vague, for it is not yet known whether X determines Y and Y determines Z, it could just as well be Z that discloses Y, and the same may hold for Y and X. The critic, in contrast, has only one variable, let us call it judgment, J, and his struggle with the book – how they love this grandiloquent, heroic description of their readings – amounts to nothing more than deriving J from X, Y, and Z, to saying, for example, the form is incommensurate with the plot, or Y has given X away.

Here is a gloomy room on a rainy midday, my cousin Ursula is inside riding her tricycle, the weeping knots in the wood peer down from the panels in the sideboard, my parents, my godfather, and his wife are having their coffee on the upper floor; I have no such conveyance of my own, I too want to trace out circles there on the madder lake red *trampivelo* with the enamel stripe; I beg, I moan, but the girl in her buttoned-up overcoat zips on past the window, over and over, faster and faster. An architectural distinction of this kind is unheard of at Menzenmang, a playspace sheltered from the wind and rain, there is no stopping the fevered pilot Ursula without stepping directly into her path, an accident happens, a hue and cry, skinned knee, grazed elbow, now the tricycle is mine, I have won it, in the interim my cousin runs upstairs to tattle, a shape appears in the veil of rain falling over the garden, before I can mount the pedals, it strides up to the French doors, a gigantic man in a long, transparent robe, right away I know it is Saint Peter, and I leave the *trampivelo* standing there, I want to run, but can't, my shoes have turned to lead as in my witch-dreams and are moreover covered in mud, Peter glides slowly toward the house, his gaze is piercing, two glowing coals transfix me, he passes through the glass like air, stands in the room in his redeemer's sandals, arms outstretched, what does he want, the rain is pounding, Except ye be converted, and become as little children, the apparition is agonizingly slow and inconclusive, I try and speak, say Peter, yes, you're Peter, and the vision is dispelled, I have to tell my parents, it was Peter, I say in the living room, where Ursula sits on my father's knee, head pressed into his chest, and my godfather, the theologian, parish priest in Grabs in those days – there was an abandoned spinning mill on the ground floor of the parish house – couldn't believe it. Even now this astonishes me to no end, he simply shook his head and laughed, he didn't even punish me for hurting his daughter, and then I heard for the first time the words that would later narcotize me time and again: "What an original boy he is." My mother never uttered them, if anyone made a scene, most times she would just stare mutely at the table, now was no different, her eyes wandered wearily over the Meissen coffee cups and saucers, We've got plum cake, with those words she tried to redeem the embarrassment of the three-year-old cheroot in the parish house claiming he'd been visited by Saint Peter.

In June of 1985, when Klärli, Kari, and Hermann Arbogast Brenner were despoiling Menzenmang to prepare for its orderly transfer to its soon-to-be owners, the Gavertschi coffin makers, I came, by chance, during the liquidation of the attic, upon the engraving that must have inspired my hallucination in Grabs, the picture, unseen for decades, used to hang over my grandmother's bed, always covered with a bright yellow duvet in the daytime, it showed Jesus on a stone with the grass-eating children approaching him, yes, and the disciples stood amid the treetrunks in long, flowing togas, one among them had a dark beard and an especially sinister stare, this was he, it came to me, my Saint Peter from the workshop in Grabs, the print had touched me, and was clearly not incidental to my early ambition of becoming a priest. Outside in the gravel lot where we used to shake the sleeping maybugs from the maple lately felled, the wagon was waiting to be loaded with my belongings, all of them useless, like this illustration of a scene from the Bible, mementos fleeting like the volatile oils of a cigar, and now, as I write this sentence, my noble Montecristo No. 2 torpedo has burned down, and again I end this *gavilla* with the sense that nothing essential has been said, we left Menzenmang as beggars, nameless passersby dug through the rubbish in the back of the moving van, one fished out an old lamp, another a shattered spinning wheel, they were mad for so-called antiques, *entiquities* my father would have said, we were given just a week to have the house emptied out and cleaned, that was the summer of eighty-five, which impacted my torment as the flesh of the gums impacts a molar's jutting roots, it must be extracted, cost what it may. We never hung a sign reading *No Begging* on the front door, my father was by nature generous and always had a little something for the wayward wanderer, but now he was no longer there to lend a hand to his brood, who were busy selling off all he had built, the yard lay unmowed like an abandoned field amid the rose beds, of which only a scattering of crippled stems remained.

15.

POCHHAMMER, PRINCE OF HELL
THE CIGARIER'S SAMPLE CASE

Climbing the twelve worn steps to the cool, mossy rock garden, former haunt of the abbots of the Muri cloister as well as the colonists and war internees, who used to spend their day's wages in the old Gormund Inn, you enter the domain where the imperishable Hombre does the honors. His name comes from *ombre,* the French for shadow, he is a shade plant, like *nicotiana tabacum,* and belongs to the family of mandrakes, belladonna, fellenwort, wolfberry, and boxthorn, he has a secret kinship to roots of all kinds employed in magic and the black arts. Bert May, whom I assume is still on his way from Castle Trunz in the Schiltal, will surely cite some pertinent passage in the *Handbook of German Superstitions.* Hombre is lord of the ground floor hunter's room, of the murk and must of the cellar, of the well house under Elf Hill, he is a dweller of the underworld, his habitus is less that of a butler like Amorose at Brunsleben than a factotum, and even then, the Latin phrase *fac totum,* does everything, is not quite adequate to this giant reminiscent of Kortschädel, for Hombre hardly carries out orders like a servile concierge, docility is not one of his virtues, nor did he ever attend a footmen's academy like Amorose in Blankenberg – if only – his masters depends entirely on his moods; perhaps this is somehow related to the proverbial hard-headedness of the colonists of the Muri wetlands, it is a sort of blessing to be assured Hombre's good graces, for otherwise, he will manhandle the porcelain like none other, his explosiveness cedes nothing to Umberer, my vassal at Starrkirch, only Frau Irlande can keep him in line, and *en guard,* if something offends his sensibilities, he'll go to the garden pantry and raise a racket of shattered crockery the likes of which you've never heard.

But today, in the same frayed monkey suit he dons to offer his assistance as orchestra lackey, Hombre steps forth from the darkness of the hallway on the ground floor, pungent of sweet molasses and incense, greets me with his beloved poem "O Valleys Wide, O Heights," receiving me as though I had never set foot here before, guides me around the Chinese plum tree ringed with pale pink and carmine red begonias, walks me past the precariously balanced stack of stones lying past the tall fir tree, and deposits me in the semicircular patch of gravel before the Virginia creeper on the southern façade, where bees buzz all around; and there, the lithesome Bert May, in his inevitable off-white summer suit, stands up from the swing to hail the Brunsleben guest with the words: "Never lonelier than in August…" I know, my dear man, this very verse will have occurred to you today, bright the lakes, the heavens mild, pure the fields that softly gleam, which suits the valley's desolation, but misses the mark, agriculturally, the wheat, the rye, the corn are still standing, you must have seen as much on the drive over, well, have a seat now, Frau Irlande will be back soon from her walk through the Bünz moor and the birch woods on the lazy little river, which would remind our dear friend Jérôme – *entre parenthèse*, how is he? – of Proust's Vivonne, and Edmond de Mog, too, you can hardly say this of the Schilt, which rushes past below my castle, nor of my Roos, if you will allow me to quote my own work; I am tempted to call it a water *chausée* in view of the sweep of the countryside, which is almost French; did you know, by the way, that the Wyna in your *Stumpenland* was tamed by polders in the days of the great floods in Reinach, *Schwirinen* they called them, already the court bulletin of 1606 attests to the variant *wyrinen* as meaning the planted surface of the landform and not the stopbank itself, the walls began under the Bären Bridge and extended down into Alzbach, practically every house near the river had its own patch of Schwiri, and the ownership of one implied the obligation to maintain it.

As always when Bert May strays into one of his excurses, I listen with fascination, for there is nothing at all he doesn't know, if I asked him right now about the mechanics of the pneumatic buffers on the Trans-Siberian Railroad, an answer wouldn't be long in coming, but the ice bucket on the table is a far stronger temptation, someone has slung, rather than laid, a few bottles of licorice-black Guinness inside, and with the heat, I can barely wait for this Nubian-brown, top-fermented brew with its mocha head foaming up visibly in the thick-walled tankards bearing the Gormund coat of arms, I realize, as I slip a pack of Toscanos – *stinkweeds* as they are called in *Anatomy of a Murder* – to the factotum, we must toast to our hostess Irlande von Elbstein-Bruyère before taking the first sip. Let's drink then, Bert May says in tacit accord, to the health of Our Lady of Elves and Moors, to her beloved Merlin, so deeply intertwined is she, like Melusina, with the elements that kobolds, nymphs, and dryads mean more to her than the spirits of the robotic age, especially Merlin, the archetypal sorcerer, house magician of Gormund, who traps everyone and everything in his spell. Cheers! Capital. Remember those famous words of hers, elves are the energy of the soul, if we take earth's benighted population as a whole, the frail heir of Trunz continued, who still grasps that the world is crossed by tracks of dreams, and man and beast and stone are one? So: what have you brought with you from the *Stumpenland?* Grateful my friend has steered the conversation onto paths that lead back to my grandfather, that he, the omniscient one, has thrown me a line, I open my Bordeaux-red sample case, a kind of pipe bag, only bigger, with leather loops to hold the cigars, a bequest from Hermann Brenner of the Waldau. First of all, just smell, this is a pan-tobacco aroma of all the varieties or family members, from the Brenner Export to the Huifkar to the Hoyo de Monterrey, from the Mocca wrapped in silver to the Bahía Export from Salvador, to be specific, from Cidade do Salvador da Bahía de Todos os Santos, city of the redeemer, more or less – it lies on the Bay of All Saints, the Mecca of raw tobacco merchants and producers, but I would no more recommend you a black *puro* at this hour than I would a glass of red before eating. The proper thing now would be a Maria Mancini, but they're no longer on the market, the meteorological conditions beg for something pale, *pajizo* or *amarillo,* try this, have a puff of a Schimmelpennig.

Bert May – and we must ask ourselves here earnestly, which one of us is recounting his tobacco past – would not be Bert May did he not respond: Schimmelpennick, you mean, Schimmelpenn*inck,* formerly Geurts & van Schuppen cigar manufacturers, founded in 1924, headquartered in Wageningen, Holland – but despite this, there is no helping him with the *cohiba* itself, as the Taino Indians designated the divine weed; he sniffs at my assortment, which spans all provinces, only to decline them and take from his pocket a sable box of Sobranie Black Russians with a gold border running around the edge, removing one of the harsh cigarettes, which look like they've been soaked in indigo, and pressing it between his lips. Do I chastise him now with that slogan created for my second cousin, Johann Caspar Brenner – *A cigarette's no luxury, cigars alone bring ecstasy?* – do I let the old religious hostilities flare up again, knowing how acidic the byproducts of this Balkan tobacco are, black paper or no, leaving the tar aside, the acidity alone is enough to cause catarrh in the lower respiratory tract? No, let us clothe our argument in literature, belletristic literature of a special sort, the only kind that agrees with Hermann Arbogast Brenner: May I remind you, dear Bert, of Harry Martinson's novel *The Road,* where the cigar maker Bolle complains around 1890 of the restlessness of the times, the turncoats going over to the side of cigarettes, a habit suited to fast living, one that doesn't cost too much, "and only then did tobacco use become an authentic vice, a slavish capitulation to hustle and bustle, to be found at every hour and on all sides," my choice for this late afternoon hour in midsummer, the mild Huifkar – technically speaking a torpedo, a sort of cousin to the Trabuco – demands a ritual capable of holding addiction at bay, but far be it from me to preach to the lord of Castle Trunz, after the debacle of Moral Re-Armament in my childhood, everything that reeks of messianism is a profound source of disgust.

So the conversation goes, and my quiet triumph is Hombre with his cigarillo coming down on my side, the bees' diligent humming in the Virginia creeper has given the day a slightly drowsy mood, and we will not conceal from the indulgent reader, who has followed along with us to Gormund and now waits, pulled into events as a kind of passive smoker, on Irlande von Elbstein-Bruyère to arrive, that the rondell where we are sitting, of 4/8 Comolli gravel in slate grey and blue, forms a sort of terrace tending southward on a gradient and flowing into the rows of apple trees, which are covered by the bushes apart from their pruned crowns draped in ivy, and as I grasp the silk band of the Huifkar, manufactured by Hamers & Co. in Oisterwyk, and remove it with the same care as in Jérôme von Castelmur-Bondo's garden, I try to orient myself to the flora, this is always an adventure, I recognize the lilac and the privet to the left, I recall that the man-high hazel hedges conceal fusoria on the far side, hawthorns and guelder roses surround the quaking aspen shimmering far into the blue sky, through its leaves drifts a soft frolicking wind from the northeast, which makes the heat almost comfortable, and I think of those Canadian giants in Menzen-mang, towering over the august hipped roof, to the right is an abun-dance of barberry with dark violet inflorescences, the blackthorns extend to the majestic standalone pines that draw the lightning, in their shade at one time were the rough-hewn benches and tables of the beer garden; the so-called bowling alley al fresco, a splintered lath platform where stone balls still thunder dully, lay on the east side of the house, and so here, beside the putti blowing flutes and ringed with nasturtiums, we really do feel the park's enchanted depths, we are linked to the French side, because the splashing of the fountains is audible echoing off the outer walls, and we know the English garden is further down below, that the *allée* and the meadow lie outside our line of sight, no matter, we are happy with the two rose bushes and the wild lilac in the back, their sky blue disclosing the depths of leonine August.

Now there is a minor commotion, with an air of storminess about it, Frau Irlande has arrived not with outspread arms and measured steps, but has returned from her walk through the Bünz Moor, blond braids undone, to ask for our help, Hombre is having another one of his days, this was the same as saying his restiveness was threatening to get out of hand. *Vat's got into him dish time,* Bert May asks, well, Irlande von Elbstein-Bruyère replies, in a fit he's tangled himself up in the hose under the black locusts, and now he's in the periwinkles stomping on it like a snake, he's too irritable now, there's no way he can do the watering, ach, he's got a good heart, but more and more often it seems *I jest kent manage him.* Bert and I join forces to free him from the hose, which is cracked and frayed from end to end, before his brute rage leads him to throw a boulder at the water tank, and since he goes on beserking, Bert opens the tap and brings him to his senses with a good dousing. The sight of this unwilling clown at the mercy of an inanimate object makes our hostess sink down in a deck chair with sweat pearling on her forehead, and a bit of time must pass before the Gormund poetess may be addressed, perhaps we should use these few minutes to mention her attire on this midsummer night, through a gossamer, translucent, white polka-dotted veil, the sea green and mauve accents of a Mantua gown are visible, along with knee-high stockings and golden, open-toed high heels, their filigree design a contrast to the heavy, wheaten gold of her hair, which Hombre is allowed to comb now and then, in his moments of glory.

Bert May says we must do something about that nightshade, in the meantime it is now half-past five, fine, three-quarters of an hour remain until Woldemar, Rex, and Czako arrive in Stechlin, where old Dubslav and Engelke will greet them on the ramp – incidentally, my dear Hermann, wasn't that a lovely idea of Fontane's, making the sick aloe, the one infected with flowering rush, *Botumus umbellatus,* the lord of the castle's favorite, but *item,* what I am trying to say is the following: we should relieve the clearly exhausted Frau Irlande of the burden of preparing dinner, it should be something light, a smorgasbord hardly fits with the character of Gormund, the former seat of the Muri abbots for me resembles the kind of *gentilhommière* where the French minor gentry of the nineteenth century whiled away their time, but for the love of God, which of these clodhoppers around here has the least idea of nouvelle cuisine? For my part, if I may, assuming Frau Irlande has not already made other arrangements, I wouldn't mind trout – that, dear Bert, is a specialty in Beinwil – there is a well-known fishery between Boswil and *Bäsebüüri* – Besenbüren – and if we phrase it to Hombre in the right way, I don't suppose he will refuse this mission. Besides, I add, I know a thing or two about preparing *truite au bleu,* I'd be happy to try my hand at playing chef de cuisine. My proposal does not meet with Frau Irlande's unmitigated approval, she nearly choked to death once on a fishbone, the thought of it still makes her gag; but the prospect of avoiding the kitchen for every second of our soiree – made ceremony now through the tolling bells of the Catholic church in Aristau – has helped her regain her composure, as if she were transformed back into Lilith before our eyes. That she too reaches for a cigarette, a Laurens Orient, we would gladly have overlooked.

As Hombre, requisite net in hand, sets off toward the forest on his army-issue bicycle, Bert May, after reiterated pleas from all round, is compelled to take a manuscript from his handbag and read. Frau Irlande is a superb poet, but a no less attentive listener, for this reason, among others, she is eternally sought out by homeless spirits set on mortgaging themselves to Gormund. I, Hermann Arbogast Brenner, denied my career in tobacco production, am consigned to the role of dilettante in this trio; true, I am documenting my cheroot childhood, but free of all ambition of composing a literary work; at best, what I am cobbling together is a memoir of *nicotiana tabacum,* the first draft of a specialist's encyclopedia of my gathered memories. Bert May, on the other hand, is now reciting in a subdued tone an account of a prince of Hell that plumbs the deepest chasms of the earth, of a man who holds the insanity of the world as a global system inside his skull, his name is Athanas Pochhammer and he leaves behind a sort of bequest for his follower at Castle Weisswasser in the high meadows of Besan, imagining this stone coffin is the ideal birthplace for his *summa philosophica;* as a consequence of his immortality, which neither physiology nor metaphysics can explain, Athanus, after his suicide, can observe his disciple's reading and predict and comment on each of his pathetic responses. This is one of those works that recall the devil's pact with Doctor Faustus, as Bert himself remarks, but in contrast to the compositions of Adrian Leverkühn, which are deemed capable of pouring a sniveling jubilation straight into the ear of God, its cryptically rhythmic prose is born under the iron law of paradoxical self-affirmation, a coldly calculating enthronement of Lucifer, with not a trace of the torridness of hell, recollecting the grave and grandiloquent labors of Poseidon on the ocean floor, Lucifer, the first-born, more perfect, more brilliant than his creator as he points toward that aeonal darkness that stood behind God when he gave shape to heaven and earth, for if not, the almighty would have despaired of that inspiration that granted him this most beautiful of all the angels, literally and with reference to the principle of becoming and those who could enter the book of seven seals only through the most unspeakable iniquity, the *hydra of despair,* how, in such conditions, seething in Gehenna's maws, could one formulate a philosophy of last words; if a *diabolus ex machina* has chewed through it beforehand, if a dead man has showered us in his contempt, how can one live in Weisswasser without living through Hühnerwasser, when, and Bert May must have intended this with a touch of self-irony, you are constantly reminded of the vanity of your merely *clever existence,* when your ego shrivels to a bloodless mollusk, when bare horror degenerates into a malignant tumor. In brief, the hint of a culmination comes when

Pochammer describes the transformation of Lucifer into Noctifer, with creation defiling the innocent and exalting the banal, and nothing is left to the universe but to go on spinning without end, with not a care for how many creatures must die because they were born, to cite the text verbatim, "I see the iron maul of a meat grinder sedately extruding a thick, red, skinless sausage," and this skinless sausage, Bert May says, is like the food of our salvation, Christ too was the son of Noctifer, when he spoke of his father, this was who he meant. The crabwalk of creation, its diminishment and draining off into non-existence, we can imagine only as collapsing in on us from all sides, like the mass grave of the universe folding over on itself, reduced to a Jupiter-like spinning top; annihilation, augured by Noctifer and brought about by Pochhammer, is the irreversible dialectical-historical progress from much to more and to still yet more and then to less and to nothing, it may be the birth of generations of descendants who will unleash the catastrophe when their great-great grandchildren have multiplied into boundlessness. This keyword, catastrophe, the author uses with reference to the elegant final solutions of the atomic age, admonishing the advocates of the peaceful use of nuclear power two years before Chernobyl, he knows quite well what the stakes are, in conclusion, Bert May says *nota bene,* and with this, it seems we have survived the reading.

I would certainly be remiss in my task as chronist or rapporteur of this scene in all its details if I failed to report what the Gormund *gentilhommière* as a whole and Frau Irlande in particular have to say about the Pochhammer papers, which were written, as the author stresses, in a single afternoon on the terrace of Castle Trunz. One thing seems certain to me, that the spirit of Noctifer, made manifest in this testamentary bequest of utter and complete annihilation, must have struck our lady friend, with her diametrically opposed, deeply lyrical nature, to the core; but unfortunately I cannot say, because it happens that Hombre, and with him our trout, has failed to appear during the half-hour or more the performance lasted, and if the culinary optimism of this summer evening is not to fall prey to Bert May's nihilism, someone must track down the fugitive factotum, and I, who else, am ordered away, for these true poets are insatiably savoring the oscillations of their prose and verse. I don't mind admitting this change of scene pleases me, a drive in the Ferrari is always agreeable, particularly if the weather fits the temperament of the convertible aficionado, naturally I restrain the thundering of the *cavallo rampante* from Maranello so the engine's roar will not disturb Frau Irlande and Bert amid their pondering – and taken literally, this is surely the aptest designation for it – on low profile tires, 205 mm. in the front, 225 in the back; off I creep, shifting straight into third at 1000 RPM. I would like very much to leave the Pochhammer colloquium behind me, drive off to Lucerne, promenade along Pilatusstrasse, dare to reminisce about the long-vanished botanical gardens, where we fourth-graders, after a listless field trip to Lake Lucerne and the obligatory history lesson, sat at the outside tables of the Rütli amid the palm trees over the lilac colored gravel, licked ice cream cones, and listened to a dreadful medley by the house violinist, and there it happened, Liliane, whom I had pretended to kiss as a prince in kindergarten to bring her six-year slumber to an end, smiled. Who was the recipient of that look, slightly puckered because she was chewing bubblegum, which glows pinkish red in my memory? Was it Schuggi, who could throw a tennis ball across the entire schoolhouse square? No, it was Hermann Arbogast, Mandü, as they called him. The luring smile was for me alone, for no one else in the world, for me, and I drifted off in silent rapture. ·

16.

FRAU IRLANDE,
PARISIENNES OHNE

There lies the noble white box with the stripes, green, black, and orange, two gold bars, Laurens Orient – does Frau Irlande think of Charly as she tears back the silver foil to reach for a tightly packed Oriental cigarette? On a Saturday night, her homework done, the child would close the windows, latch the doors, and ceremonially smoke the single cigarette she was permitted, a Parisienne, oddly enough, a non-filter, the femme fatale of the tobacco world. It is the smoke alone that makes the landscape in the wallpaper become reality. She is waiting for Charly, the colonist, has fallen prey to a criminal, to his accordion art. How I would like to know, Frau Irlande, what his instrument looked like. Was it a Hohner, an Olympia, an Akkordia? With ruby-red mottles or mouse-grey stripes, what did the sound holes look like, were they volutes, agraffes, fragments of clefs? And the keys on the hand grip, were they mother of pearl, nicotine yellow, worn, veined in blue? How did

Charly pull open the bellows, how did he press the harp together, was it diatonic or chromatic, did it have black and white piano keys or buttons that sprang back automatically, and if so, did some of them have little cross-shaped grooves? What is Hermann Arbogast really asking, squinting through the cigar smoke like his grandfather at the Waldau? *Parisiennes Ohne* – unfiltered – that was the order of a young farm boy who came into the inn one very bright afternoon, and Olga or Elda or Imreli or Greta or Rösli slid open the glass-walled tobacco case and reached for that prismatic straw yellow box that embodied the wide world of Paris. It distinguished itself from Boston and Javana, from Turmac and Laurens, from every other brand with its high-rise shape, its square silver closure, which showed the goods packed tightly side by side as soon as you tore the foil from the corner, what a contrast between the brown of the crumbs and the white of the paper. Aunt Margrit with the gravelly sonorous voice and the blond hair in curls, the Greta Garbo of the Upper Wynental, used to smoke Parisennes Ohne in the Bertrand house, the filterless Parisiennes gave her that brittle she-wolf voice, she used to suck the blue haze deep into her lungs and breathe it out when she spoke, laughed, cursed, sang. By then, Grandfather Hermann was no longer alive, he died of esophageal cancer on September 20, 1943, and in the family photo album, dressed in a white soldier's uniform, he holds me in his left arm over his knee, his right index finger is raised, and there stands the historic phrase: *Ven ye ken tek de hill,* the hill meant the shortest route from Menzenmang to the Waldau, the grass path over Hans's hill and through the Röllis' farm, or the ruins of their burned-out stables, to be exact.

In South America, particularly Brazil, cigarettes were already popular in the eighteenth century, and seem to have spread from there to Spain. Casanova writes about them in a chapter of his memoirs devoted to his adventures in the land of grandees. We are told that one of his Spanish acquaintances rolls *cigarritos,* enveloping her tobacco in fine white paper. Cigarettes are rumored to have first been manufactured in France in 1844. It is possible that paper pipes, as they were once called, were discovered two times independently, or even more, such things have been observed repeatedly in the course of history. According to one tradition with a certain anecdotal charm, the cigarette owes its existence to a chance event that made a virtue of necessity. When Ibrahim Pasha (1789-1848), who rose from a poor tobacco sorter to viceroy of Egypt, laid siege to the fortress of Acre, he presented one of his artillery battalions with a considerable quantity of Kavala tobacco. The soldiers smoked it mixed with their Smyrna in the only water pipe left to them. When one day a Turkish projectile shattered it, a soldier looking for a solution espied the cartridge powder wrapped in paper cylinders and hit on the idea of rolling up their tobacco in strips of this very same paper. Allegedly this makeshift form of cigarette spread from Ibrahim Pasha's artillery to Turkey and southern Russia.

The cigarette penetrated through to northern Germany by a totally different route, accompanying the Spanish soldiers in 1807, as a contemporary report from the *Lübeck Gazette* states: "When the Spanish troops marched into our city, one saw the majority of the soldiers smoking tobacco rolled up in paper. For many reasons, the custom is highly pernicious. First of all, the smoke is too hot, second, too much of it enters the mouth, third, the smoke and heat are too close to the eyes, and fourth, the smoke of burning paper is extremely dangerous, doing inestimable harm to the lungs and eyes…" A few years later, a merchant from Hamburg, drawing on his long years of experience in Cuba, attempted to manufacture *cigarritos* wrapped in cornhusks and paper. He failed, the cigarette's hour had yet to come in Central and Western Europe. But after the Crimean War, the paper pipe seized half the world, and from then on, its triumph was unstoppable. The first German cigarette factory was founded in 1862 in Dresden, which until its destruction in the Second World War was the capital of the German cigarette industry. The first *cigarritos* the Austrian Tobacco Monopoly produced were so-called double cigarettes with two tips that had to be broken in half before smoking. Within a year, consumption rose from three to six million units. One of the first prominent cigarette smokers was Napoleon III. Smoking offered an ideal addiction and indulgence for his nervous, restless character. Just as Bismarck swore by his cigar and as the Lord of Friedrichsruhe reached eagerly for his Ulmer pipe, so the cigarette became the second French emperor's accessory *de rigueur*. It is pleasing to imagine these two antagonists in their essentially irreconcilable smoking postures: the ill-starred monarch frantically smoking one butt after another, and the impenetrable chancellor who loved to shroud himself in thick Havana smoke in the midst of negotiations.

Toward the end of the last century, the number of cigarette smokers kept rising, but there seemed to be little point in the Schlottmann and Havana fathers switching horses to join their sons swayed by fashion, cigar manufacture took on a whiff of the patriarchal, indeed, an entire chapter could be written about smoking behavior among fathers and sons, what fired the youth were the signs of a new vital sensibility, a protest against the values of their ancestors. The domestic cigar makers of the Wynental, bent over their old-fashioned work tables covered in leaves of Langkat and silk grey Vorstenland, saw the cigarette as the irruption of machinery into the tobacco workers' craft, and were no less unsettled by it than the weavers in Silesia or the Luddites in England. This was a profession in which, formerly, it had meant a promotion if, after a half-year's apprenticeship, an employee was permitted to roll a Donna Elvira. The year 1862 must be seen as historic, when the Russian cigarette manufacturer Joseph Huppmann opened a branch office in Dresden under the name "Laferme" and started up production with the help of manpower from the East. Though other cigarette makers would soon crop up in the region, houses like Jean Vouris, Sulima, and Georg A. Jasmatzi, reports from the National Tobacco Survey Commission state that even as late as 1887, no more than 187 million units were manufactured, a third of them for export. It took nearly a decade for the cigarette to make inroads into the broader population, and it did so thanks to the invention of machines capable of bulk manufacture, which represented a considerable reduction in cost for producers. There followed a period of intense competition among the various firms, with hitherto unseen outlays for advertising. This, in turn, led to the democratization of cigarettes. The tobacco historian Jacob Wolf writes in his book, *The German Cigarette Industry:* "Since work life has grown more hurried, pauses for enjoyment are shorter than ever, and hardly anyone has the spare time to devote to a cigar, which may take as much as twenty or thirty minutes to smoke. Contemporary smokers demand satisfaction quickly, and the cigarette is the answer. Moreover, contemporary habits have grown more refined, and many customers find the pipe or cigar too harsh or heavy, our nerves being different, more excitable than those of our forebears. Today what one likes is mildness, mellowness rather than heft, and to find these, we reach for the cigarette, the most readily tolerable way of enjoying *nicotiana tabacum*." The 187 million units produced in Germany in 1887 rose to 600 million in 1893 and eight billion in 1910, with 407 different firms employing some 14,500 workers. The tobacco used was exclusively from the Levant. Most of it came from Turkey, and was set apart from varieties grown elsewhere by its small, typically golden leaves, which were tender, with little veining. Its outstanding qualities included its sweetness and its ambrosia-like aroma. Before the First World War, the trade distinguished between two categories of product: from European and Asiatic Turkey. In quality terms, the first was better and more expensive. In European Turkey, tobacco was cultivated above all in Epirus, Thessaly, and Macedonia, the major export centers were Salonika, Kavalla, and Dedeğaç. No discussion of the most important plantations in Asiatic Turkey is complete without the Trabzon Vilayet, which includes the Samsun region and the municipalities of Bafra and Çarşamba, the southern foothills of the Taurus mountains, the coast of the Aegean sea and the Sea of Marmara; further away in Syria, in the coastlands of the Saïda Province, Latakia and Abu-Riha were grown, and then there was the Upper and Lower Koura in Lebanon. Smyrna,

Bursa, Trabzon, and Beirut were the major harbors. Yearly production over the entire Ottoman territory amounted to 40 million kilograms of brown gold.

Cultivation was and still is, for the most part, carried out as follows: sowing takes place in specially prepared hotbeds from the end of February to early March. In mild temperatures the seeds germinate in twenty to twenty-five days, but if it is cold, this can last from fifty to sixty. In May, the seedlings are transplanted to a well-tilled and richly manured field, with about ten centimeters between them. During harvest, from the end of June to the end of July, the leaves are picked, as everywhere in the world, in waves, from *viso* to *volado*. They are then mounted on cords to dry out in the open air. Around September they are taken to a covered tobacco cathedral where they remain until September, and then they spend a month under a press. Now begins the laborious work of sorting, with the farmers dividing their wares into two classes before packing them in bales, which the commissioner will then deliver to the wholesaler. Once the tobacco has changed hands from farmer to buyer, the latter undoes the bales in his warehouse and sorts it into four categories: Dubek, Maxoul, Sira-Pastal, and Refuse, of these Dubek is the first class, Maxoul the second, Sira-Pastal the third, and Refuse the fourth. Thus divided, it reaches the hands of the *dengçi*, who goes through it one last time, leaf by leaf, to eliminate the scraps. The bales are then repacked, and fermentation, zymosis, begins. The wholesaler must restack the bales frequently to keep the leaves from charring. In August, the tobacco is ready for shipping. Only the harvest from the previous year can be cleared for exportation. In Germany, Dresden was the main distribution center, the majority of vendors had offices there, though I do not know whether my grandfather, Hermann Brenner – and all the jargon employed above already belongs to his era – had any contacts in Saxony or Thuringia. Via Hamburg and Trieste, tobacco made its way through the whole of the German Reich. 4,248 tons were imported from European Turkey in 1911, another 2,344 from the Asian side. In 1910, the quantity of unworked raw tobacco housed in Dresden reached 4,448,338 kilograms. Manufacturers placed orders with wholesalers on the strength of samples delivered by traveling salesman, or else made their purchases on-site. The average price per kilo of Turkish raw tobacco on the wholesale market in those days was around two marks, not including import duties.

And so, when tobacco arrives to the producer, it is already prepared for manufacture, and the most important process, the blending, can proceed without delay. For reasons of taste, no smoke except the *puro* contains a single variety, and even then, several provinces contribute to the final product. The best producers rely on technicians, so-called master blenders, the compounding of the arcana being a procedure of utmost subtlety. These are generally Greek, and have grown up around the plant, and they fiddle, mix, shuffle, and taste until the blend is perfect. The leaves selected for the blend are piled up and sprayed with water, this is necessary to prevent them from crumbling to dust when they are chopped. The indispensable instrument, far more important than the knife, was the Greek cutting board, where the worker carefully laid the tobacco out lengthwise and held it taut with his knees. He would swing his knife back and forth while shifting the leaf along the surface. The Russian hand cutter from the fifties of the foregoing century marked a significant advance: an infinite screw fed the leaf automatically into a blade that swung up and down. By the First World War, this work was entirely in the hands of machines. The Ferdinand Flinsch model from Offenbach consisted of two main parts: a belt for the intake of tobacco and a slicer with rotating blades. The leaves were pressed and fed through a corrugated cylinder of cast iron and two grooved rollers. A crank handle could adjust the cut to as fine as ten millimeters.

The blade was manipulated with two levers that were only greased at the fulcrum, for hygienic reasons it was essential that the tobacco never come in contact with the oil. Adjustments could be made to account for wear and tear so the quality of the cut was unaffected. The corners of the machine's intake were rounded, and the cut was never perpendicular to the Uch-alti or Dip-üstü leaf, but instead set at an angle determined by experience. The steel fittings were attached to a special bronze plate, and could be repaired or replaced without the need of hauling the machine off to the workshop. If the worker overloaded it, the feed would freeze, thus avoiding clumping and breakdowns. It was essential not to force the tobacco through the machine, or else it would fray after cutting. The rollers pulled it in automatically and pressed it to the precise degree required for the cleanest cut. The knife had to be razor sharp at all times, so there was a sharpening machine in every cigarette factory. The process inevitably ground a certain percentage of the raw material into dust; as this could not under any circumstances wind up in the finished cigarette, the tobacco, once cut, was sifted in a drum composed of eight chambers lined with wire; dumped into a hopper, the product, once cleaned, would fall into a crate lying at the ready. The leftover dust, unfit for consumption, was sold to farmers as a fertilizer. Even this byproduct was purchased and taxed at full price. The manufacture of cigarettes requires not only the finest Macedonia and Kavala, but also the ever-dubious paper. Here, Hermann Arbogast Brenner pauses after treating himself to a Turmac, to reflect for a moment that this same substance – and not a folio of tobacco leaves per se – is the raw material fed into his typewriter; however much he struggles to dupe the indulgent reader into thinking what he is writing on is a *gavilla* from Vorstenland, the prose industry will never transcend the outmost layer of the cigarette, and so it is right that we pay tribute to the distinctive poetry of this most modern of all smoking habits.

At this, we will turn back to Frau Irlande's box of Orients lying on the table on the rondell in front of the wall of Virginia creeper buzzing with bees, delighting in the gold signet with the two stylized gamecocks, we verify their twenty-six milligrams of *goudron* and 1.3 milligrams of nicotine, we open the vault of the box top, see the red trademark, *fondée en* 1887, nervously crumple the foil paper sealing the aromas of the two rows of cigarettes, and help ourselves to one of these tightly packed marvels. The Orient the poetess von Elbstein-Bruyère squeezes in her ageless fingers throbs with arcana, in spirit we observe as it is harvested in stages, starting with the *dip-alti*, which corresponds to the sandleaves, then the *dip-üstü, Ana I, II*, and *III*, the *kovalama, outch-alti*, and *outch-ustu*, which grows at the same height as the *corona*. A connoisseur of cigarette culture – which we are not in the least –

would immediately distinguish the *gusto* of the various seasoning tobaccos, which must enter with the filler into a marriage of convenience, like a composer who shacks up with his housekeeper. Initially we taste the Bosphorus sweetness of the Turkish blond, which harmonizes ideally with the neutral, rather incense-like sharpness of the paper. In drinking terms, it is at least as bitter as the mocha lather of a Guinness, a sting of kif is perhaps detectable as well, touching our addictive predisposition such that the dying away of the first cigarette's impressions on the palate already harbors the desire for a second. We resist inhaling, as we have since our boyhood, that time when we went green and yellow in the face, instead the smoke hovers up in soft curls and lightly strokes our nose, through the scent organ it proceeds into the upper respiratory passages and then, brightly, into the brain, tanning it in this way like a pelt. When the kitchen work was done at my tobacco grandfather's inn, when the Waldau *Raumschnitzel* or *Poulet* had been served, my favorite aunt Ideli would sit down with a guest, a traveler, perhaps, still in her white apron, with a turban to protect her hair, and smoke a Laurens Orient – filtered – inimitably elegant as she squeezed the butt between her fingers and blew the smoke, lower lip bulging, up her face like a curtain, while the guest most likely asked to have something brought to him from the cigar cabinet, splurging even on a *chopsigarre,* perhaps.

The cigarette factories sourced paper of two types: sheets for hand-rolling and bobbins for machine production. The bobbins were placed on rollers and the paper unraveled in strips. At one time, the sheets were sent to a lithographic printer's, stamped with the company logo, and sometimes fitted with a cork or gold foil tip. The cutting was entrusted to a device invented by Karl Krause of Leipzig that featured mechanized precompression, in 1910 it cost around 3,855 marks. The workers then treated the precision-cut paper with glue and curled it around a bar into individual rolls. They inserted the tobacco in two ways, with paper cards and with a measuring tin. The contents were stuffed into a brass tube the same width as the cigarette, then pushed from there into the housing; for filter cigarettes, an empty space was left at one end. An experienced worker, a lady – cigarette rolling was generally women's work – could stuff a thousand cigarettes in seven hours, and needed another two hours to assemble the rolls. One of the first machines was the Durand, which performed the following functions independently: retrieving and stamping the rolling paper, gluing it and rolling it closed, shaping the tip, filling, smoothing, and sealing the cigarette, and packing it into the carton. The French tobacco monopoly was already employing one of these by the end of the eighteen fifties. Lebland, Abadie, and Decouflé would later produce similar models, in all cases, they functioned more or less as follows: the machine pulls a strip of paper from the bobbin and cuts it into tiny sheets. These are wrapped around a bar, turned, and glued, then pulled through a rubber ring that smoothes them out into finished housings. A revolving drum or step feeder brings these to the packing line. The chopped blend is deposited continually onto a leather belt and pressed between two molds to give the rod its final form. Then, just as with manual production, a pestle shoves this sculpted produce of the Orient into the prepared housing, and the cigarette is finished, a single machine could make up to 20,000 per day.

In May of 1881, Otto Bergsträsser filed his initial German patent for the first machine employing three conveyor belts to feed and roll tobacco. With this, he invented continuous production. His specifically German contraption soon reached America. Bonsack modified and perfected it and put it on display in Brussels in 1882. It had two shortcomings to begin with: first, it was only capable of producing unfiltered cigarettes, second, it could deliver twenty million a year at a time when annual consumption in Germany topped out at five million. Bonsack was forced to return to America a failure, only to see a countryman of his, a fellow by the name of Strouse, take his brainchild to all the countries of Europe. It was another twelve years before the Dresden cigarette firm Thessalia bought a test unit of the machine, this later came into the possession of Eckstein & Sons, who were still using it in 1903. Schilling & Brüning in Bremen acquired all the necessary patents, but in doing so, put the cart before the horse, because supply continued to outstrip demand. After the Bonsack, another machine with the same continuous operation, the Eliot, came on the market, like the Victor, the Hilal, the Calberla, it could turn out 90,000 units in ten hours, when two blades were mounted, output rose to 220,000 filterless cigarettes. Then there is my pocket roller, the Elwa Extra, German patent number 916302, a slightly bowed, stippled silver box filled with Van Nelle Halfzware – *demi fort*. When you push the cloth to the back, it forms a kind of satchel behind the roller, you lay a long hank of tobacco inside, place a JOB Bleu rolling paper behind it, moisten the gummy strip, close the top, and a finished cigarette pops out of the slot. This would have been the crown jewel of my boyhood treasures, to own such a thing as a Menzenmang street urchin. At Rohr, the tobacco shop on Zwischen den Toren in Aargau, I bought, along with the Van Nelle, one of those packs of Parisiennes Ohne the Greta Garbo of the Upper Wynental used to ask for at the Waldau: a prismatic bundle of silver and bright yellow, between citron and straw, F. J. Burrus, Boncourt, the emblem of lions rampant framing the family's coat of arms. *Les cigarettes Parisiennes carrées, de fabrication traditionnelle, sans filtre ni colle, sont faites de véritable Maryland, importé directement.* Maryland, in America, capital Annapolis, looking out toward the Atlantic Ocean, bordered by Pennsylvania, Delaware, and Virginia. Maryland, a cut tobacco used notably in the Luxembourg brand Maryland Cigarettes. The categories for harvesting are heavy leaf, thin leaf, seconds, ground leaf, and scrap, then there are ten further color gradations. *Nicotiana tabacum,* in this expression, is exclusively air-cured, the texture of the leaf is supple, the aroma mild and sweet. Packed in wooden crates weighing three to four hundred kilograms.

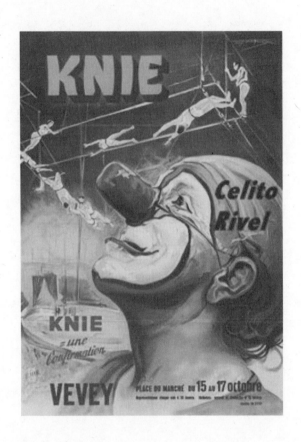

17.

BIRTH AND THE CIRCENSIAN,
HOYO DE MONTERREY DES DIEUX

It was not at my parents' home in Menzenmang, in the *Stumpenland,* where I first awoke from the chaos of myth and the muck of the divine, from the sepulcher of the universe, from the fiery rain of meteorites, the brackish, swampy wasteland where Ur breeds with Ur in Paleolithic lechery, thence to gaze upon the lights of this world, no, this happened elsewhere, in a completely separate realm, one that has held me under its spell my whole life long. Let us first try and get the scent, for as I learn, puff by puff, from the volatile oils and resin of my Hoyo de Monterrey Des Dieux, Flor Extrafina, from Vuelta Abajo in the province of Pinar del Río, it is those scents we track down in an animal manner that draw us into the deepest shafts of childhood, amber, ess bouquet, lavender, heliotrope, musk – not to mention, at least not for now, the kaleidoscopically exotic blend of aromatic spices in my cemetery-grandmother's kitchen cabinet, the musty rancidness of certain jam jars on the wine cellar's rotting shelves, the vapor of Zahn's flour soup on wash day, all these sorted scents from the colonies of my childhood spirit can only be imported to the present through a merger of Menzenmang with Brunsleben, of the villa in the Upper Wynental with the Stechlinesque Chaistenberg croft, just as the Sumatran Deli wrapper fuses with the Javanese Vorstenlanden binder, renowned for its dappled ash. I am straying into tobacconistics, but surely the indulgent reader will not blame me if I extend to him an open cedar box and tell him to help himself, let us join one another in a tobacco colloquium, of the kind Frederick William I, the Soldier King, was wont to hold in Castle Charlottenburg, and that lives on now in my conversations in the fumoir with my landlord, Jérôme von Castelmur-Bondo, when our words dissolve into the steely haze hovering over the alder-paneled ceiling.

At present, the Hoyo is glowing superbly, with no canoeing, that is always a sign the dilettante doesn't know what he's doing with his *puro,* the aroma is capital, a composite of manifold constituent aromas, magnesia, elephant urine, contortionist-perfume, clown makeup, and estrus of predatory beasts, an osphresiological symphony under the marquee, but no placard shows a market crier's potpourri of tiger mauls, white clown faces, and the teeterboard acrobats who seem always to come from Yugoslavia or Romania and bear the surname Cretus or Marinoff — the anticipatory pleasure of the whole thing bewilders me, the event itself, undoubtedly suffused with acute giddiness, as when an acrobat vaults over the audience, remains mired in that darkness I have dubbed mythological, for we all emerge from the mythos and strive to return there, immersed, the exception to this is the spectacle of the three jesters Célito, Rogelio, and Fofó. My life, which owing to an infaust diagnosis is drawing to a close at forty-six, was determined by three high Cs: the Cemeterian, the Cigaristic, and the Circensian. Reddish dim light reigns in the tent, it must have been a children's show in the wake of the war, I still remember the puling brood amid the raving madness of the swimming baths near the cemetery on the Angermatt in Menzenmang, the bitter reek of the arena wafts up high, on the highest bench, furthest back, flush with the right aisle, my father sits there, grimaces, turns his Menzo hat in his hand, looking up at him I cannot tell if he is laughing or crying, he runs his hand through his raven-black hair, slicked back with Canadoline, pats his thigh, gasps, giggles, and grins, and this fiesta-mimicry is at least as frightening to me as all that is unfolding in the circle lit by four floodlights glowing under orange tulle, where three marvelous beings are romping around a weather cabin, two with bulbous red noses and pants checked yellow and brown and a third who calls the shots, a glittering angel in baggy, frilly garb, with a white mask and white sugarloaf hat, his wondrous apparel glimmering all the way to his knee stockings, transforming from kingfisher blue to emerald green to cotton candy purple, depending on which way he turns, and he doesn't stride in his ballet flats, he dances pirouettes, holding an octagonal instrument adorned with ruby red flames, a concertina, it is called; you could say he's trying to play it, but the stupid Augusts keep cutting in and thwarting him, one of them has climbed onto the roof and is swiping at a butterfly with his net. But before he can catch it, the roof gives way, and he rolls from the door in a cloud of white dust, *shnow* my father shouts in my ear, *meteorology,* a word still present in its craggy ungraspability, then the incessantly beguiling concertina music rises up again, *shqueezebox,* Hermann, the insurance inspector, informs me, why is he playing the interpreter, I have grasped every bit of this, the ur-chromatics, the chameleon synthesis of harlequins, the accordion tremolo, the brandy-sweet colorplay of tones, the mother-of-pearl yearning, Father's sputtering was hardly able to disclose anything more, and I feel the tears come, tears of dry drunkenness, if you will, the white clown enthralls me to my very core. Here is the sound of the circus orchestra, its entire specificity encompassed by the capering Lipizzans, the trapeze artists in flight, the lions' roars, what refinement in the arrangement of these evergreens, now the clarinet leads the saxophone melody, as in Glenn Miller, butter-soft, now the trombones reverberate in unison over the percussionist's ur-forest rhythm, if you study the notes, the hard tones predominate, E major, B major, and C major, only the most circensian of all, *Oh! My Papa,* demands an A flat major, it may be that was what Célito, the white clown, played on the concertina, *Oh! My Papa,* the so-called *serenade.* Unlike smoking, which grows dreary in the darkness, so that even a true connoisseur, blindfolded, cannot tell a Sumatra from a Brazil, a circus band heard only on the radio forfeits not an ounce of its glamor, of its glitz and glissando glimmer, those accents so kitschy to ears inured to pageantry, but which to mine sound frankly divine, that trumpet-gold, artifactic-polyphonal, hymnal quality, in brief, and the music stands, spruced up with advent calendar glitter, contribute to the balsamic-seraphic epopoeia, to the saxophone-sexy virtuoso exploitative *crescendi* and *decrescendi* of this metallic melos, an Emperor's Artificial Nightingale, in a way, but with eleven heads instead of one.

And there the unprecedented occurs: my father, a Grock in the flesh, lost his hat, which fell through the wide gap between the foot boards, and he put me down and hurried down the steps to find it right as the floodlights dimmed and the clowns chased each other up the aisles with torches to perilous and ghastly effect. I must, in order properly to set this tremendous scene, light myself a Brenner Mocca, a classic cheroot from a silver bundle with a cardinal purple emblem, its packaging reminiscent of the giant jute bales from Langkat. My father was gone, no doubt, neither he nor his hat would be at lost and found, staff is not responsible for et cetera, the stomach of the immense predator prowling beneath the risers had swallowed him at the very moment Célito, Rogelio, and Fofó began their wild torch dance; they popped up amid the public now here, now there, the viewers raved, my hat has three corners, my father has gone into the circus's underworld, a subartistic pandemonium filled with chimeras, now one of them is right in front of me, no frilly smock, no blundering shoes, face painted with the same chalk the wolf inhaled to hoodwink the seven goats, ears pasted on with something like icing, a red dab of nose, white candy cane in his white glove, the hand vanished behind the spangled robe, when it came back it was empty, this silver bird had countless hands and all at once they grabbed me, heaved me high over the crowd, and hauled me down inside the funnel, where the fire dance in the meantime was coming to an end, in the tent's firmament the torches whirled, eyes of tango red, eucalyptus green, ischia blue. I didn't cry, didn't fidget, it was the most ordinary thing in the world, they would feed me to the tigers now, just as they had my father, and then the white clown sat me on a black horse with sky blue tack, a woman held me up, motley feathers covered her body, they tickled me – she looked like the Pfiffifix, but I would only find that out later, from a picture book, *Mineli and Stineli,* at the Waldau – on her arms shone golden bracelets, with the crack of a whip the Arabian hopped, and the circus spun faster and faster like a mad spinning top, the tin kind with the plunger, spraying Ceresit sparks all round, I caught sight of the curtain, purplish red blotched velvet, and now and then a pedestal for the elephants behind, it was black night at midday, and the woman squeezed me hard against her belly, squeeze, cry, press, I was skidding off the bobsled, hurtled through mazes large and small, a casualty of centrifugal shock, a hook from the left pelvic wall caught me in the liver, I shot through the Straight to the exit of the tunnel, first the Gunter Sachs, then the long left-leaning Martineau, at last the circus run-out, pressure 4.5 G, no bridles in hand to steer with, the Siorpaes tin coffin followed the racetrack blindly, shot under the overhang, yes, at last there was light, a clap on the bottom makes the infant exult at the bobsled baptism now behind him.

Of course, as a cigarier frankly oblivious to the novelist's bag of tricks, I have allowed myself to conflate my mother-birth and circus-birth, have given, in these leaves subject to countless fermentations, the fate of which is still unknown, a glimpse of the artificial to Hermann Arbogast Brenner, the floodlights, the tango red, ischia blue, and eucalyptus green, before he has seen the light of the world *tout court,* again

this may – isn't that right, Adam Nautilus – betray that awry understanding of the artistic I have gathered *en passant* as the not-quite-settled
companion of the lord of Brunsleben; abundant lessons I have learned
from the Emeritus's far-ranging excurses, but far more I confess, from
the anatomy of the cigar itself, which consists not only of filler, binder,
and wrapper, but of the pneuma that unites me to my ancestors and the
gods. An understanding of the artistic – what does that mean? Because
the arena is older than the world, the artistic outranks the bloody mess
of life, which is always contingent and never amenable to law. And if I
have declared that the determinants of my existence are the Cemeterian, the Cigaristic, and the Circensian, I must immediately add the
prestidigitarian and illusionistic, which may be adjoined as a fourth C
under the term of art *Comedy magic.* It is not true, though, that on the
morning of July 10, 1942, clear at first, then muggy, then roaring with
thunder and hailing here and there, I was brought into the world in the
midget car at the Circus Knie by a country doctor rustled up from the
audience and only weakly acquainted with gynecology, no, that cannot
have been, because everything suggestive of fairgrounds and showmen
was deeply foreign to my mother, and that family spectacle run by
Louis from the fourth generation and Fredy from the fifth, which was
still rather modest in those days, performed that day not in Reinach, but
in Biel. Nor, *hélas,* is it true that my mother died during birth, or that I
was raised by a governess, a *bonne* from the Latin lands, from Dijon or
even Paris – it *was* possible, my father *could have* met her during his
studies at the Académie Leger – and such a figure would have brought

an undreamt-of, speculative-erotic aspect to my games at Menzen-mang; the things I experienced holding my grandmother's calloused, gnarled hand would have come to me under the tutelage of a French-woman, and my existence, owing to this minor detail, would have taken an utterly different direction, especially if this *petite dame* in the redoubt of her mansard had smoked Parisiennes Ohne and had initiated me into tobacconistics with that brand with the citron yellow box and the silver strip on the upper edge; the heart flutters, surely the enchantment would not have ended with nicotine alone. Now, as my son Matthias likes to say: *eff only*.

Such a thing wasn't really in the cards for me, and it seems to me becoming of the thwarted tobacco maker to approach the happy times through byways, to deal with the bloody mess as sparingly as possible, and so I consult, with the aid of a light-equipped magnifying glass from the Eschenbach firm in Nuremburg, technical data 2.5 volts, .2 amperes, a shrunken photocopy of the *Aargau Daily* from Friday, July 10, 1942, vol. 96, subscription price 22 CHF – the very newspaper my mother likely leafed through to distract herself in the women's ward of the canton hospital in Aargau, if her inborn obsession with cleanliness didn't hinder her from bringing black printer's ink in contact with the white of her duvet. Did the mail-schlepper Hansueli, the postman in Menzenmang, slip it into the mail slot on the Sandstrasse for her along with the *Wynentaler* news and the *Neue Zürcher Zeitung,* de rigueur for members of – here it is again, that lovely genitive – the *fabri-kants* class? I can no longer say. On that same day, the USA recognized the military authority of Charles de Gaulle, the supreme command of the Wehrmacht reported without comment the annihilation of two hundred eighty-nine enemy tanks to the north and northwest of Oryol and the successful defense of a bridgehead on the Volkhov Front, which must be viewed in the context of Hitler's troops' penetration of a five-hundred-kilometer-wide stretch to the west of the Don; United Press International reported that in Turkey, former Foreign Minister Saracoğlu had replaced Prime Minister Inönü; Havas, ironically named after the king of the gutter press, the crookedest broadsheet of all time – thence the Swiss adage, *you're tellin eh Havash* – detailed a discussion between Roosevelt and the Chief of Naval Operations; in domestic news, the War Industry and Labor Office of the Federal Council was authorized – how ominous this word is! – to organize a handover of rubber tires and tubes, which tractor drivers, in particular, were hoarding; the citizens of Aargau were informed of the July 12 cantonal referendum on the financing of war and crisis measures, the levying of a cantonal surtax over federal defense contributions, and the freezing of the price of salt; a resourceful housewife gave advice in block letters on the virtues of sugar as a preservative; below the fold in the feuilleton section was the day's installment of A.J. Cronin's novel *Lady With Carnations;* in Buchs, Ernst Furrer, an eighty-five-year-old railway employee, died while unloading a handcart; in a poem printed in italics on the occasion of the local fair, local bard Gustav Meier wondered whether *all of us are children of paradise;* Radio Beromünster would be sending marching songs off into the ether; Wullschleger's lingerie shop in Hintere Vorstadt was advertising made-to-order corsets; and – cruel coincidence – my future children's home-cum-concentration camp in

Amden flogged itself as a health resort; according to a registry kept by the cemetery groundskeeper, there were seventeen burials and nineteen cremations in the second quarter of 1942; in the crossword puzzle, seven down, *I* in Italian, spelled backwards.

I have always been of the opinion that only the local is truly poetic, I could smoke a La Paz Sumatra Import and amuse myself for hours in this panopticon of the black arts, the *bon mot* "nothing is older than yesterday's news" becomes less and less mordant the further back you page in time, for Hermann Arbogast Brenner there is nothing more thrilling than to retrace what his parents may have read on the day of his birth, the story, for example, of the high-flown summer fair, that orgy of local patriotism, when "an expectant, festive mood suffused the venerable Telliring amid proud trees and colorful pennants," when Gellert's protégés, looking like button mushrooms in their snow-white garb, sent "The Heavens Are Telling" sonorously into the summer heights, the editor or journalist dubbed the midday catering "the feeding of the ten thousand," a violent storm toward evening drove "the older sort" from Schanzmatt, so we have a mix of the good and bad weather programs, which must have meant a changing of the flag on the tower of the Stadtkirche. In dialect, Vice-Mayor Eduard Frey-Wilson asked himself whether the young people gathered there would grow into a "valiant race" capable of conserving the Swiss spirit of yore, whether the strapping cadets would make able soldiers, of the Swiss maidens he simply pleaded that they "man the hearth" – a bit of transvestitism there – for their husbands, the looming war was described in meteorological terms, the phrase "to the last man" rang out. In his full fraternity uniform, flanked by two new pledges, Gustav Siebenmann, a boy from the canton school, spoke of labor in service to one's country with an address devoted to a certain *Schtineli,* the diminutive of Christine. Parochial-festive, then as now, Old Aarau in its pure state, while in Room 23 of the gynecological ward the suckling must have been in awe of the post-natal storm, this remains the favorite mood of nature for Hermann Arbogast Brenner, even at Brunsleben, where the clouds mass over the Chaistenberg and in the past year, lightning has struck the tenant cottage.

According to the family album, my mother dined that evening on trout. Eight pages of photos are devoted to the *great ocasion,* another typical spelling error of my father's; the bill from the Aargau hospital notes an advance payment from *unnamed* in the amount of CHF 100. *Unnamed* was my tobacco-grandfather from the Waldau, the innkeeper loved far and wide, the mushroom authority, hunter, angler, soldier, singer in the Frohsinn Men's Choir. A precipitate birth, delivered successfully at 6:00 AM, Hermann Arbogast Brenner was the first grandchild at the Waldau, and the flags flew not only in the capital at the local fair, but also from the balustrade of the schoolhouse in Burg, giving a feeling of home. If you caught the WSB in Leimbach and took the long stretch past the Reinach Moor, you would see the Swiss flag flapping in the storm. When a new citizen, a future man, is welcomed into the world, the custom in my home region is to fly the nation's colors; with a girl, the blue-and-white Aargau flag is good enough, perhaps in remembrance of the folk song *Et's two lovers en Aargau,* in which a boy, entering manhood, goes off in the fields to work whilst his darling stays true to the three stars and three waves that represent her native soil; the young lady may look forward to the charming Aargau folk costume, while the stiff fatigues await us men around age twenty, and all too often, the path from getting fitted for a green jacket and getting measured for a wooden suit is a short one. I can hardly expect the indulgent gourmet of the present tobacco leaves to grasp what might have come of me if my grandfather, who died at sixty-one on September 20, 1943, had lived to eighty-one instead, or if Mandi – here he is on September 23, 1942, the second to break away from this family of eight, on page thirty-two of the thick volume, *Three Generations at the Waldau* – had met Gertrud Emmy Pfendsack five years earlier. Why, O generations, could you not grant me the sorely needed advantage of a mere two hundred forty months, so I could take over the inn on the hill in front of the Stierenberg and the tobacco business, get hunting and fishing licenses of my own? Even if a pink line running from September 23, 1941 to July 10, 1942 shows that everything proceeded smoothly and according to schedule, there was never a chance for Hermann IV to escape his doom. On his deathbed, Grandfather's shares in Brenner & Brothers, the raw tobacco firm, went to Bertrand senior, while I was still lying fettered in my playpen, and in fifty-six, the inn was sold off, not long after *Mueti,* my grandmother Rosa Brenner-Suter, died. At the cadet's ball after squad formation on the Fluckmatt soccer field, where I forfeited right forward by stumbling into the penalty area while giving orders, I sat, a gangly stranger, in the dining room across from a woman I never dared to ask for a dance and smoked my North Pole filters.

I am still this same person in my late period at Brunsleben: a smoke-bellowing outsider, a failed tobacco vendor, dispossessed of Menzenmang in strict accordance with inheritance law; custodian of castle grounds, companion to Jérôme von Castelmur-Bondo, who didn't want an intellectual, but a robust gardener, someone who wouldn't demur when the cold congealed the heating oil and the furnace had to be hooked up to portable tanks, who wouldn't complain when lightning struck the rooftop studio and the green plasterwork crumbled in the entryway; but still, thanks to my tobacco pension, arranged by my second cousin, Johann Caspar Brenner, who manages the parent company in Pfeffikon, my livelihood is assured, and I can smoke the noblest leaves at my leisure, ruminating over my childhood in the *Stumpenland* in the knowledge that we may only undertake the search for lost time in earnest when our own hour has irrevocably struck.

ZWIEBACK HUG

18.

THE VANISHED PICTURE BOOK
TOBAJARA REALES BRASIL

Yesterday's weather report: still pleasant and hot, possible storms. The thermometer climbed to thirty degrees, the zero-degree line lay at four thousand meters. The Thursday afternoon satellite image of Europe, captured from a height of thirty-six thousand kilometers, shows a band of clouds stretching from Biscay over western France and from the North Sea over to Iceland. The nights are mild, and the weather frog from the Zurich daily paper advises me of a phenomenon very beautiful to observe when the skies are clear. There will be many shooting stars between the tenth and fourteenth of August. They belong to the Perseid meteor shower, which appears at this time every year. As Friday is a new moon, the nights will be relatively dark, and this circus arena of indigo blue taffeta is favorable to the radiance of heavenly bodies. A maximum of seventy shooting stars per day will be visible. Further developments: the westerlies sweeping across the northern hemisphere will continue to affect the southern edge of the Alps, bringing in warm to very warm air masses. The low-pressure trough will affect Switzerland sporadically, with an increased possibility of thunderstorms. In general, though, the weather will continue to be influenced by the Azores High as it expands toward Central Europe.

I chose to take my evening meal in the country inn at Böttstein Castle overseen by *patron* Torokoff, the rush had filled the terrace, so I opted for the dining room with chandeliers, a space of some hundred square meters with two windows overlooking the Aare and four glass doors leading to the garden. A lush arrangement of hortensias in yellow and blotting paper pink goes beautifully with the rocaille stucco above the windowpanes, this in turn lends a Mozartean tone to the nitrate-polished bric-a-brac of Maria Theresa lamps heavy with rhombi, quails, and teardrops, and the appliques with their three or five candles protruding from the whitewashed walls. After the *truite au bleu* with brown butter, I had a tomato salad with mozzarella and basil and, to accompany it, a half-bottle of Yvorne Clos de Rochay. With the cheese course, a Château de Fieuzal 1978, *grand cru classé*, then I quit the castle to smoke my Romeo y Julieta Cedros de Luxe in total silence in the Ebnet as I waited for the shooting stars to come. When the first luminous body arced across the southern sky, I wondered whether I should still wish for something, now that the three classic desiderata of love, health, and professional success all lay behind me. Was it not best to simply content myself with the view in the Ebnet from the bench at Castelmur? Andromeda and Cassiopeia in the east, Aquarius, Pegasus, and the Pisces, in the south the Altair with an apparent magnitude of

.89 and the rarely to be seen Sagittarius in the meridian; the shallow arc stretching elliptically through Capricorn, Sagittarius, and Scorpio; over in the southwest the few fixed points of Libra that remained visible. The band of the Milky Way began high in the southeast and tugged obliquely toward Aquila and Serpens. And there again whished a shooting star from the Perseid cluster. No, Hermann Arbogast Brenner would wish for nothing more than to come to grips with his childhood, with the heartward burning intarsia of his earliest years in Menzenmang.

And again I awaken, as I set the Tobjara Reales aglow, in a strange bed, in murderous pain, which pulls like stitching crosswise over my groin, like little daggers twisting in my stomach. In the lamplight I see my mother's weary face, a blue eye blazes over the door, two eternities pass before the nurse comes in with her starched bonnet on her head to pour a thimbleful of tea over the fiery desert in my throat, a few scant drops hit my hot tongue, the acme of hallucination now is a bottle of Orangina, I must already have known well the assortment of lemon fizzes in the cobweb-draped vaults of the Waldau cellar, I was given a choice as a little man on the mend and rejected the purple Virano, the Nubian-black Vivi Kola, and the seltzer-clear Eglisana in favor of the paunchy Orangina, best equipped, in my estimation, to bring the havoc in my lower abdomen to an end. When I groan, my mother turns toward me on the cot, glasses off, without them her eyelids look strangely like mussel shells, they are closed, she has a migraine, as she will in the middle Alps on Plän Vest later, or maybe that was all around the same time. I must possess this image in a definite form, and so I open the smallest of the family albums, in the hospital photo on the day of the *great ocasion* – yes, I will let my father's misspelling stand, the way he butchered words is dear to me – is a woman, pretty as a picture, one Gertrud Emmy Pfendsack, her eyes settle on the newborn with his fettered little mitts, the precipitate birth appears to have come off with no complications, just a slight snag with the preliminary contractions: Mama had, on the evening of July 9, 1942, made preserves from Schiltal cherries, nibbling on the fruit the whole time, and had mistaken the jabbing pains in her stomach for cramps, it wasn't easy in the middle of the war to scare up a taxi after midnight to take us – yes, I am already counting myself – from Aarau to the canton hospital.

Now we have checked in together again, this time at the local hospital in Menzenmang, and I awaken with the razorblades in my lower abdomen – already once, during the operation for an inguinal hernia, I awoke, frightened, from the anesthesia, and heard our neighbor, Doctor Axel Auer, a true lout of a male midwife, say: This one'll make a brave soldier. Then a damp cloth smothered me. No one can yet say whether Hermann Arbogast Brenner fulfilled this prophecy as a tank driver in winter recruits' school in the Thun barracks in 1962, though I, given the circumstances, always thought of myself as valiant when I had to stand sentry in Gantrisch while my comrades in their snow-packed fort peppered the mountains with ammunition from a G-13 cannon. After four hours' hiking in furs, with skis and a radio transmitter on my back, I reached the abandoned hut, the floor coated in white on account of its leaky shingles. In a rusty bathtub left as a testament to God knows what sanitary culture, I made a fire despite the lack of paper, drawing on my four years as a scout. But unfortunately, I was on the wrong side once the shooting began, and the Swiss army, in the form of a tank recruit class under the command of First Lieutenant Gläser, turned its sights on me, I heard a whistle as the first shell exploded, not over but inside me. It was the most dreadful second of my young life, knowing I was done for because some idiot behind a cannon was incapable of judging distances. As the shells felled the firs in the protected forest a hundred meters beneath the hut, I yelled into my radio to the command post: Are you out of your goddamn mind, who was that? Then came the voice of my corporal, Jenny from the Zürich Goldcoast: Brenner, you all right? Not at all, you dogs, my watch duty ends as of now. Who was that? Now our unit lieutenant intervened: Brenner? Well done. That was Recruit Wider, he was supposed to have it set to neutral. Lo and behold, I thought to myself, shivering – the fire had long since gone out – neutral Switzerland puts its own in danger because Recruit Wider, in the heat of combat, doesn't know how to control his weapon, this must be the screw-up of the week, here's what you get when our esteemed officers laugh the hick off the drill ground at the Stockhorn Front because he can't even manage a backward roll. Tank Commander Brenner, the lieutenant closed the discussion – promoting me, at least in name, from recruit to soldier – First Lieutenant Glaser will personally revise the distance settings on each of the artillery pieces. That put an end to any possible objections to the piping of the grenades, which fell according to program in the Gantrisch hollows and loosed avalanches of dust.

When day at last comes behind the long drapes, freeing the yellow wall of the single room in Menzenmang hospital from its former ashen tone, my mother leaves me, and I scream bloody murder, what holds for the new mother holds for the first-born son, too, neither should ever be asked to suffer a pain worse than the cruelty of childbirth, what comes now is a torment, a passion, a torture beyond compare, remaining even a single second alone in my room is unthinkable, there is a rotunda past my window in the garden of the clinic, the infirmary, it is sulfur yellow like the plaster on my walls, and the nurse rushes in, warns me my sutures will burst if I put up such a fuss, I don't care, and my mother can hear me all the way down by the school ground, she later reports, what a vile idea, stowing me, the only child, away in a private room, but how could my parents have guessed I would have suffered less, not more, in a dormitory with eight young patients. They only wanted to do right by you – how often have I heard that sentence, intended as an absolution of guilt, we meant well, that is what all well-bred people strive for, but in the abject fear of making a single mistake, they overlook the basic ground rules, for example: that distraction is the best remedy for homesickness.

But a visitor comes, and my grandmother removes from one of her unspeakable handbags – checked onion-soup-brown and cat-food-ochre – a red Märklin dining car that once belonged to my Uncle Hans on the ridge, along with three sections of straight track. When we went for a *saunter* to Aunt Klärli's, I always used it as a locomotive, because the five-axeled CS 65/13020 with the two pantographs and the bulging headlamp over the slitted grille remained sealed up in a cardboard box, *Bobeli* from the Sandstrasse, as I was known all round, could not yet be trusted with a machine of this kind, then there was the inscrutability of

Uncle Emil, *Emiu,* who shuffled into the parlor in his slippers, a Toscani Black stewing in the corner of his mouth, and swept away the entire railroad as he strode toward an instrument in a carved oak frame, muttering *vat's de berometer shay,* meteorology was all he seemed to care about, but here in the sickbed – and I take this lesson deeply to heart – a scar across the belly is also a warrant, and I am free to set up the cinnabar-red Mitropa carriage with the open doors and massive bogies on the dead-end track, to push it endlessly back and forth, I can still see the tiny brass handles, the sharp corners on the windows delight me, the stop-block, the slots for the accordion gangway, and my cemetery-grandmother outdoes herself from one visit to the next; however much my heart's longing for an Orangina goes unfulfilled, I get by in the afternoons on tea and a bit of Zwieback, the HUG packet on the nightstand holds me in its spell, in the medallion on the label framed elegantly in silver and matte black, a distinguished-looking gentleman looks at the far smaller oval of a miniature sleeve of HUG Zwieback and asks himself: How long does the series go on? For on that same miniature package, the same man is portrayed, he asks himself how long, and so on and so forth, the mirror effect reduplicated lessened the hours of waiting when I turned to face the infirmary rotunda, whence strained cries emerged now and again, the tortured protests of the patients, I would hear them again decades later as an inmate on the open ward, passing the barred windows of this freight yard of human refuse on my walks in the Friedmatt and in Königsfelden.

Here it is, then, the book, I relight the Tobajara, *charutos finos de alta qualidade,* Handmade in Brazil, a soft beige label framed in cinnabar green, it helps me forget the pains in my stitched belly and the grainy texture of the longing for home, *Edwin's Pretty Mama,* from the archives of Uncle Otto Weber-Brenner, time stops as I look to my heart's content at the bizarre kobolds and animals, a thin mist of dust rises through the sunbeams as I turn the pages, leaving behind a sweetish scent of dry wood shavings. The back-and-forth between hijinks and full-page tableaux leads me to think it was modeled on the Munich picture sheets, but the research I have embarked on at various stages of my adult life has turned up nothing conclusive. Do not fear, indulgent reader, Hermann Arbogast Brenner will not take up yet again his philippic against his rubbish-siblings: he knows the dazzling colors of the discovery on the floor beneath the hipped roof of the Menzenmang attic will wither with the first glance, that the mischief of the dwarf jumping onto the fisherman's plank, knocking the bearded man backwards and catching the silver-scaled perch in his hat held at the ready will never seem so clever as it did in the hours of childhood. Here is a black rubber Knorrli dancing out in a meadow, doing splits in the air like Rumpelstilskin – how nice, no one knows I'm here – but the two roosters have something else in mind, they peck at the kobold and pull him apart until his flesh-toned face is a distended oval, and when it hangs there in the grass, drawn out into a thread, they let him fall. How could a living being, even a contortionist, survive such a stretching? Here is the crookbacked peasant playing away on his bass fiddle in front of the carpenter's workshop, the carpenter glowers out the window and wonders how he can bring this racket to an end. In a pause, while the musician drains a filigreed tankard of beer, the philistine craftsman exchanges the bow for a handsaw, none the wiser, the gnarled man proceeds with his recital, saws off the instrument's body. Now he stands there, appalled, fingerboard and scroll in his left hand, the mangled resonance box rolling like a beetle's belly on the ground. Two things concern me here: the technique of presentation and the weight of inevitability in the unfolding of events. Not so much the moral content: certainly it moves me when the pair of love birds in the little cottage with the cozy fireplace leave the woodpecker knocking at their door in the rain, until finally the sopping wet solitaire twists the gutter into their chimney, the rush of water crashes out the door, and the two turtledoves watch all their happiness stream away, but I am more curious as to the interior, nothing is visible save a gaping hole, there is no fluffy nest like the one Father showed me when he pointed out the busy little damsel flying in and out of the pear tree. O eternal childhood question: what holds together the center of the world, what do you see when the accordion is torn open?

Naturally I destroyed one or two as a child, an old model, for example, because they forced me to take recorder lessons at Aunt Lili's house in Ölberg and I didn't get to learn the diatonic system with pretty Elvyra on the Waldaustrasse like my friend Peter Häggli-Brenner from Burg. No blind arches adorned the instrument in question, as on moody Riemi Weber's chromatic organ, how his crinkled parchment face contracted when he used to hear the glasses being washed, he had perfect pitch and found that impure F sharp a torment; no, it was a dusty, moth-eaten monstrosity, the cloth patterned with peacock eyes, the bellows leaked, the bass was wheezy, various mother of pearl buttons were worn away, others were stuck in droning ostinato tones. One morning I got a pair of scissors from Mother's sewing kit, or Father's office perhaps, dragged the wreck from the dark belly of my toy drawer in the buffet in the *doble claro* brown parlor, and cut it down the middle, I wore myself out in this work of destruction, but I wanted to know where the enchanting music came from, those howls, still divine even coming from this abject specimen, and when the two halves fell, one to each side, I saw: it came from nowhere; true, there were reeds with red rows of caps, and this explosive red seemed related, somehow, to the brilliant itineraries of Riemi Weber's mealy fingers as they wandered across the ivory keys, but still, this shabby wooden mesentery was the furthest thing from the android mechanisms inside a music box, and this squeezebox dissection on a rainy Sunday in a manufacturer's villa in Menzenmang set the mood for the miserable disappearance of my tobacco childhood in the ordered world of adults, who wished to keep me from becoming a country minstrel. On those sultry nights when the storm god stood at the southward-facing window of the den, staring into the fiery veins of lightning, Irlande von Elbstein-Bruyère fell prey to the colonist Charly, who played lumbering tangos and marches set to goosestep rhythms at Gormund, in the afternoons I would sit at the grainy grille of the radio cabinet in the living room and listen to folk music concerts, Scottish virtuosities, mordant skipping polkas, musette-sniveling, which brought me to tears, because it sounded like Lisa Tetzner's *Journey to Ostend* set to music – Ostend, this coastal refuge lay as many miles from my homeland as I, the petrified boy, lay from Father and Mother – it was then that I could taste my eventual exile on my tongue, the sale of the Waldau, because my pretty aunts had wearied of wasting away behind a stove, the first loss of Menzenmang, when I married and moved to Aarau, my expulsion from the paternal paradise; my family's move to Mörken in 1987, the fire sale of my parents' home two years earlier, my quasi-Margravian days at Brunsleben. Alas, instead of a tradesman, I have become a kind of minion, a professional colleague of Amorose and Hombre and Umberer in Starrkirch.

Here is the Elektromobil, the cream-colored landau with the cocky city dwellers in the front; in the middle of the street walks a dotty peasant lady and the wizened egg vendor, the auto honks and honks, but the two women won't step aside, a nasty way to cause a smashup; things go topsy turvy, the two bumpkins are now behind the wheel, and the elegant lady in her foppish finery stands alone in the dusty road, surrounded by a blessing of eggs. It seems to me that then – and this image belongs to the primeval images from my mythological past – that I was allowed to accompany Mother to the theater at the Hotel Sternen, where the tobacco agents from Bremen used to gather at the turn of the century, after arriving in one of the narrow-windowed baggage cars of the Wynentaler line, we were going to see *Samichlaus* – Santa Claus – and here is the green stretch of cloth with a hilltop street like the one from the vanished picture book and the painting of the wayside cross in my parents' bedroom, and – how he has managed it, I do not know – I see Saint Nicholas come down the path with a strand of eggs, the illusion is flawless, this is my first contact with the stage. Again, it is the ruses in the picture book that captivate the child in the district hospital, staring out at the yellow rotunda of the infirmary: the misadventure of an artist whose painting of a lass in a blood red kerchief so inflames the bull in the meadow that he charges at the canvas, and his snorting nostrils, his garlanded head appear over the peasant girl's clothes, here it is again, a game within a game, a picture in a picture, and I check the details of the figure in the portrait, seeing which ones reappear, for me, each apron string, each blouse button is indispensable, the naïve observer's brain agonizes over the complexities of naturalism and abstraction, the design on the HUG package, telescoping into infinity, demands an ever stricter simplification, but still, you know the black dot is the head, the little hook the hand, these symbols are dependable; but what technique do you resort to at the minute limits of representation, I try to imagine this grey zone, the Nirvana of appearances, the Bermuda triangle of dematerializing signs.

With bated breath, I await the full-page tableaux: here is Jonah and the whale. These particularly German pedagogical illustrations, diaphanous and dark as smoke, revolve around a single principle – when the cat is away, the mice will play – and here the children with their geriatric faces have transformed the duvet on their mother's bed into a pale fish, for the jaws they use the silverware case, the forks and knives for teeth, a full moon with puffy cheeks blows water through a hose into the room – just imagine a world where such things are permitted – and the youngest, whose scream will return to me later when I stand before Edvard Munch's painting, appears to be caught in the shark's fangs; most unsettling though is the narrow crack in the door, because through this gap, the night presses in, and the mother is standing just past it in a poison green Biedermeyer dress and looking in on the scene with feigned repulsion – outrageous, it is not the children, but a respectable adult here doing the snooping, why does she not intervene? The patient with the inguinal hernia learns something of the spiritual cruelty of German women when he creeps, where else, into Jonah's skin and spins out the horror of imprisonment further until his feathery asphyxiation. Hermann Arbogast Brenner no longer knows how his parents replied to the gnawing question of why it had to be the youngest boy; it was true he himself was oldest, but only because he had no siblings, and that evening, he must have included in his prayers: Dear Lord God, gentle Father in Heaven, please send me a little brother or sister, that he was there did not suffice to bring true happiness to his begetters on this earth, he alone could not make Mandi's and Gertrud's marriage a family.

Here, now, is the crowning tableau of the vanished picture book, the dark-paneled parlor transformed into a sea, once again in the absence of adults, for otherwise, how could they have dragged the zinc tub out onto the parquet, a broom stands in for a mainmast, the sailor boy crouches in a basket with his spyglass and stares into the storm, and on the headrest of the settee stands a proud, conquering captain, one foot stretched forward as if about to touch land, a red conductor's bag slung over his shoulder, and if I am not mistaken, and if the beatitude of memory is not piloting my pen, he is holding, in place of a helm, a spinning wheel in his hand, and the youngest – yet again – sits in a skiff that has drifted away, sheltered by an umbrella, manning the crank handle of a coffee mill of the kind my cemetery-grandmother used to hold between her knees in the *kitchinette,* letting me shake Jamaica-scented beans from Uncle Herbert's fund of colonial goods into the hopper, again the fine, crabbed wrinkles on the children's worried faces lend something bellicose to this sea-parlor tableau, I might call it the Imperator effect, after my Anker stone blocks, that deeply German thoroughness not even fantasy can escape. And here is the last page, torn, the wrecked golden carriage, like a tabernacle, with the Christmas child in a pink dress stranded in the brambles, the dwarves hurry over from the roadside to help out, get tangled up and bleed to death, what must the illustrator have had in his mind, sitting in Nuremburg or Munich or Bremen, when he chose to steer our imagination down such roads, how putrid, how scarred must his heart have been to hit on this gruesome combination of the Sleeping Beauty and the secret of Christmas, bringing the whole thing to grief in the Hell of the German fairytale forest? In any case, it was Uncle Otto, the builder of the house in Menzenmang, who bought the picture book on a work trip and brought it to young Mandi in the Wynental, it was waiting for me under the table in my cemetery-grandmother's kitchenette, along with Buster, the calendar for the blind, and the standard work on mountain railways, and before the latecomers could tear it to shreds, it marked Hermann Arbogast's imagination indelibly.

Here is the frogs' harvest festival and the nuptials of the rats, here a wanderer sits exhausted on a toadstool, which shoots up in the sky at night, and when he opens his eyes in wonderment, his legs are dangling over the abyss: this is just how perfidiously the world is arranged, the mushroom takes you hostage before you have time to blink; and as I trace back today in the courtyard of Castle Brunsleben, with the Brasil Import between my lips, the adventurous entanglements of long ago, the question arises whether the hand of the colorist seated where the Munich picture sheets were printed, or in the offices of the *Fliegende Blätter,* did not shape us more powerfully than our immediate superiors from the world of the old, than the bamboo rod of our teacher pointing at the ABCs. And here comes my Pretty Mama's great redemption, a birthday reception is prepared for me at home, on the little child's table in front of the flowerbed window, decked with a cloth for the occasion, the liter bottle of Orangina stands, more seductive than any beverage since, and next to it is a trumpet and a gingerbread house baked by mother, the panels are adorned with icing, Hansl and Gretl punched out to scale, a row of roof beams glows especially bright in memory; everything was correct, and yet all of it was meant to be eaten, Father laid me down on the wicker-bottomed sofa beneath a painting of this-tles in undersea green executed by Grandfather Pfendsack. The mirac-ulous rascal smuggles boxes into the parlor, drawing them from his jacket pockets like a magician: he assembles the tiny tracks of chocolate brown wood, connects a coal-black bakelite transformer, puts the red locomotive body over the wheel set from the tram, hooks up two pas-senger wagons and a slate grey gondola car with two little boxes of Ovaltine inside, flips the switch with pursed lips – do I not stand there like a *goddam fool* myself – and look, the Wesa Lilliput sets off on its maiden voyage, and the joy of surprise brings with it the higher school of renunciation of this sister brand of Märklin, the die is cast: no, I do not get the Buco HO, made of tin, with the wide gauge tracks that would have stretched out into the living room; not the king of brands from Göppingen with the hotly yearned for Krokodil; no, it was the small-gauge trainlet from Inkwil, which would bring the Apostolic church of the Wynentaler line into my childhood bedroom, and like all well-bred boys, I piously concealed my disappointment. But when my sons Hermann and Matthias came into the world, I pounced, and spent long afternoons in the Märklin section of the Hemmeler toy store in Hintere Vorstadt, in the lifesaving workshop of my friend, the literary critic Adam Nautilus Rauch. Except ye be converted, and become not as the fathers.

19.

TROUT DINNER IN GORMUND,
ROMEO Y JULIETA CHURCHILL

In the assorted pubs deemed possible hideouts for the absconded Hombre, I indulge abundantly in elderberry brandy, but we do not strike gold at the Bahnhöfli, the Löwen, the Rigiblick, or the Sternen in Boswil, none of the waitresses we speak with will admit to having served the onetime colonist or even laid eyes on him, so as I tip my glass at the bar, I must consider which is the most fruitful direction in which to broaden the radius of my search – or has the lech accepted an invitation proffered with batting eyelids to enjoy a torrid hour in some rooming house? To cut things short, I call Muri from the Rigiblick, ring up the Alpenzeiger, the Frohsinn, the Wartegg, and the Lindenberg. That I do not wish to make a dinner reservation, but am rather on the hunt for a trout-toting personage in a black tux, proves more and more vexing with each number I dial, and after the Adler makes clear to me that their *gueshts* are not in the habit of bringing along their own fish, they recommend me the recipe *à la mode du chef,* meunière with lemon and capers, flour-dusted, but lightly, or else the crisp brown skin will turn to a doughy mush. After Othmar Seiler and Verena Hasenfretz from the Hirschen in Bünz leave me in the lurch, I have something approaching inspiration. Where does an old swamp-dog go, what dull ache pangs his factotum's belly on this picture-postcard day, how does he overmaster the desolation of the valley in Upper Freiamt? When I turn onto the square in front of the station in Muri, I am utterly sure of myself, the ineffable station buffet for second-class customers for local transit on the Gotthard stretch – there is no first class – is the only solution to the riddle, wanderlust is the word, even if the timetable only grants him this pleasure twice an hour, he wants to hear the trains go past, to weave from them his southern dreams – and there he is, dozing in the corner by the pastries, beneath a punched tin sign for Feldschlösschen Brewery, an army of empty Rittergold bottles on the table, the national beverage of Freiamt, hard cider, turbid, bubbly, cool, evocative of spider webs in cellars. The trout in the plastic sack are not unharmed. Hombre in a Ferrari with six specimens of *salmo truttae* in a town known for its poorhouse strikes me as a quite extraordinary sort of taxi service on a late Saturday afternoon, especially when we shoot past the garden of the madhouse, where the ochre attrition of the crumbling walls merges with the corn yellow of the upper floor of Gormund, and my culinary optimism is once again on the rise. We two – in this group, the only true reverencers of tobacco, so I stop at a kiosk to treat my guest to two South Sea blue boxes of Toscanellis, *Fabbrica tobacchi Brissago, fondata nel 1847* – return like apostates, the first has run because he can't bear the heat of the oven, the second is likewise averse to the infernal glow of Bert May's prose.

While I busy myself in the kitchen, Hombre, in his astoundingly anesthetized state, is put to bed in the hunter's room, the lord of Castle Trunz sets the table on the roundel, and Frau Irlande, with her youthful enthusiasm, decides to decorate the garden for dinner with lanterns that will give the darkening evening an urbane nocturnal note, a bit of the cachet of nearby Lucerne, the city of lights. She hurries up- and downstairs, rummages under the gables in the room behind the Sleeping Beauty window, then in some Renaissance chests in her bedroom, I would like to help her, because looking for something and finally finding it is a succinct joy that leaps up inside you like a spark. But my task is somehow to bring back into shape six trout that Hombre has crushed – I wonder, did he use them as pillows? They've already been gutted, so we prepare the court-bouillon in a large copper casserole, *au bleu,* I still remember this from my Waldau aunts, recommended for fresh-caught river trout, *truite de rivière,* also for carp, rainbow trout, and arctic char; though we use the term "boiling" when referring to this basic preparation, the fish should never be subjected to high temperatures, we poach it, to be plain, let it simmer, we must distinguish here between *caisson au court-bouillon ordinaire, caisson au court-bouillon blanc,* and *caisson au bleu,* where the blue coloring is an effect of the slime coat, under no circumstances to be stripped off when removing the entrails. Since I need the help of no one, I light myself a Brenner Tambour, in the finer kitchens this is actually forbidden, but I rely on the pneuma of home for inspiration of any kind, I am careful, of course, to make sure the broth doesn't cloud, and so, we take four liters of tap water from the Gormund spring, a half-liter of white wine, from the Vaud, if possible, three deciliters of vinegar, sixty grams of salt, a so-called *paysanne de légumes,* white garlic, onions, carrots, a sprig of parsley, a bit of thyme, and three bay leaves, the onions should be studded with *nägeli* – cloves – a pinch of black pepper, too, but not whole kernels, this is a common error among chefs, there should be nothing that will do harm to the fish's tender flesh. We will put these ingredients – without the vinegar, of course – to simmer for a good quarter-hour, but first we inform ourselves as to the preparations for the feast, everything seems to be going ideally, the damask-white tablecloth is glowing in the twilight, Irlande, a royal blue phantom, feels her way through the bushes and branches, not wanting to injure a single twig, and attaches the accordion and ball lamps, Bert May has just stepped out of the hall with two bottles under his arm, the ice bucket is newly filled as well, the carefully cleaned trout are marinated briefly in the vinegar, we only drop them in the court-bouillon when we have dipped our finger inside to make sure it's warm but no longer hot, reboil, skim, let it simmer a few minutes, now is the most delicate phase of the poach, in the basin the fish begin to shimmer a beautiful slate blue, this is the time, if we wait longer, the flesh will lose its suppleness, and you won't manage to separate it from the skin without mashing it to bits, Wedgwood platter, lemon wheels, a bit of greens, no salted potatoes, that's a yokel's accompaniment, no, we want it pure as a *puro,* pristine as a Bahía export, are all those gathered ready to savor this work of art?

Chapeau, Frau Irlande, I would not have expected a white Bordeaux so fine as a Pavillon Blanc de Château Margaux, 1974 vintage, to have come from your cellar. Hombre in his present state cannot reasonably be expected to serve us – we hear the echo of his snores behind the grated window – but I am utterly in my element, each person receives one trout, those remaining will not be placed back in the broth, my God, what an unpardonable sin, instead I cover them with a warm serviette to keep them at temperature. Who will offer the toast, not I certainly, not the cook, and never the master of ceremonies, the hostess is out of the question, and so it falls to Bert May, who takes it upon himself to celebrate this occasion with a Stechlinish twist, invoking the table talk in Chapter Three, true, the heir of Trunz notes, in the book they are having carp, Captain Czako raises the question of how the magnificent creature on his plate would have behaved in Lake Stechlin when the geyser rose up and the red rooster shot forth, like a fellow revolutionary or a weakling; would he cower like a bourgeois in the marsh, only to ask himself the morning after, are they still shooting? But the trout's element is mountain streams, and this makes him turn now from Fontane to Goethe, *In furrows round the peak / he hunted colored stones,* this hunter's disposition, if you will allow me, determines the trout's temperament, it is an ur-symbol of vitality, and this is why *au bleu* is the only way to enjoy it. Here I would like to interrupt my friend from the Schiltal, who is audacious enough to mention the eternal hunting grounds of Frau Irlande's father, and will surely make reference to that appalling scene in *The Heron Hunter From Gran Chaco* in which the storm god, after migrating to South America, poisons twelve alligators with strychnine to reach a heron's nest. The episode has been authenticated, but it is hardly favorable to the appetite, Irlande von Elbstein-Bruyère agrees, for some time now she's been waving him off so we may start filleting out the little cheeks – what would trout be without these almond-shaped delicacies! The surface of the white wine, lemon-toned in crystal glasses, shines like a faint star, we toast to Gormund, to Trunz, to Jérôme von Castelmur-Bondo, and the poetess, who more and more is queen of this midsummer night, wants to know the truth behind the geyser and the red rooster at Lake Stechlin. Though a dilettante of literature, I do know this novel quite well, but knowing something quite well inevitably means knowing a shade less about it than Bert May, he even refers to Fontane's source, *Folk Customs of the County of Ruppin and Environs,* Karl Eduard Haase, Neuruppin, 1887, which relates the story of a fisherman by the name of Minack who was surprised by a storm and choppy waters following a plentiful catch, and a red rooster emerged from the deep and knocked him into the lake. Minack's tale, says Bert May, is really a mermaid story, the nereids that approach men are often seen in red hats. Because it forks in the direction of the wind, the Stechlin is unusually exposed, even amid calm winds there are considerable waves. The Slavic fisherman who gave the lake its name were already aware of this peculiarity, according to the Slavist Julius Beck, *Stechlin* derives from the Proto-Baltic-Slavic root *tek,* meaning flow or shift, and so the translation, *wild, uneasy waters* is an apposite one; as far as the red rooster, the explanation certainly lies in the flammable swamp gas, methane, which is created through the decomposition of organic matter, in olden times you often threw your net out by the light of pine torches, and rising methane bubbles could ignite, causing explosions.

You cannot expect, Frau Irlande protests, a Melusina like myself to accept this scientific interpretation of Minack's story, especially as it says nothing of the events surrounding the Lisbon earthquake of 1755, what can you tell me about that, then, Hermann? Well, my dear, if you are referring to my abandoned minor in hydrology from my semesters at the ETH, I don't have a great deal to add, only what Fontane's teacher and the director of the Berlin Vocational School has said in *Contributions to Mineralogical and Geognostic Knowledge of the State of Brandenburg,* published in 1837, namely that such movements have been observed in Lake Stechlin to the west of Fürstenberg, *such* here refers to a related thesis of Brating's, but limnologists' investigations have been unable to corroborate the reports of witnesses conclusively. What is a limnologist, Hermann? Well, limnology is the study of inland waters, from the Greek *limne,* pond or lake. The Stechlin, the deepest of all Middle German lakes, reaching down seventy meters below the surface, is not known to have subterranean connections to any rivers. You know, Bert May added, the legend of the red rooster as a tectonic alarm was given new life in 1929, when a boat supposedly gliding across the smooth surface of the water was thrown five meters into the air and capsized. Whatever the case, Fontane's artistry lies in his reinterpretation of the original mermaid myth as a dialectical-insurrectionary symbol, the red cockerel at the novel's opening anticipates what will reach full expression in little Agnes's red stockings at the story's end, and what is granted to the idealized Brandenburg Junker, the lower nobleman Dubslav von Stechlin: a heart for social democracy.

It is not yet completely dark, but the night is far enough along that Frau Irlande, full of delight, draws our attention to the spectral illumination in her garden, the crepe paper lanterns, which flickered a bit at first and now have settled into a warm, rich glow, the haphazardly placed garlands in the quaking aspen over the putti point up toward the pitch-black fir; boldly grinning, the Chinese tangerines sway softly, the barberry leaves, sawtoothed in eucalyptus green, bring to mind angina, apple juice, eternity in a pediatric bed, in the middle of the blackthorns grow plump and juicy citrons and oranges, while the aquamarine face of the moon lacks any geometric corporeality and seems to rise up from the bushes like a balloon. The crinkled accordion lanterns hang slanted, lighting fairytale motifs in wavering pink and lilac, almost immodestly the Swiss red flaps, its white cross slightly blurred, a purple flower flickers amid the stands of conifers. Will neither of the esteemed versifiers take a bit more trout? No, Frau Irlande has had enough, Bert has already lit one of his black cigarettes, betraying his boorishness *par excellence,* but Hermann Arbogast Brenner, as per previous, will not stage a war of religion over the sore point of dry drunkenness, he gathers the fish scraps as his cemetery-grandmother used to do, and while poetess and poet amble off into the garden, perhaps to recite in tandem Hesse's "Lanterns on a Summer Night" in the niche or next to the gurgling fountain, I take the plates to the hunter's room and try to persuade Hombre, still sleeping off his stupor from the cider, to partake of a cold fillet of trout. He is lying there beneath his woolen blanket; his smooth skull, dotted with warts, moles, and pimples, is tucked into the crook of his arm; he has not even removed his coattails, and I think to myself, no one incapable of describing such a soul's inner life deserves the title of poet, for on the brackish surface of its waters, where the fires of eau-de-vie burn, skim the wrecks of svelte ships that poetesses have sent forth sailing into night, it may be, I think heretically, staring at the serpent in the spirit jar, that the eminent Georges and Rilkes and their like thrive in a soil of profound inhumanity; men like Hombre are the base matter their hearts transform into sublimity, the fate of the nameless is the price paid for the crystalline phrases printed in cursive in the *Neue Zürcher Zeitung,* the elf-queens suck their blood, inhuman, because their verses tread on corpses. The precious essence of O-so-noble compassion is only to be had at the cost of someone else's going to the dogs. And this is the basis of the thoroughgoing mendacity of the artist's calling, because what the public sees is the twinkling diamond and never the fathomless shafts where the kaffir breaks off the precious stones, it's a fact, the lyricist's trade is Apartheid.

And yet, Hermann Arbogast Brenner too delights in the garden, pregnant with the spirit of August, and it seems to him as if an accordion were sounding from some garden inn decked with gaudy hanging lamps in the distance, as if a tipsy Charly were playing a tune off past the Reiterswald or even the Reuss, now and then the wind conveys a dominant seventh, and the resolution lingers in the dark. Now is the hour of the Romeo y Julieta Churchill. We should not forget, the British Prime Minister would have needed a hundred years to smoke all the cigars he was credited with. No one has truly lived – not Frau Irlande, not Bert May – who is ignorant of this pleasure. For the plant known as *cohiba,* described in a document in the Indian Archives in Seville as a grass with fleshy leaves and a soft and velvety touch, discovered in lieu of India after Columbus's months of errancy, allows us to discourse with the gods. More than two thousand years ago, the father of history reported that the Massageteans on the isle of Araxes would sit together around the fire and throw the fruit of the hemp plant inside, and in this way they became as drunk as the Hellenes on their wine. The Greek geographer Strabo discovered something similar among the Mysians of Asia Minor, whose name means "those who eat smoke." This designation remains a just one, even today we say of a Havana's vapor that it has *bite*. Smoking takes us back to the earliest traces of humankind. Even if the indulgences of modern man as he idly blows his clouds of smoke will hardly be confused with any sort of sacrament, still, a Romeo y Julieta transports him to that peculiar state of limbo halfway between volatility and the solidification of thought, an initially harmless rapture that drags the addict further and further from life itself. The calumet of the Indians enclosed the entire world in a pipe, and its smoke is like a fiery breath of pneuma, the people will live on so long as the custom of the peace pipe is preserved. With their tobacco rolls, the Mayan priests communed with the temple gods, I on the other hand am satisfied with the apparition of my Waldau grandfather, who used to say: he who serves for nothing will end up serving for nothing, an ironic allusion to the innkeeper's profession. Let us not forget here that botanists include tobacco in the family *solanaceae,* from the Latin *solare,* to soothe, hence banning smoking from hospitals is the greatest inanity of all times.

The isolation illness gives rise to is best overcome with the aid of a cigar, did Hermann Arbogast Brenner himself not say: Never lonelier than at Gormund? Frau Irlande has her home and her verses, Bert May his mathematics of darkness, I have only tobacco and a terminal diagnosis, but both are more gratifying to me than your spiritual bounties are to you, because the Romeo y Julieta demands no adoration, no adepts, no apostles. Now the darkness has advanced so far that the lanterns are luciform bodies, to elude their magic – glassy purple, emerald-edged, spherical sapphire – you would have take a saw and cut them from the night. And the longer one stares and sinks into this chromatism, the more stygian the shadows grow, and the further one falls into the furrows of the universe, the more the plenitude of space glides toward the sidereal crosshairs. Magic word, Andromeda, magic word, Capella. Lilith, according to Frau Irlande, speaks of light years and astral miles the way others talk of road-kilometers and nautical miles, and darkness alters the specific gravity of the soul. Strange, I feel the urge to play jass, spades trump, that would do the trick, throw out the Jack, follow up with the nine, third card is Ace of Hearts. But there's nothing doing. So I content myself with my being as a cigarier, hear the name Novalis uttered from afar. With this highest of all pleasures as the apogee of the trout dinner at Gormund, Hermann Arbogast has been left alone, soon he will stride alone over the frontier, no shilling under his tongue, no passport in hand. The Bruns men's choir will sing the song *Friendship,* and hoarfrost will settle overnight. A good companion, that is how they will remember him.

20.

MENZENMANG LANDSCAPE ARCHITECTURE, OFFAL

O ffal is the term for leftover tobacco from the manufacture of cigarettes and cigars, a sack of these *nicotiana* crumbs stood in Rüedu's cellar, his mother worked at the cigar plant and was allowed to gather as much of this coveted waste as she wished to fertilize her flowers; in doing so, she had no notion that she was providing the raw material for the first tobacco colloquium of my life, for he and I carved wooden pipes of copper-gold horse chestnut, climbed into the uppermost nest of branches next to the chapel, and puffed away on these calumets, from the French *chalumeau,* which originally denoted something like a reed; who knows, perhaps we felt linked to the seven secret rites of the Oglala Sioux, passed down to the medicine man Black Elk from the eternal guardian of the peace pipe, the elk's head itself. The ethnologist Joseph Epes Brown summarized these with the words: "As soon as the pipe is forgotten, the people will be without a center and they will perish." I never did get round to Karl May, but Zane Gray I read by the yard, in his Wild West romances, which filled up half a bookshelf in the Menzenmang library, the gentle Colt Girl always won. The production of the present tobacco leaves, which we laboriously assemble into *gavillas,* gives rise to offal of its own, for Mneme favors compartmentalization, and whatever doesn't fit in the cubbyholes of our night porter's lodge gets left behind as strips of Mandi Angin or Vorstenlanden, naturally we can blend this into the filler, and the high cost per bale of these prized wrapper leaves will raise the price of a bundle thus prepared. We may also proceed through the concept of the off-shade, discoloration, something utterly distinct from the irregularly blotched appearance of inferior-grade cigars that all good manufacturers throw out. For the puzzle of childhood to prove credible, according to Ludwig Reiner's handbook on the epic technique, it is essential that all this not be omitted, there are even customers who place orders for discolorations of a certain sort, who feel a closer bond to the miracle weed in its natural, resin-dappled expression – this is something the jeans generation, which has elevated the triangle to an aesthetic precept, will understand especially well. We may even go so far as to say only malpractice makes perfection bearable, that the strident mewling and wolfen howls of the barrel organs are what stirs us most, who would not commend the Italian masters for including in the formal plan of their works the void of unfinished details, in the Valais, it is reported that budding brides paint the features of corpses on their face.

If we confine ourselves strictly to the anatomy of the cigar, and study the offal and the practices surrounding it in the workshops at the

parent company of Johann Caspar Brenner, we encounter a new technique suited to our Menzenmang undertaking: snippets of binder,
strips of wrapper, and scraps of leftover filler are placed in the center of
the mixing box, which is already suffused with the arcana, and what
emerges is a sort of *tutti frutti* cheroot; with pleasure I imagine how its
spice swells the palate in the same way as double-cooked sauerkraut.
Only what is left over after this stage will be discarded as offal, packed
into bags and sold off to gardeners. If a green thumb is required for our
tobacco leaves as well, we should see – I will have to ask Adam Nautilus
Rauch – whether it is advantageous for us to spruce up our plantation
with a little *Schusterfleck*. Naturally this presupposes we have succeeded
in establishing something like a guideline for composition, a set of
judgments we may pass along to the indulgent reader. What is style after
all? For the wanderer, the way he sets one foot before the other, his red
cable-stitched stockings, and his checkered shirt are mere ingredients.
Style is a matter of rhythm, of selection. What I suppress may leave a
deeper imprint on my memories than the designs apparent on the
surface. Offal is whatever I cannot *make fit*. Here is the main street in
Menzenmang, the *feshtivil mashks* are frolicking in a wild dance by the
sawmill, they keep coming closer and closer. Where, though, are we
watching from? Perhaps my father heaved me up onto his shoulders to
pull me away from the whirl of the paper serpent, perhaps we fled to
the tower in the post office, horrified by the mask and gestures of a
red-wigged woman in a feathery harlequin balloon skirt. So the scene
closes, the splinter in the kaleidoscope, a figment in the panopticon of
early childhood memory. What pressed on afterward was the fear

mechanism alone, and so here I must prospectively remember or retro-spectively invent a trip with my father to the observation tower in Homburg, a four-legged curio mimicking the Eiffel tower in Paris, how he lifted me up over the railings and vertigo gripped me when I was faced with the abyss. Everything depends on whether we choose to be the chroniclers or inventors of our lives. And here again, I must praise the medium of the cigar. It is ruminative, depending on its aging, its moisture retention, and how it burns, it lowers us more or less deeply into that shaft its aroma opens for us as a kind of Ariadne's thread. The smoker cannot give the order: Memory, arise, ur-image, come to me. He must instead cultivate an infinite degree of patience. Now the indulgent reader, following my precedent, perhaps, and reaching when-ever possible into the cedar box, will rightly ask if by offal what I mean here are misbegotten episodes. To gauge this, we must stress the ways my Brunsleben workshop differs from a regular writer's place of work. The author by trade proceeds by cobbling together chapters, then sketching out a rough draft; he thinks this over, lets it ferment, sprays the leaves again, maybe saucing them up with something contemporary, conceives of variants number one, two, three, and four, files the text down until every detail sits right. Like an architect, he takes pains to assure that the accents harmonize with the proportions of the whole. His goal is reached when his form has the clarity of crystal. Hermann Arbogast Brenner has no such intentions. He quite simply no longer has the time such an effort would require. In the castle keep, in the tenant's cottage, the materials are piled on the tables, chairs, beds, and floor. He sits, as it were, on the captain's bridge and runs the mass of it through the Hermes 3000 he rented from Mathys Office Supplies. As he does so, he listens to records that remind him of the happy times, when he used to play dance music in the Pete Hiller Septet as a schoolboy, then later in the Paul Weber Orchestra in Menzenmang.

The chaos that reigns in the stockpile has its advantages and disadvantages. When I had hoped to describe the crate of books in my cemetery-grandmother's *kitchinette,* I imagined it was enough to take from the shelf at the junk shop an antique copy of the calendar for the blind I happened on. But it was not so. And yet, my tragic search for the blind calendar brought me to that forgotten notice of the canton hospital in Aarau that documents the progress of my birth. The question now is whether the corresponding passage about the relics from my grandmother's is not more authentic precisely because all I have at my disposal is the image of a boy feeling his way around a green hill wreathed with sunbeams. As I raise this conjecture, I suddenly recall where that keepsake from the Swiss Association of the Blind may have gotten to, and I set forth on a new expedition, lie on my belly before the overflowing piles, eat dust, defile each heap with the letter opener, and look, there it is, faded grass green. A writer would take this occasion to leaf through it once more and reacquaint himself with the moment. But for what? The indulgent reader has never seen the booklet, he must accept whatever blind calendar I offer him. He must, like the boy with his eyes sewn closed, wreathed in sunbeams, look inward. And I can turn the pages for him as I wish. The strips of images like woodcuts for the months, the plow wheels of animal zodiac signs, the banners reading January, February, March, April, stretched out above them like awnings – my reader knows nothing of this. Only if I wish to share how this seasonal emblematics in my cemetery-grandmother's kitchen put me in mind of something motile, how behind each and every object I perceived the automotive principle, how even the brittlest missionary tractate meant something if the just eye of God in the isosceles triangle so frequently espied on the gravestones saw fit to give nourishment through them to my imagination – only then does the offal turn to filler. In my manual cheroot maker, I press it into a roll, let the mechanism seal the wrapper and the binder, and light up the product that emerges. That the material dissolves into fugitive clouds instead of returning to the soil is the root of my fascination with the tobacconist's calling, I smoke my childhood to its end, grateful to the indulgent reader who affords me company in the meanwhile, for the arid grace of a dear cigar is doubled when it's shared.

Back from the district hospital, I go out and reconnoiter in the garden, here is the sun-warmed water in the tin tub on the terrace beneath the tent roof of the red-and-yellow marquee, here is a sea of gravel you can wash, put in your mouth, and then throw back out of the ship. The group of photos labeled *And now little Bobeli can stand on his own* shows a nipper with stumpy legs and a bright, fleshy face under hair combed to a high gleam, what torture, binding his hands to the mattress with rubber straps. Of the stuffed animals all around me I no longer have any memories, but there is one possession that becomes a trademark for the two-year-old, the frying pan I drag back with me from my explorations. What insights a psychologist would manage to take from that! He had a sense for the histrionic early on. Or: his mother always kept an eye on his whereabouts. But no, the pan was just my wheelless trailer, you could load it and pull it from the gravel lot down the steps to my cemetery-grandmother's shadowy kingdom. Here, beneath the shimmering grandeur of the Canadian silver birches, which I still hear rustling every night before I fall asleep, is the henhouse beneath the thickets of exuberant blackberries, not a shack surrounded by a rickety fence, but a god's honest house made of wire like you see in zoos, in front of the hip-roofed hut, the *biddies* mince up the ladder, the black one, the one I get to go in and feed, my hen, I see repeated on the base of the yellow bowl when I spoon up all my soup like a good boy, the crockery rests on a tin tray painted with teddy bears, not only is there a fancy border, but even a little channel to catch the spilt broth. If I have said elsewhere that nature never interested me, that I never collected grasshoppers and butterflies, that is untrue, at least as regards my early garden and chicken coop studies, self-evidently a black chicken with a red comb stands out from the white average and in this way, for a child, is something utterly special, like the pottle-pleasure of driving the scoop into the feed sack and scattering corn among the cackling brood. If Menzenmang possessed the character of a Margravian estate, it was not least of all because of this rustic cabin precinct, where my grandmother, actually my great aunt, worked and fiddled, leaving the stately rooms and the southerly ornamental garden to my parents. The three entrances to the house bespoke its different realms, the heavy oaken door with the ornate grate over the window was where Father walked in when he returned from his insurance inspector duties, it was also where the postman slid in the mail. The welcoming terrace door led from the far too gloomy parlor to the raised gravel lot with the embankment descending precipitously to the grass parterre, passing through it was almost a recreation. The cellar door, beneath the roof linking the sheer east façade and the woodshed, unveiled a world of tools and planters, to say nothing of the hole in the wall for the cat door. Here on the laundry rack, where we would one day practice our forward rolls, hung a walking stick carved to my measurements, a gift from Uncle Arnold so I could do like him and tap grandiloquently on the pavement as we walked together up the path to the Waldau. Here I stand at the fountain in my *jumper* gulping down a drink of *shyrup,* and here is the grated rabbit tunnel with the guillotine door, you can move it and let them nibble on a new patch of grass, there is a great temptation to raise up the warped, bluish barrier and let the bunnies with their bloodshot eyes hop off into freedom. Here is the muck barrow, a heavy, monstrous vat on iron wheels, and father is standing splay-legged over the open cover to the manhole behind the house and scooping out the brown brew with the *dipper,* the stubborn scent stuns you, but you stare rapt at the open pit, for in a place like this, surrounded by sharp instruments like the hoe, the pitchfork, and the *shickle,* danger is surely lurking, yes, here is where they kill the *coneys* that Grandmother's frying pan transforms into blackish-brown, crisped-up delicacies of shoulder, shank, and ribs. Strangely, though, the witches in my dreams always came into the house through Sandstrasse entrance, the proper one, and never the cellar door.

Here the kingdom of plants and berry crops opens before me, with the gravel path between the lower henhouse and the birches leading to the paved road, here the channels tamped into the crumbly soil of the geometrical garden beds branch out, Grandmother kneels down next to them and picks potatoes or beets or kohlrabi, low on the slope that divides our immense hacienda from the Aschbach place are the raspberry thickets my mother reaches into in gauze gloves while I stand there dreaming up words like *kranschpautscht* and *hatschipatschami,* past the fence stands shifty Margrit calling out for *Bobeli,* I've never known where that name came from, I suppose it alludes to my tubbiness, from all the provinces past the Menzenmang frontier you can hear it shouted out, *Bobeli.* The neighbor boy with the Buco train set, Philipp, calls me that, and one day, at Pan's hour, a shifty teenage girl stands in a strawberry dress with white polka dots on the steps to the coal chute by the hiba trees, grabs my hand, guides it under her skirt, presses my finger into the damp slit, and orders me to sniff it, the smell is acrid, rotten, mossy, indistinguishable from the turds Rüedu and I squeeze out in the needles under cover of the furs and that blowflies buzz around for days on end, Margrit, summer-spry, laughs at me, one, two, three fingers of my little mitt vanish into her hole, her heavy breasts heave under the thin summer fabric, just behind there, where you *evacuate,* is anathema, the grief-stricken green of the hibas binds it with the cemetery earth of the Angermatt, she tugs down my shorts and eggs me on, telling me to piss in her cleft, this may be the archetype of the navel-woman who haunted my dreams in Amden. I am uneasy as I find myself in Father's ornamental garden, which starts below the bank with the mahonia hedge and its poisonous blue berries. In the magnolia corner, presided over by a brick red female torso, is the sandbox where I squat barefoot and bake madeleine cakes from loamy mud, dig tunnels, spill water from the trough inside, use building blocks as bulldozers; give the child a hand shovel, a pot, some cookie cutters, and he will stay busy there for hours, Father pushes the lawnmower in orderly rows, I can still remember the stuttering whirr of the blade as he ran the machine along the edge of the rose, phlox, and lockspur beds, pulling it back with one hand, a cheroot ever in the corner of his mouth, now and then the metal clanged brightly when a stone made it into the cylindrical housing, *ye goddamn fool* he would say before pulling it aside. When I am thirsty, I hurry, dragging the pan behind me, to the shadowy district of shed and henhouse, by the espaliered wall that runs along the level gravel lot, my grandmother rests on a two-slat bench painted cypress green, Emiu is there, he's brought a sackful of feed and is puffing his pipe with his cane between his knees, *tobacking,* we used to say; Aunt Ida is holding the raspberry syrup bottle in one hand and the eau de vie from the cellar in the other, the smoker gets a cider glass, I get a mug, and the sticky sap pools on the bottom and flames up bright red and foamy when the clear stream from the fountain courses in, my memory, recreated from one cigar to the next, tells me it was always my cemetery-grandmother who looked out for my vital needs, on the green bench beside her were a wedge of *zöbeli* – cervelat – a few slices of speck with onion rings, and dark bread, which she cut into slices, *shlivers,* pressing the loaf against her jabot with its ivory brooch.

Early on, I was already a cellar creature, more often under the house than in the orderly domain of Gertrud, who used to kneel in the currant bushes with a floral kerchief around her head or trifle with the hothouse plants and the tomatoes; the shed is where the vehicles were kept – the barrow I helped push when we got fodder from the mill in Pfeffikon, the slurry cart, the hay wagon, here was the flap door that led to the nesting boxes where I was allowed to retrieve the eggs, here the axe and mallet and spading fork hung on the wall, and underneath the airless roof it smelled of dried grass, blanched chervil, and sun-dried cardamine, and in the cellar maze on muggy days the main water ran in trickles down the pipes. O syrup in narrow bottles, names written on compote labels, O rubber rings from canning jars, perfect for fashioning a slingshot, O black roasting drum from grandmother's hoard where Rebecca bore her kittens, O ancient tea tin full of screws and knick-knacks and hinges, O grape press in the washroom, O cement floor cool and damp, where the barefoot child partook of the sepulchrousness of Menzenmang! In *Little Peter's Journey to the Moon,* the picture book I used to page through on summer evenings in my barred crib in the corner of my parents' room by the veranda, gawked at by the holographic kobold-asters in the beige wallpaper, I saw my sandbox swell into a paradise. The little sandmen crept into Peter's room, sprinkled sand in his eyes, and carted him off to their mine; the bustling dwarflings streamed in through numerous tunnels and dumped out barrowsful of yellow baking powder on a hill, the metal wheels shone Bordeaux red against the shafts in the background. Then the band flew to the moon, which had a wooden house in a deep green meadow. Before it had been a crescent puffing its pipe in the night sky, but now it greeted the visitors as a smooth round lunar face with teeny ears and a ring of keys around its belt. And he received them in his garden with an enormous ring cake and a barrel of syrup, then cried, resplendent in the firmament, as Peter's captors floated back down to earth with a parasol.

Just as my nose and palate today are attuned to the noblest produce of far-flung provinces, so my child's soul in those days was sensitive to these stories, which I begged to hear told over and over, making anxiously sure the grown-ups didn't change a single detail, that they didn't say Little Peter and then a moment later Little Hans, that what had today been a mine did not become a sandpit tomorrow – for what was one to rely on if, in the world of images, the unimaginable was possible, even a night jaunt to the moon? And here is Aunt Picki – and this too falls into the category of offal – who used to come by and sit at the Pfaff sewing machine and who tickled my skin with needles, she brought another book from which a single sequence abides in my memory: the yellow glow of a night-blue house with Auntie Tempest inside, throwing her bolts over the stucco walls while the thunder cracks in a fiery span across the sky. Most people, if they bother with their childhood at all, find nothing but this kind of tobacco debris, which they sweep together in their cellar dungeons, intent on a well-ordered biography, sprinkling sawdust over the top of it to soak up the damp from the floor. But on torrid summer nights, when they sit with a beer at a garden table and smoke an Export or a Rössli Aromatico, the question overtakes them, accented by the cloudbursts on the horizon: *ye shtill remember ven?* It is a grandfatherly question, asked by those who stare into sunsets. Memory addicts are romantics, for this reason my Stechlinesque cottage, which resembles, as Jérôme von Castelmur-Bondo remarked, a haunted castle in Eichendorff on these hot July and August days, is the perfect workshop for my you-still-remember-when enterprise. This is something distinct from the storyteller's métier, which starts with Once upon a time. I am not certain that what I bring together in my tobacco leaves actually ever was, whether it is not merely the dreams and schemes of a cigarier who remained asleep from birth to death, who, because he found no haven among men, never bothered to drag himself out of bed. Hence my method is the perpetual subjunctive of the collage: this piece you can paste in one way, this one another. And of the three Cs of the artist's trade it is the third I like best: Contrive.

If August comes and brings no rain, in winter snow will shroud the plain. Heavy dew in August foretells stable weather. No dew means storms, heat, and rain. Because night dew covers the fruits and fields, apples should be washed before eating. What August doesn't sear, September won't cook through. For the second time this summer, an unusually powerful Monday night storm has struck Zurich. At the Swiss Meteorological Institute on the Zurichberg a total of 80.4 millimeters – corresponding to 80.4 liters of water per square meter – were collected, one of the highest measurements registered for a single day in August in the past one hundred years. Even stranger when you keep in mind that 71.2 liters fell in under one hour. In Brunsleben, too, around half-past three, a malevolent ulcer opened in the sky, my white jumbo thermometer measured thirty-two in the shade of the courtyard. The oppressive silence, broken by the muffled cries of birds, hinted at the possibility of a cyclone. My rented Hermes 3000 clacked ever slower, the tobacco clung in sheets to the heart, which had to pump violently to maintain the circulation of memories. Shortly after four I could hold out no longer, I packed my La Perla briefs into the open-topped Ferrari, drove to the cooling baths of the Aabach in Leonz-burg-Combray, and jumped, still in my clothes, utterly parched, under the first free shower I could find. Then I swam a few laps in the big pool and imagined myself in the loamy tides of Tipaza, where the sun shines so bright that the land is burnt black. Weather forecast till next Sunday: the even pressure distribution of the past few days favors the buildup of storm cells. Further on, a new offshoot of the Azores High stretches up toward Western and Central Europe. Weather conditions in Switzerland will be affected from midweek on. At the same time, the Bise will reach slightly into the midlands. On Thursday and Friday, the high pressures will predominate, and temperatures will rise again to thirty degrees. Calendar for Wednesday, August 17, 1988: 33rd week, 230th day of the year, saints' days: Amor, Benedicta, Hyacinth, Severus, and Liberatus. Sunrise: 6:25 AM, sunset 8:34 PM. Lunar phase: waxing.

21.

HERMANN, THE TOBACCO GRANDFATHER,
ORMOND BRASIL JUBILÉ

Here is the historic photo taken on the Menzenmang terrace, with my grandfather in his white soldier's dress, holding me on his knee and saying, supposedly: *ven ye ken tek de hill*. The grass path over Hansi Hill, past the burnt remains of the old Rölli estate, is the shortest route from the plateau to the Stierenberg with the restaurant and the lookout at the top. Yes, Ätti, whose bulging goiter hinted at his ailing esophagus, must have been proud of his first grandson, if not he wouldn't have given a hundred francs to the Aargau hospital in the name of *unknown*. That he died unexpectedly when I was fourteen months old had greater sway over my life than my horoscope at birth would have dared augur, this much is clear to me as I look back from Brunsleben — for had my grandfather lived to eighty-one instead of sixty-one, I would have hoofed it over *de hill* twice weekly to sit in at his office with its trout pond. On page three of the large-format album

Three Generations of the Waldau, we read: Ätti, born January 26, 1882, attended parish school in Burg, district school in Reinach, left for Neuenburg in 1898 and for Bellinzona in 1899. His father sends him to Bremen thereafter, because he wants to make of him a good tobacconist. And here my element unfurls itself with its sepia brown veins, samples of Java, Havana, Sumatra, Brazil, bundled into *stels.* Just imagine if the two of us, an Ormond Brasil Jubilé between our lips, had tested the wares' softness and elasticity together, knowing that everything in the raw tobacco business depends entirely on the five senses, on the nose, the instincts, the hunter's discernment, the fisherman's patience. Had I been schooled in the ancestral trade, I would not have to slave here over this printed *gavilla,* companion to Jérôme von Castelmur-Bondo and gawker at the queendom of Irlande von Elbstein-Bruyère, I would instead be one of the last of the cigar barons of the Upper Wynental. The page would not be complete without a hand-drawn arabesque, an *oscuro* brown trabuco and a finely nerved corona. This was my father's narrative style, the sepia of the cadet photo and the pale Van Dyck of frayed twine endue this page of the album with a you-still-remember-when veneer.

And here, read and reread, is the obituary from the Wynenthal paper: The Waldau, a beautiful home with a sweeping view of the valley, was the destination Thursday morning of countless people dressed in mourning come to pay their respects to Hermann Brenner, businessman and departed owner of the Waldau Inn. The news of his death has deeply touched his relatives, acquaintances, and his many friends. At eleven, the crowd of the bereaved was still growing. The singers from the Burg men's choir and the Frohsinn choir in Menzenmang gathered in a half-circle around the coffin, which loving hands had adorned with splendid autumn flowers in honor of the deceased. Solemnly at first, in a mysterious, wondrous melody that rose like a storm wind to pound at the *doors to other worlds,* the singers' words rang out like an everlasting bequest. We must imagine here our Hermann as a young, enthusiastic member of the Frohsinn nearly forty years before, how for a few years he marched in front of the group in his snazzy officer's garb, how for decades he stood out in the ranks of the Burg singers. O you schnapps-bright weeds and gouty mushrooms ennobling with your melancholy the sylvan backdrops of dances in country gyms, which of you still knows that classic slow and solemn funeral song, "The Bard" by Friedrich Sucher? *There lies the singer in repose / Ear pressed to Heaven's gate / His voice returns when the runnel slows / With the sound of springs sedate.* In the second part we descend from D major to B minor and then back to the dominant E. At a men's choir rehearsal recently I asked about this song, and Surleuly, the second bass, told a story right away. *Ye know Hans Richter, ye know how he is, type cudn't help but get up in arms, en he says te me, ven my time comes, y'ell not be singin "De Bard" fer me, dat en etself took eh good bit eh gall, who's he te say who sings vat fer who, den wouldn't ye know, Murer Miggu pipes in en says, widout eh shadow of eh doubt, once you're dead, dat's et, time's up, zilch, amen, closed curtain, thank ye very much. As et happens, Hans Richter did die right early, en de Bruns men's choir shtuck te his vishes, en dey sung de motet et his grave, ye know de one, yev heard et on de radio. En naturally dem vat veren't dere come along en asked me all shocked en shnivelin, how cud ye do such a thing, en I say ye know it's vat he vanted, of*

course we cud eh sung "De Bard," he vouldna known no different. And damned
if Murer Miggu dint pipe up en ask: are ye sure?

Dear Ätti, for your sake, at least, because we are not certain you can't
hear it, I sing in the Bruns men's choir every Thursday evening, first
bass, following the tuning fork of our hot-headed *dompteuse* from Löp-
fen, na-na-na-ing and down the scale, preach the "Rhine Creed" at the
top of my lungs, raise a glass to "Saint Peter's" in Salzburg, trot superbly
through the "Elizabethan Serenade," sneak a few teardrops from my dry
libation as the tenors guide us into the misty minor key. When the
pause comes, I consume my obligatory cheroot. My ode to these musi-
cal-political fraternities has yet to arrive, for now, what I know of my
grandfather is, in the main, nothing but hearsay. He probably did not
engage all that seriously in the trade of leaves from Java, Sumatra, Cuba,
and Brazil, he certainly didn't spin the weed into gold like my uncle,
Bertrand the younger. The photos in the Waldau album show him as a
jovial *bon vivant* and affable friend to all. Slender, with short hair and an
elegant moustache, he poses with Rosa Suter for their wedding photo
on July 25, 1907 in Teufenthal at the *Herbrig*. Father even managed to
dig up the wedding menu, it merits mention for its *richesse*, which
reflects the optimism of the young businessman, the poem runs: *Con-
sommé printanier royal, Truites de rocher au bleu à la sauce hollandaise, Pommes
nouvelles natures, Côtes de bœuf à la bordelaise, Ris de veau aux petits pois,
Asperges d'Argenteuil à la sauce Mousseline, Salade de laitues, Parfait à la
vanille, Tourtes au citron, Fruits et dessert.* My grandfather must never have
prepared a dinner of this kind as an innkeeper, his specialties were the

seasonal dishes that would make the Waldau famous, frog legs in spring, still legal at the time, in May spiced wine with woodruff, in summer blackberry ice cream and selected forest fruits, and when the horns echoed through the Stierenberg, Hasenpfeffer and Venison Tenderloin Baden-Baden; the savory mushrooms depended on the season, there were chanterelles with onions and garlic and black trumpets à la crème. Not to be missed were the house poulet, the cream schnitzel, the trout fresh from Uncle Bertrand's pond. My grandfather's menu was modern without trying, it is common knowledge among today's restaurateurs that the recipe for success is exclusivity: and if Hermann Arbogast Brenner received a license for an establishment in Brunsleben, to give some competition to the nearby Hapsburg, he, too, would stick to that formula, the schnitzel-and-fries-at-all-hours ideology is the very height of tedium, especially in summer, when a crisp salad of iceberg lettuce, diced speck, and croutons gives succor to the soul. Nothing is more exasperating, am I right, dear Grandfather, than a desiccated strip of Dover sole when the occasion calls for a *blanquette de turbotin et saumon.* The selection can be limited, but everything handmade, like a Havana. The beef fillet with mushrooms demands a well-seasoned cast-iron skillet to sear shut the pores in the hot fat. To get the long loins for his ten-centimeter cuts, Hermann Brenner did not balk at driving to every butcher on the Lindenberg. And if the first blanket of fog settled over the Wachtel meadow below the three oaks, he knew a proper country inn owed its guests a bona fide platter of meats with farmhouse bread baked on the premises, the sausages used to hang on broomsticks over the back steps that led from the kitchen to father's sculpture atelier, not a crumb would be left behind, after a long summer the whole world seems to be starving.

Eh deep philosophy stood behind my grandfather's approach to work, my father used to say, and to my dismay, his kind has disappeared from the hospitality sector without a trace: the all-rounder who can swap out his spatula for a jass baize, can trade the diamond trump for the billiard cue, the billiard cue for the hunting rifle, the rifle for the fishing pole, and so on. My favorite aunt Ideli told me that on Saturdays, when they used to boil down the hocks, ears, and tails, my grandfather would sit down around 5:00 PM to set a good example; Gautschi and Turi would follow suit, and soon the plate would be empty. They say too many cooks spoil the broth, but the opposite is indisputable: no one knows how to season it better than the boss himself. That is another gift he passed down to Hermann Arbogast, whose illness prevents him from ever making good on it: a genius for sociability. Here we see a half-page image, Ätti with his hunting partners. Bertrand's felt hat is pushed back for drinking, he is pinching a cheroot in the corner of his mouth, rifle slung over his shoulder. He is the adventurer, the *shkylark* wherever they go, my grandfather is lying comfortably in the grass with Barry behind the pot where the stew is simmering, cigar in his domed hand, the portrait of cozy respectability. There was a man you could trust, whose advice was sought far and wide by workers and captains of industry alike. True, he was grumpy, as my father always said, when he stepped into the rundown kitchen after a long night of sleep or shooed the brood out of bed, *if you don't rise early, you're stealing the day from the Lord*

God, that said, he wasn't often to be seen in the church, his religion was the forest. We grandchildren came to realize what the Stierenberg meant to my grandfather when we went to pick mushrooms with Aunt Ideli or Aunt Irma, he had passed down his knowledge of toadstools to his daughters, not to my father, who would sooner stomp on a morel than pull it up out of the leaves. Here we see the custodian of this little piece of paradise along with Else and the twins, all three in white ruffs that look like neck braces and brightly printed fabrics; Else I would reckon to be fourteen, so Hermann the cigar-muncher is thirty-eight, in his best years, at that age I had still my family living with me in Starrkirch, but his bushy moustache and his cheroot make him look older. In no time, if we cede to the collage technique, the sophisticated grandfather of the early pages, who paid by subscription for Sumatra tobacco in Amsterdam's Frascati Theater, has transformed into my stalwart grandfather, in a sweater with a fustian shirt buttoned up under his goiter, in the frame hanging in the insurance inspector's office above the telephone that chained my father to the all-powerful Swiss Life Insurance and Pension Company headquartered in Zurich; with his broad, flat nose, fleshy ears, and narrowed eyes, he looked down at his son's labors, which must surely have made his Mandi-Agin more bitter still, and if I speak of the downfall of our branch of the great Brenner line, I see it in the growing abstraction of our occupations: while my ancestors trafficked in raw tobacco, my father dealt in figures, premiums, and annuities; while the tobacco men in the curing halls and the sample rooms of the big firms – Brenner & Sons, Hediger & Sons, Weber & Sons, and Opal Eichenberger, all Ltd. – could lay their strong, leafy goods across the counter, for his own customers, Mandi spread out actuarial tables and application forms.

The Waldau, same as ever! reads one title. Wherever possible, my father let the pictures speak and wrote nothing. Of course it wasn't always the Upper Wynental idyll we take it for now, the day-to-day running of a family business doesn't permit cozy evenings in the living room, but the ice saint still dropped in on Christmas eve in his woolen hat to collect his two double shots of eau de vie; if Christmas festivities had to be interrupted, it was usually Grandfather who sat with the guest, not entirely irked at the disturbance, in all honesty *Silent Night, Holy Night* was a bit beyond him. But the vista his obituary praises made the people who grew up here big-hearted and free. To appreciate this, there is no better place than the terrace over the dining room. From the outside tables, you can see the modern porch with glass doors, like a wood-framed drawer slid out from the brick restaurant. A steep staircase with one twist led to the overlook, where a half-dozen tables fit comfortably. Many group portraits of the family were taken here, the heads always rising over the ridge of the Sonnenberg, on clear days, you could see the Lindenberg and the row of hills behind it; to the left, over the roof of the Haller's villa, stretching from the Brenner moraine to the Rein-ach Moor, the Homburg, the *Böiuwer Höchi* rose up to greet you, and on starry nights, a glimmer, the lights of Zurich, overlaid it. In the narrow-gauge Waldau film, there are two sequences that magnify my childhood as through a glass: in the very beginning, my grandfather steps through the door from the courtyard, lights a cheroot, puts out the match with an entirely typical movement of the hand, it means something that the fire must die no sooner than the burning has begun. Some time later, the corona has migrated to the terrace, and Hermann the cigar-muncher traces his finger over the horizon, pausing a while at some distant point. It is not the gesture of a monarch, saying all of this belongs to me, that would be a crass misunderstanding; rather the gratitude of a man given tenure over a beautiful stretch of the earth, who wants to call his family's attention to it. To the south stand two landmarks, the Schwarzenbach churchtower and the Burg schoolhouse, the eerie brain folds of the molasse valleys overtake the transverse undulations of the Alpine foothills, cut off by the Rigi, which glimmers in the silver mist. To take in these visions from one day to the next must have restored his good humor and eased his spirit, so often beset by businessman's worries; in this gift of nature lie the roots, it strikes me, of my father Mandi's proverbial generosity.

How often in my life have I met people whose feudal bequests have made them stingy and *shmug*, because their material wealth lacks such horizons. This phenomenon struck me all the more when my father taught me the essential principle of success: invest before you look for a return. After Black Friday in America, when the hosiery where Otto Weber's protégé was named artistic director went belly-up, the young man, a diploma-bearer from the Académie Leger, was pushed to the edge of the abyss, and found himself cleaning milk cans from Uncle Herbert's store. In entrepreneurial terms, this was the low point of my father's existence, already it must have eaten at him that he'd not gone into the tobacco firm. And yet, it was this same adversity that made him generous. Not principally as regards money, but more a willingness to give. The skinflint holds his possessions to his chest, the smallest sacrifice pains him. This is a spiritual ailment, often concealed beneath the cloak of Christian charity, the purest hypocrisy, since the Bible says it is better to give than to receive. And the parish – reduced all round to a troupe of seven upright men – whose example shall it follow, when the preacher himself cashes in wherever he roams? The pastor's greed makes manifest the utter bankruptcy of Christianity, all talk of God's mercy with its boundless love turns hollow when those who preach the gospel are unable to bestow this gift themselves. Taking what we might call the clerical-economic approach reveals to us the angst of the pious before the great deception. Worldly existence is supposed a vale of tears with only the beyond promising a life in light and truth. Whoever strives for that is damned close to a penny investor wringing his hands, never certain if his deposits will pay out. And so we come to the paradox that the legatees of Christian charity are the greatest egoists, cheese-parers, and cheapskates, because the guarantee of eternal bliss throws them into an identity crisis. Naturally they won't admit they chase on Mammon's heels like every other so-called materialist, but are too tight-fisted ever to treat themselves or those around them, they hover like blowflies round their earthly possessions, far more than the nonbeliever, because they are never entirely certain they won't be taking their bank book with them when they go.

In this sense, my tobacco grandfather was a realist, he died of cancer of the esophagus, suffered dreadful pains, did not lament his preference for the Stierenberg over the church in Menzenmang, departed after a full life at sixty-one years of age, I would happily sit with him at one of the garden tables with a bottle of Beaujolais, as I do sometimes in dreams, scoffing at God and the world. The Waldau as it was back then: clematis climbs from the studio corner up to the window of the back door, where I used to huddle shut away for hours and eavesdrop on the guests, in the front garden, the Swiss flag whips in the wind. The wisteria has overgrown the staggered fence, and the closed shutters on the first floor of the brick restaurant wing speak of darkened bedrooms in an everlasting summer. In the background, the mossy fountain gurgles. Here, the gabled façade looks out into the countryside, welcoming; there under the eaves is the almond-shaped vent. Ideli, her black hair pulled back, is gathering vegetables in the *gartin,* Elsa is pulling Barry toward her and dreaming of the Vorstenlanden, Greti sits on the railing of the Lindenberg terrace looking out for the cheeky American, who will drive past in his open-topped Buick, Rösli, the eldest, is playing her part in her white flowered dress, Irma – a cancer – the chef of the group, stands gracefully in the door to the *salï;* Mandi, with his Modigliani eyes, breaks the hearts of dark-skinned women he will never dare his whole life long to speak a word to; this was the big family I would have wanted, schlepping the mattress to the upmost balcony on hot summer nights to sleep out under the stars. And when, in June of 1941, Mandi broke away from this commonwealth, the second member of the family to do so – there he is, down and to the left of the title, in what seems to be a deep conversation with my grandfather, and again on the opposing page introducing his first born, who reaches for Ätti's spectacles beneath the legend *ven ye ken tek de hill* – the die was already cast, the Waldau will not pass down to the fourth generation, the inheritance will come too late. The wedding photo in front of the Menzenmang terrace, Hermann II in a tux, head heavy on his trabuco-like body; my mother, the city girl from St. Gallen, is wearing a tufted wedding gown, Father is sticking his nose into the bouquet of roses, Grandmother from Schneisingen is leaning on her son, perennial lace jabot atop her sagging breasts: the manufacturer's villa will remain with the family forty-four years in total. I cannot omit here that my Ormond Brasil Jubilé has burned down to a chilled cadaver that clings to my lower lip. I didn't have the strength to take the reins when my parents' home was sold off, I was laid up at the hospital in Königsfelden and endorsed the calamitous documents, though it is a humane imperative not to exact a life-altering decision from a patient in an acute state of depression. Now I am long gone under, grey of heart, grey of hair, but is my pertinacity to the bitter end at Brunsleben not a last demonstration of the Waldau spirit? Am I not reliving my grandfather's legacy as I seek solace in the next cigar, pour a glass of Château Lynch-Bages, *grand cru classé,* light a few lanterns, sing "On the Heath, the Last Roses Still Bloom" with the men's choir? Am I not still a memory for all of you, so long as I sit here at my table in the palace courtyard filling these tobacco leaves?

Schweizerischer
Blindenfreund
Kalender

XXIX. Jahrgang 1950 Preis Fr. 1.
(inkl. WuSt)

22.

APPRENTICESHIP WITH GRANDFATHER, HABASUMA

Had three generations at the Waldau given me the chance, had the wife of Hermann I, the founder of the excursion restaurant, given birth to my grandfather a little later, let's say in 1892 instead of 1882, had Mandi been the firstborn and married in 1935, then my coveted apprenticeship as a tobacco merchant would hardly have been impossible, I would, after secondary school, have trained as a salesman – my father did this, and he hated it – lodging in the Brenner brothers office next to the trout pond in Uncle Bertrand's garden, that prototypical Upper Wynental counting house with its innumerable hunting trophies and its view of the green valley – I salute thee a thousand times; the sedate figure in his sixties would have offered a cigar to his underling, guiding him over to the map of Cuba, deep yellow, almost brown, from age, pointing out where the tobacco was grown: Look here, *mon compagnon,* these are the provinces of Pinar del Río, that's the origin of Vuelta Abajo, the king of all leaves, Partido comes from outside of Havana, Santa Clara is famous for Remedio. The produce is gathered in *manojos,* that's a thick bundle of leaves squeezed together. Partido leaves are lighter than those from the powerful Vuelta Abajo, sometimes they have a light green tint, especially when they're used for wrappers. Around eighty *manojos* make up a bale or *tercio,* which is packed in palm leaves, often wrapped in tissue, a *serón* is the antiquated term, in the sixteenth century they used to reach the port of Seville wrapped in silk. Apart from the provenance, Vuelta Abajo, you divide the leaves into the following categories: for *capas,* 1 ½*, ligero, seco, viso, viso seco.* For *quebrados: ligero, seco, fino, medio tiempo, maduro. Capas* are destined for wrappers, *tripas* for the filler, the binder we will get to later. *Tripas ligeras* make for a lighter filler, *tripas pesadas* a more substantial one. Then there are *puntillas,* which add zest to the blend. *Botes* and *hojas* are loose leaves, *barre suelo* the tiny sandleaves. Stamped letters stand for a number of attributes: M for *maduro,* MT for *medio tiempo,* C for *capa dura,* which are little full-bodied leaves.

At this, Grandfather would have pulled a few samples from a bale and bundled them into what the Dutch call a *stel,* a tuft of the kind handed to wholesalers bidding on subscriptions in Bremen or in Amsterdam's Frascati Theater so they could check the edges of the wrapper leaves, test their elasticity, confirm their color, thinking always of the sumptuousness of the final product, and concerned, in all instances, with clarity. Make a note, Junior, the classic triad of Habasuma: Havana, Sumatra, and Brazil. Which tobacco sultanates produce the finest wrappers in the world? Two mornings in, Hermann Arbogast

Brenner would already have known: Langkat, Deli Sardang, and Padang Bedagai. Correct, the first Sumatra lots came on the market in 1864. Plants are cultivated on large plantations, the best known being Deli Maatschaapij and Senemba Mij. Sorting and baling take place on the premises, this is called the estate system. The stamp usually tells plantation, color, leaf length, and harvest year. The bales are also marked with a lot number and a declared weight. Roman numerals are used for length when the bushel is superior grade. Here is a page from a subscription book: up for auction is a lot of 711 bundles of Deli Maatschappij, delivered on the Palembang, Length I, 125 Pn., leaf portion 209. LV means *licht vaal,* slightly pale, as is true of the mouse-grey sand leaves. For a tobacco to be seaworthy, it must first of all be baled with the right degree of humidity. Wares packed in a damp hold run not only the risk of mold or spoilage, but also of uncontrolled fermentation, darkening, sometimes cooking themselves to death. Here Grandfather would have shown me his Danneman and said: what we want is a black Brazil with snow-white ash, but never one fermented to death. Write that phrase in your notebook: *fermented to death.* He progressed following his pedagogical instincts rather than ironbound principles – nothing at all like Basler, my teacher from Burg – though he would emphasize a basic conceptual framework. Now, as for proper stowage on a ship, the freighter's steel frame must either be padded or the cargo insulated with wood scrap. The floor must be laid with fabric, even the supports. Tobacco can't be stacked too high, because the pressure will damage it. Incidentally, can you tell me the export harbor for Río Grande in Brazil? Porto Alegre. Correct. The tweendeck is ideal for loading if condensation buildup can be avoided. With summer shipments, when the brown gold continues to ferment as it travels – this happens with Oriental tobacco, among others – it must be covered with great care. No ventilators. Pay attention here, junior, in the end, all these things are the responsibility of the raw wholesaler. Sweaty freight, as we call it, poses a special danger to the bales: ores, fresh corn, wood, spices with strong aromas. If there's any of that around, you have to put special barriers in place.

Throughout his disquisition, Grandfather would walk repeatedly to the window, keeping a lookout for incoming guests – a good host neglects no *arrivée*. Bahía tobacco is seeded in April or May and reaches the trade market in December, packed in canvas bales of sixty or seventy kilograms, the shippers stamp it, the names printed underneath the logo, as with Suerdieck, Danneman, and Barreto before. The quality center is Mata Fina, important towns and villages include São Félix, Muritiba, Cabeças, Cruz das Almas, Sapeaçu, Baixa do Palmeira, Conceição do Almeida and São Felipe. The docked leaves are sorted into the following grades: Patente finissima, Patente Patente Patente, Patente Patente, Patente Flor, Prima, Segunda, Segunda Baixa, Terceira Alta, Terceira Baixa, Folhas finas and R (Refugo, the rejects). Now for a bit of morphology: the twisted three-piece cigar, what we call a crooked dog, is known elsewhere as a *culebra*. The long one there, rolled from a single leaf, that's a *veguero*. On the table we have a perfecto, it's shaped like a fish, narrow foot, long and pointed head. From the Spanish styles, we have yet to look at the coronas, which run from *petit* to *gran,* with robustos, toros, and Churchills in between. Ecstatic, Hermann II would have opened the sample case then to show me the nuances, hardly visible to the eye, of the Regalía, the Regalía Media, the Millar, the Entre Actos, the Londres. I would have grasped all this in no time. Why bother wading through thick tomes when you can learn it all with your nose!

In the cargo port, inspectors often receive the tobacco, and are tasked with properly storing the goods and forwarding them along to the customer. On the wall of the counting house with the hunting lodge accents hangs the image of a narrow street between old brick buildings with sharp gabled roofs – old tobacco storehouses in Bremen. O, Bremen, my grandfather sighs, looking over toward the Reinach Moor, Hanseatic city of the patrissians, patrissians with a long hissing S, that's how they talk up there, you know. That one is the Schröder house on the Langenstrasse, those are the workers' buildings with the broad halls and oriels. Here is the somber North German shipping port for malvasia, olive oil, muscat, and gold-laced brocade. Those are the big beer trucks on the harbor streets, the scent of malt hangs over the docks. When the bales of Havana, Sumatra, and Brazil are stored in the warehouse, they require the same attention as during shipping. Avoid concrete floors, wood grating is really best. Now and then, you must rotate the tobacco bales, same as during fermentation. Too much light is harmful, windows should be covered or painted blue. Oriental bales especially need to be restacked every month, Kalum and Samsun six units high, Bashi Bagli eight. In Samsun we distinguish the following provinces, Samsun-Maden-Dere Bashi Bagli, Samsun-Alatcham Bashi Bagli, Samsun Bashi Bagli, Baffra Bashi Bagli, this is Yaka, very rich in aromas, but not as spicy as the Xanthi varieties. It burns excellently, the leaf is smooth, similar in shape to the Kulaksis, darker than Macedo-nian, ranging from brownish yellow to smoky topaz. The jewel of these counting house hours at the foot of the Stierenberg would have been the shift from the discussion of districts to an ever more intensive tast-ing of the tobacco itself, in the handing of which my grandfather would have been a master; he would have rolled the core of the cigar one leaf at a time, without need of a mold or pattern sheet, would have cut the wrapper from the outspread, deveined leaf with his *chaveta*. This is how you smoke at the auctions in the Bremen harbor, where the quality experts from houses like Brenner, Burger, La Paz, and Suerdieck bring *bonches* of their own product to test how they marry with the Mandi Angin on offer. Three years ago, my cousin Johann Caspar Brenner took me along as his guest. That was a modern lesson in attentiveness, in four days of hard work every last sign of overfermentation was rooted out and noted down. In the makeshift offices, which some joker had hung with No Smoking signs, not the least vestige remained of the romanticism of the Frascati Theater in Amsterdam as my grandfather was able to experience it, with bidders looking to buy select portions of a given lot climbing up over the balustrades of the loggia at the risk of breaking their necks. The subscriptions, *inschrijvingen* in Dutch, are doled out by blind auction. The advantage of this for the plantations is that the producer or wholesaler must offer the highest price he is will-ing to pay from the very beginning if he wants any chance of getting his hands on an allotment. *De makelaars van het kontor,* who have con-ducted this business on behalf of the importers since time immemorial, take samples from the bales and bundle them into *stels* or sheaves, with each wholesaler getting a sample. Subscriptions are for whole lots only, which comprise bales with marks of all kinds on them. From the letters and symbols in the subscription book, the initiated can tell how much of the tobacco is *spikkel,* marked with brown spots, how much is shatter and offal, whether an assortment will likely show a lighter or darker tint. In the first four days of an auction week, brokers will hand the samples over to their customers in their offices. Leaf after leaf was laid in the Brenner stall over the half-cylinder board and tested according to strict criteria; a hunchbacked *mynheer* from Dentz & van Breggen zipped around constantly and pounded his foot like Rumpelstiltskin if the product was too damp or crumbly. The tobacco was tested for combustibility and the consistency of the ash, and the arcanum specialists – in this matter, Hermann Arbogast Brenner could claim no expertise – bandied about expressions specific to the métier, *a hint of onion, a tinny aftertaste, a slightly cloying sensation,* this sandleaf has a touch of Kentucky to it, there are rust spots on some of the viso leaves, the SA 1 from PPN Yogyakurta is too green, better the SH 1 and 2, say thirteen or fourteen bales of the full-bodied stuff, a third of the SO is *clunky,* in the PB Tamarin the SH 1 has heft, from the SKK lot not one bit is salvageable. The Sahara beige subscription book, published by the German-Indonesian Tobacco Trade Society, LLC, shows an order for 8,466 bales of Sumatra, mainly Maden Estate, Sampali, Batang Kwis, Bandar Klippa, Helvetia, Paja Bakung, Bulu Tjina, Tandjon Djati, Kwala Begumit, but many others, too, lots were stored at the warehouses of the Bremer Lagerhaus-Gesellschaft, known today as the BLG Logistics Group.

Subscription bids were placed on Friday, with the bid – a prospective purchase price in DM per half kilo – delivered in a sealed envelope to the brokers at Denz & van der Breggen or submitted to other firms like J. de Keijzer or Köster & Schriefer and then forwarded to the plantations themselves. The contract went to the highest bidder. No sooner was Brenner & Sons declared winner of the PB than the secondary purchasers stormed the stall and besieged Johann Caspar Brenner; calculator in hand, he had to decide on the fate of the PSK and PSO. Hand over his mouth, he said to me: if I can't get rid of the surplus lots at a profit, I'm ruined, I just can't warehouse this much Sumatra. This would have been my world, this and nothing more. The successful broker naturally showed his magnanimity, pouring, at the Bremer Hof, Johann Caspar Brenner's favorite Bordeaux, a 1979 Lynch-Bages *grand cru classé*. Such was my experience in the merchant city where my great-grandfather had sent his son Hermann from the Waldau to make of him a good *Tubaker*. Older Sumatra freaks still recalled the young huntsman, the singer from the Menzenmang men's choir, had kind words for his inn and for his beautiful daughters, had heard of the fate of my aunt who had gone to Java and gotten married. In the rooms of the Bremen exchange in the harbor, no smoker needed recoil, contrite in his blue haze, only the cigarette smoker could expect a sneering glance. As always in specialized circles, I was given a role, which I played to the hilt, all the more so as it was tailor-made for me: on account of my last name, Brenner, the competition set to asking who this new bigwig from the renowned firm in Pfeffikon might be, and more than a few secondary purchasers came to me directly, thinking it would be easier to fleece a greenhorn than

Herr von der Osten-Sacken, the old warhorse in charge of the German subsidiary; after the count, with his monocle, observed this turn of events, he encouraged me to start bargaining, and, to the despair of van der Breggens, I was the one to push the price for the high-karat PB down five more pfennigs in the final seconds, the broker watched his lot slip away, and with it his entire business, but my instincts were correct, we had overbid our Dutch arch-rivals, who were keen on the Suerdieck leaves for wrappers, by a single pfennig. I gathered the bids, placated a sore loser here, a PSJ hunter there, proved my usefulness and in this way justified the outlay on my hotel. It is not ill-advised for the man without home, job, or family to enjoy the illusion, at least, of playing his part in society now and again, it gives him a sort of nest egg of self-assurance for the rainy days when he's dangling from an IV in the Friedmatt or Königsfelden, though it must be said that the depressive, during his phases of tablet-somnolence, is hard to convince of the wisdom of nurturing himself on recollections from his lucid intervals; he is more like a gastro-intestinal casualty who has eaten a bad bit of fish – no pike ever again, he declares, and the mere thought of a beer-battered perch brings him to the verge of vomiting. I know the comparison is a lame one, but the image is appropriate, in the endogenous deeps, there is nothing to do but gag, what is buried inside erupts forth, the stomach turns inside out like the pocket of a vest. But *nicotiana tabacum* is a solanacean par excellence, and in these dark times, the cigar alone offers us a certain consolation, for the Havana or Brenner Habasuma is not a boundless gustatory pleasure, but instead serves the function of cardiograph or spirometer, as long as the smoke ribbons gather and furl, we can be certain we are still here.

Far be it from Hermann Arbogast Brenner to plunge the indulgent reader into the shadowy fate of the depression-plagued, O no, this is one lesson I have grasped, it is tactless for one to inventory his assembled torments and bid the incurably healthy to forfeit their earnestness in the enjoyment of life; and yet he will point to one peculiarity in the existential strategy of this species of chronic invalid, namely that our kind must achieve in three, four months what the psychologically stable, those pampered by God, may dawdle over an entire year. To Jérôme von Castelmur-Bondo or Bert May or Irlande von Elbstein-Bruyère or Adam Nautilus Rauch, to all those who can confidently fill in their agenda, one wants to cry out: *try it my way.* We would like to beg them for a bit of sympathy for the immutable terror that lingers when we light a cigar, never knowing, when the cadaver sits dead in the ashtray, whether we will not lie devastated on the floor until nine. This phrase too demands an apology. As a drudge in the fields of literature, particularly in matters lyrical, I let a quote from Benn glide in now and then, the verses of this Berlin dermatologist and specialist in venereal diseases are the only ones I can adorn myself with from the annals of the world's inwardness: *There are songs and melodies / that make certain rhythms soar / they maim you inwardly / and till nine you're on the floor.* Depression proceeds in this very same way: it maims our soul, knocks us down with a low blow, cares nothing about good sportsmanship. When this happens, we can kiss goodbye to all our plans, call for the ambulance, put ourselves into psychiatry's hands. If I speak so immodestly of all this, it is only so that

the reader of these tobacco leaves, who savors the smoke of my childhood, may grasp that Hermann Arbogast Brenner never could strive for
the writer's ideal of immaculate prose hardened in the hearth of
self-critique. He may have had the desire and patience, but sadly, the
capacity to work was often wanting. Every page I type on my rented
machine may be my last. For months, at least. And so it would be point-
less to anticipate a motif, for tomorrow the meat wagon may drag me
off again, and then what I had to say will linger there, unresolved in
space. To make a virtue of this immense impairment demands an
entirely new aesthetic. Where the true novelist is right to slip pleasantly
into Book One what will reach its resolution in Book Five, I am living
hand-to-mouth, and must keep my suitcase packed next to my desk,
waiting at all hours for my arrest.

Expounding upon these matters rather longer than I had meant to,
I am compelled to put forward assorted factual constants concerning
the most dreadful mental illness that has ever haunted humankind. It is
commonly said that someone's fallen down in the dumps. A man who
tumbles into a crack in a glacier will not express himself so euphemis-
tically. Nor does one buried beneath meters of snow go on believing
in avalanche dogs with casks of brandy around their necks. And yet,
compared with us, the daredevil tourist has an advantage: everyone can
see his misfortune. The rescue party is called to action, because even a
child can imagine how terrible it is to slide down twenty meters among
the seracs. Such a fate is stirring, alpine folklore, if you will. It grips the
imagination of thousands upon thousands, and with a sample of this
size, the odds of finding a Samaritan are fairly high. Add to that another

factor, not to be underestimated: no matter what happens, the recovery operation is destined to be spectacular. Tabloid headlines are guaranteed. The rude elements – ice, cold, snow – are a challenge, and people rise to the occasion to defy their rigors. The depressive must get by without any such heroic prerogatives. Even in the midst of the most critical danger, he walks upright among the living, and this makes an SOS out of the question. I am aware of the dimension I have introduced with this concept. There are no theatrical laurels to be harvested by caring for the patient with neurotransmitter deficiencies. His protracted suicide occurs in utter silence, in isolation from the public. If there were, in the health care system, something akin to patent law, it would prohibit a prognosis more dreadful than terminal cancer, such a thing, in diplomatic terms, would quite simply not be recognized. A curious detail in this regard. The brochure for the euthanasia society Exitus, entitled "What Is the Most Practical Way to Kill Myself?" is available for a lending fee of twenty francs to the life-weary of all stripes. But not to endogenous depressives. Whoever finds himself in the unenviable position of having to accept therapeutic treatment for his mood disorder is disqualified from suicide by euthanasia. Membership in this minority means being saddled with the verdict: you get no chance.

When my beloved wife and two sons, whom I coddled like seedlings in the soil of Vuelta Abajo, fled Brunsleben like rats abandoning a sinking ship after years of attrition from my illness, one and all among my circle agreed that I couldn't hold it against them. My friend Fernanda Blanca of Blankenberg shot me a stare hot with indignation: Don't you understand, no one could take all that. Her feminist-tinged protest suffers from a single logical failing. There is one person who must take it, and that is the depressive himself. And here is where the glaring injustice lies: he is forced to cling to the war hero's code, the kamikaze mentality of *fight to the last man.* O numberless dilettantes of mercy! A rule-abiding *Exitus* exitus with the help of one hundred tabs of Vesparax could still be portrayed as euthanasia. Do you not see that Hermann Arbogast Brenner could more calmly make his peace with the world if a higher court would lend him a thoughtful hand in view of his life's unbearableness? Do you not see his salesman's pride prevents him from taking the blame for this *faillisement?* But no: all others have the right no longer to stand him, he alone is condemned to endure his own sinister company. And he will never forgive you this grave offense: that in your schadenfreude, you left him to smolder in his hell. Let us temper that a bit: he *would* never have forgiven you had he not discovered in the Stechlinesque spirit of Brunsleben a medium that unmasks your diabolical self-righteousness – in tobacco, a potion against the danger of earthquakes in mind and spirit. Turning back to my cigarier apprenticeship amid the hunting trophies in my grandfather's Waldau counting house: he, too, had hard days in his life, one of my aunts told me of a conversation in Ätti and Müeti's marital bed in which the wine lover and trout fisherman admitted: I wouldn't at all mind doing myself in. The question now arises whether a smoker of some thirty cigars and cheroots a day is not in the midst of shoveling his own grave. We can only respond by introducing the principle of intensity into the debate. The person who renounces tobacco for the sake of health has adopted a clear strategy of becoming as old as possible, no matter the price. In doing so, he overlooks a certain paradox. He is running the risk of having to remember at ninety years of age how he said no to a Havana or a Brazil after his wedding. And for what? Nothing, not a single thing save this tormented recollection. Especially as an impenitent is sitting there next to him at his usual table, still alive despite indulging in tobacco since the days of his confirmation. How insulting. He was allowed to sin unpunished, what about me? One or another of my indulgent readers may now object: not so fast, sure as night follows day, the other guy's got a smoker's leg. And so? Is it not far worse, more frustrating, to have to renounce life's sublimest pleasure hundreds of thousands of times over than to pay for the decades of wishes granted with a narrowing of the vessels in old age?

Note now that I digress philosophically here without having read a single letter of Kant, Schopenhauer, or Nietzsche. But I do seem to remember a sentence of my grandfather's: he had tobacco to thank for so many good years that he'd gladly take a few Mays off his old age. And his approach seems to me wiser than the ascetic aspirations of the vita-min-marathon superheroes who eschew dry drunkenness only to recall when they are old as Lazarus every cigar they ever turned down. A miser is not just someone who pinches pennies, who doesn't like to splurge or give, it is a person who never treats himself. He labors under the delusion that a little ledger exists in Heaven with an annotation in the profits column stating that he made it to a hundred by shopping at the organic market. All the world's misery originates with underachiev-ers. Hitler had to kill millions for failing to achieve his dream. Had he known, like Churchill, how to savor a Havana, there would never have been a Second World War. I admit Hermann Arbogast Brenner was late in taking this lesson to heart, in Caux, at the conference for Moral Re-Armament, he was raised in the opposite tendency. He learned to suppress his drives, to contemn the yearning to sleep with a woman as a Communist subversion of morals. He paid for this school, which his parents threw him into, with complexes, psychosomatic disturbances, and eventually endogenous depression. But a true Brenner is like a reed, he bends but doesn't break. He drew from his experience an ironbound mirth. The worldwide anti-smoking hysteria, an alibi for those for whom the grapes of true enjoyment hang too high, could not keep a single Brenner Export from his hands. And the entire bewitchment of Moral Re-Armament, veiled as anti-Communist ideology, collapsed like a house of cards when a beautiful woman was not only willing, but even keen to share a bed with him.

This brings me to a further question, why we always smoke after lovemaking. In the orgasm, as psychologists say, we suffer a little death. For the passionate cigarier, it is logically an aesthetic failing when, especially in French films, the afterplay ends and the lovers reach for a Gauloise. Nothing stimulates a woman of the world so much as a corona. Not only does it help us gather our scattered thoughts, it is a tonic for the soul, and promotes potency – because the Havana, Sumatra, and Brazil actually satisfy, whereas the cigarette serves only to bridge an awkward interval. In a social setting, the aromas drifting from a Romeo y Julieta may strike women as offensive, but in the intimate realm, they generate an aura that lets a lady know: real men smoke cigars. This has nothing to do with the superficial phallic symbol, it relates to erotics in the broadest sense of the term. A man who understands tobacco in its natural form knows how to proceed with women. Like a Montecristo, they want to be taken patiently, not pawed at in a fever. They may place value on their impeccable complexion, but it would offend them if a man, led astray by it, were to ignore the quality of the filler. Their red hair is a sign for their admiration of Rilke. Their carmine nails hint at the metrics in their innermost depths. And so they are advised to seek consummate tenderness not from a chain smoker, but in the arms of a mature connoisseur of *nicotiana tabacum*.

At this point, at the latest, Hermann Arbogast Brenner must bring this analogy to an end, for a lover never is and never will be a luxury good to be savored, but a person with her own contradictions. A cigar can be procured when the craving strikes, a woman who shares not just our bed, but our miseries, cannot. To meet one is a gift, a bit of mercy, even. Love is not an exchange of hormones, but the highest, happiest hours this crippled planet holds in store for us. You can be happy alone with a cigar, but not in love. The blue haze gets lost in the ether, our wish to be understood by someone will never go away. If it did, we would be lost forever. The rose may bloom without ifs and buts, and unfold its splendor in a graveyard. But it can only be called happy when it is found and plucked. This brings me, through byways, back to the nonsmoker and his health-oriented ascesis. His behavior is bold, for he renounces the scent of temptation, deprives the five senses of an aroma expressly made to produce camaraderie. A class reunion only comes to life once a box of cigars makes the rounds. Friendship is the anteroom of love. Whoever has made it to the age of Hermann Arbogast Brenner and yet hopes to meet a noble lady should not renounce these ingredients lightly. This is not in the least a play on the Stuyvesant cigarette jingle: *The fragrance of the whole wide world*. What's in the Stuyvesant? A little Maryland, a bit of Kentucky, the same old trimmings from Hamburg you find all over in the cancer stick business. If anyone is destined to bring the entire palette to life, from Cruz das Almas to Vorstenlanden, then it is the passionate cigarier, for he alone knows how to appreciate nuances. And nuances, in the end, are what matters in the interpersonal as well. Nowadays, any woman who wants can be blonde, but not Titian red. Each individual is a unique and irrepeatable child of nature, and the highest thing he has to give, his love, may bring him a partner who acknowledges this unicity. All subordinate forms of affection are prostitution: far commoner than monetary corruption is the horizontal traffic in illusions. I belong to you because you take me to be what corresponds to your ideal. Millions of marriages follow this pattern. The cigarier, who devotes decades of study to distinguishing authentic Brazilian black from a Bahía leaf fermented to death, is less hasty in succumbing to contemporary delusions.

I had wished simply to communicate to the indulgent reader that at the end of his days, despite the hard blows of fate and bodily misfortunes of all sorts, Hermann Arbogast Brenner is not unhappy, because each of the cigar boxes stacked on the floor with its persistent bouquet of cedar or Gabon wood reminds me of countless hours of concentrated attention. And this brings us to the blunder of many present-day cavaliers: they do not realize the woman of their heart yearns for fire.

23.

CHILDREN'S HOME IN AMDEN,
CULEBRA

G reat is the joy when my father one day explains: From tomorrow on, you won't be alone any more, we're putting you in a home with lots of children, all of them your own age, and you'll get to play with them. Though I pray every afternoon, no little sister or brother is ever granted me, I drag my pan like a cursed prince through the park, eventually exploring it all the way to the woods in front and the arbor in the back, and the iron fence overgrown with hedges, which rises up as an espaliered wall toward Gütschstrasse, turns to a veritable cage imprisoning me in my relentless boredom, Rüedeli in Aschenbach is still too young, Philipp comes to see me sometimes on his wooden tricycle, but then there's usually a fight, my mossy-slit trysts with shifty Margrit are confined to forbidden moments behind the house. I must pause now to withdraw a Partagás Culebras from its foil sleeve. This is a twisted bundle of three breva-style cigars, in Germany it is known as a crooked dog. I have long wrestled in vain with this section, have tried to evoke once and for all this most cursed time in my Menzenmang childhood with the help of Brissago lung-busters, assorted Virginias, even chewing tobacco. The memory burns like dirt in a skinned knee. We spend a whole day traveling by rail, then take the yellow post bus with the open roof up a steep wooded road through a mountain pass, it resembles the way to Soglio, I have no idea what country they are taking me to, over and over I ask, what are the children's names? If, in the present tobacco leaves, which I hope have not fermented to death, Hermann Arbogast Brenner repeatedly sings the praises of growing up alone, this is, to a degree, a distortion, for in those days, before Amden, he had imagined something promising might well come of a group of playmates, yes, I approached society full of hope and good intentions, but would soon find this love was not reciprocated.

The inmates, or must I say pupils, sit at a long table in front of their soup bowls on the veranda of the dark brown chalet. It smells sharply of varnish, the sun is blinding. A sister takes me to my seat, Father watches from the doorway. She ties a bib in a knot around my neck, squeezing it tight against my wart. I will soon learn to detest the resolute grasp of these hands with their scent of curd soap. The boy next to me looks far older than I. He has fire red curls and a freckled face. Because I know this name from a fairytale, I ask him: Are you Siegfried? No, he answers dismissively, I'm Adrian. What's your name? It's still a riddle to me why I lie to him, in this way putting myself at his mercy. Perhaps it is the instinct of a criminal, who never willingly reveals his identity. Wolfgang, I say. Well now, who's afraid of the big bad wolf? Do you have seven goats at your house? Already we are trapped in a dialogue of subordination, and I will never break free from this nickname I've pinned on myself. Father nods to me, maybe says to the old woman in the starched headdress: Look, he's already found a friend. Every time I try to eat a spoonful of my soup, he nudges me with his elbow and says, as my groats spill out: One spoonful for Red Riding Hood, one for Soupy Caspar, *I will not eat this soup, I won't,* and the children join in with an unholy racket, all of them have finished their meal. Now, for the first time, the five-year-old asks himself in dread: What are they going do to you? Adrian won't stop bumping me, my bib is soaked. And as I look over toward the veranda door to appeal to a higher justice, I see that my father is gone. He is far down the hill, walking the path into that foreign village high over the Walensee. This cannot be true. But it is, and now the latch turns closed. Thick tears slide down into my cold gruel. Adrian bangs his spoon on the table and shouts: Sister Margrit, the wolf won't eat his soup, he has to wear his bib all afternoon. No one helps me loosen the tight knot around my neck, our warden vanishes into the labyrinthine interior of the witch house, the children run past me to the field to play. Except for Adrian, who pulls me in back of the chalet and commands me to crouch on the gravel. If I wait long enough, someone will come untie my bib. He corrects my posture with a hazel switch. He is wearing grey-and-red checked socks and green lederhosen with edelweiss on the suspenders. *Git down,* he orders me. You stay there till you hear steps. Repeat what you're to do. I stay crouching till I hear steps. That's right! Even his knees are covered in tiny, rust red freckles. I turn toward the wall, Adrian vanishes into the underbrush, the woods descend sharply behind the children's home toward a creek. After hours of waiting, when I try to get up, my joints are completely numb, and stones fly from all sides toward my face. My tormenter stands suddenly before me with crossed arms, spits at my feet, and asks: You know what you're being punished for? No, I say, and again, a hail of stones. You still don't know: Yes, I tried to get up before someone came. Lookey here, Adrian continues, someone's feeling guilty. My mom says a clear conscience is a good pillow. We'll give you another chance. I turn back toward the wall, which looks just like the tarry brown laths of the Menzenmang baths I walk past holding Grandmother's hand when we take the path along the Wyna into the village on our way back from the cemetery. Down in the meadow I hear the children playing a game called Uri, Schwyz, and Unterwald. Rescue is so close and yet so far. I crouch so long my legs give out, now I am kneeling on the sharp gravel, and I tuck my head, covering my ears with my hands. But no stones come, the leader and his lackeys have long since stolen away.

The sister makes a stern face: Where'd you get off to all that time? I never even think of telling on Adrian. He is the stronger one. I am passed over when sweets are handed out before bedtime. A helper scrubs my eyes with a soapy rag until they burn so horribly I can't see. In the dormitory, which opens onto a broad balcony, I lie pressed against the wall, squeeze the sheet in my fingers, and feel *it* running out of me, warm. How awful that this still happens to me. When darkness breaks in, and the boys have crawled under their blankets, I hold my breath, listening for sounds in the hallway, on the stairs. A soft click-clack tells of footfalls. Someone has it in for me, someone is tiptoeing up the stairs. Lying, legs sticky, in my cold, wet puddle, I wait for the pillow to smother me. Jonah and the whale. Then there is a murmur, a groan, a moan, a padding, a tapping, a drone. The ghost glides soundlessly through the locked door and hides behind the dresser in the corner, where it glowers at me. I can't move a limb, and I feel my hair bristle. My teeth start chattering and give me away. Is it the Klabautermann, the phantom dog, the Rye Aunt? In the darkness, a basilisk pins me in its stare. And again, a slimy rasping sound! In torment, I turn away, but now I have given the nightmare beast my back. It is best to play dead. For that sputtering and crackling thing could be a reaper, a gnome, or a huldra. Or an elf or nixie, some unspeakable incubus with tentacles and suckers that has found its way up to Amden. Hermann Arbogast Brenner is aware of the pitfalls of drawing on concepts that for the child do not yet exist. He does so only because all these hellcats and spawn of the underworld, these sylphs, trolls, and kobolds, are prefigured in our souls, which make as though to banish the horror through distance, for the terror we can name we can domesticate. Morning begins with my vain search for my teddy bear. I look all over, at the foot of the bed, behind it, under the covers, in the nightstand. Then someone chuckles: Time for your morning tinkle, Wolfie. My stuffed animal is in the chamber pot, head down, dark yellow with urine. Still, I press it to my body, maybe this teddy bear from Menzenmang will protect me like a talisman. I coughed, and Adrian said: Our bedwetter's sick, we better give him a shot. Four of them gather around the bedframe, I obey the order to push my bottom up in the air. One of them rolls up my nightshirt, and the boy with the red hair slowly presses a needle into my flesh. Better now? he asks. The tears flow with the chiming of the bell. Instead of going to church like everyone else, I am made to stay behind in the dormitory. Later I will learn this is a Catholic home, I am the only one from a different denomination; with unerring instinct the gang has figured out which one of us is the outsider. A bronze torrent engulfs my heart, it saps me when I think of Menzenmang, of the big magnolia tree by the sandbox, the water trough in the grape cellar, the hiba trees behind the house. Edwin's Pretty Mama in a high-necked dress, her hair in curls. But Father and Mother will not answer at the manufacturer's villa, they are off attending the Moral Re-Armament conference in Caux. They did their homework, the current Agape Center in the hill country of St. Gallen came highly recommended. They could not have known, during their "quiet time" while they waited for a message from God, that I was living through a small Hell, a children's camp mortification.

Why did they have it in for you, what made you different from all the others? One day I promise myself I *will* heed the call of the bell, will run down the hill, through the steep woods to the lake, climb over the seven mountains, and return home to my Anker stones, my colored pencils, and the vanished picture book. The strange thing is that the world where Adrian reigned fit so easily in the overall order of the home, with its mealtimes, naptimes, recess, swimming trips, even bedtime stories. In this system, the bully is the model child, and the sisters hold him up for us as an example to be followed. He washes himself cleanest, polishes his shoes brightest, picks the prettiest flowers, has the best table manners, helps out drying dishes in the kitchen. No one would believe he carries out such infamies with me behind the building. In the middle of a ballgame, I see him wave. A few boys break away and vanish with their ringleader into the forest. I follow at a prudent distance, so no one will mistake me for one of these gangsters. The gravel lot is abandoned and shadowy, the scattered firs rustle, in their shadows the holiday home transforms to Dracula's castle, the scent of garbage wafts up from the brook. I know what I have to do, I crouch down in my corner of shame, my hands clasped over my knees. I have gradually grown used to *hunkerin,* but I never know how long my bailiffs will stay waiting in the bushes. That is part of the punishment. It can last an hour, maybe more. Sometimes I run away after a few minutes and no one throws a single stone, and I find Adrian on the playground playing the Samaritan and bandaging up some girl who's fallen and gotten scraped. In a conversation on Lake Hallwil, Adam Nautilus Rauch rebuked me for using the term *concentration camp* to describe the children's home in Amden: Whoever says such a thing has no idea what he's talking about. True, what I suffered through two years after the gruesome discoveries in Auschwitz, Buchenwald, and Bergen-Belsen cannot be compared to the Nazis' vast death-and-inferno machinery. True, the words *concentration camp* are so laden with specific atrocities that they reject employment as metaphor. We ate no potato-peel soup, no one tore out our gold teeth, everything was quite simply much, much worse. To describe Amden as a children's concentration camp is an inadmissible understatement. If I am taken off to the showers, I don't know what is happening to me, and once the gas streams in, the horror is over. But these weeks of arbitrary terror above the Walensee, indirectly perpetrated by Moral Re-Armament, were endless, and the perversity of childhood savagery was that it could play out right under the eyes of the sisters in their cornettes. The inmates of Auschwitz could appeal to no higher power, their fate befell them without any semblance of justice. Murder behind the barbed wire was at least a certainty, straightforward, like cancer as opposed to the inconclusiveness of depression. Here I must respond to my friend and critic that Hermann Arbogast Brenner is no historian and need not conceive things in relative terms. His persuasiveness depends on mingling materials the scholar keeps in different drawers. I do so in awareness of my right to subjectivity. This in no way restricts the compass of my remarks: a personal point of view, the primordial ownness of my perspective are my weapons. Can you not see, Adam Nautilus, that what was trampled underfoot in those days was an only child's sense of justice, and that this destined the castoff to a Kohlhaas nature? I was tortured in accordance with the law.

And yet I do have one friend, a gangly boy with greasy hair named Buser. Only he can't help me, because his left leg is crippled. In the afternoons on the veranda, we lie side by side in cots and communicate with one another through signs – talking during naptime is forbidden. Not even the sisters can understand this language we've invented with our hands. O, how we enjoy it when we impart some trifle and everyone around us racks their brains trying to suss out our hidden code. There it is in the sweltering heat under the orange shutters, the explosiveness of secrecy. Buser gets around on two small crutches. When he watches the other children walk on stilts, he sometimes stands on his healthy leg and hops around in the grass. He is so pale that the blue veins in his temples show through. Buser is kind. I tell him in our deaf-mutes' tongue about my torments on the gravel lot. He follows along so intently that sweat starts to drip down his forehead. Then he sinks back on his cot, exhausted, and writes in the air with his crutch: I am your friend. I look at his lame leg, all skin and bone, which bends slightly in its bandage and splint. If I had a leg like that, I say to myself, no one could ever make me crouch down. Buser shakes his head, he has read my thoughts. No, Wolfgang, at home you can run free, I will never do that again.

The indulgent reader will long since have worked out that the roots of my fascination with magic, the nucleus of my calling as an amateur sorcerer, lie in my experience at the children's home. No one in my life has left such a mark on me as Ehrich Weiss, alias Harry Houdini, the greatest escape artist of all time. The handcuff king broke out of all irons. If today I can effortlessly thread together three strings complete strangers have tied into separate loops, my passion for repeating the feat over and again with an audience and without a cover or a backup plan comes from the plight of the five-year-old who knew no trick to escape Adrian's clutches. But I would like to stress that he who takes refuge in illusionism has despaired of reality with its physical and juridical laws. We must pass first through the hell of defenselessness, only then do we become masters of our craft. Later, one afternoon when the foehn is blowing over the veranda, Buser signs with his crutch over the view of the mountainside: Fire. The call goes out like a siren's cry into the oppressive silence, even the birds have stopped chirping. The children stand up terrified from the deck chairs, Adrian first of all. Their hair down, still in their underclothes, the sisters run out of the bathrooms. Thick, black smoke billows up from behind the firs. The scent of burning clings to the inside of your nose. We stand in a circle around a brightly blazing building just a few hundred steps from the home, watching in despair as men with sooty faces hurry past with buckets of water. The flames rage so wild against the beams, it sounds like roaring thunder. Chairs and pillows fly from the blackened windows, cattle bellow. The heat singes our hair. Girders crack, joists break open, laths splinter, lintels snap, the flames dance like a mantle of sparks over the roof. Nostrils flared, we stare into the catastrophe, not grasping how a stone structure, the most secure of all human shelters, can vanish in a tornado of fire. The bell tolls in the village. By the time the first firemen come scrambling over the hill, there is nothing left to save. I see the sister who watches us in her open cloak, thrown over her naked shoulders in haste. She stands like a goddess in the rut-red light and breathes heavily, massaging her heaving chest with her hands. She has completely forgotten her charges. I sense somehow that this misfortune, which has left a mountain family homeless, is pertinent to my own life, particularly in this camp, because the protection of my mother and father has been withdrawn, put out of commission, and yet a certain feeling of security does not elude me, in this great devastation, my own torments become more bearable. Everyone pulls together, as in the aftermath of a flood, and at this hour of chaos, not even Adrian has power over me.

In the *Struwwelpeter,* which I take to bed with me on rainy afternoons, I see my apprehensions expressed. Just as in the vanished children's book from the archives of Otto Weber-Brenner, the disobedient children bear the traits of surly adults, they move like dolls with stiff wooden legs and arms, the devil must be somewhere behind the backdrop pulling the strings. And, as in the children's home, there is no sidestepping doom. What a sad sun god, with his wild wheaten mane and his long thorny nails, standing splay-legged on the pedestal in a red waistcoat and poison green stockings, what is he railing against? And *cruel Frederick, see, a naughty, wicked boy was he,* he torments the birds, whips his Gretchen, beats the dog by the fountain, whence comes the wickedness in the minuscule face of this half-grown beer carter with a blue billed cap? I investigate the stories with my index finger, count the potted trees at the foot of the sloping stairway, lose myself in this unorthodox chronology, in which the thing announced above, where the distant village greets you over the plains, is already occurring on the path down below. The horrors of the conflagration live again in foolish Harriet's temptation, her Biedermeier dress seems made of crepe paper, the matchbox is so alluring, how full of foreboding the cats, Minz and Maunz, implore her, how they warn her of the dangers of the fire, but it cannot be otherwise, the girl with red ribbons in her hair simply must go up in flames, she is of the same substance as all these sorry marionettes, the same as Jonah in the whale at home alone. No sooner has this chubby-cheeked governess's girl struck a match than the dragons engulf her, the tongues of flame jut up from her garment, she tumbles through the room, arms aloft, as if hoping to jump out a window, and I, the inmate with the urine-soaked teddy bear, cry bitterly with the two kitties when nothing remains of her but two tiny shoes in front of a pile of ashes. Yes, I ask with Doctor Heinrich Hoffmann, where were the poor parents, where? The same drama appears in the tale of Little Suck-a-Thumb. One day, Mama said *Conrad dear, I must go out and leave you here.* How can this dreadful mother in her doll-like skirts, whose face remains hidden, leave the house so calmly, knowing, as she must, how dangerous the man with the shears is? Already in the first illustration, which makes plain her malevolent indulgence, the scraggy tike, patent leather belt cinched far below his waist, offers his thumbs for the cutting. Then there is that sphinxlike mask over the door, a rudiment of the Attic chorus narrating the events. No sooner than he is left alone, the sinner brings his thumb to his mouth, bends his knees, offers us a view of himself in profile. Conrad sucks his thumb because he doesn't know what else to do, he has no brother or sister, no toys to play with, and just as in a Greek tragedy, fate takes over. The loggia where the castration occurs reminds me of the orange veranda with the geraniums in Menzenmang. Boom, the door opens. How self-assured the man flies in, how confidently he slices, this lecherous master tailor, his horizontal hair, coattails, and measuring tape attest to his haste, his eagerness to make himself available. His top hat hovers in the archway to the right. Three drops of blood, a puddle in the shape of a red handkerchief, Conrad like a puppet with missing limbs. And the mask grins silently as he stands there with his stumps, black boots angled inward, the very image of violated childhood. It would have frightened me less had the cutter dragged the recalcitrant thumbsucker with him into the parlor, the perfidy resides in the architecture itself, which offers no shelter to the boy left alone, this is a house with hidden doors in the walls and traps in the floors, the demons have access from all sides, and in bed in the children's home, my mute question was: Who will punish the tailor for his swollen nostrils, who will take to task the children who shout *Johnny-Head-in-the-Air* in unison, who will forbid Harriet's parents to leave matches lying around? These stories, panic in its concentrated form, do not explain, they leave me all alone with my indignation.

Sometimes, when I have tired of these pictures, I pull my nightshirt up under my neck and feel my nakedness, a delightful tingling, under the covers. Then a dream overtakes me, and I savor it down to the last detail. I see myself plunged into an underworld of roots suffused with dull light and filled like a washroom with hot vapors. The deeper inside I go, the hotter the illicit lust between my legs, and the greater the impulse to tuck my *dingle* so my stomping around will massage it. From a corner in the depths of the murky root-kingdom, a fat matron comes forth, cups her hands like a violet, and draws me toward her with beguiling words. No doubt, she is the *Näbi,* the navel-woman. Despite the grey haze, her doughy body is clearly visible, arms gleaming with sweat and sausage thighs teeming with freckles, she is buck naked but for two elbow-guards of faded yellow elastic. These accessories of the underworld hetaera excite me enormously. In a corner is a changing table where, with her cracked washerwoman's hands, she unfastens the triangle of fabric between my legs. The removal of the diaper, the over-coming of my shame, all this pushes my dream-lust to such heights that I feel the urge to let my urine flow. I know, of course, I am in a prisoner's bed and this is absolutely forbidden. But the *Näbi's* tempting voice is too potent, she demands this act from me. And when she takes me on her lap and buries me under her soft masses of flesh, I can stand the temptation no more, and I let it run out warm and onto her belly, and this streaming brings with it a deep satiation as she lets me suck at her heavy breasts. The precision of my imaginings is such that I can show my cemetery-grandmother on our *saunters* to Pfeffikon to feed the animals the very house – the Siebenmanns' on the upper ridge – where the entrance to the underworld lies, it's a winter vestibule in front of their door, the same piss-yellow as the elastic elbow protectors. When dirty little Jean-Pierre later shows me a crinkled condom in the shade of the fir trees in the garden of the Eicifa villa, I don't yet know what you use it for, but its kinship with the slip-on pads is immediately clear. And when I hear the word *humping* on my way home from kindergarten, again I imagine nothing concrete, but recall the forbidden longing of my washroom dream.

One time, when my nightshirt is rolled up high, and I have just emerged from a fit of animal lust for my navel-woman, the sister comes into the room to fetch the *Struwwelpeter*. She looks at me long, hesitant, then jerks back the cover lightning-fast and asks in an icy voice: What are you at then? Stupefied with shame, I lie there, a martyr to her gaze in my pool of urine. Shame, says the woman with the fire-red face in her cornette, shame, shame, shame. She takes her crucifix from her neck and thrashes my backside with the stinging chain. Go, off to the latrines with you, you piglet, you'll have plenty of time there to think over what you've done. Shivering and naked, I sit in the closed stall, my skin burns from the lashes, Adrian knocks at the door and calls: Bedwetter, bedwetter. Later the sister orders me to the washroom, soaps up my groin, and scrubs me clean with scalding water. She pinches my penis as though trying to tear it off, and says: You're the only one here who still pisses his pyjamas, that comes from having dirty thoughts. Keep on with it, and your parents will have to put you in an institution. Your thing will swell up one day and fill with pus, and they'll have to cut it off to keep it from infecting your whole body. Understand? Conscious of my guilt, I believe everything the headmistress says, she speaks of mortal sins of the flesh, of fornication with the devil, and what is this *Näbi* I'm on about, it even sounds like *knob,* she's a hedonist, naturally, a temptress sent from Sodom and Gomorrah, in another version of the dream she has me roll around in my own feces. Lust only escalates to the degree that it is suppressed, and often I am happy the entire day because when darkness comes, I will be allowed again to pee on her maternal body.

In the gully there's a playground, a wood table with two benches, here is where our schemes are sometimes hatched. Adrian has the idea to build a cabin, and for an afternoon, his tyranny is forgotten, the circle of the great accepts me as one of its own. I am allowed to bring branches, sharpen stakes, spread out moss carpets, I almost forget I ever wanted to run off over the seven mountains. When the wooden house is finished, we discuss who should go in first. One boy says: The witch sleeps here at night, if we wait till sundown, we'll hear her creeping through the

bushes. She'll catch whoever isn't in bed by eight, when the gate closes.
Everyone looks at each other incredulously. What's the witch's name?
the redhead with the freckles asks. Without hesitation, the boy answers:
Jordibeth. You've never heard of Jordibeth? She lives down by the river,
she wears a kerchief that's red like a flame. She kills children. At night,
she gets thirsty for blood. She steals babies from their mothers and
debones them. She has gout, so her bones crackle. They also call her the
Fire Witch. Sometimes she sets a house on fire so she can eat her victims cooked. You think that house that burned down last week just
caught fire all on its own? No one recognized Jordibeth because she
was dressed up as a medicine woman. We sit there as though rooted to
the table. One boy, pallid, asks: Is that true? It is, Adrian's helper replies,
I can call her right now. He walks over to the cabin, curls his hand into
a megaphone, and shouts three times into the forest: Jordibeth! And a
crackling sound comes from down by the stream. The leader gives the
order: Get a move on, now! We gather the scattered tools, throw them
in a two-wheeled handcart, and storm the path to the chalet. The
barred gate is closed. Boy after boy climbs over it. Help me! I beg. Then
the cart rolls away from us and crashes against the cabin down in the
clearing. Adrian says: Wolfgang should go get it, he's the youngest, we'll
try and open the gate in the meanwhile. There's nothing I can do, I will
never make it over the hurdle. I walk down the hill slowly, one step at a
time, my empty eyes not shifting from the black hollows below. There
are rasps and whispers and whimpers and hisses in the trees. Quite
clearly, I hear a distant, malicious laughter with a mannish hoarseness to
it. At any moment a red kerchief will emerge from behind the witch's

house. Panic gives me strength. I pull the handle toward me, drag the heavy handcart uphill, spurred on by the giggling at my back. I think I see two glowing coals turn toward me in a window. As in a nightmare, my steps are sluggish, they sink into muck, there is no way for me to move forward. I stumble, scrape my knee, smell the forest floor, scour myself on the nettles. Stones come loose below me, clatter down into the gully. My Sisyphus journey grows harder with each step. But with a strongman's exertions, I manage even to run the last stretch. And when I reach the locked gate at the top of the hill, I dare to try something I would never have thought possible. I land on my belly on the gravel torture-lot, and it grows dark all around me, once more I seem to have descended into the mythological dark, the brackish swamp where Ur lies with Ur.

24.

AMDEN MATERIAL,
DANNEMAN FRESH BRASIL ESCURO

A gorgeous journey takes us from Montreux via the Furka-Oberhalp Line through Chur to Amden, where we pick up little Hermann from the children's home, so reads Father's entry in the family album. There my parents sit in the dining car of the Glacier Express with their coffees, Mother is wearing a pillbox hat with a mesh veil, she doesn't yet know her luck, four pages later a great event will take place, on May 6, 1948, at 8:00 PM, my brother Kari, 3.1 kilograms, will be born. Hence, despite the measures promoting absolute purity, he was conceived during the Moral Re-Armament conference in Caux. This surprises me, for in the fifties, when Hermann Arbogast Brenner came to know the movement, it was strictly forbidden for marriage partners to sleep with one another, even onanism was scorned with the lapidary phrase: To pleasure oneself is communism. In the group portrait with two of the sisters behind the *home,* on the same lot I learned to hate for four weeks in that humiliating crouching posture, the hastily spruced-up, beaming tike shows no signs of his torments or hardships, a miracle, my parents are here, I am free, my affliction is at an end. At the sight of this harmonious scene, I take a deep draw on my Danneman Brasil, for once more, the relief of escape brings tears to the eyes of this master of dry drunkenness, O yes, it shocks and distresses me again to see the spire of the Amden church over the misty Walensee against the backdrops of the Glarus Alps, which I did not dare climb over at the time. Once, in despair, when I hid under the firs by the meadow where we played and let myself roll away down the hill, the postman intercepted me.

It can only strike one as derisive that my parents' ideological bleaching in service to a well-intentioned goal – the postwar reconciliation of all peoples across the boundaries of race and religion – took place at the same time as my childhood concentration camp internment, especially when we realize it could easily have been otherwise had the factory owner's wife in Niederlenz who offered to take me into her care not canceled at the last minute. The Danneman holds its own splendidly against the authentic Bahía Export, it has the same Mata Fina spiciness and an unbroken snow-white ash. I returned to the scene of the crime when I traveled to the Grisons five years ago. I would not care to bore the indulgent reader with an exordium on this staid village that has gone from health resort to hiking center to alpine ski station, I will simply inform him that the memories returned as soon as I found the footpath leading up to that chalet that ruined for me for all time the art of my home country's carpenters. The leader of the Agape Center now housed there welcomed me cordially, it was no sure thing that he would show me around there in the middle of a weekday. I allowed him to hand me the green pamphlets, promised to study them, even if, when I was an inmate there, I had seen nothing of the fellowship of communion, the nourishing grace designated by the Greek word *eukharistia*. How small and harmless the gravel lot appeared in the shadow of the decorative firs, how paltry the slope of the forest path the handcart had slid down! The stream didn't flow through a ravine, just a tiny gulley right past the playground that had degenerated into a dump for tin cans and assorted rubbish. I never managed to find the chicken coop in Soglio, but during this visit I did investigate the architecture of fear with firm footsteps, unfortunately I wasn't allowed to light a cigar. Yes, there was the veranda where I had spilled my soup, to the left the common room where the sisters refused me sweets before bed, the staircase, the lavatory, the primitive washrooms, on the upper floor the dormitories with the angular balcony – I hadn't remembered it that way, but now, standing at the window, I could see a boy – Buser, the cripple? – pushing a little red truck along the ledge. Not a trace of the crimes committed there, no, joyful pictures of trees hung all around and wooden plaques with engraved proverbs. The kitchen where I had once gotten lost in the vapor while waiting for a glass of Ovaltine was still there in the cellar, I looked up the slope where the burnt house stood, the event must be recorded in the local archives, but I refused to research any further. There was the craft room where the puppet shows occurred, and just then another anchor lifted, when I saw the slightly smoked wood and rustic paint of the shoeboxes in the hallway, I recalled a long-vanished scene in the midst of all this unclarity. There was a girl named Ursula who kept watch over me, who helped me tie my shoes, I sat there on one of these trunks holding two looped strings in my hands amid the storm of rampaging brats, unable to bring them together, my God, of course, Ursula, who brought the coloring book and didn't shout *wrong!* when I colored the gardener lady's handkerchief yellow instead of blue. My mind was relieved as I saw all this, it couldn't have been so many children, then, a dozen, maybe, and I had to ask myself as I strode over to the flagpole whether I wasn't, in reproaching my parents with this grave childrearing error, laying it on a little too thick.

The question, Hermann Arbogast Brenner surmises from his current Brunsleben exile, is most likely posed wrongly, what counts is always our inner truth. Our task is not to clarify whether Amden can be justified in human terms, no, we must confront its devastating consequences. I will reserve for a later *gavilla* the witch dream that made me plead for years, after I was moved from my parents' room into my own, for the jib door to be left open so I could take a trusted sliver of light with me into the infernal night. But I absolve Father and Mother of all responsibility for the aftereffects of Amden, the demons that would awaken in the children's home slumbered within me – in me and me alone. I had to fight them, and I did so badly, as all well-bred children do. It would be nonsensical – particularly if we are striving after a Stechlinesque serenity and sobriety in the service of Jérôme von Castelmur-Bondo – to lodge a complaint about the failed socialization of the only child from Menzenmang, the little cheroot who was certainly spoiled to boot, the youngest, incidentally, incidentally the weakest, incidentally the only one of another faith. We are stuck with this role forever, and there is no urbarium that states man has a right to mercy.

After politely taking leave of the Agape leader, I drove to Näfels to dine there at the renowned Hotel Schwert: two trout with salted potatoes and brown butter, and to smoke, a Hoyo de Monterrey from my traveling reserve. In my briefcase I had the *Struwwelpeter,* which I must not have opened for decades, and I leafed through the eight illustrated tales with an eager *aha* feeling. In the end, Amden had also brought me that book, and it stunned me to realize what the boy left alone in the dark-brown-varnished holiday chalet had already grasped so deeply: that in drawing and painting, the how is what matters. One formal reminiscence after another rose to the surface. If I registered every detail of the artist's treatment of the satchel as it floated off in the tragedy of Johnny-Head-in-the-Air, if I saw there was no need to redraw the river in every scene, that the narrowly hatched waterway already suggested distance, this was the discovery of an important aesthetic principle: the representation of the general through the particular. I turned my entire attention to these details now. Here were the three fish. They jumped from the cool water as Johnny stepped over the wall of the quay, they swam off in haste as he tumbled inside, bunched together they observed as he was pulled out with a long pole, with a laugh they looked up at the sopping wet dimwit. This was the foundation for my success as a draftsman in all the contests held by clothing brands, department stores, and automobile factories that I sent my sketches to. I must thank Amden for this, in part. For it was pain that made me see. Would I have wished, in all honesty, to be one of the dozen children not delivered up to Adrian's savagery – would I have wanted to be among those cheerfully making onion calendars or playing Uri, Schwyz, and Unterwalden? The indulgent reader is perhaps unfamiliar with the idiocy of ballgames of this kind. Every player was assigned the name of a canton. The leader throws the rubber ball in the air and cries *Uri*. While Uri goes to catch the ball, the others scatter in all directions. The one who's *it* tries to tag another person, and if he does, he gets to shout the name of the other canton, and Schwyz has one life less. It seems to me more dignified to ask why Flying Robert lives in a church, why there is a rooster atop the spire in the stormy heath and a cross on the main building's roof. Why, the diner in Näfels asks himself, did you never realize his parents' home lies outside the drawing? Robert doesn't live in the house of God, he has just wandered past it out walking in the rain. True, but the castoff boy at Amden had understood the effects of framing. Inside is where the totality of events takes place, outside is no man's land. Far more seductive were the endless who-knows than playing with the clunky wooden steamroller on the cellar steps: which of the three boys Saint Nicholas dips into the inkpot has the most enviable appurtenances, Edward with his flag, Arthur with his pretzel, or William with his hula hoop? At the time it was simply a philosophical question, these symbols represent the world of toys, and you had to ask yourself, does vexilology, baking, or technics suit me best? Hermann Arbogast Brenner was sick so long, he let his internists, urologists, dermatologists, and cardiologists convince him to try a psychoanalytic course of treatment. He broke it off the day he decided to put his Menzenmang cigar-childhood to paper. But an error must be avoided here. This confrontation with the lived experiences, dreams, and fears of the early years is not a working-through in the therapeutic sense, but is rather to be thought a particularly refined form of smoking for pleasure. Whoever lies on the couch and reveals his innermost secrets is hoping for catharsis or clarity to ensue. The psychiatrist helps him, sometimes with canny reticence, sometimes with gallant theorizing, to understand who he is. We are intentionally dispensing here with jargon anyone can bone up on and presenting this model in the most primitive terms possible. Health, it is said among the Coryphaei, is when we succeed in reliving the spiritual notes of childhood under the protection of an adult who will not leave us in the lurch the way our mother did when she hid away behind the seven mountains, or Father when he turned his back to the veranda where his son had been marked out as a sacrificial lamb. To remain with this metaphor, the psychological disorder would be something like a gastro-intestinal disturbance. And this is where Hermann Arbogast Brenner's doubts about this verbal sand castle begin. Having me puke out again what I already vomited once in Amden can never make it palatable for me, even if the poisoned meal will finally stay down once I am dead. Nor do I want to go on paying someone to let me bemoan it to no end. I would prefer, through my bond with the high culture of smoking, to enjoy it from cigar to cigar. Bert May had a difficult childhood, too, he too writes along the fault lines, but with the outlandish claim that the sense of suffering provides the artist with a form. Just think of the punishment he subjects himself to: the front hip turn he couldn't manage in the gym he must now execute on the aesthetic high bars! Such striving is foreign to me. I fill my tobacco leaves with nerves and veins to master my inventory of cigars. I do not say, I have written three pages while smoking a Danneman Brasil, that would be putting the cart before the horse.

Returning to the psychotherapists: over and over they want to know, what does that mean? I could discuss the symbolic meaning of the primordial image of the *Näbi* in one marathon session after the other, why she lived in the root kingdom and not in the mountains, how steam, feces, and urine are related, the spiritual significance of the elastic elbow pads, what role the freckles play, where this mother-archetype comes from. Such considerations were broached in my sessions with Doctor Jesenska Kiehl. But even if my mother was obsessed with cleanliness and fretted over whether I went peepee and caca when I was supposed to, the fact remains that it was my interior that produced, from the navel outward, a primeval figure whose fecal embrace provoked in me a blissful satiation. And even if, as an adult, I could not have sex with a woman except by re-enacting the ritual of this cryptic episode, this still would be no grounds to go on wringing my dream out like a damp rag. Analysis – and this is the perfidy of it – robs us of our myths. It proffers a concept of health concordant with societal clichés of normality. Let's assume, on the basis of his prepubescent hallucinations, Hermann Arbogast Brenner was destined to become a latex fetishist, that the only sexuality he knows is defecating with big-breasted hookers in red-lit brothels. I contend it would still be more sensible for him to share his money with a woman in possession of the proper attributes than spend it on therapy where his tics will be analyzed away and no analogous pleasure granted him as a stand-in.

We should realize our dreams, not throw them away. No one misses the noble feeling of a loving wife until he has known it. The same cannot be said of the cigar, of course. Not to have experienced *nicotiana tabacum* in its purest expression is tantamount to a primary deficit – and here I do not shy away from jargon. But Hermann Arbogast Brenner will not repeat here what he has already dwelt on in his portrait of his grandfather. Far be it from him to stand before mankind as a pedagogue. He just cannot grasp how something so peaceful and nebulous as blue haze can divide the world population into two camps. Smoking is a privilege of the mind and of the senses. Whoever willingly forgoes dialogue with the priceless aromas of Havana, Sumatra, Java, Santo Domingo, and Brazil has bet on 'the wrong horse, on a being without myths, on a religion of health without pneuma. Naturally only one who has suffered has the right to declare that health is not the highest of all goods. And he refuses to place medical intactness on the upmost pedestal, because he has known from very early that in the case of the depressive, there is no relying on stomach, kidneys, lungs, heart, joints, transmitters. Even a normal life, says Gottfried Benn, leads to an infirm death. Death has nothing to do with health and illness whatsoever, it obeys its own designs. This is something the majority of mortals fail to see. As death cannot be cordoned off from life by construing it as the highest illness, trying to jog your way to a hale old age remains a delusion. The only thing we extend by doing so is our uncertainty as to last things. The cigar smoker is calmer in his movements, having observed his own progressive incineration as measured in units of coronas. My pension is a tobacco pension, I do not count the Havanas I have left, I would like to lament neither the first one nor the last.

25.

FAREWELL TO MENZENMANG,
PUNCH

Whoever has a choice has the agony of choice: the Lonsdale or the demi-tasse, *doble claro* or *oscuro,* Domingo or Malawi – from *gavilla* to *gavilla,* from *stel* to *stel,* this has been, throughout the present bundle, a question of worldview. When Fidel Castro came to power in Cuba, he nationalized the island's two most important exports, sugar and cigars, because for him, the traditional brands, Partagás, Larrañaga, Hoyo de Monterrey, Bock, Ramón Allones, and Punch, were no less passé than the brocades and medallions and luxuriant old pinks and sky blues of the decoration on the boxes they were sold in. Instead of nearly one thousand different choices, there should be a single *puro* in a few shapes that every man could afford, a symbol of the triumph of the revolution over free enterprise. Zino Davidoff writes in *Memoirs of a Tobacco Czar* how he followed these events from Geneva, where he had tens of thousands of Havanas in his luxurious shop, which was frequented by princes, industrialists, and sheiks. After just a few months, two meek emissaries stopped in and complained: What should we do, no one wants our people's cigars, the sales numbers keep dropping and dropping. In long discussions with the representatives of Cuba Tobacco, Davidoff made clear that Fidel was ruining the market forever, he failed to see that the wealth of their country lay in its variety. The owners of the expropriated plantations rebelled against the new order, lodged cases with the international court in The Hague, or resolved to move production to Florida, the Philippines, or the Orient. Many owners, rumor has it, pulled up their best plants and acclimated them to other skies in exile. The most experienced cigar makers followed suit, engaged in a scorched earth policy, and destroyed the vegas forever, so that the royal wrapper leaf could never be grown in the saintly rectangle of Vuelta Abajo again. Castro's Siboney still exists today, but no one asks for one outside of Cuba, what customers want is an Upmann, a Romeo y Julieta, a Montecristo, all of which are now produced under the supervision of the Cuban state.

Now, as he is taking his leave of Menzenmang for a time, as he passes the indulgent reader the yawning box with the last cigar, Hermann Arbogast Brenner, seasoned in Brunsleben's Stechlinesque spirit, knows full well the perishable nature of socialist depictions of unity in epic undertakings of this sort, and nothing would be less appropriate than to try and foist off on the connoisseur of his tobacco leaves a centrally planned novelistic fantasy. We must leave our customers with the agony of choice, we can only hope that it has been to his liking, that sooner or later he will return to the blend we leave behind in our mixing box.

Here and today, amid the encroaching grey of this Sunday morning in late August, I must depart not only from this *Stumpenland* village in the Upper Wynental, but also from the indulgent reader himself, and I rise to meet the pain of separation with a Punch from the box with the olive green edging. Once again, the long-familiar ceremony: testing of the suppleness through slight pressure of thumb and forefinger, gentle warming of the corona's shaft, a dry taste of the *puro* to verify: wrapper from Isabel María, filler from the Semi-Vuelta. The striking of the match, the careful toasting of the foot, the virgin draw, capital. We, the indulgent reader of unknown provenance and the thwarted tobacco merchant Hermann Arbogast Brenner, have met one another by chance thanks to that question which even today in every global metropolis permits us to address a word to a complete stranger: Got a light? Our common passion was dry drunkenness, that rush of arousal and appeasement, distinguished by its freight of memories from the drifting numbness of alcohol and heroin with its hallucinations. He and I, we abandon ourselves to *solanaceae,* to the consoling wellsprings of pneuma, and I permit myself, when I say we have found joy in one another's company, to presume the feeling was mutual. Perhaps he will be surprised to hear from Hermann Arbogast Brenner, companion of Jérôme von Castelmur-Bondo and beneficiary of a tobacco pension in Brunsleben, that the teller of a story, no matter what kind, knows more about the reader than the reader does about the packager of the present tobacco leaves, for language attracts language. He, too, the person bent in apparent silence over these pages, has spoken unceasingly of *seco* and *volado,* and the tissue of his life remains there between the veins. No fear, I will not divulge what has been entrusted to me here, things often more intimate than those revealed behind a psychiatrist's padded door. Cigar smokers are a discreet race, and magicians even more so, we know how to keep a secret.

What do we mean, though, when we speak of imaginations stunted by a state monopoly, abortive as Fidel's Siboney? When novelists set to work, they do so as though they sat at the levers of power, as though they knew more about the inner and outer lives of their characters than the gods – whom they make offerings to, like the Mayan priests with their rolls of *cohiba* – know about them, the narrators. And now there is the bad habit of relativizing what is portrayed through formulas denoting discrepancy and uncertainty, burdening the reader with the illusion that it all might have been quite different; the coy interventions *Let us assume, Let us imagine, Supposing that* are merely loutish variations on the dictatorship of the author – a socialism of the imagination of a kind that functions nowhere in the world. Hermann Arbogast Brenner, whose only wish was to be a passionate cigarier, may well be less well-versed than his professional colleagues, who put the present in the pluperfect, spontaneous outbursts in indirect speech, the factually indisputable in the conditional, and the logically interdependent in dismembered montages, this makes him a straight shooter, like his grandfather at the Waldau. The indulgent reader will allow me a brief excursus on magic. The pass is a splendid trick by which we bring a card from spot X in the middle of the deck lightning-fast to the top or bottom. But like every gimmick it comes with a risk: even if we are quick-handed enough to prevent another's seeing what has happened, the onlooker may still realize he's being had, and that kills the trick. For this reason, though I can execute the pass eighty times in one minute, I will never do it if there is a simpler way to pull the Queen of Hearts from the deck. My great professor in the art of card magic, Wolff Baron von Keyserlingk, explained to me once that the simplest method of forcing an Ace of Spades is to have at hand a deck consisting entirely of Aces of Spades. To dare this most brazen of all illusions, I must first perform other tricks with common cards of the kind you find in any restaurant. If I am successful there with, say, Forcing Number Three, then no public will later insist on investigating the prop with the singled-out Aces. If I choose now to pass, glide, or palm, this would be like Picasso showing off his paintbrushes in the gallery. And that is the thing that bores me about modern novels, how the writers insist on flaunting their proficiency in juggling the *consecutio temporum*. They have to drag their indicative-subjunctive orgies off with them to the Frankfurt Book Fair because they – cigarette smokers, most of them – aren't sure they have any substance.

Hermann Arbogast Brenner is unfamiliar with such tribulations, because the kingdom of the cigar is of this world, and the fluidium of tobacco sustains him. Rent by uncertainty whether he should explicitly present or subversively suppress the conjunction *and*, O so deeply estranged in metacommunication, shimmering androgynously in the arbitrary space between *signifiant* and *signifié*, the hypersensitive language skeptic introduces himself to the TV cameras and literature magazines with a body-snatcher's hat-tip to Lord Chandos, trumpets about all the sleepless nights he needed to dismember his plot – incidentally not worth a trifle – into segments, so that the raw horror of condemnation to silence shimmers through the cracking skin of form, in telescopic syntax, yes, as soon as the spotlights dazzle he is all too happy to climb up on the highwire – and in full possession of Dornseiff's word fields, with the whole of Grimm in his beleaguered head, he complains he has lost his naivety as a novelist, and so on and so forth to forestall the child's fateful cry in the tale *The Emperor's New Clothes*. With a verbally null flap of the hand, he cites two syllables of Celan, the poem at the crater of silence, but heroically, he has hung on in the literature biz, has squeezed six hundred pages from his fabulation-abstinence, and the critics fawn over him with full-page reviews, for he has held fast to the iron rule of the game – not to frighten them with something new, let alone with a prose one must read from the first line to the last – already after the first *interruptus* in the prologue you know, from his fragile-fragmentary idiom, that here we have stuck one hundred percent with the tried-and-true. That's what you get, says the dilettante Hermann Arbogast Brenner, when you make writing the center of your life, familiarity turns to tedium and the beginner's potent fluency dwindles from prize to prize into the dribblings of a eunuch.

Farewell to Menzenmang, for my courage to live is broken, the demons have been stirring for days now, it is time to pay them their tribute, the dread gnaws at the walls of my heart, I will dive down into the unnamable, will be hooked up to the IV tubes at the offices of

Professor Pollenleitner at the Friedmatt, a destitute mental serf of *vita minima* – for this reason, then, a last word about my illness. Radiation treatments or surgery are performed on terminal cancer patients even when their salvation appears hopeless. But whatever mechanical medicine does to him, it will never be permissible to plant in the survivor, like an underhanded gardener, a new carcinoma in place of the old. But when the cyclical endogenous depressive makes it to the surface without the aid of drugs, they confidently strike the blow that will eventually metastasize into further depths. As regards the children's concentration camp in Amden, I have named my core wound: the humiliation and violation of my developing sense of justice. Depression, a comprehensive retraction of the veil, is at once the instinct to play dead and a demonstration of the most extreme distress, the transmitters stop firing because the ill person wants for a metaphor that can scream to the outside world: This is how miserable I am! And so long as psychotherapy is incapable of providing him with the one thing that might help – erotic affection – it will never, ever be possible to hinder these breakdowns. It brushes iodine on the wound without cauterizing it. And once again, things have come this far, Hermann Arbogast Brenner, still in his midsummer fury, and burning the candle at both ends, can no longer bear the sum of injustices committed against him. That his wife left him in his darkest hour, that she took his beloved sons with her moreover, that his parents' home, sold off for a song, would fetch two million today – though he would not let go of it even for that price – that his churlish siblings squeezed him for a signature at the foot of the inheritance contract in the Königsfelden hospital cafeteria, all this weighs so heavily on his soul that he is withering like a parched plant. Does no one on this entire crippled planet understand? No, not even Exitus, the assisted suicide organization, whose brochure "What Is the Most Practical Way to Kill Myself" can be sold to the whole gamut of injured parties, but not to depressives.

No, no one will share with me this desert, I alone am king of the crunching sands, which coat all my feelings and thoughts. And so I must make haste to bring these observations to an end. I will take them with me to Basel, these tobacco leaves will finish drying out in the Paul Pavilion. But before I close, I would like to take a last look at the brown faienced plate with the grey die-stamp of the Berlin cathedral, which hung in the Menzenmang villa over the sliding door to the living room, here is the high tambour of the dome overlooking the park with the projecting gabled portico flanked by two narrow pillars, a rainy cloudy sky, and I must have had a dream when I was young that I wandered down the broad curves of a snaking avenue, my mother's hand in mine in the foreign capital; for the first time I hear the magic sounds of Brandenburg, even as a little cheroot I am *mittenmang* – in the midst of things – I romp around the Molkenmarkt, stand in front of Saint Nicholas's church under the broom shapes of the late autumn trees, cross a beer cart on the Mühlendamm, hear the crackle of the electric tram taking the Leipzigerstrasse down to Tietz department store, where Hundreiser's huge statue of Berolina stands, there is chainmail on her breast, her left hand is outstretched, yes, Alexanderplatz, the globe in its clock-socket giving promises of worldliness, and the view into Fried-richstrasse with its glow of the boom years, countless advertisements, the Mercedes, the Crown Prince's Palace with its stern pilaster strips, the presentation balcony over the four pillars with Corinthian capitals, St. Hedwig's church lowering under its deep dome, the obelisk at Potsdamer Platz, the traffic chaos at Oranienburger Tor, the Schiffbauerdamm with its sloops in the September mist, on the plate at Menzenmang was a hazy light, the transition from summer to fall, and I hold fast, before I settle into the psychiatric clinic, to this fragment of memory, because here, in Castle Brunsleben, my Fontane readings have made me grasp how deeply Prussian the vanishment of my childhood is, a German division has run through my life ever since the pillage of Menzenmang, an Oder-Neisse Line; whenever I take the Wynentaler over the border into Reinach-Unterdorf, past the shady Hediger & Sons villa overlooking its stands of hardwoods, I realize it, after the unspeakable inheritance war, the victorious parties, brother and sister, were able to dictate to Her-mann Arbogast Brenner their humiliating terms. Naturally there is also something wistfully beautiful in this Margravian segregation, I think of the Effi magic on the terrace beneath the Brandenburgesque sun, the high and sweetly swaying mauves, their powdery grey pink, the purple of the asters amid the buzzing wasps.

It's been twenty-two years now since I sat in the wicker chair in the melancholy hours of hammered brass and was startled by a phone call at mid-morning, the fiancé of my later wife told me in a sepulchral voice that Flavia Soguel, the jurist from Davos with the Undine-blonde hair, had tumbled over the balcony the night before, this was the moment, more or less, when I fell abruptly from my paternal paradise, for I wanted to stay by her side, no matter if she was left a cripple in a wheelchair, and I assured her of this when I visited her in the Zurich Polyclinic. Love was stronger than the fear of invalidism, and as I note this down, on September 1, 1988 — a sunny day under the influence of the foehn, with clouds on the Alpine Divide, storm weather expected in late afternoon coming in from the southwest, zero-degree line holding steady at 3500 meters — a Frank Sinatra record is playing "Strangers in the Night," her favorite song: *Wond'ring in the night, what were the chances we'd be sharing love, before the night was through. Something in your eyes was so inviting, something in your smile was so exciting, something in my heart told me I must have you.* That was the hit we danced to on hot July nights at the Corso or the Terrace. Two decades later, when Hermann Arbogast Brenner had grown into a deranged stranger, the jurist from the Grisons did not apply the law equally, instead she took off like a rat from a sinking ship, and this tort weighs so heavily on me today that again I have to suck it up, hoe my own row, and ready myself for travel to my martyrdom in the Paul Pavilion in the Friedmatt. The endogenous depressive is the runt of creation, he wastes away in the Stygian mist, with no power to end things on his own, nor would doing so be logical, in a way, because for those left behind he is already dead, behind closed shutters he hears them haggling over his estate.

We should like to go ahead and put things in order at Brunsleben, particularly as we do not know whether it will ever even be possible to get back to processing our tobacco leaves. I disassemble the bookshelf under the awning of the entrance to the guest house, throw out the stacks of tobacco journals and the *Wynentaler Daily* damp with dew, bundle together the unopened mail, struggle through the saltpeter green hall where the bags with cigar literature, model Ferraris, and empty cigar boxes pile up, give up before the *tohu-wa-bohu* in the castle parlor with the booked-up Biedermeier niches, for this is where it crashes over me; like sediments of humus, the magic props overlay the expired invoices, plantation maps, WSB schedules, and scraps of paper. This inconceivable mishmash continues through the library and up into the attic room, where the three drafting tables in the chilly chapel or ossuary with the skewed wooden beams run over with photos, receipts, pages from calendars, magic coins, rotting socks, reference works, record sleeves, sheet music, fountain pen cartridges, research envelopes, file cards, flyers, family albums, automotive magazines, copperplates, and medicine boxes, and on the bedpost – better said on the gallows over the bed – Flavia's black, high-heeled dancing sandals with the white rose still hang, they remind Hermann Arbogast Brenner not only of the nights of dancing he missed out on, but also of the blondine's first visit to Menzenmang, at that time in the company of her fiancé, the architecture student from Bern. She lost one of these fabric roses on the gravel terrace, my father handed it back to me with the words: She's a keeper. And now I see the two of us standing there just as my tobacco grandfather stood in the orchard of the Waldau with his own son twenty-five years before, in his white summer jacket on the occasion of the latter's engagement, and Hermann II seems to be saying to Hermann III: You've made a fine choice, Mandi, you'd have to be blind in both eyes not to see what an exquisite woman this Gertrud Emmy Pfendsack is, it's true she's a city girl, but she'll get used to it out here. Yes, this repeated itself a generation later when my father found the rose from Flavia's shoe, and I thank the gods, to whom I offer up the blue haze from my Punch, that he didn't survive to hear my wife utter the words: For me, the Hermann Arbogast Brenner enterprise is officially dead. It was on New Year's Eve at her parents' house in Davos, in the midst of the festivities, streamers were flying through the air, confetti rained down, balloons were popping. In the midst of the revelry, the dance to ring in the New Year, the death verdict, and I got into my car and drove through the Prättigau on a breakneck journey along the Walensee to Brunsleben, just to hear the bells ring at midnight on the highmost of the castle's Italianate terraces, and it took me back to Amden, when the ringing from the Catholic church tortured me. I sat there in my fur coat, a glass of champagne in my hand, and knew, you are now completely alone, what's broken will never again be made whole, the last pillar of your existence has buckled. After seven excruciating years of depression, interrupted by brief manic intervals, I had hoped we would get through it together, just a hundred meters more, I begged Flavia, crawl with me for this last stretch over the cinder track, if not for me, then for the children, but it was over forever, *finis,* the same word I now scrawl beneath these observations before departing to atone again for months for these few transitory weeks when things went well for me. I will, when the suitcases stand packed in the

yard – oh, one doesn't need much, a few pairs of pyjamas, some under-
wear, a half-dozen shirts – climb once again to the Ebnet, light a cigar
and look southward, toward Menzenmang behind the iron curtain.
Unto ashes thou shalt return, for nowhere is it written man has a right
to a modicum of bliss.

AFTERWORD

BY ADRIAN NATHAN WEST

I ndeed, he was a freak – *er war ja ein Freak* – these words were my introduction to Hermann Burger, glimpsed in the opening of his novelette *The Laughter Artist*. *Skurril,* bizarre or outlandish – in Arnold's day we still said "scurrile," meaning characteristic of a buffoon – is the adjective most often seen alongside his name. Did he choose it himself? It wouldn't have been out of character for this image-obsessed author, who had his own public relations consultant, wheeled around in a Ferrari in costly white suits, did magic tricks for Helmut Kohl, and showed up with a rifle to a reading of his *Schuss auf die Kanzel,* a bitter tale of vengeance against the ecclesiastical authorities who evicted him from the parish house where he wrote his first novel and where his two sons were born. At twenty-three, he told a friend, contradicting Wittgenstein, "death is the most important event of life." He claimed to know how the dead felt in their coffins, to possess an "authentic memory" of eternity. His mature work began with *Schilten,* the tale of a village teacher whose lessons seek to prepare his students, not for the brief life ahead of them, but for the never-ending darkness that will succeed it; twelve years later, he would compose a treatise on suicide, the *Tractatus Logico-Suicidalis,* a collection of 1046 "mortologisms" on voluntary death. Following its release, he declared in an interview that by exploring the theme, he had exorcised it, and embarked, grandiosely, on a proposed tetralogy for his new publisher, Suhrkamp. By then, he was estranged from his wife and children, living in the guesthouse at Castle Brunegg – Brunsleben, as it is known in the present volume. Friends would call the plan for a multivolume cycle bluster, the fruit of manic ideation; but a hundred pages of a second volume do exist, slapdash, cryptic, and moving. What you hold in your hands is Burger's final published work, and he committed suicide a few days before its appearance.

LIFE

Hermann Burger was born in 1942 in Menziken in the canton of Aargau in German-speaking Switzerland. His father, Mandi, was the son of a local innkeeper and tobacco trader; his mother, Gertrud Pfendsack, came from an eminent family in Sankt Gallen, which, with its 50,000 citizens, qualified her as a "city girl." His brother and sister were born in 1948 and 1949. From an early age, Burger showed talent as a writer, artist, and musician. He studied architecture for four semesters before changing his major to German language and literature. His first published writings appeared in the early sixties. He was married in 1967.

Signs of his mental instability appeared soon afterwards: manic depression, impotence, the "genital migraines" that would become the major affliction of his alter-ego, Wolfram Schollkopf, in his second novel, *The Artificial Mother* (Burger blamed his problems on mother's mania for cleanliness, his precipitate birth – the German, *Sturzgeburt,* sounds more drastic – and an operation at age five for an inguinal hernia). Things improved after the publication of *Schilten,* and for a time, he enjoyed the fruits of success: he was picked up by the German publisher Fischer, took part in the Ingeborg Bachmann Prizes, wrote fluently, gave readings, saw his work adapted for the screen.

His maturity was marked by oscillation between frenetic activity and crippling dejection. It is to the first that we owe our image of him as a consummate eccentric. In preparation for his story *Diabelli,* he studied magic and took an oath never to reveal the secrets of the sorcerer's art; as a reporter for the *Frankfurter Allgemeine Zeitung,* he took a bobsled certification course (the ice track is one of his favorite metaphors for the ordeal of coming into the world, and appears here in Chapter 2); he was a toy collector, gourmand, Rotarian, saxophonist, actor, choir singer, smoker of up to thirty cigars a day. He lived hard, the toll was heavy, and as time went on, he spent increasing amounts of time in therapy and clinics.

He was a difficult person, and embittered friends and family alike, particularly in his readiness to blame them publicly and in writing for countless injustices he believed he'd been subjected to. One scholar mentions his "regressive concept of genius," his Romantic notion of the artist as hypersensitive, spiritually fragile, attuned to values unperceived by ordinary people. In a play, *The Apparent Dead,* one of his characters declares: "In the most extreme cases, the artist safeguards his neurosis against the desire for recovery, he knows his illness is his capital."

He must have been hard to live with. A study of his life and works reveals him to be a man wounded, but also one with a compulsion to find fault, even for largely imagined offenses. Emil Kraeplin's now-obsolete concept of "querulant psychosis" fits him well: he was monomaniacal, narcissistic, attuned to the least slight on his person but capable of immense cruelty to others, as he reveals over and over in writing about his family. He justified this with recourse to the therapeutic process his art represented – even if his increasingly bizarre pseudo-Freudian suppositions about the origins of his sorrows only seem to have aggravated them – and by his view of literary achievement as the highest of all goods.

Suicide is everywhere in Burger's work, a corollary of his idea of life as performance. He portrays birth as being shoved onto a stage, forced to amuse an often hostile audience. His heroes choose their absurd vocations in thrall to strange pretensions and obscure torments and often dream of unshouldering their burdens. Emblematic is his prestidigitator Diabelli, who responds to an invitation to entertain at his mentor's birthday with an unsolicited curriculum vitae and a brief history of magic as the effort to compensate for inner emptiness before announcing that, for his final trick, he will make himself disappear. More mundane factors obtained as well. In 1987, Burger and his wife separated, and she moved away with their children. He lived extravagantly, and his debts were catching up to him. His last years were a blur of lectures and publications, punctuated by manic fits and hospital stays. When lucid, he dreaded the return of his depression and the loss, perhaps permanent, of his ability to write. His landlord, Jean Rudolphe von Salis – here fictionalized as Jérôme von Castelmur Bondo – had heard him say in private that he would kill himself when the *Brenner* tetralogy was finished. "I knew this: a drowning man, he had made more than evident to me his wish to *bring things to a close.*"

CONTRE PROUST

Brenner is unique among Burger's works. Readers may balk if I call it lucid, and I could certainly devote an essay to my exertions to resolve its many uncertainties. Still, there is a levity, a wistfulness in its style rarely seen in his other major works. Burger typically presents the reader with dense blocks of unindented text, an impasto of endless subordinate clauses, neologisms, and foreign or obsolete words that can make Thomas Bernhard's style feel dainty. He craved fame, but ignored the demands of the public, eager instead to best the writers he admired – and as a young man, he would diagram the sentences of those he considered masters, copying their structure until he had mastered it inside and out. The results could prove impenetrable for all but the most dedicated. His benefactor, the great critic Marcel Reich-Ranicki, did not doubt he was one of the greatest writers of his time, but feared he was "too strange, too demanding."

Brenner is Burger's attempt to one-up Proust, a writer he seems to have known only secondhand. What mattered to Burger about Proust was not the technique, but the gesture of the *Recherche*, the paragon of the book to end all books, the monument that leaves the competition speechless; and then, the association of the madeleine and involuntary memory was one Burger felt tempted to recreate through the "pneuma" of the cigar. Originally, *Brenner* was to consist of four volumes with four place-names: *Brunsleben, Menzenmang, Waldau,* and *Gormund.* There were to be twenty-five chapters in each, corresponding to the twenty-five cigars in a case, and the individual chapters would bear the names of cigars, some authentic, others the product of the imaginary family firm Brenner & Sons Ltd.

If *Brenner* is gentler, more charming than Burger's earlier works, it may be because here, for the first time, introspection is freed from imprecation and from the obsession with tracing the author's ailments to cruelties inflicted upon him in the past. The key episodes remain – his mother tying him to the bed, the bullies trapping him in the chicken coop – sources of bitterness that appear repeatedly in his work; but for the first time, there is forgiveness, a gesture toward reconciliation, and skepticism toward the psychoanalytic constructs long used to justify his vehemence. I have read that the receipt of a terminal diagnosis often calms a hypochondriac's nerves; in the same way, the recognition that everything would soon be over freed Burger to write with unaccustomed generosity, reflecting on the sources of beauty and pleasure in his life and for once attempting to see things from others' perspective. Not to exaggerate – *Brenner* contains passages offensive in their intransigence, and its final pages, when the narrator looks on the wreck of his existence before packing his bags to return to the mental hospital, are among the most forlorn in all of literature. But the cigar, for Burger, is more than an occasion for meditation; it also teaches one how to die with dignity. And so a serenity, a muted playfulness, permeates these pages, and the author's barbs are duller than before:

> The cigar smoker is calmer in his movements, having observed his own progressive incineration as measured in units of coronas. My pension is measured in tobacco, I do not count the Havanas I have left, I would like to lament neither the first nor the last of them.

MORAL RE-ARMAMENT

Burger's parents were members of Moral Re-Armament, and he blamed it for strains in his relations with them as well as for facets of his sexual neuroses. Though elements of it remain in its distant relative, Alcoholics Anonymous, the movement is no longer well known, and it is worth saying a few words about it here.

Founded by American evangelist Frank Buchman in 1938, Moral Re-Armament was an extension of the spiritual principles that had inspired his earlier organization, the Oxford Group. Influenced by the

Wesleyan idea of the "second work of grace" that sanctifies the life of the believer, Buchman contended that the major problems facing the world were not political or economic, but the result of individual dishonesty, selfishness, and fear. His call for moral rearmament in 1938 was the consequence of this belief, and inspired the most ludicrous episode in his biography: his attempt to meet Hitler to dissuade him from pursuing war (for their part, the Nazis thought Buchman was a spy, censured Moral Re-Armament's subversive teachings, and imprisoned its leaders in occupied countries).

The Oxford Group had already made inroads in Switzerland when, in 1946, a group of Swiss families bought the luxurious but by-then derelict Caux Palace Hotel, which their spokesman saw as "a place where Europeans, torn apart by hatred, suffering, and resentment, will be able to meet each other." That same year, 3,000 adherents to Moral Re-Armament would visit. Over the years, attendees would include Konrad Adenauer, Nobusike Kishi, and Habib Bourgiba of Tunisia. MRA's successor organization, Initiatives of Change, continues to hold events there today.

The family's attraction to the movement was above reproach, judging from the excerpts from his father's scrapbook Burger quotes in *Brenner*. It is easy to imagine two young parents being drawn after the war toward a project that promised revolution in favor of the unity of mankind, and if it is not quite just to call Buchman a charlatan, he was skilled at casting MRA's achievements in the best light. Detractors (among them actress Glenn Close, who lived with her parents at Caux) consider MRA a cult that attempted to control all aspects of its members' lives. Burger blamed his mother's obsession with sexual purity on the group, and in therapy would come to embrace the psychoanalytic cliché of the neurotic son of the withdrawn, frigid mother.

The greatest importance of Moral Re-Armament for Hermann Burger was as the cause-in-fact for his stay at the "children's home-concentration camp" in Amden in 1947. Neither his grandmother nor his aunt could care for him for the four weeks his parents spent at the conference in Caux, and another sitter his mother asked refused at the last minute. The boy's parents told him he would enjoy being with children his own age; after his operation, his doctor had even recommended he spend some time in the mountains. Burger would later remember the harassment he endured there as one of the most harrowing experiences of his life and the moment when his sense of justice was irrevocably destroyed.

THE RIGHT TO SUBJECTIVITY

The idea of psychological trauma – of there being a threshold past which a shock or upset becomes a categorically distinct, generally permanent impairment – is a little over a hundred years old. For much of the twentieth century, it was rarely encountered outside of clinical literature. Its current popularity owes much to the self-help craze of the eighties and nineties, and to tabloid talk shows that offered a boundless array of exhibitionistic wretches recounting their histories of abuse and degradation for the delight of daytime television audiences in the eighties. If Bruno Latour is right and novel concepts triumph not because they are *true,* but because they appeal to the interests of diverse actors and institutions, then the consecration of trauma in contemporary thinking reflects in part the growth of the therapy industry, which purports to relieve trauma's burden, and in part the belief that the experience of trauma confers moral authority on its victims. Both aspects are present in the writing of Hermann Burger: his convictions about the psychological origins of his afflictions were as unshakeable as they were unprovable, and he never doubted that they justified his caprices and his indignation. In *Brenner,* Adam Nautilus Rauch – a stand-in for Burger's friend, the literary critic Anton Krättli – objects to the narrator's characterization of Amden as a concentration camp: "Whoever says such a thing has no idea what he's talking about." Burger agrees that the Nazi concentration camps admit no comparison, that he saw nothing akin to that "vast death-and-inferno machinery," but then objects – rebarbatively – that his own experience was worse.

> Here I must respond to my friend and critic that Hermann Arbogast Brenner is no historian and need not conceive things in relative terms. His persuasiveness depends on mingling materials the scholar keeps in different drawers. I do so in awareness of my right to subjectivity. This in no way restricts the compass of my remarks: a personal point of view, the primordial ownness of my perspective are my weapons.

Übertreibungskünstler – exaggeration artist – a term associated with Thomas Bernhard, applies just as well or better to Hermann Burger in these moments of delusion; still, he touches here on a real dilemma. Niklas Lühmann locates the transition from modernity to post-modernity at the moment when the discourse of subjective values overtakes the discourse of universal rights, throwing the significance of individual experience into confusion; under conditions of postmodernity, no one can say for certain whose pain is feigned, whose vindications are genuine, what constitutes a trauma and what is an idle complaint. The only person who can tell you about me is me – this is a very contemporary sentiment, and one Burger would subscribe to.

SWISS GERMAN

Dialect is a curse for translators, and is generally dealt with badly. The typical solution is lots of apostrophes, lots of *y'alls* and dropped final consonants, giving readers an impression – itself stupid, because everyone in English drops final consonants – that they've come upon a misplaced Alabaman in a novel set in Senegal or the Maldives. At the least, the translator must ask what dialect means in context, what of that can be communicated, and how. Often it's best to just leave it out. The reasons dialects exist, the reasons they are spoken, are many, and not all of them are interesting to outsiders.

Swiss German appears in *Brenner* from the very first page, and has a significance I felt it would be improper to omit. It is not just Burger's mother language, but the ore or bedrock of his words, inseparable from his private attempt to recover lost time. Readers of standard German can only decipher it imperfectly. Burger's publisher, Siegfried Unseld, asked for a key to be placed at the end of the book; this exists in the archives, but was left out of the published text.

To me, the best solution has been to devise a new sort of English, one that has no ethnic or class associations – something artificial, that preserves elements of Swiss German phonetics and older English formations similar to the antiquated phrasings still current in Swiss usage. I cannot say whether this is successful, but it has the virtue, at least, of signaling to the reader when a passage in the narrator's mind has the sound of home, of the ur-tones or primal sounds so important in the novel.

OFFAL

No translation has given me the headaches *Brenner* has; I hope no other ever will. To clear up doubts, I have paged through hundred-year-old tobacco wholesalers' catalogues in Dutch, corresponded with Swiss aluminum manufacturers, looked at antiquarians' photos of trains and toy cars, stared at dozens of cigar boxes and cigarette labels, read Ernst Voges's *Tobacco Encyclopedia* cover to cover. In the end, the words are translatable; the sensations they inspire are slipperier. Several times throughout *Brenner,* Burger invokes the conventional writer to make plain what his project isn't. It *isn't* a novel as such; it isn't concerned with the perfection of form.

Hermann Arbogast Brenner has no such intentions. He quite simply no longer has the time such an effort would require. In the castle keep, in the tenant's cottage, the materials are piled on the tables, chairs, beds, and floor.

To describe his method of bricolage, Burger hits on the concept of offal, the waste product of tobacco processing that falls to the factory floor. Offal, he writes, is what he cannot make fit. But then he questions the principle of order: "What I suppress may leave a deeper imprint on my memories than the designs apparent on the surface," and like a collagist, he juxtaposes disordered recollections redolent with the truth of having lived. At times, these are almost irredeemably obscure: I think of the description of Villa Malaga's facade, where "checkerboard triskeles alternate with chessboard pawns, curved corbels like abstract caryatids hold up the cornice, licorice-black W's divide window from window, toreador white squares off against oxblood red." Picturing such things is difficult, but the minimum the reader must take from them is a dying man's retrospective affection, which lingers over the tiniest salvageable detail.

INTERTEXTUALITY

Hermann Burger described himself as a man made of words, and his works are self-consciously literary. Essential reading for *Brenner*: Thomas Mann's *Tonio Kröger,* Theodor Fontane's *Stechlin,* Heinrich von Kleist's

Michael Kohlhaas. Burger refers to Gottfried Benn, Hermann Hesse, Swiss novelist Ernst Halter's *Die silberne Nacht,* his own story "Zentgraf im Gebirg oder das Erdbeben zu Soglio," Ernst Loesch's *Der Sog.* Sections of the book are lifted almost unchanged from Georg Böse's wonderful cultural history of tobacco, *Im blauen Dunst.* There must be much else I have missed. Occasionally incomprehensible passages are to be explained by hidden references: "Poseidon, lost in his endless calculations on the ocean's floor" and the equestrian qualified as "not tubercular" are nods to stories by Kafka – "Poseidon" and "Up in the Gallery" respectively. Much that seems to be true is not, and vice-versa – Burger spoke often of his favorite technique, the glancing intersection or *schleifender Schnitt,* the constant play with the point where credible and incredible cross over into one another. The most important reference here is to the *Struwwelpeter,* Heinrich Hoffman's horrifying book of didactic poems for children. An English translation, by Mark Twain, is a classic. It takes ten minutes to read, is available online, and will greatly aid readers in understanding *Brenner's* final chapters.

ACKNOWLEDGEMENTS

Simon Zumsteg is the preeminent Hermann Burger scholar and the curator of Burger's legacy. He assisted me at several stages of this translation. Uwe Schütte and I worked together on a short essay for *Asymptote* that was instrumental in my finding a publisher for this book. Friederike Barakat was helpful in matters of rights. Flowerville checked the musical sections. Jeremy Davies and my wife, Beatriz Leal Riesco, advised me on numerous passages. All of them deserve my thanks.

archipelago books
is a not-for-profit literary press devoted to
promoting cross-cultural exchange through innovative
classic and contemporary international literature
www.archipelagobooks.org